I0822467

SK HORTON

THE CROWNED

HEIR OF EARTH AND SKY BOOK THREE

aethonbooks.com

THE CROWNED
©2026 S.K. HORTON

Aethon Books
www.aethonbooks.com

Cover by Steve Beaulieu. Print and eBook formatting by Kevin G. Summers.

Published by Aethon Books LLC.

ALSO BY S.K. HORTON

HEIR OF EARTH AND SKY

The Concealed

The Captured

The Crowned

To Mom and Dad:
For helping me believe in life's endless possibilities.

CHAPTER 1
CATE

The phone slid from my fingers and bounced to the floor, the sound dampened by the static buzzing in my ears. The words from the text burned like fire in my brain.

Come find us or he dies. You have two weeks.

"Ma'am. Your Highness." Emma's muffled voice vaguely registered while I stared sightlessly through the wall of windows in my suite, the view from the top tower of Caelum Castle a blur. Her hand fell to my shoulder. "What is it?"

My maid had never seen a cell phone before, unless she'd opened my nightstand drawer where my dead iPhone still sat. These last few months, I'd tried to conserve the battery, only powering it briefly to stare at photos of Mom, Dad, and Jack when I most needed a reminder of my past life in Oregon. The life I'd left behind to fulfill the prophecy. The bar had dripped lower and lower until one day, the phone wouldn't start.

And now, with this delivery, I had a picture of the three of them again, yet I wished I'd never seen it. My breath bottomed out, unable to shake the image of the Embers' leader, a knife at little Jack's throat. The terror in Mom's eyes. Dad's mouth, a grim line of despair, holding it together for them.

The phone arrived mere moments ago by messenger. Rowan must have traversed a portal not long after we'd parted in order to reach my family and deliver it in the short time between now and murdering the king. I'd barely managed the royal funeral today.

And now this.

"Cate." Her fingers squeezed my shoulder.

She never called me by name—it should have seeped through the haze—yet I still struggled to focus. I finally turned to Emma's hovering form, rounding the sofa to retrieve the abandoned cell. It lay face down on the plush rug, an image of the Oregon coast on the case. *My mom's case.* Tears burned, and I swallowed the thickness growing in my throat. Emma sat beside me, placing the phone between us.

"It's Rowan," I whispered.

Her brows creased together. "Who?"

"The Embers' leader. The one who killed Father. He went through a portal and..." I exhaled slowly. "He has my other family. Where I grew up."

Emma's expression twisted in a mix of disbelief and horror. "I thought the portals were closed."

A hot tear escaped and slid down my cheek. "So did I. He says I have to be there in two weeks or he's going to kill my little brother."

"But isn't it... impossible? No one knows how to get through them anymore except Alana. And she's..."

Dead. Just like my father. Alana closed every portal when she hid me in America as a baby so I'd be safe. Somehow, the Embers found a way. Maybe the entrance I came back through with Daniel and Lucas reopened. Or they've had one of their own all this time.

"What can I do?" Emma bit her lip, her eyes welling with tears. She might seem shy and timid, but she was stronger than she appeared. I wouldn't be alive if it weren't for her helping me take down the Ember that entered this very suite those months ago at The Great Battle.

My mind spun from one appalling thought to the next, focus weaving in and out. How would I make it to Oregon in two weeks? And the portal. Was it even open? I'd see my family again—which would mean confronting Rowan. For a second time. The last ended with Father lying in a pool of blood. Panic and dread sat like a ragged stone in my chest.

I don't want to do this alone.

"Daniel." I turned to Emma. "Will you find him? And Lucas, too."

She rushed out of the room, leaving me with nothing but my thoughts and the phone. Mom had probably captured more pictures over the last several months. Moments I'd missed. But I couldn't bear to touch it. Not yet.

Lucas arrived first, with Mya tumbling in behind, brushing dark hair from her cheeks. "You're not going to abandon us at the dinner tonight, are you?" Lucas called, then stopped short when he saw my face. "Oh. It's been a rough day. For all of us. Sorry. I'm—"

"Always making jokes at the wrong time," Mya finished.

Mya's presence took me aback. I automatically thought of Lucas and Daniel because they'd been with me at university through the portal, though I should have known these two would be together. Mya and Lucas had been inseparable since sharing a cell in an Ember prison. I tried to stand, then sank back onto the sofa, wobbly knees giving out.

"Hey." Lucas's soft tone nearly undid me. He came to sit beside me while Mya stood tentatively near the door. I motioned wearily for her to join us.

"What can we do? Your maid said you wanted to see me?" Lucas asked.

"I..." My throat closed, and I choked on my tears. I took a couple of deep breaths. "Daniel's coming. Let's wait 'till he's here."

He exhaled dramatically. "Oh, good. For a minute there, I thought he'd done something horrible, and that's why you called me. I didn't want to have to beat him up with his sister here." He flashed a small smile to Mya. "I'm doing it again, aren't I? Sorry. Give me a quiet room, and it happens. Seriously, though. Daniel didn't do anything dumb, did he?"

I shook my head. I'd missed Lucas when he'd been gone. Somehow, his joking on the day of my father's funeral felt right.

"I liked your speech," Mya spoke up. "You're going to be a good queen."

The coronation. It was in three weeks. How would I make it back in time? What would happen if I didn't claim my crown? Graftonberg was sure to find a loophole to take over. Bitterness that my father chose the baron as my regent once again welled up in my chest.

"What did I say?" Mya asked, noting my sour expression.

Daniel stopped me from answering by entering, followed by Emma. Lucas made room and folded his long legs across from me, and Mya perched next to him on the chair's arm. Daniel sat beside me, his dark brows knitted in concern. He placed a warm hand on my knee. His power to sense emotions was sometimes difficult for him to bear, and my distress likely washed over him like the ocean at high tide.

"What's wrong?" he asked. "Emma said it was important. You have a dinner full of diplomats in thirty minutes downstairs."

I held back more tears, hugging a throw pillow.

"But we can totally skip it," he added quickly. "My father's down there. I don't want to go either."

No one wanted to see King Dryden. But we had more important matters. I carefully lifted the phone and put in the passcode—my dad's birthday. The wallpaper flashed, showing my family at my high school graduation. All of us so happy. So unsuspecting of things to come. I pressed on the text icon, and the photo of Rowan holding a knife to Jack's neck opened with the worded threat below. Rowan's stance mirrored the position when he'd killed King Aldridge. I blinked back visions of the blood from that day. Visions that haunted my dreams. Haunted every moment.

My hand trembled as I handed the cell to Daniel and looked away. I couldn't bear to see his reaction. The guys had used phones the month they'd been in England, so they were somewhat familiar. Daniel's sharp intake of breath was followed by Lucas's.

I didn't have to explain the significance. They'd both seen photos of my family on my old phone and on my desk back at university.

"What are we going to do?" I whispered.

"We'll go after them," Daniel said without hesitation.

"But what about..." I trailed off. The million problems. The portal. My coronation. The baron.

"It will all keep." Daniel slid his hand into mine.

"Wait. Where are we going?" Mya asked.

Daniel's grip tightened in irritation. "You're not going anywhere."

The Embers had captured Mya because she trailed along to the disaster of a peace treaty when she wasn't invited. She seemed to be developing a habit of wanting to be included, even when she didn't have the training or know-how.

"Through the portal," Lucas answered Mya. "Rowan has Cate's adoptive family."

Mya sat up straighter. "To England?"

"Yes. Then to America." Lucas spoke with confidence, though I couldn't help noticing the tightness in his jaw, and his steady gaze held on me a bit too long, as if to reassure both of us.

I scooted closer to Daniel, and he wrapped an arm around my shoulders as if he could shield me from this nightmare. "Two weeks," I said. "It doesn't leave any time to plan. We're not even sure we can use that portal. What did Alana tell you guys about it?"

Both boys fidgeted, waiting for the other to say something. Lucas finally spoke, "Alana said it was unbalanced. She traveled with us up north and stabilized it the last time we went through. She set it up for the full and new moon to keep the Embers from following, which obviously didn't work."

"I wonder if they might have their own portal near their lands," I responded. "It makes more sense. Remember, they were chasing us and then never showed up when we crossed? They should have been right behind us."

Daniel shifted to face me. "We wondered the same."

Mya spoke up, "What does it mean when you say the portal was unstable? That's been the story for years. It's why fewer and fewer people crossed over, even before Alana closed them. I've asked about it, especially around the time Cate came. No one bothers to explain anything."

"Who have you been asking?" Daniel's voice lowered. "And why?"

She shrugged. "Curious."

Daniel narrowed his eyes at her, navy in the dimming light. "Mya?"

"I was jealous, okay? I wanted to go to England. Why couldn't I have gone too? I'm tired of being left behind."

"Because the council *elected* us. It was dangerous, if you recall. We weren't going to parties and sightseeing." Daniel pulled his arm from around me and leaned forward.

"Well..." Lucas chimed in. "There were *some* parties."

"You're not helping, mate." Daniel stood to pace. "There are bigger problems to solve than whether Mya gets a holiday. And to answer your question, some people... just disappeared."

I remembered the portal. For a few moments, I had been lost in a hurricane, both metaphorically and physically, tossed in the melee. It was nearly impossible to focus on willing myself through. Ultimately, it was thoughts of Daniel that propelled me to this world.

"Alana's gone." My heart ached for my mentor, killed in battle. "How do we go through safely? Did she teach anyone? Who taught *her*?"

"That's what we've got to figure out," Daniel said. "I wish King Aldridge were here. He might have some of those answers."

We all wished the king could help us, no one more than me. "Who else would know?" I asked.

Daniel's lips creased into a thin line. "Unfortunately, I have an idea where to start. My father."

CHAPTER 2
DANIEL

All eyes hit the floor at the mention of King Dryden. He'd been a thorn in my relationship with Cate, and the thought of needing his help once again placed further disquiet in the room.

Cate turned her attention to Emma rather than addressing my comment. "Has anyone been to Alana's quarters? Is there family? Has it been cleaned out?"

"I'm not sure, ma'am. I'll be happy to check."

"Thank you. Why don't you do that now?"

The maid shuffled her feet, started toward the door, then backtracked. "Are you attending the dinner? Because your…" She circled her head with one finger.

"Tiara is crooked," Mya finished. "And your hair has escaped in a few places. I can fix it for you."

"I hate to waste time at that dinner." Cate sighed after Emma left. "Maybe we can use it to ask around about the portals. There'll be some powerful people there from both kingdoms."

"I'll see what I can find out," Mya responded.

"That," I said, "I completely approve of. You're the best choice." Mya's ability to influence the emotions of others usually helped her wheedle her way into getting what she wanted. Although only the two of us knew it. We'd made a pact to tell no one about her talent.

Lucas straightened. "And we keep the phone message a secret for now."

I nodded. "Agreed."

"Speaking of secrets…" Mya pursed her lips.

I glared at her in warning.

She shot me a pleading look. "Lucas already knows. I had to tell him. For our escape."

This was the first I'd heard of Lucas finding out about the family secret. Although I couldn't influence others, I was able to sense emotions like my father. Lucas, a former rival having this information, sat uncomfortably against my Terran roots. I'd have to ask Mya later if she divulged everything Father and I could do or only her own secrets. Resigned, I gestured, palm up, for Mya to continue.

She proceeded to explain her power. How when she projected certain emotions, it could lure others to feel the same about a topic. Cate took it in stride, barely able to concentrate on anything else but the ticking clock of her family's survival, her fear a tar-like heaviness across my skin.

"Just… use it for good," Cate said wearily. "If we're going to find out anything down there, we'd better get moving." She stood. "I need help with this hair. Offer still stand?" she asked Mya.

Cate hated formal affairs. She looked gorgeous in her fitted beaded dress from the funeral, though it wasn't the clothes she disliked so much as the small talk. It had been an enormous adjustment for her to transform from student to princess. Coupled with her anxiety and grief, this night would be difficult. I'd have to keep a close eye and step in where I could. Watching her wouldn't be hard. I could barely take my eyes off her in normal circumstances.

The girls headed into Cate's bedroom, leaving me alone with Lucas. We hadn't talked much in the two weeks since he'd escaped from Ember prison with Mya. He'd been busy with Caelum soldier business and was away for several days visiting his mother. It came as a relief when he hadn't taken Mya with him. I wasn't ready for my little sister to be *that* serious with anyone.

I leaned back into the sofa and crossed an ankle over my knee. "Have you told my father about you and Mya?"

Lucas leveled a glare. We never did get on much. "He just arrived today. I've been on duty during the funeral." His features morphed from annoyance to worry, his eyes crinkling at the edges. "How do you think he'll take it?"

"Not well. For example, he threatened to make a deal with the Embers to invade Caelum unless Cate traveled with the rest of the soldiers to your rescue. There're a whole lot of Terrans who aren't interested in peace, including my father." I gave him a wry half-smile. "So, the two of you cozying up? Not a picture of an ideal match for his daughter."

"Not only *my* rescue. King Aldridge. And his own daughter. You'd think he would have cared about that."

Yeah, I'd thought so too. I raised my hands. "Just a warning."

"And what about you? Are *you* interested in peace?" Lucas leaned forward. "I haven't stopped protecting Cate. Not only is it my duty as a knight to the crown, but delivering her safely through the portal wasn't the end of my assignment."

"Nor mine." I huffed a sarcastic laugh. "I'll protect her with my life. And of course I want peace. It's baffling that so many people expect Cate to fulfill the part of the prophecy about defeating the enemy. Then ignore that bit about uniting the kingdoms."

"People like *your* father."

And there it was. It always came back to that. Living under King Dryden's shadow haunted me, simmering beneath every conversation. "Look," I sat up straighter, planting my feet in the plush rug, "I believe we both have Cate's best interests in mind. I also think we both want the entire prophecy fulfilled. If the two of us can't get along, I can't help wondering how the rest of the kingdoms are going to manage."

Lucas crossed his arms, settling himself in the chair across from me as if he had all the time in the world for me to convince him.

"You're right," I continued, ignoring his silence. "King Dryden is the elephant in the room wherever I go here in Caelum. I can't escape him. Our ideas of running a kingdom don't align. Unfortunately, I haven't much influence on him. And since you're in a relationship with my sister, you'd better start understanding the family dynamics. He doesn't know Mya can sway emotions, and that's a secret I'll keep to the grave, as should you. He can never find out. As you're aware, that power of hers isn't perfect. We'll have to see if she's able to persuade him that you two won't topple the kingdoms by being together or such nonsense."

Lucas rolled his eyes.

"He's allowed me to be with Cate," I continued, "but only as long as the alliance works for him. One day, I'll have to defy him. Maybe even turn my back on Terra to be with her. A warning: I'm not sure Mya is prepared to do the same."

"I don't want any of us to be forced into that choice." Lucas pulled on his lip and let it bounce back, sighing heavily. "Mya's not ready. Neither am I, honestly. I like your sister. A lot. My gut tells me I'd burn down the kingdoms for her. But my brain is more cautious. We've talked about it, and we're taking it day by day."

At least he was being sensible. "Are you willing to leave her and go through the portal for Cate? We could use another person familiar with that world."

"I'll be there," he said without hesitation.

Heat rose at the back of my neck. Is it Cate that he'd burn down kingdoms for, not my sister? I tucked the feeling away. Now wasn't the time to jeopardize Cate's family because of my jealousy. She'd chosen me. Not Lucas.

"We're ready," Mya called, gliding into the room with Cate on her heels.

Lucas and I both stood, admiring the girls. Cate's honey-brown hair was resecured into a braided crown of sorts, and the tiara, now straight, sparkled in the light. Her cheeks glowed, likely from makeup wizardry because she'd been pale from shock earlier. I reached out to sense her feelings, a mixture of determination, nerves, and grief.

She linked her arm with mine. "Thanks for being here for me."

My heart ballooned. "Always."

The gathering space outside the dining room bustled with crowds when we arrived, mere minutes before dinner was to be served. Nobles from Caelum and Terra traveled to pay their respects to King Aldridge, murmuring in low voices, setting a somber mood. Cate arranged the seating so she would be at the head, me by her side, and my father at the foot. She also sneakily sat Baron Graftonberg away from us. She'd been in a daze for most of the funeral arrangements, though self-preservation had prodded her to make this one request. I scanned the room, searching for the older members in the group. Those who may have crossed the portal when they were eighteen, as was tradition before the passages became unreliable.

"Dinner is served," called a footman.

We filed into the enormous dining room. Polished table leaves had been added to accommodate the crowd of around fifty. I heard Cate's breath catch before I saw the problem. Graftonberg had ensconced himself at the head of the glossy table.

Cate's arm slipped from mine, and she gracefully stepped toward him, shoulders pulled back. I followed on her heels.

"Princess," the baron said loudly, "I wasn't sure you would grace us with your presence. I've heard you abhor these events."

Cate's cheeks flushed beyond her carefully applied blush. "Queen," she said quietly. "I'm the queen." She needed to be coronated to rule, but the right was still hers, at least in name.

A hush fell over the room, vultures watching the spectacle. It seemed every time Graftonberg and I were together, I wanted to punch him in those wobbly jowls. Nails bit into my palms through clenched fists, though I held back to give Cate the space to decide whether to show strength or graciousness.

Cate turned to the room. "The baron takes his role as regent extremely seriously." She eyed Graftonberg again. "Thank you for ensuring the seat would be filled in my absence. As you can see, I've arrived. Everyone, Baron Graftonberg!" She swiped the nearest goblet from the table and held it aloft.

She'd chosen both—graciousness and strength. Pride swelled. The baron stood, took a ridiculous bow, and edged to sit on Cate's right. "That's my seat," I whispered. The guests' low chatter muffled my voice as they found their places. "And mark my words, you sit there, you'll either get a fist to the face or be humiliated. My money's on both."

Graftonberg's hooded eyes narrowed. "You'll see who wins in the end." He tried to jostle me as he passed, but I stood my ground. I hadn't needed him to show me his hand. We'd been suspecting he'd attempt a coup for some time. This just gives us more insight into his state of mind. *Overconfident.*

Rowan's threat against Cate's family couldn't have come at a worse moment. Caelum's power hung in the balance. If anything went wrong when we traveled through the portal, it could be catastrophic for her reign. Because if she wasn't back by her coronation next month, Graftonberg would step in. And once on the throne, removing him would be no easy task.

CHAPTER 3
LUCAS

Mya and I strode into the dining room together, the space glowing with crystal goblets, beaded dresses, polished wood, and gleaming silver. I wished we were arm-in-arm; it was always tempting to move closer to her like a honeybee to a lily. Instead, a good meter of space separated us. We'd speak to King Dryden about our relationship soon enough—if he hadn't already guessed. King Aldridge's funeral reception was not the place. Cate had kindly assigned Mya and me to sit together, placing us toward the middle of the table.

Graftonberg shouldered through the crowd, his jowls reddening further when he stepped on a few women's silk skirts as he stomped toward us. Faces huddled together, murmuring as he passed. Cate stood at the head of the table, Daniel by her side, her jaw set proudly.

Mya and I exchanged looks. "Wonder what we missed?" she whispered.

When she leaned in close, her lavender shampoo wafted, and I forced myself to move a step back before I did something dumb, like take a giant sniff in front of all these people.

"The usual, likely." I discreetly angled my head toward Graftonberg. "Keep a lookout for opportunities to extract info."

She fluttered her dark lashes at me and tilted her lips into a coy smile. "Of course. I thought we already established I was the better spy?"

I covered a laugh. "That we did." Mya had proved excellent at ferreting information and instrumental in our escape from Ember City.

We'd arrived at the meal after Cate and Daniel because Mya wanted to stop by briefly to say hello to Dev, who was still recovering in the infirmary. Cutting it close, we almost missed the seating time. We'd filled Dev in, who immediately tried to barrel out of bed like a blond bull to help before we settled him. He'd probably always have a limp from the leg injury he incurred while fleeing with Cate and Daniel after Aldridge was killed. Supposedly, he would be released from bedrest in a couple of days.

We found our places: me next to an elderly Dame Martha Hemlock, part of the Caelum aristocracy, on one side; Mya on the other. Graftonberg sat kitty-corner across from me, and I dutifully avoided eye contact. As regent, he was my superior, but I'd much rather take orders from General Dixon. Cate had elevated Dixon from colonel after leading the charge to rescue us from Ember City.

Dame Hemlock straightened the already perfectly aligned silverware as I slid into the seat next to her. Even with my knight status, I was likely the lowest-ranking person here, at the invitation of Cate. I'd grown accustomed to it, often a guest of King Aldridge in the same manner. He'd been friends with my father and taken me under his wing when an Ember struck him down five years prior. Now the king had met the same fate. A familiar ache pulsed in my chest. When would it all end?

"Sir Lucas," the dame greeted. Her graying hair contrasted with her dark skin and was piled on top of her head, curling in a halo around her face. "Nice to see you back. I heard you ran into a little trouble."

"That I did, ma'am."

"Something about dragons? King Aldridge told me before…" She trailed off. She didn't have to finish the sentence… *before he died.*

"Molly, my dragon, convinced a group of dragons to leave without supporting the Embers during The Great Battle."

"Yes, I've heard that. Weren't you going to get some sort of medal?" She peered over half-moon spectacles with gray irises.

I chuckled weakly. "That might have been before I was captured. We tried to convince the dragons in the north not to side with the Embers anymore. It didn't go so well."

She sniffed. "Apparently not." Her voice turned wistful. "Not so long ago, they were our friends. We rode them up and down the cliffs. A few even kept them as pets, much as you do with your dragon. My family never had one, but I do remember a particularly lovely Blueback here at the castle. Flying on him… it's like nothing else in the world, don't you think?"

Even with the dame's wrinkles and beaded buttoned-up dress, I could imagine her soaring over a sparkling Caelum Castle. She had that hidden air of adventure tucked beneath a sour demeanor. "It must have been a sight. Dragons circling the castle, every color of the rainbow. They were dwindling when I was young, but I still remember a few until they defected. They wanted their freedom."

"Some of the dragon masters were known for their cruelty. To keep them in line." She sniffed and straightened the silverware again. "Wasn't right."

It would kill me if anyone were cruel to gentle Molly. "It's unfortunate people didn't figure out they were pushing the dragons too far." I paused, working to sound casual. "Speaking of old times, did you ever go through the portal?"

She shot me a dubious look. "I'm going to start thinking you know nothing about this kingdom. Aristocratic women have never been allowed. We needed to be here. Making proper marriages, of course." Her tone indicated how little she thought of that rule.

I bit my lip. I *had* known. "I suppose I was just confirming."

"Before the portals became unstable, some probably went secretly, but not anyone in my circles. By the end, most of the passages would send someone there, and no one knew when or if they'd return."

"What, you'd go a young man and come back old?" Why hadn't this been publicized?

"Sometimes. More often, people would return the same as they left, but years had passed here."

I tried to act unconcerned, even though this news sent my head spinning. "I thought Alana closed most of them and stabilized the ones that remained? Until Cate was born, of course."

"She did. Some people would go off on their own, taking their chances for… adventure? A new life? That's what prompted her to seal most of them."

Was the one we traveled through the first time more reliable? Would her enchantments still work now that she'd died? "Since Alana was a woman, I would have thought she'd let any female through, no matter their rank. Were you tempted to ask her?"

"Not to speak ill of the dead, but we didn't get on well. She was always so serious."

That was *definitely* true. "Who *was* Alana friends with?"

"I don't know. She struck me as lonely." She tapped her index finger to her thin upper lip. "Actually, she was close with her mentor… what was his name? Oh, it will come to me. Don't ever get old, young man."

"Alana had a mentor? I'd always thought she was self-trained—the only person except Cate with both Caelum and Terran powers."

"Oh, you are naïve, aren't you? Of course, King Aldridge and Catherine's mother weren't the only two to ever fall in love from the two kingdoms." She leaned over me to glance at Mya, who was speaking to the tablemate on her right. "It's a well-kept secret, that's all."

Apparently, we hadn't been as subtle as we thought. I glanced down the table at King Dryden, who met my gaze with a dark, steady one in return. I grabbed for my water goblet to wet my suddenly parched throat.

"Everything okay?" Mya asked when I set my cup down a little too hard, sloshing a few droplets onto the white tablecloth.

I swallowed again. "Fine." King Dryden knew, I was sure of it. Alerting Mya wouldn't do any good. With her ability to sense feelings, she probably had more insight than I did. Actually, it was likely that very power which prompted her to ask how *I* was doing.

The soup course arrived, saving me from additional conversation and inspection. I don't know why funerals were always accompanied by so much food. Surely no one had an appetite. Cate took a tiny mouthful, eyeing the group for an opportunity to search for answers about the portal.

"They're not working hard enough." Graftonberg's voice rumbled across the table. "We need to do it like the British did with the island sugar workers."

My head shot up. He spoke to another prominent landowner, not caring who listened.

The other man nodded enthusiastically. "Then we wouldn't have to pay them at all."

"Slaves?" Mya asked. "You're talking about bringing slavery to Caelum?" Her dark brows arched in a deceptively curious position. However, she'd never approve. Particularly after being captive and essentially a slave herself recently.

"Of course not," Graftonberg replied. "We provide food and shelter. They work. Seems like a fair trade."

The aristocracy were supposed to take care of the people who lived on their land and villages by letting them keep what they earn, except for a tax paid to the nobles and the crown. Graftonberg's idea would upend our entire economic history and freedoms.

"And who exactly will fall under this decree?" I leaned forward, pushing my bowl out of the way. "My mother lives in Orangeshire. She's an herbalist. You going to make her turn over all her earnings? With a husband who died serving this country?"

"I'm sure we can make exceptions," the baron answered smoothly. "We're still working out the details."

"Cate would never allow it," I said.

"The princess doesn't understand how this kingdom runs. She hasn't even been present for any of our council meetings."

Dame Hemlock placed two fingers on my forearm, stopping me from arguing. "Well, dear." She craned her long neck to glare at the baron. "She's been off trying to save everyone, hasn't she? Then, grieving her father. And," she set her hand under her chin, "I do believe she's our queen, not the princess. You might do well to remember that. Hmmm..." She swiveled to me. "Is treason still punishable by death?"

"I believe it is, ma'am."

"Ah, you *do* know this kingdom's history." Her lips turned up, and she leaned in to whisper, her attention focused on the baron, "We're going to have to keep an eye on him."

She was right. We all knew it. If only we weren't traveling through a portal that apparently had serious issues with the space-time continuum.

CHAPTER 4
CATE

"Glad that's over." I collapsed into the cushions.

Daniel, Lucas, Mya, and I had returned to my suite—the only place to be sure we'd be alone with so many guests in the castle.

"My father behaved himself." Daniel, seated next to me, stretched his legs onto the coffee table. "Mostly."

King Dryden, fortunately, hadn't created a scene, although he did stare down his nose at the Caelumites, who comprised most of the guests. He'd made important "announcements" one too many times in the past to influential gatherings, which often skirted the truth, leaving me edgy the entire meal. The supper was supposed to signal a remembrance of my father, yet it turned political, as everything did at court.

"I found out a few things about the portal and Alana," Lucas said, leaning against the arm of the chair across from me. "Turns out we might get there, but who knows when we'll return. Years may pass while we're gone, or just a day. As if that doesn't create enough problems, it makes your coronation a little tricky."

The thought of being unable to help my family deepened the torment beneath my ribs. "I have to save them. It doesn't matter."

"I've been thinking about that," Daniel said. "Maybe… now hear me out, maybe you stay here, and Lucas and I go. We'll bring a tactical team."

"No," I said. "He'll kill them if I don't show. He won't hesitate. You know he won't. I can't sacrifice them."

Mya raised her hand tentatively. "Aren't you kind of sacrificing yourself? Even if you make it through the portal, he means to kill you. Your family is bait. This whole thing is just to get rid of you."

"He'll be missing his powers there." I tried to pretend Mya's words didn't affect me. This was the first time anyone had said it aloud. We all knew Rowan's plan, but the chilling statement swept through like a winter storm, quieting the room.

After a moment's pause, Mya continued, "Neither will you, right? Didn't you guys struggle to use the energy when you went?" Her gaze flipped from Lucas to Daniel.

"We did. Daniel used it only once," Lucas replied.

"And sorry, Cate," Mya said. "You have trouble in the best of times here."

Annoyance sparked. "Thanks for pointing that out." It was true. I'd grown much better, especially with Daniel's presence, but I'd grappled for months to make rain, only recently having success. I hadn't tried since my father's death.

"The only hope we have of saving my family is for Rowan to see me. And yes, I'm fully aware," I swallowed thickly, "that I'm the bait. But as long as we set a trap, we'll have a chance."

"Well, I guess that's settled." Lucas patted his thigh. Next to me, Daniel stared at the floor. He wanted so badly to protect me. To wrap me in cotton and shutter all the pain away. I loved him for it, and I'd have to fight him because of it.

"Anybody heard of Alana having a mentor?" Lucas asked. "Dame Hemlock mentioned someone trained her."

"Really?" I glanced at Daniel, his familiar, chiseled profile still broody. "I guess that makes sense. So, who is this person?"

"The dame couldn't remember, although I suspect he's a Caelumite if she knew of him."

"Alana did spend more time here than Terra," Mya said. "I could ask Father. He might know. At least he acts like he knows everything." She cracked a grin. No one smiled back.

"Did you get a chance to talk with him?" I asked her.

"I'm meeting him in the morning. Too many people downstairs tonight."

"Just you or with Daniel? Or Lucas?" I didn't envy Lucas having a relationship conversation with King Dryden. Been there, done that.

Neither of the boys jumped at the opportunity.

Daniel finally spoke up, "You meet with him first. I'll just put him in a bad mood. Afterward, I'll follow up. He should be told before he returns to Terra."

"We're telling him about going through the portal?" Mya asked.

"How *I'm* going? Yes. I was planning on it." Daniel rolled his eyes at her. They loved each other, but Mya knew just how to push his buttons. He still hadn't completely forgiven her for tagging along and getting herself captured at the Embers' sham of a peace treaty.

Lucas stood. "I'll go with you tomorrow, Mya. And I'll walk you out. I'm sure Cate could use some rest."

Exhaustion ached deep in my bones, but the underlying strumming of nerves meant I wouldn't be sleeping much. I waited until they left before tilting my head onto Daniel's shoulder.

"We'll solve this. We have to," he whispered, and drew soft circles on my knee, the pad of his finger bumping across the beads of my gown.

We sat in silence, as we often did when overwhelming news crashed upon us. Comfortable enough with each other to not have to speak, we both let the gravity of the situation do the talking. He never doubted that we should go after them. Never faltered. My heart ached with both love and sorrow. The energy, always present when we were close, blanketed us in invisible strength.

It would be strategic to sacrifice my family. To take the throne and leave them to Rowan would be the strongest choice for my kingdom. But I couldn't bear the weight of any more deaths. My father surrendered his life to save his men and me. I wouldn't let anyone else I love die because of me. A tear snaked down my cheek, the overwhelming helplessness setting in.

Daniel shifted and wrapped his arms around me, his fingers sliding up and down my spine. The dam finally broke. I tore the tiara from my head, the sting of hair ripping from my scalp adding to my frustration, and sobbed into his chest. So many deaths: my father, Alana, and all the men who fell in battle. Daniel's arms comforted, though a longing to be held by my mom surged. Flashes of her soft smile, the way she'd tuck a loose curl behind my ear, and dinners of spaghetti and garlic bread around the oak table. Dad's presence was always steadying—quick to laugh, he knew how to make light of even the toughest situations, reassuring us that everything would turn out. Even when the bills piled up and we weren't sure the family store would remain open.

"I know. I'm sorry, Cate," Daniel whispered into my hair.

It felt like my insides were being ripped apart—the sick anguish threatened to consume me, spiraling and spiraling into darkness. Then Rowan's confident smirk flashed. The man responsible for this pain. Sorrow morphed into anger. The hurt was still there, but a fire kindled to stop this man. To stop all the Embers once and for all.

I sat up and dabbed my still-dripping tears. He handed me a handkerchief. Sometimes, it was hard to believe I lived in a world where men carried handkerchiefs instead of a wadded-up, off-brand Kleenex. The reminder helped ground me—bring me back from the edge. "Thank you for being here." My grief affected him. He was drowning in my emotions, the heartache reflecting back at me. I needed to spare him—make him leave. I wiped my nose, then blew out a breath. "I'm okay. Why don't you get some sleep? It's been a long day."

His blue eyes, dark in the low light, searched my face. Feather-like fingertips brushed a stray tear and cupped my cheek. "I don't want to leave you like this."

"I'll be alright. I'm exhausted. Really. I'll be asleep as soon as my head hits the pillow. And I can't wait to get out of this coffin of a gown." I stood and pulled the fabric at my waist; the form-fitting dress not giving a millimeter. The clock in the corner ticked midnight. I'd already worn it for over twelve hours.

Daniel leaned in and kissed my cheek. "If you're sure?"

I nudged him toward the door.

When he left, I stripped off the beaded garment and sighed in relief at the absence of its weight and scratchy fabric against my skin. Next, I donned the softest gown in my wardrobe, the cotton soothing and light. I didn't quite lie to Daniel. I *will* fall asleep when my head hits the pillow. It just won't get there for a while. I straightened the loose strands I'd pulled when yanking off the tiara, then headed out the door. Because every moment I wasted was another second my family was in enemy hands.

The darkened shadows of the library, the branches knocking against the window, gave an eerie effect to one of my favorite places in the castle. I clicked the heavy door shut, turned the lock to keep a wayward guest from disturbing me, and flicked on a few sconces to browse the shelves. I was looking for… well, I wasn't completely sure. Something with information on portals—no idea what that would be listed under. I skipped my usual haunting ground of fiction and moved toward the far recesses for dusty history tomes. I slid my index finger—*bump, bump, bump*—along the spines until one caught my eye. The gold lettering read, *The Two-Way Kingdom*. I pulled it off the shelf. Two more equally vague titles followed, and I hauled them to a nearby table.

The first volume opened with a creak. From the looks of it, the last person to read it might have been the author himself. I scanned the text, finding no mention of the portals. There were hundreds of pages, so it was hard to be sure. The oversized gold clock ticked just past one in the morning, yet my body would not settle. Every second I slept was another wasted.

The clock chimed two. Still, I persisted. After fifteen minutes more, I was flagging. The emotions of the day—a speech in front of thousands, the burial, the threat to my family—were too overwhelming. I blinked blurry eyes and turned another page. The word "portal" caught my attention. I hunched in the dim light, my spine aching in the solid wood chair.

"When a portal becomes weak, the powers of both the air and earth strengthen it," I whispered aloud. *That must be why Alana could manipu-*

late them. I read on, "Working together is the only way to continue our passage back and forth."

The door to the library rattled with a bang. The lock held. Who would be here at this time of night?

"I know someone's in there. I can see the light under the door," called the unmistakable blustery voice of Baron Graftonberg. "I'll wake up one of the servants for a key if I must."

A long sigh escaped. I might as well let him in. Someone should inform him that the kingdom's future ruler was once again risking her life.

"Coming." I marked the page and stacked it with the others before trudging to the entrance.

When I opened the door, his eyes narrowed. He peered past me into the low-lit library. "Who else is in there with you? Not having a dalliance, are you?"

My hand went to my hip. "If I wanted a 'dalliance' as you put it, I'd surely do it in my own suite. I don't need to sneak around." I sagged into the doorframe. "I'm alone and didn't want to be disturbed by guests. How can I help you?"

His features slackened in disappointment at not catching me or someone else in a compromising position. "I found it difficult to sleep, so I came down for a book. Your father's funeral… wasn't easy for me." He tilted his head. "Nor for you either, I imagine. May I come in?"

This civilized Graftonberg was unexpected. Maybe his attitude was due to lack of anyone else to posture in front of. I stepped aside to let him through, then proceeded to a set of overstuffed chairs near the darkened windows.

He sat and tugged at his waistcoat, glowering. "I realize you don't approve of me and my methods. But whatever you think of me, King Aldridge was my friend. I held him in great esteem."

"Thank you for that. He's missed by many." Somehow, when others spoke of my father, my throat closed, and I could barely hold myself together. With the baron, probably because he was correct when he said I didn't respect him, I could speak freely without letting my emotions run wild. "I wish he'd never gone to that treaty."

Graftonberg shook his head. "I told him—"

"We all know you were against it. Saying 'I told you so' isn't going to help me feel any better." The reminder that my father should never have fallen into Rowan's trap sent a trickle of foreboding slithering down the base of my neck. Yet, I was preparing to do that very thing.

He harrumphed. "I suppose you're right. At least we learned once again the Embers can never be trusted. We must do everything possible to strengthen our defenses. And for that, we need money. The coffers—"

"I have to tell you something," I blurted, not having the patience for an economics lesson.

He arched his brows and gave a go-ahead gesture, palm up.

Nerves took flight in my belly. *Just say it quick, Cate. Like ripping off a Band-Aid.* "I've received a message. From Rowan. He's traveled through a portal and has my family, the one I grew up with in America, captive. He'll kill them if I don't meet him in Oregon. I have two weeks to get there. And I will. I have to."

He opened his lips like a largemouth bass and closed them.

Right. It did sound absolutely asinine, even to my own ears.

"Your father would have never allowed it," Graftonberg said.

King Aldridge's hard edges and uncompromising personality wouldn't have let his daughter enter into such peril. He'd finally started to let me in—let the love for me slide through a few cracks in the armor—when Rowan had struck him down. He wasn't perfect, but he'd been trying, and that was good enough. Graftonberg's statement didn't need answering. No reason to argue fact.

"As regent, I should forbid it as well." He pursed worm-like, full lips. "But I say, let the people see what kind of queen you are. They'll decide if saving your family and going after Rowan is admirable or abandoning your kingdom is foolish."

"I'm not abandon—"

"You are," he cut in. "And even if they shouldn't, it's the people who believe in you, not me." His eyes lifted skyward.

There was no doubt that Graftonberg would like to see me disappear so he could run the kingdom himself. Sure, there had to be a small part of him, the part allegiant to King Aldridge, that would be stricken with remorse if I died. Maybe he'd convinced himself he was a good person because a sliver of compassion still resided within. But his greed for power and elevated ego had also convinced him he would lead this country better than I ever could. Prophecy or not.

He rose and started for the exit, not bothering with the book he claimed he'd wanted when he arrived. "Good luck with your trip," he said, turning back. "And don't worry. The kingdom's in excellent hands—mine." He shut the door behind him with a thud.

That was exactly what I worried about.

CHAPTER 5
DANIEL

Last night, rather than sleeping, I made lists. Who to talk to that might help us understand portals, what to bring, reminders to find our contacts—Brian and Lucy and their address for when we arrived, and who I should say my final goodbyes to. Deep down, I knew that no amount of planning could make this trip safe.

I knocked on the door to meet Father in Cate's favorite sitting room. She hadn't hidden her annoyance when she discovered Dryden had claimed it during his stay. When I entered, Lucas and Mya were already there. They sat in club chairs across from the king, Lucas ramrod straight, the muscles in his neck corded.

"Daniel." King Dryden inclined his head at my arrival, appearing tidy, as usual, in a Terran-green jacket trimmed with gold braid. He lacked the circles under his eyes the rest of us sported.

I pulled a chair from the corner to sit beside Mya, so the three of us would face Father together, then settled in, trying to appear relaxed, though struggling with the wooden hardback I'd chosen. I lowered my shoulders, exhaling, always conscious that the king could read my emotions.

"These two were just about to ask my blessing for a relationship." Father glared at Lucas while he spoke.

Apparently, I made my appearance too early. Now I'd have to witness this conversation.

"We haven't even mentioned—" Mya started.

"No need. Why else would you be here together? And then there were those eyes you two were making at each other last night. Now, the entirety of both kingdoms is aware." He sighed. "Mya. You must realize how it looks. You were locked in a prison cell together for weeks."

"No one knows we shared a cell. We were smart enough to keep that part a secret," she said.

"They certainly imagined that you did," he snapped.

I'd hoped to discuss Father's knowledge of the portals, not my sister's relationship. I could feel the king's blood pressure rising, which would do little to help our cause.

"Your Highness," Lucas interjected. "I promise, nothing untoward has happened between your daughter and me. My role was to protect, not accost her. I give you my word." He took a deep breath. I sensed his nerves ratcheting. "Besides, we have other important matters to discuss, and I'd like to request your discretion. I'll be leaving on a trip soon."

Father crossed his arms. "And how does that involve me?"

"Because I'm going with him," I spoke up. "Across the portal to America."

The vein on the king's forehead bulged, his temper no longer in check. "Absolutely not. Why would you want to?"

I proceeded, with Mya's help, to explain Cate's situation. We were counting on Mya's talent for influencing emotions. I could sneak away without his permission, though it would be nice not to have to defy him again.

"It's an excellent opportunity to take down Rowan in a location where his powers are useless," Mya said. "Our best chance."

Her angle was clever. And she was right. This mission *could* work in our favor.

Or be our downfall.

"Our biggest hurdle is crossing the portal without Alana. Any advice?" I asked.

Lucas added, "Someone spoke of Alana's mentor last night, but she couldn't remember his name. Is he still alive?"

Father leaned back, the tension easing. Asking for his input usually helped. "I seem to recall a Caelum man. Harlow, I believe. You mustn't try without getting help. Sometimes people would go on their own and just... disappear. Back before Alana closed them."

"Maybe they wanted to stay," Mya suggested.

"Perhaps. But others would follow through a more stable portal to search for the missing. A few ended up being stuck on the other side. They never found most of them. The uncertainty for those of us who remain here is... not easy." Father stared off in the distance. "My cousin was one of them. There was a portal near his home, and he couldn't resist. He'd had a fight with the girl he was seeing. I warned him not to go, and they were the last words I spoke to him." His voice drifted lower, lost in the memory.

Silence hovered in the space. "Where would we find this Harlow?" I finally asked. "Is he alive?"

"I don't actually know. He was something of a hermit, I believe. I'll ask around." The king stood, glaring daggers at me. "You are not to step foot in a portal until you know it's safe. Understood?"

"Yes, Father," I replied dutifully, though I'd do whatever it took to help Cate.

We all rose with him, unsure what to make of his demeanor. The king exited, and we eyed each other with a mixture of relief and *disbelief*.

"We didn't learn much." Mya smiled up at Lucas and took his hand. "But nice job distracting him from the two of us."

"I think he's hoping I go through that portal never to be seen again," Lucas joked.

"I've not exactly been his favorite offspring of late," I said. "Perhaps he's hoping the same for me. Otherwise, he would have locked me in the dungeon. He could start fresh with Mya as the heir."

She wrinkled her nose. "A woman in charge of Terra? Hardly."

"Wouldn't that be something?" A small smile crept in. "Both kingdoms led by women." After a few beats, the words sank in. After all, if I didn't return, Cate likely wouldn't either.

"Well. Shall we find the queen and give her an update?" Lucas asked, starting for the door.

To no one's surprise, Emma informed us that Cate had holed herself up in the library. We found her hunched over a giant tome, asleep. My heart ached for her. She must be exhausted.

"Wake up, sleepyhead," Lucas called. "And you have a little something..." he pointed to the side of his mouth, "right here."

Cate lurched to a sitting position and scrambled to wipe the drool with the back of her arm, flushing. "I—must have fallen asleep." She frowned. "I found some things, but I want to cross-check them. I was thinking we could search Alana's house together. Emma asked around, and apparently, it's been untouched. No one knew what to do with it."

"Let's talk timeline first," I said. "We can do research for a millennium and still not understand how to go through that portal. And we obviously don't have that much time." I leaned against the table. "I've been thinking about why Rowan gave us two weeks. Presumably, he thought it would be difficult, but not impossible. It will take five days to reach the portal from here. Then a couple of travel days to buy tickets and fly to Oregon. That leaves us seven—wait, now six days to meet his demand."

"Barging in won't do us any good. We should get there early and scout out the place. That's where we'll need Cate." Lucas angled his index finger toward her.

"I do have the home-court advantage." Cate closed the book she'd been reading.

Lucas, Mya, and I shared a glance; none of us familiar with the expression, but we figured out the gist. Cate's knowledge of America, and specifically her own house, would be key.

"So, why did Rowan leave us extra time?" I asked.

"He must be allowing wiggle room for both us and his messenger to travel." Cate tilted up a shoulder. "Because the ultimate goal for him is to make sure I arrive so he can..."

"Spring the trap, yes," I finished, not willing to say, or even think the words, *so he can kill you.*

"Well." Mya crossed her arms. "We have six days left to play with. How many extras do you want on the American end?"

"A couple, and add another for travel," Cate said. "It might be hard to find flights for us all on short notice. Plus, we'll have to go to pawn shops and trade jewelry for cash."

"Sounds like we leave in three days," I said. "Let's get to work."

Alana spent most of her time in a cottage several kilometers away. Her spartan rooms at the castle produced nothing of interest. The four of us saddled our horses and rode the short distance.

"It's cozy." Cate circled the main room filled with oversized chairs and plump pillows, with bookshelves lining the walls, and soft throw blankets draped over cushions, all in serene beige and dark blue.

A desk sat in one corner, and I beelined toward it. "I'll search for correspondence with this Harlow fellow." I rifled through the drawers, cubbies, and papers stacked neatly on top, but found no mention of him.

"I'll head to the bedroom," Mya said while Lucas and Cate examined the bookshelves.

The kitchen was small but serviceable, with a few drawers that yielded nothing.

"Found it!" Mya called, racing into the space. "A letter. Signed," she held it up, "with all my love, Harlow."

"With all my…" Lucas repeated, his jaw hanging open.

This didn't fit with how any of us imagined the austere Alana. Was he a friend? Or something more? Guilt pinged my conscience for not having ever thought of her as someone who might have a significant other. Someone who she cared for and loved her back. Someone who would be devastated by her loss.

"Is there an address?" Cate asked.

Mya scanned the envelope. "It's here." She handed it to Lucas. "Know where it is?"

He nodded and looked to me. "Why don't you and Cate stay here —see if Alana has journals or anything else that might help—while Mya and I visit him."

Cate answered, "Good idea. Find out if he trained Alana. And if he did, would he help me too?"

Mya and Lucas left, leaving me alone with Cate. She continued to search the shelves. Her emotions ranged from determined to desperate, strung tight as a bowstring. I came up behind her and slid my arms around her waist. "Don't forget to breathe," I whispered.

She turned and buried her head in my chest. "Thank you for agreeing to this crazy plan. Supporting me, no matter what."

"I'd follow you to the ends of the universe." I stroked her silky hair. She'd left it down today, likely for ease, but I always liked it better when it was free, so I could run my fingers through it.

She stepped back, and I loosened my hold.

"You might have to." Her green eyes searched mine.

"At least we'll be together." I slid my palms down her arms. I wished she could feel my emotions right then, like I could hers. She'd know my love bubbled over, uncontainable. She was supposed to be the savior of our kingdoms, and instead, she'd saved *me*. I'd been destined to forever fall in my father's shadow, encased in a shell of indifference. Now that I'd let myself experience love, I couldn't imagine that life, half locked away from the world. From *myself*.

Her gaze drifted downward. "I'm scared. Scared I'm leading us all to our deaths. Maybe I should go alone."

My fingers stiffened around her biceps. "You are not sacrificing yourself to Rowan. Your people need you. *I* need you."

"Who said anything about sacrificing?"

"You've been training, but facing him by yourself? It's a suicide mission. Using you as bait is bad enough."

She chewed her bottom lip. "There's no good answer. Will I end up bait to help us get to Rowan, or for him to get to me?"

I turned her words over in my mind, goosebumps rising. "I'm afraid, both."

CHAPTER 6
LUCAS

Mya and I slowed our horses after an hour's ride into the forest from Alana's house, stopping in front of a small cabin with overgrown greenery flanking the door. Mya hopped off her horse before I could even offer assistance.

"I would have given you a hand, you know," I teased.

"It looks like I'm going to be on my own for a while soon. Might as well get used to it." Her features clouded before pasting on a smile. "See. Obviously, I manage just fine." She tied both our horses to a tree. We were sheltered from the house's direct sight by the overgrown brush.

I reached for her hand. "Of course, you do. But…" I hesitated. Our relationship was new. We were still feeling out the other—her putting on a brave face, me searching for signs she'd miss me. "Are you okay? This is a lot to pile on you at once."

"What, both my brother and you being thrown into the aether in three days, never to return? At least I'll be first in line to rule Terra," she said airily. Her dark, winged brows arched, as if challenging me to argue her point.

Maybe that's what I liked about her so much. She had a tendency to deflect like me. I stroked the pad of her thumb. "I'm going to miss you."

Her sooty lashes furiously blinked back watery tears. "Don't do that to me, Lucas. We're not doing goodbyes. Not yet, anyway."

I leaned in close to kiss her cheek, then lingered, feathering another below her ear. "Aren't you going to miss me?" I whispered.

Her cheeks were now a pleasant shade of rose. She shifted and kissed me full on the lips, wrapping her arms around my neck and pressing close. "Yes," she breathed.

Our mouths moved in desperation as if melding them together could somehow stop us from being pulled apart. Could hold this perfect, fragile thing in one piece. She trailed nails down my spine, and I kissed her neck, the smell of her lavender-scented hair driving me mad. Finally, I forced myself to step away before I plucked out her pins and ran my hands through the dark tresses.

"We have a job to do," I said.

She sighed. "We do."

"You don't have to help."

She crinkled her nose. "You know I hate being left out."

I linked her arm in mine, elbowed her, and started toward the house. "I'm aware. You won't let anyone forget it."

She scowled. "Because literally everyone will! Years of being confined to the ballroom. I mean, sure, I know the exact cut and color to wear, how to flip my fan—"

"Yes, yes, I can't take my eyes off you in one of those fancy gowns. And I promise," I placed a hand over my heart, "I will never discount you." We came to the door, and I gestured. "Would you like to be the one to knock?"

She rolled her eyes. "Thanks."

It took a few moments, but an older gentleman with sagging skin, giving him a hound-like expression, arrived at the door. "Yes?"

"Hello, sir. I'm Sir Lucas Bradbury. I was friends with Alana. Are you Mr. Harlow by any chance?"

"It's Matthews. Harlow's my given name." His gray brows furrowed. "I don't recall Alana speaking of you."

"What he means is," Mya cut in, "he's friends with Queen Catherine, and by proxy, Alana. I'm Princess Mya of Terra. We were hoping you could help us with something."

His mouth gaped, then he stepped back, widening the gap in the doorway. "Please come in." Harlow gave a small bow to Mya. "Your Highness."

I inwardly smiled. We should have led with Mya's royal status—her presence certainly carries more weight than mine. And here she thought she was always ignored.

Books covered nearly every surface of the cramped cottage, piled in corners, on tables, and in most spaces to sit. "Forgive me. I'm happiest out here alone in the woods with my readings. Sometimes I forget…" He shook his head. "It's been a long time since I've had company." He cleared a spot on a worn sofa and stacked more volumes next to a chair for himself.

"What news has traveled out here?" I asked. "Have you been to town recently?"

"Oh, yes. I go about once a week. I'm aware of the king's death." His gaze fell to his lap. "And Alana's."

"We heard you were her mentor?" I asked.

"Oh… that was a considerable time ago. It didn't take long for the student to surpass the teacher."

"The queen—Cate, was hoping you could help her. She needs to get through the portal."

He grunted. "Unless her powers are stronger than I've been led to believe, she shouldn't try it alone."

"I'll be with her." I tried to sound like my presence would somehow make the passage easier when, in reality, my only role would be to protect her from outside dangers.

"And my brother, Daniel, is going too," Mya said.

He turned to Mya, his gaze questioning, yet judging at the same time. "And not you?"

"No, I'll be staying here. Traveling back to Terra with my father, actually." That smile I knew so well turned false.

"They'll need another," he said. "I sense you would fulfill the circle."

Mya and I exchanged looks. I cleared my throat. "The circle?"

His mouth twisted downward. "You know nothing. Do not attempt it." He started to rise.

"But we have to," I said, stopping him. "We only have a few days."

His bushy brows went up. "Caelum just lost its king, and now the heir is fleeing? No, I cannot help you. Besides, there's too much training… practice."

"It's to rid us of Rowan," Mya explained. "And save Cate's other family."

The folds of his wrinkles hardened like crags in stone. "A few days? She'll be lost forever, and you will condemn us all to a kingdom in turmoil. And you—" he focused again on Mya. "Are you prepared to be the next in line for Terra? Because you're dooming your brother. Especially if you choose not to assist them."

Mya's chin lowered. "What do you mean? That's exactly what I'm doing here. Helping."

The biting gaze disappeared. "Never mind. No matter. There's not enough time."

I leaned forward and lowered my voice, holding back from shooting out of my chair and looming over the man in frustration. "Harlow. We're going whether you help us or not. If you have information that could assist your queen, you best produce it."

The man's shoulders sagged along with the rest of his body. His clothes, a size too big, the bags under his eyes, and his countenance rounded out the appearance of a tired, lonely man who'd given up. And now I'd kicked a dog when it was down.

"You must bring the queen here. We shall see if she possesses enough balanced energy to stabilize a portal. Otherwise, you will need a full circle."

"Forgive our ignorance," Mya said. "We don't know what that means."

"To correctly balance the portals, the strength of energy from both Caelum and Terra needs to be in harmony, which you've probably surmised given Alana's success. Long ago, we discovered that a group of four with power from each side would also work, though they should somehow be connected for the best results. It's why the portals became unstable in the first place. They began to require simultaneous Caelum and Terran energy between individuals from both sides working together to combine their power. As you're aware, there hasn't been much cooperation between the kingdoms in centuries."

"You're saying the portals went haywire because of our feuding?" I sat back, stunned by the revelation sitting in front of our noses this entire time.

"I believe so, yes."

"And Alana knew this?" I wondered why she never shared it.

He cocked his head. "If she did, would it have changed anything?"

I wanted to argue. To say if we'd only known, things might have been different. Truth is, tensions ran too deep between the kingdoms. If what he said was true—that a connection was needed between those stabilizing the portal—then finding participants wouldn't have been easy.

"Alana hoped the prophecy would pull us together through Catherine, then she would share the information. Only…"

Her death hung in the air, a heavy presence in the small space.

Mya cleared her throat. "So, we need to bring Cate here, and you'll somehow be able to tell if she has enough energy to do this balancing thing?"

"We will try. There's a reason my cabin sits out here in the middle of nowhere."

He let the words dangle until curiosity got the better of me. "And why's that?"

His sad eyes met mine, taking on a sharp edge once more. "Because I'm guarding a portal."

CHAPTER 7 **CATE**

After searching Alana's house, we found nothing else useful. The books on her shelves were largely fiction, which surprised me. There was so much I didn't know about her. Was it because she'd been unwilling to share, or I'd never asked? It left me aching to have one more sunrise conversation, sitting on that cold marble bench in the castle gardens.

As we rode home, Daniel recited the lists he'd created last night. Clearly, neither of us had slept much. I'd tried to grant him a respite from my emotions, yet he had plenty of his own.

"Also," he said, "I'm having a set of clothes made for Lucas and me. Mine from last time are at Terra, and I'm not sure what happened to Lucas's. I presume you've kept yours?"

They were tucked away in a drawer—my treasured Nikes, Oregon hoodie, and jeans.

"We'll buy more when we get there. You'll provide the jewelry for the pawn shop?"

He was trying to distract me, it just wasn't working. Ever the planner, he'd plot every last detail to mitigate the risk of any situation. And I loved him for it.

"Mmhmm." I stared off into the countryside. "Unless Graftonberg stole everything." Two riders approached in the distance. Mya's mint-green dress stood out in the late afternoon light. I slowed our horses and waved.

"We have to turn around," Lucas said once they came close. "Come back with us—Harlow is willing to train you."

Finally, something other than a dead end.

"You up for it?" Daniel asked me.

A constant whirlwind of training had assaulted me since arriving to this world. It felt like a lifetime ago, but only a touch over four months had passed. At this point, learning and struggling had become a way of life. The burden to always be better—to harness the power without draining my own—was a stone constantly around my neck. Adding one more weight might lead me to stumble or make me stronger.

I'm not sure what I expected, but Harlow wasn't it. I'd imagine anyone loving Alana would be fastidious, tall, and austere—instead, a stooped figure with a few stains on his loosely fitting waistcoat and baggy trousers answered our knock. A peek inside the door showed what appeared to be a library in the midst of a reorganization. Either that, or someone who belonged on one of those hoarder TV shows.

He bowed. "Your Highness. I—I wasn't expecting you back today. The mess..."

"Is fine." I stepped through the entrance. "It looks like we're kindred spirits. I love to read. Are you doing research, or is it for pleasure?"

The lines around his mouth softened. "Some of both. Come, sit."

We navigated our way to the seating area, careful not to topple any piles. "I hear there's a portal nearby? It would save time if we didn't have to travel to the one up north," I said. It was hard not to be annoyed that this old man living out in the woods was guarding a portal we could have been using all along.

"I'm afraid it's quite unstable," he answered. "Alana gave up on it and usually traveled to the one you came through. Mine is for practice only. Though I must warn you. Alana worked for years to understand them. Only allowing yourself a couple of days is a fool's errand." He ducked his head, his mouth forming a wry smile. "Forgive me." He closed his eyes, growing absolutely still.

It wasn't clear if he was asking for forgiveness for calling me a fool or for suddenly closing his eyes. When they remained shut after what seemed like a full minute, I exchanged glances with Lucas and sent him an, *are you sure about this guy?* stare. The silence began to grow more than awkward—the only sound a ticking clock somewhere on the mantel, obscured by books. Daniel gave a tiny shrug, then slipped his arm behind me on the couch and absently stroked his fingers at the base of my neck, sending tingles into my scalp.

"There." Harlow's lids flipped open. "There's your energy." He folded his hands in his lap. "It's much weaker than I expected, especially for one with such power over water. But it surged just now."

Those same tingles turned into the heat of embarrassment at realizing the spike was due to Daniel's touch. Although I'd been working on my powers while distancing myself from him, there was no doubt he helped strengthen them.

"Even so. I suspect it won't be enough," he said.

Mya spoke up, "You can feel how much energy someone has?"

"Oh, yes. It's one of my abilities. I found Alana by sensing her in town one day. The strongest I've felt to date. Although, to be fair, I haven't been near enough to either king to make a proper judgment." His eyes flickered from me to Daniel.

"We only have a couple days. Can we get started?" I asked.

Harlow's attention centered back on me. He'd seemed distracted since we arrived, now laser-focused. His demeanor had been odd, wavering from deference to near defiance. Maybe it came from living out here alone so long, or maybe he didn't want to help and hid it poorly. "Your Highness," he sat up straighter, "I'm asking you not to do this. Don't travel through the portal, and please… please don't force me to train you." He swallowed hard. "This won't end well."

He was asking too much. I couldn't give up on my family. Couldn't be responsible for more deaths. But I was responsible for Lucas and Daniel, too. The weight of so many lives hung on my shoulders, adding to the ever-growing burden, his foreboding words chilling. My fingers had clenched into fists, nails digging half-moons into my palms. I exhaled and slowly opened my hand, taking Daniel's.

"I have to try. Please?" How could I live with myself if I chose anything else?

He hesitated. "We'll visit the portal, then decide. Is there enough daylight for you to see it, and still get you home?" He stood, leaning over to peer out a grimy window at the setting sun.

Lucas pulled out a pocket watch. "It'll be getting dark soon. We'll be back first thing in the morning."

Harlow stopped at the cabin door. "I'll bid you good night here. You must all come tomorrow, not just the queen. She'll need you."

"My sister isn't traveling with us," Daniel said, his voice firm.

Harlow straightened his sweater, a motion I'd started to identify as a nervous tick. "Bring her anyway," he replied. "Please," he added, as if remembering he'd spoken to a prince.

Mya's reckless behavior gave Daniel pause. I didn't particularly want to depend on her either. In the short time we'd been together, I liked her well enough, but she seemed like a liability—unfamiliar with my world, untrained in fighting, and a distraction for both Lucas and her brother.

We mounted our horses and headed toward the castle, the air turning cool with the golden sun setting behind us.

"We have two days," Daniel said. "Then we pack up and go."

"Three days," Lucas replied. "I've been thinking we should take Molly. She can carry all of us. It won't be easy for her, but she'll do it. We'll travel faster that way."

I'd ridden Lucas's dragon only once before. It had been an exhilarating yet terrifying experience.

"You trust going that far north with her?" Daniel asked. "We might run into other dragons."

"I'm more concerned about an Ember ambush."

Lucas was right. We'd been so worried about a trap on the other side—what if they were waiting for us at the portal over here?

"Thank you." I placed a hand on Lucas's shoulder. "I know how much Molly means to you. We'll take you up on that offer." When Daniel remained silent, I elbowed him.

"Yeah. Thanks, mate," he mumbled.

The two of them had better start getting along. I'd need them both.

Daniel turned to Mya. "Why does Harlow want you there?" He sent her a pointed look as if to ask what she'd been up to.

"Something about a circle," Mya replied.

Lucas went on to explain that a connection between four members of Caelum and Terra was stronger, especially when they shared a bond.

"That backs up what I read in the library," I said.

"You're still not going," Daniel told Mya.

She looked away, but not before I caught the hurt flashing across her face. After a moment, her features now smooth and cold, she said, "I'll be staying here with Father, working on becoming even more useless, if that's possible. Someone has to." The bitterness in her tone was unmasked, showing just how much she hated being under King Dryden's thumb.

Daniel's shoulders deflated. He, of all people, understood how hard it was to be left alone with their father. "I'm sorry. I really am. I talked to Dev about getting you set up with self-defense training, and… I'll speak to Father to see if you can be more involved."

"Come tomorrow," I said to Mya. "It might help us understand what the energy should feel like. We can practice with and without you in the circle."

"I'll think about it," she said, watching Daniel.

I didn't miss the glance of longing Lucas sent her, while nervously flicking his attention back to her brother.

"Daniel?" I moved North to ride closer to him. "It can't hurt to let her come tomorrow."

His lips curved into the barest of smiles. "Thanks for keeping me from falling into the overbearing brother role." He exhaled. "Again."

"You want to protect her. I get that." Sometimes others didn't realize what a huge heart Daniel hid under his shell, and how thin and fragile those walls he'd erected really were.

"Not sure she cares what I think."

"Tell her anyway and find out."

"I'll pull her aside when we get there," he said.

"Thank you," I mouthed.

"We should hurry." Daniel urged Raven on. "Big day tomorrow. And we only have a few left."

His words echoed, starting me down the anxiety spiral. *Only a few left*. What if we couldn't get through the portal? Or worse, what if we never made it back?

CHAPTER 8
DANIEL

Once we arrived at the stables, I called out to Mya, "Care to talk for a few?"

Her gaze lingered on Lucas, strolling to the castle, Cate by his side. I, too, fought back that old pang of jealousy. Not as strong as it once was, but somewhere in the back of my mind, I always worried I'd lose her—the best thing that ever happened to me. Probably because I'd never deserve her.

Turning my focus back to Mya, I said, "I want you to come tomorrow. Cate does too."

She pursed her lips. "I thought this was going to be another one of your lectures." It came out sharp, but the edge hid the obvious hurt.

"I deserved that. I've been hard on you. Honestly, Mya." I fiddled with the leather tack hanging on the barn wall beside me. "I'm scared, and I'm not entirely sure how this portal traveling is going to turn out. I'd feel immensely better if you were here to look after Terra."

Her lips formed a teasing lilt. "Immensely?"

I ignored her ribbing. "You want to be in the thick of things. I get that. In a lot of ways, your job is harder. Sitting here. Waiting. Dealing with Father. I'd hate it too." I dropped the bridle. "Forgive me?"

She eyed me skeptically.

"I don't say it enough, but you really are brilliant." The reality of leaving indefinitely set in, along with a desperation to mend this rift.

"The kingdom is lucky to have you. Remember when we were kids, and you'd beat me at chess? Every. Time."

She smirked. "Of course. I remember when you stopped playing."

"And why would I have done that?"

"Because your male ego couldn't take it?"

She had me pegged. "I do hate losing." I slipped my arm into the crook of hers and escorted her to the castle. "See you in the morning?"

She smiled—a genuine one, her dimples flashing. "I'll be here."

I stopped by the infirmary to visit Dev before returning to my room. My oldest friend was raring to leave his bed.

"I feel useless here, staring at these four blank walls." Dev flung an arm out in exasperation, sitting farther up in bed and glaring at the untouched broth on the table beside him.

"Are you well enough to travel back to Terra with my parents? I'm sure Mother will let you ride in the carriage."

Dev snorted. "Well, it's better than riding horseback next to your father for days." He held up his hands. "No offense."

I stifled a grin and sat at the edge of the bed. "None taken. I've been meaning to talk to you about something." I proceeded to explain Cate's dilemma, the portals, the circle, and how I was afraid I might not return.

Dev's frown deepened the more I spoke.

"I need you to look after Mya. And… I support her to be queen. But if Father won't name her as his heir, I'm going to recommend you to be the next in line."

His head cranked back. "What? No. I won't do it. It has to be Mya."

"You know my father and his opinions on women. Advise her. Support her. I trust you to be fair and bring peace between the kingdoms, and if the time comes, you'll step up and be king. You will. Father likes you. And yours is the second-most powerful province in the kingdom. It's a natural choice." Plus, I'd hope to skip over Dev's father, the Duke of Earlington, if anything happened to King Dryden. He'd be as bad as Graftonberg.

Dev's throat bobbed with a swallow. "I don't—Mya's the better choice."

"She is," I replied automatically. "And you're the next best."

He flopped his head back on his pillow and stared at the ceiling. "Whatever you need, mate."

Silence settled in the space as we both contemplated our uncertain futures.

"When do you leave?" he finally asked.

"Not for a couple of days. We'll talk again. You'll be on your way to Terra the day after tomorrow? I'll see you off with a proper goodbye."

"You know I love those." He smiled wryly.

The knots in my belly continued to tighten the more I spoke of this trip. Cate would never give up on her family. And I would never abandon her. So, here we were. The heirs of both kingdoms potentially setting themselves up to disappear forever.

The next morning, Cate was already at the stables when I arrived. She wrapped her arms tight around my waist, settling her cheek on my chest. Her touch, sometimes a balm, others a match to my flame, now intensified the sorrow floating around her. "Hey. You okay?" I murmured.

"I was up early and decided to go to the bench where I used to meet Alana at sunrise." Her head somehow felt heavier against my ribs. Her breath shuddered. "It was good. Centering. I just miss her, you know? Miss my father, too."

I held her, stroking her back. Nothing I could say would make it better. I'd learned recently from Dev that sometimes just being there was enough.

She pulled away, exhaling noisily. "We have to move forward and stop looking back. Which means no more regrets."

I took her hand, fingers cool in mine. "It's impossible not to have regrets. None of us is perfect. It's how we choose to learn and change from our mistakes that matters."

Her eyes shone with unshed tears. "I have so many. I—"

"Shhh." I slid a gentle finger across her lips. "We're going to fix this. I promise." It rang hollow, that promise. We both knew neither of us could count on it.

Mya and Lucas strode into the barn, hand-in-hand. "You guys ready?" Lucas asked, heading for his horse's stall.

"As I'll ever be," Cate answered.

We headed out and reached the cabin within an hour. Harlow greeted us, and we traipsed through the woods to the portal. Apprehension hovered like fog, rolling heaviest from Cate. The damp earth created a spongy cushion as we hiked farther into the forest, finally reaching a clearing.

I shot my arm out. "Stop."

Cate halted, glancing around. "What is it?"

"The portal," Lucas answered, also holding out a hand to prevent anyone from moving.

"You can't feel it?" Mya's brows scrunched together.

Cate almost unwittingly stepped right through the thing. From her expression, I could tell she felt nothing. She took an unsteady breath, stepping closer so that our shoulders brushed. The hair on her arms rose.

"There," she called out, now sensing what we all did.

Instead of the harmonious buzz of the molecules that usually moved in concert, a discordant movement jostled the air just in front of us. My foot shifted involuntarily backward. Something about the energy felt… off.

"Is that what the other portal was like?" she asked.

"No," Lucas and I said in unison.

"How?" Mya asked. "How did it feel to go through?" Her constant desire for adventure glowed bright behind her questions.

"When you stood next to it—at least the one Alana fixed—there was a pull," Lucas said. "All the energy seemed to be traveling in the same direction. Not," he jiggled his fingers, "whatever this is."

"Yeah, it feels so disorganized." Mya rubbed her arms. "Angry, even."

"Going through feels like weightlessness," I said. "You have to remind yourself to focus. Then poof—you're on the other side."

Cate held an uneasy expression.

"What? You don't agree?" I asked her.

"It was different for me. Kind of like being in the movie *Twister*."

Later, she'd confided that she'd dreamed I'd called to her in the portal. That we'd almost kissed, which of course was a bit of an ego boost. Even then, she'd been drawn to my energy. And I to hers.

"Cate," Lucas tilted his head, "you've gotta stop doing that to us. No one here has seen *Twister*."

"Sorry, I'll stop mentioning pop-culture stuff."

"Pop-what?" Mya asked.

"Never mind. Anyway, when I went through, there was a lot of wind. I thought I was going to die. Fun times. I made it, but not exactly in the same place as the guys."

Lucas laughed. "She was at the bottom of a volcano crater."

"Didn't seem so funny at the time," she muttered.

Harlow cleared his throat.

"Sorry, Harlow," Cate said. "I think we've established that the portal doesn't feel right. So, what do we do?"

"You'll need to harness it," Harlow replied, "smooth out the edges. Make the energy go where you wish."

Another seemingly impossible task. "If you taught Alana," I hesitated, "then can you control the portal?"

He straightened his cardigan. "I certainly wouldn't leave it in such disarray if I were able to manage it. My father tried to teach me, but we discovered I held neither the talent nor the power. This portal was once frequented by many in Caelum, and my family lived in that house for generations, maintaining it. Long ago, I could align the energy. As the years passed, it became more and more unstable. Too much for me. Then, when I came upon Alana…" He took on a nostalgic expression. "I thought she might try."

"Did she ever use it? Even once?" I asked.

"Never. As I told you, she could tell it wasn't safe. You'll have to travel north." He crossed his arms.

The portal swirled with ominous energy. Everything about it felt wrong, as if it warned us not to enter. I slipped my hand in Cate's, letting the soothing energy that always accompanied her flow around us.

"Feel it?" I whispered.

"Listen to it," Harlow said. "Learn its pattern, then you will work to tame it. Just don't let it overtake you."

The portal almost seemed to react to his words, the negative energy shooting through me, in one side and out the other, like a ghost. A shiver scaled up my scalp. "How might that happen?" I asked warily.

I took a step back, pulling Cate with me. "How much danger are we in? I thought we were just practicing."

The bags beneath Harlow's eyes sagged heavier today. "If she cannot at least do this with you as an anchor, then much higher danger lies ahead."

Cate squeezed my hand. "It's okay. I'm good."

"Should we make the circle?" Mya asked, her shifting feet crunching the dry leaves.

"Let me try first," Cate said. "Get a feel for it."

We all stood in silence, the discordant energy of the portal pouring over us. I tried to tame it too, because, why not? Except I couldn't sense any change. My eyes met Lucas's, and he shook his head subtly, his mouth a grim line.

Cate released my fingers. Her lids fluttered open as if coming to a decision. "Harlow, how do we form the circle?"

"You two." He gestured to Mya and Lucas. "Come around to this side."

I could see what he meant for us to do—literally encircle the passage. Even with our arms extended, we'd have to take two more steps closer to touch. The thought of edging nearer was repellent. Cate nodded reassuringly, but when I checked her emotions, they trembled with anxiety.

We squished together until I clasped Mya's hand, arms outstretched, and Cate grasped Lucas's.

"Because of the mix of both Caelum and Terran," Harlow began, "you should come closer to taming it. The connections you share—use them. You're familiar with the other's energy, whether you realize it or not."

I already sensed Cate's, and with concentration, I could feel Mya's high-pitched hum, though it took focus to overcome the dissonant energy of the portal.

"Good," Harlow said, his voice low and soothing. "I can tell you're joined. Now expand your mind to the portal. Catherine, grab both the Caelum and Terran inside you. Take the strength of the others and smooth them into one."

The energy ricocheted off itself, then expanded, its speed increasing. The buzz grew louder, infiltrating my skull and crawling under my skin. Wind rushed, my hair whipping across my forehead, catching in my lashes and making me yearn to brush it from my eyes. The energy gained strength, becoming more erratic, even as we all tried to fight it. I longed to release Cate's hand and rub out the uncomfortable sensation pulsating across my body. It was like Father transferring power into me. And for a moment, I relived the torture. Relived the nightmare. Me in the fetal position. Him looming above me.

I tore my attention to Cate, blinking back the unwanted images. Her skirt ripped in the gale, but her face remained placid, eyes closed. She must believe she can control it. *Maybe she can.* A crinkle finally marred her brow as she bit her lip. Across the circle, Lucas and Mya watched, wide-eyed, no longer pretending to attempt to control the chaos.

The winds shifted, pulling us toward the center. The buzz turned to a roar, my heart slamming against my chest. *This can't be right.* The last portal felt nothing like this.

"Cate," I yelled.

She remained stoic, her grip iron in my hand.

"Let go if you can't control it," Harlow shouted. "Break the circle!"

I tried to release Cate, but she held fast. Mya's hand also stayed glued to mine, as if bound by the energy.

"Let go of me!" Mya's dark brows slashed into a V, her high-pitched tone a mixture of annoyed sister and fear.

"Cate," I screamed. "Stop!"

Yet the force only strengthened. I leaned back to combat the pull.

"Break it!" Harlow barked.

Lucas struggled across from me, attempting to wrench his hands free, twisting his arms so the girls nearly staggered to their knees to avoid injury.

Cate remained almost in a trance, unfazed, as if the energy controlled her instead of the other way around. It swirled and trembled around us. A branch broke from a nearby tree with a *crack*, debris flying. I put up my own energy shield for Cate and me while Mya did the same. But it was no use.

My feet slid.

First, a few inches, then the portal sucked Mya in. She tumbled headfirst into the abyss. Panic streaked across her face, sending a shudder of terror through me. It flashed right before the momentum pitched Lucas, then me, into the void. I glimpsed Cate, the final one to topple into the vortex, still gripping my hand in a dream-like state.

And then there was nothing.

CHAPTER 9
CATE

I couldn't stop. It was as if the portal's power took over, sinking into my skin and embedding itself, burrowing deeper and deeper until its frantic rhythm became one with the beat of my erratic heart. As soon as our circle joined, it was as if the entirety of energy from Caelum and Terra thudded through my veins. I'd never experienced such power, and my body didn't know how to handle it.

Such a thing couldn't be tamed. It was alive, energy swooping and swirling into every crevice, into our very beings. My world turned dream-like, a hazy fog tossing with the whims of the portal. My mind wanted to grasp at something, but all my thoughts had turned slippery, like oil on a pond. A tiny trigger of sadness awakened a memory.

I'd lost the others.

I felt no one. Only the pulse of the portal as I careened through the mouth of its grasp. The haze intensified, wispy thoughts intangible. Suddenly, I was back in my childhood twin bed with the pink bedspread, and the panda bear stuffy tucked beside me. Mom caressed my forehead. She peered at someone across the room. I couldn't see him, but I knew it was my dad. Knew I was safe with them.

"Should we call the doctor?" Worry stretched the lines around her eyes. "The fever's so high."

"I gave her more Tylenol. Let's see if it breaks this time," Dad replied, his voice low and steady.

"I'm scared. It's like she's somewhere else."

The day returned in a patchwork of memories. I'd ended up in the ER from dehydration and fever, mostly incoherent. Now… it was like I could see both sides. I hadn't actually been *there* all that time ago. I'd been *here*—in this portal, floating in the haze halfway between worlds.

I slipped back to that bed. Mom's fingers on my brow, the dip in the mattress. I could fall asleep. Stay forever. My eyes fluttered closed. *Home.*

An echo of my name drifted through my thoughts. *Mom?* No, the voice was male… not Dad, either. Another joined it. I wanted them to stop. Stop bothering me so I could be with my family and never have to worry about them again.

"Cate!"

Daniel. The name intruded into my childhood dreams and wormed its way as something important. Vital.

Fingers pressed across the flat of my hand.

The portal came rushing back, bringing with it a torrent of wind and a shot of adrenaline that sent my heart racing. Daniel and Lucas's shouts came into focus. I creaked open my lids, squinting in the gale. All of us were still linked, yet I thought I'd been alone. Illusions—reality and memories blended seamlessly together. Had the scene with my parents been real? The flashback, previously long forgotten, now shone in technicolor, beckoning me to the little bed with the pink comforter.

Focus, Cate. Daniel and Lucas shouted at one another, their voices spinning in and out of consciousness. Mya, across from me, floated, her features serene, eyes closed.

"Wake them! The whole circle has to focus," Daniel shouted.

"I'm trying!" Lucas jerked his arm, sending a jolt of pain through my shoulder.

"I'm here," I whispered, my throat sandpaper. "I'm with you."

"Cate. Look at me," Daniel said.

I turned my head slowly, the disconnected, feverish sensation overwhelming. His blue eyes shone with intensity.

"I love you," he said. "Hold on to that. It worked last time, remember? Don't fall back asleep."

A sensation tingled across my fingers. Daniel's energy. *Our love.* I honed in on the feeling and realized I could faintly sense Mya's Terran power, too, the current traveling through Daniel's feelings for his sister, then warm and bright through Lucas. His Caelum energy filled the cracks, solidifying the rest of my hazy thoughts.

The circle. It had to be the key.

I focused on pushing all that energy through the boys into Mya. She jolted awake as if I'd shocked her—*perhaps I did?* "Mya. We need you!" I shouted.

The power surged. "I can do this—no, *we* can do this." Suddenly, the answer seemed clear. "Concentrate on the circle. Ignore everything else. Stop trying to tame it. It will conform to us." The portal's chaotic energy led us into its disorder and fed off our fear and confusion.

The dissonant chords streamlined into a steady hum, the deep bass of the Terran energy combining with the higher tenor of Caelum. The air's power required more, as I was half of each, ribboning around us into a lopsided ring. I pushed to balance it, but it wasn't enough.

"Lucas!" I shouted. "We need more."

His reassuring nod, even if just for show, bolstered my confidence.

The winds decelerated. *We* decelerated, as if someone pressed the slow-motion button on the remote.

Then the world went silent.

Two seconds. Three.

I landed on my tailbone with a jolt. Our hands had unclasped, and in a panic, I jerked my eyes up to find the bewildered faces of my companions. The startle of a booming, low-pitched noise assaulted our ears. A long, yellow strip painted onto asphalt stretched before us. My heart seized. We were in the middle of the road with a semi-truck fast approaching, the wheels screeching, the clatter of the brakes pumping beneath the blare of the horn.

"Move!" I yelled, scrambling to my feet and lunging toward the side of the street. The semi barreled closer.

They weren't going to make it.

Adrenaline must have kicked in some of Daniel's Terran energy, because he raced to my side with lightning speed. Lucas smashed into Mya, sending them flying. The truck squealed by, unable to stop, skidding inches from Lucas. The ground vibrated, the rush of the draft skimming my cheeks.

I gulped the cool air and took in my surroundings, pulling Daniel farther from the road, while Lucas and Mya crawled to the side. Farmland lay behind, rolling acres of verdant green, bushy plants. The semi slowed, must have seen us in its mirrors, blared its horn, and continued on its way. A few more cars passed, including a newer model. My shoulders lowered a fraction. At least we didn't time travel back to World War II or something.

"Where are we?" Mya dusted off her skirts with a shake.

"Not Caelum, that's for sure," Daniel replied.

The rectangular license plates weren't the shape of any in the US. "Europe somewhere," I said. "Probably Great Britain."

"Definitely not at the other portal. I would have remembered nearly getting squashed like a bug." Lucas straightened his tunic.

I giggled. We all looked like we'd escaped a Renaissance faire.

"What are you laughing at?" Lucas frowned. "I have something in my hair?" He ran a hand through his trimmed blond locks.

"We won't exactly fit in dressed like this." I glanced at my own fitted pink riding gown.

"My lists," Daniel moaned. "All the things we needed. Clothes. Money. Directions to our contacts here."

"Wait, what?" I pulled on his hand. "You don't know where they are? I thought you met with them last time."

The crease in his brow deepened. "We did. But I only know the general direction. Finding the university would help. Lucas?" Daniel peered in his direction.

Lucas squinted into the horizon, as if he could somehow see where we should go. "Maybe if we get closer, I'll remember. When we were here before, we had maps."

"Right. Okay." I swiped my hair out of my face, my heart rate kicking up, and told myself this wasn't a big deal. We could handle this, right? Just because we were in the middle of nowhere with no money and no idea how to find the people who could help, all while Rowan still had my family…

No, it all seemed like a *very* big deal.

"At least we're together." Mya linked her arm in mine, her attempt at positivity easing the panic spiral I'd started to descend into. "Which way do you think?"

I looked around. "Most of the cars are going there." I pointed in the direction the truck had been heading.

"Okay, then. That way it is," she said.

We started walking along the road. I shifted Mya to the side of the embankment because she kept drifting from the gravel to the asphalt.

"It's easier to walk there," she insisted.

Its surface *was* paved and flat, but I didn't trust she'd be able to dodge a vehicle in time. "You've never been around cars. They're much faster than horses." To punctuate my point, a motorcycle zoomed past.

I covered a smile at her shocked face. "That's no ordinary bicycle," she said, taking another step from the road.

"Nope."

Daniel and Lucas trudged with us, one in front, the other behind. The sun occasionally peeked through clouds overhead, indicating well past midday. On cue, my stomach growled. I'd been too nervous to eat this morning. Instead, I communed with Alana's spirit at dawn. By this time, we'd already walked for an hour, my feet hurt, and even if we found a town, we had no money.

Daniel slipped his hand in mine, displacing Mya. "I'm hungry too." That must have been one angry stomach growl for him to hear. At this point, Daniel was used to my hunger pains.

"Is someone talking about food?" Lucas asked.

"How we want some, does that count?" I called behind. He'd joined Mya, the two of them a few yards back.

Guilt began its steady, venomous spread. This was *my* fault. Why couldn't I break the circle? Daniel had explained what happened, only I didn't remember the part where Harlow and everyone else yelled for me to stop. It's almost as if the portal took over my body.

"I don't know how it happened. Earlier. I—I'm sorry."

"You're sorry?" A harsh grate rang in Daniel's voice. "It's Harlow's fault. He never should have let us practice there."

I huffed a sarcastic laugh. "Not sure we gave him much choice."

"A little warning would have been nice," he grumbled.

He was trying to make me feel better, and it actually worked. Why should I take all the blame? We had no idea it would happen, and it was Harlow who insisted on the circle. Now Mya was stuck here with us. Daniel tried to hide it, but I knew he worried about her. I leaned over and kissed his cheek.

"What was that for?"

"For being you."

He whispered in my ear, "If my sister wasn't behind us, I'd kiss you until you're breathless." His hot breath in the shell of my ear shot tingles up my spine.

"And what about Lucas back there?" I blinked at him, wide-eyed and innocent-like.

"He can watch." He pulled away and sent me a cocky grin.

I shook my head at his male posturing. Although his distraction worked. A smile remained pasted on my lips.

After another hour on foot, neighborhoods spread out on either side. A man with a knitted stocking cap walking his little, fluffy dog headed toward us.

"Excuse me, sir? Which way is town?" He eyed us with a mixture of surprise and amusement. *Right. Our clothes.*

"Keep going. You'll run into shops in another two kilometers."

"We've been a bit out of touch recently. Off the grid," I nodded knowingly, like it was the most natural thing in the world to be wearing an old-fashioned gown on the side of the road. Nerves swarmed my belly at my next question, but I had to know if it was too late to save my family. "What's the date?"

"January twentieth," he answered, one eyebrow quirking up above the blue cap's fabric.

A tiny frisson of relief coursed through me. We'd calculated this same date before we left. I'd arrived at Staton University in September, but it'd been spring in our world when I first went through the portal. Nearly four months had passed in Caelum, meaning it should be winter here. "The year?" I asked.

He hesitated, picking up his tiny dog, probably wondering if we'd escaped from a mental institution at this point. His answer reassured us that we hadn't lost time.

"Now we just have to repeat it on the way back," Mya said after the man hurriedly passed.

"Sure," I responded, only partly sarcastic. I appreciated Mya's confidence, though I wasn't looking forward to passing through that portal again.

We reached the town, which spread out in all directions. Although more than a village, it was hard to estimate its size on foot. A woman in a tweed jacket, focused on her destination, approached.

"We're searching for a pawnshop," Daniel said.

She glanced up, surprised that we'd spoken, then shook her head and kept moving. I didn't know where to find a pawnshop in my hometown either. We tried three more people before someone could give us directions.

"What exactly are we selling?" I asked, eyeing a gold ring on Mya's finger with an emerald-cut green stone. Likely part of the royal collection.

"My signet ring," Daniel replied.

I stopped walking and stared. "What? You can't give that up."

He cocked his head, dark hair falling over his brow. "We're going to need loads of money, aren't we?"

"My ring. And earrings, too." Mya touched her ears where gemstone studs glittered.

They were probably all priceless, but Daniel's ring? Not like I needed *more* reasons to feel guilty that we'd ended up crossing the portal unprepared. I hadn't even thought about jewelry this morning, rushing to rise with the sun and spend time with Alana's memory. My fingers were bare.

We arrived at our destination to find a peeling sign hung above the door with the innovative words: *Pawn Shop*. The bell chimed as we entered, signaling our arrival at the empty store. By this time, I was absolutely hangry and ready to splurge on the fried chicken dive next door.

A man with a shaved head and dark beard arrived from the back to stand at a case of glittering jewels, his own diamond earring winking in the light. His biceps were as large as my thigh, with forearms sporting tattoos. The rest of the store stocked a myriad of curiosities: gleaming swords hanging on the wall behind the clerk, silver clocks, antique boxes, a coat of arms, and even a dusty armored knight.

"You buyin' or sellin'?" he asked flatly, a line he likely gave everyone who entered. When he spoke, a missing canine tooth created an unusual gap. He eyed us up and down as if he just now noticed our clothes. "What are you guys 'sposed to be?"

"We're in a traveling theater," I provided.

His smirk was more mocking than polite. "Mighta changed first, but to each their own."

Daniel and Mya carefully set their items on the glass counter, which bore more than a few grimy fingerprints.

"Hundred pounds," the man leaned a palm down, a good indicator of who most of the smudges belonged to. He hadn't even examined the jewelry.

Mya angled closer, a demure smile on her lips. "Oh?" She picked up her ring. "This is a real emerald. I'm sure my mother told me."

"That bright of green?" he scowled. "It's fake."

He likely hadn't seen such a quality stone in his life. "At least look for any inclusions," I told him. Mom's addiction to late-night shopping networks had taught me a few things. Thinking of her unwinding on the couch in the dim light, the TV flickering softly made my chest snap and tighten like a rubber band, wondering what she was doing at that moment. I couldn't imagine Rowan letting her enjoy that guilty pleasure. "Lab-created wouldn't have any," I added.

Mya's brows furrowed. "Lab?"

A tiny shake of my head served as a warning. The shopkeeper sighed and picked up a jeweler's loupe to examine the ring. He whistled through the gap in his teeth. "Well, I'll be… there is a small inclusion here."

Mya's hand rocketed to her hip. "I'll have you know—"

I rushed to her side. "It's fine. Almost all good stones have a little something extra in there."

Her mouth hung open before she closed it primly. "Of course."

Next came Daniel's signet, which was pure gold, petite emeralds flanking each end.

"Three hundred for the lot," the man said, crossing his beefy arms.

"You mean three thousand," Daniel replied.

I wondered how much money this man could give us. He might only have a few hundred lying around. We just needed enough to reach Staton or even London, where there would be better jewelers. Knowing the ring was likely at least five hundred years old, it was probably worth a hundred times that. But selling to this guy should raise fewer questions than at a more experienced jeweler.

"Just the ring," I cut in, "that one." I pointed to Daniel's and stepped forward. "Five hundred." Daniel's head cocked back in surprise, and I gave him a pleading, *trust me,* stare in return.

The man acted like he was thinking about it, but I knew he'd bite.

"Sold." He palmed the item and slid it under the counter.

"How far is Staton University from here?" I asked. "It's our next stop for the tour."

"Staton? Never heard of it."

We exchanged looks. "How about London?" Lucas leaned casually against the case.

"Not from around here, eh? I'm not Google Maps. Check your phone, mate."

"Yeah. That's just it," Lucas said. "We—"

"Had our stuff stolen," I added. "Which is why we're selling things. No phones either. We're trying to catch up with the rest of our group."

"Wales is quite a distance from London. Train station's here." He pulled out a scrap of paper and drew a rough map with a blue ballpoint pen, demonstrating several turns. "About a mile. Best of luck to you." He counted out the cash to Daniel, who pocketed the bills.

The relief of actually having money in our possession helped ease at least some of the tension. I took Daniel's hand as we left the shop. "Step one complete."

"We're going to finish this." The intensity of his voice assured promises he couldn't keep. "We're going to save your family."

He almost made me believe him.

CHAPTER 10
LUCAS

My stomach growled at the delicious smells wafting from a storefront next door, where a colorfully drawn chicken held a red-and-yellow bucket. It looked ridiculous. Undignified.

I had to try it.

Before finding the pawnshop, we'd been walking for hours. And now Cate and Daniel were locked in some sort of tender moment, and my belly wasn't having it—neither the sappy looks nor the lack of food.

"Hate to break this up, but anyone else starving? This place smells decent." I jerked my thumb to the restaurant, for some reason acting casual as if every fiber of my being wasn't screaming to sample the entire menu.

Mya wrinkled her nose. "Is that chicken eating itself?"

Sure enough, it held up a drumstick, beckoning to pedestrians passing by. "Must be good then." I smiled and headed for the door.

"Really, Lucas?" Mya hissed in my ear. "How about someplace more respectable?"

I inwardly laughed at the princess being forced to compromise her standards. She'd been a good sport while locked away in an Ember prison, though the topic of conversation frequently circled back to food, often the fancy concoctions of the Terran palace cook.

"You're the one who wanted to see England." I gestured for her to enter while I held the door. "Let's try something new."

"I did *not* say I wanted to go through the portal." She crossed her arms, blocking the doorway.

I shot her a look as if to say, "Really, Princess?"

"Well, fine. I did. But Daniel's right. Terra does need me. It's not like it's my fault the portal grabbed me, too."

We entered together, and I gestured to the counter. "Well. Let's make the most of it, shall we?"

Her brave expression as she stepped forward ignited a surge of affection. She really *shouldn't* be here, and we'd need to figure out a way to keep her protected, though I couldn't help feeling the glow of happiness from having her by my side.

Cate ended up ordering for us, being the most experienced. Mya covered her mouth when she realized we would be eating chicken out of a brightly colored paper-product bucket.

"I've never been to this place, but they're all pretty similar," Cate said, eyeing the menu. "American fast food infiltrating other countries."

We sat in a primary-colored booth. The Terran siblings primly placed paper napkins onto their laps.

"You'll want more," Cate said, tossing out napkins like confetti. "It's finger food. You've really never eaten fried chicken?"

"I, for one, am excited to try it." I leaned in as Cate set the container in front of us, along with another box, brightly decorated like the rest of the place.

"Rolls," she said, sliding them to me. "This might be the last meal for a while. We need to make sure we have enough money to get to Staton." She tore open the bread and slathered it with what I assumed was butter from a tiny container. "Wonder how much the tickets cost. We'll likely have to transfer more than once."

"Have you been to London?" Mya asked me.

"Nope. The portal is near the university. Didn't have a reason to." I bit into the crispy crust. Salty, greasy, crunchy deliciousness burst on my tongue. "What in the name of Caelum is this?"

Mya raised a brow. "Told you not to eat it."

"No—it's made from magic or something. Try it."

She obliged, taking a dainty taste. Her eyes widened. Not bothering to answer, she took another enthusiastic bite. We all ate, pretending to forget our predicament for the next few minutes, the only sounds appreciative murmurings.

"So that's fried chicken." I plucked the last crumb from Mya's paper plate. "I'm in."

"It's pretty bad for you," Cate replied. "But it does remind me of home. Wish we had money to spare to find some good coffee, too." She touched my arm from across the table. "You would not believe the—"

"Alright, Cate," Daniel interrupted. "We'd better get going."

"But," I stood with the rest of them, "I want to hear about the coffee."

Cate shot me a conspiratorial smile. "Tell you later."

Reluctantly, we left the warm restaurant to a darkening sky, the air now cooler.

"According to the map…" Daniel stared at the paper the pawnshop clerk drew.

I swiped it from him, the scratched lines looking like a preschooler had drawn it.

"That way." We both pointed in different directions.

Mya sighed. "Really?" She popped her head back into the shop. "Which way to the train station?"

Through the window, I could see the guy behind the counter pointing where Daniel had indicated. I turned the map once, saw my mistake, then handed it back to him without a word.

"Looks like women are the ones to ask for directions in both worlds." Cate smirked. "Come on," she linked her arm in mine. "You're just in a chicken-coma. All that grease slows down the brain cells."

The grating feeling of being shown up by Daniel left me irritable, erasing the food-glow. We continued on our way and found the train depot without difficulty; the only light now illuminated from the streetlamps. The station held a small collection of wooden benches, with maps lining the walls. We discreetly browsed, discovering we were in Northern Wales, quite a long way from Staton. A middle-aged clerk at the window sat bored at the mostly empty depot. Cate approached to ask for directions. He brandished several pamphlets accompanied by a lengthy discussion. Daniel listened by her side while Mya and I waited, taking a seat on one of the hard benches. They trudged toward us after thanking the clerk, Cate's mouth a grim line.

"Bad news." She flopped next to me. "We have to go through London. A train doesn't leave until early morning. We could take a bunch of short connectors, but it's more expensive, and we'd run out of money. Buses aren't any better."

"Should we go back to the pawnshop to sell my emeralds?" Mya asked Cate.

"Probably closed now." She slumped. "And we can't stay here. The guy told me they don't allow it. They'll call the police on us."

I clapped my hands together. "Hey. We've been in much tougher spots than this. I can sleep anywhere. We have full bellies—what more can we ask for? Let's find a patch of ground somewhere."

Mya's eyes turned skyward. "A bed, perhaps?"

I elbowed her. "You'll be fine." She'd survived the Ember prison, after all.

"Okay, let's get moving." Cate stood. "Some towns don't allow vagrants. Hopefully, the cops won't kick us out."

"We can take them." Daniel erected a fighting stance.

Cate laughed. "The police? I'm not interested in getting entangled with the law, thank you." Cate hugged Daniel's arm. "I know you'll protect me from anything, though. Thank you for offering." She looked up at him with adoration. I tore my gaze away, catching Mya watching my reaction. I hadn't really thought I was jealous; it was my distaste for the prince. Not wanting to further examine my feelings, I followed the others out the door.

A light drizzle started. I plastered on a smile. "At least Cate's not responsible this time, right?" Presumably anyway. From my experience, using powers in this land was limited at best.

"Not that I know of," she called back. Apparently, she still didn't have complete control of her rainmaking abilities, even now.

We passed awnings from shops, though we figured it would be too conspicuous to settle down on the main road. I wished we were in the country and could sneak into a barn. As the sun set, the cold settled in.

"Over there." Daniel pointed across the street.

An open grassy area dotted with wooden tables and a covered awning spread before us. Some sort of fort-like apparatus stood nearby. "What is it?" I asked.

"A park," Cate replied.

"And that?" Daniel pointed to the wooden structure with a rope web and ladders.

Cate chuckled. "A jungle gym. You guys didn't see much last time you were here."

Her explanation made no sense, but I let it pass. We welcomed the covering over the tables and benches, all of us now wet and chilled through. The tables were the best place to lie down, but only three sat beneath the cover.

"I'll share with Mya." Daniel strode toward his sister, not so subtly knocking into me.

The wooden surface was hard. And cold. Small cracks in the slats let wind seep through, chilling me from both sides. I sat up. Streetlamps illuminated the area enough to see the outlines of Daniel and Mya back-to-back, sharing their warmth.

"I'm cold," Cate whispered.

"Me too." I shivered.

Daniel's head shot up to look at Cate. "You okay?" He ignored my complaint, of course. "I didn't think it was that bad."

"That's because you're sharing heat with your sister," I said.

Daniel started to Cate. "I'll move over to you."

"Hey," Mya exclaimed. "You're going to let me freeze?"

Daniel swiveled between the girls. If he went to one, the other would be cold… or I would share with one of them. Watching the cogs turn in his brain was almost comical. *Who ya going to choose, mate?*

"I'll be a perfect gentleman." I hopped off the bench toward Mya to save Daniel from his head exploding with undesirable options.

His gaze flipped between the girls. "Fine. I'll be watching."

Yeah, like I would try something in the middle of town on a table in Wales with her brother six feet away. I looked skyward and waited for him to move. "Maybe it's *me* who has eyes on *you*. Cate's still my charge," I countered.

"You might be protecting me," Cate responded, "but pretty sure I'm now in charge of *you*. Sorry, Lucas."

"You don't have to rub it in." I grinned through my retort. "Sleep well, my queen."

I snuggled next to Mya, savoring her warmth and softness. Maybe Daniel was right to warn me. Perhaps I would try something if I weren't being monitored. I inhaled her lavender scent. "Sleep well, my princess," I whispered.

"*Crack*." The sound startled me awake. A shadowed man, silhouetted by the streetlamp behind, slammed our table with a stick. Another whack reverberated through the wood. I sat up with a jolt, heart thundering.

"Time to wake up," he said, his voice low and steady.

The others slowly stood. Daniel slipped beside me while I tried to figure out if this man was the police. He shifted, the light catching differently. No uniform. He wore a jacket with a logo. If my time here was any indication, likely a sports team. Definitely not a copper. Another step sent light glinting off what he held in his other hand.

A knife. And it looked to be a wicked sharp one. Mine had toppled to the ground when I'd startled awake, lying in the dirt, still in its sheath. Hot shame flooded my skin. I should have been ready. It was my job to be ready.

"Empty your pockets." The man gestured toward the table.

A few train maps, a key that must fit something back in Caelum, and a pocket mirror were emptied onto the wooden surface by the group. I didn't know where Daniel hid the money, but it wasn't among the items on the worn wood. None of us held much; our possessions were all left at home.

"Where's the cash?" Closer to him now, I could see dirt ground into his clothes, his curly hair greasy. The blade remained angled toward us, though it wavered with a tremor.

"Why do you think we're out here?" I asked. "We have none."

"Sir," Cate spoke up. "Look at our outfits. We're traveling actors and have already been robbed once. We're stranded."

The man's gaze fell to Mya. She'd apparently hidden her ring somewhere because her fingers were bare. "Her earrings," he barked.

"Paste," Cate replied. "We're actors, remember?"

His eyes flashed with doubt, then realization. "You've got to be worth something." He shook the knife at Mya. "Her. You're coming with me." He discarded the stick and reached to grab her.

Everything happened at once. Daniel and I both sprang forward, while Mya struggled violently against the man's hold, her unbound arm swinging wildly, making it more difficult for us to free her.

Daniel changed course and rounded from the side, crashing into the ruffian. At the same time, Mya gripped my shoulder, pulling me toward her, and all four of us started to fall in a tangle. I tried to unsnarl myself, but propelled by Daniel's momentum, the man tumbled on top of me.

My breath expelled violently under both his and Daniel's weight. Something sharp burnt into my side. Mya scrambled free, and Daniel pulled the man off. I started to rise, coming up on my knees, hands reflexively shooting to my belly, finding the knife embedded in my side. My fingers came away hot and sticky. The world listed like a sinking ship.

Someone screamed my name.

I collapsed onto the gravel, the park spinning. The noise of Daniel fighting grew muffled, as if my ears were filled with cotton. I wanted to pull out the knife, but I couldn't move. The burning in my side intensified, a hot brand blazing deeper.

"Daniel, watch out!" Mya's voice called.

A dark curtain drifted over my vision, hazy and black. Inescapable. I fought the darkness, but it was no use.

This was the end.

CHAPTER 11
DANIEL

Mya's screaming echoed through the night air while I grappled for my life, sweat dripping despite the cold. The man had procured another knife, the steel glinting from the streetlamp across the lawn. I dodged his swings, my movements unsure and sluggish without Terran energy.

"Just go," I huffed between breaths, taking care to keep myself between him and the others.

"I can't leave—" he lunged again, "empty-handed."

At closer range, his dilated eyes flared wild with animal-like frenzy.

Shouts rang out in the distance.

"Help," Cate yelled. "Call the police!"

"See?" I sidestepped another blow, watching for an opportunity to wrench the dagger free. "If you leave now, you can escape."

He took a step back, gaze shifting between Lucas and me before he turned and ran.

The girls huddled over Lucas's still unmoving body. Sick tendrils of guilt climbed up my throat. I should have given up the money. Lucas had been many things: nemesis, sparring partner, enemy, and, when confronted with his possible death, I'd call him friend. Nausea built deep in my stomach with worry that it might be too late to tell him.

Cate started to turn him onto his back, and I rushed to help. "He has a pulse," she said, her voice breathy and faint.

A dark stain bloomed across the left side of his upper midsection. I plunged my hands against it to slow the blood flow. He needed a healer. *Now*. "Hold pressure," I instructed Cate. "I'll see if anyone called for help." A few people stood on the sidewalk across the road, likely too afraid to investigate. I sprinted toward them, shouting, "Someone's injured. It's bad." Cate would know the procedure of finding a medic more than I, but the knot of men huddled next to the street could be friend or foe, and I couldn't risk her safety.

"I called." A short man in the back raised a finger. "They'll be here in a moment. Good luck, mate." One of them, wearing a thick trench coat, gestured to the others, and they hastened in the opposite direction.

Worry settled deep in my chest. Worry I'd have to rely on these unreliable-looking men who didn't want to stick around for the police to arrive. Worry it would be too late to save Lucas. I'd seen plenty of wounds in battle. This one—the stain on his tunic flashed in my head—the location and the sheer amount of bleeding required care quickly. No one could survive steady blood loss like that for long.

"Someone called for help," I said as I jogged up to the girls. "How is he?"

"Alive," Mya replied.

Cate pulled her attention from Lucas, her features contorted with fear. She shook her head to convey the severity, not wanting, or not able, to say it aloud. The lump in my throat thickened. I stooped to find a thready pulse in his neck, his skin clammy under my touch.

Sirens blared in the distance, the sound a beacon of hope. Flaring lights lit up the space. Each brief flash amplified Cate's and Mya's expressions, frozen momentarily, then changing at each illumination like flipping through the images of a gothic novel. Fear. Love. Determination. Anxiety. A single moment's painting come to life. Lucas's unconscious face remained unchanged, the only constant in the scene.

A man and woman dressed in similar clothes—green jackets and a logo on the chest approached. "Step aside," the woman elbowed her way to Lucas.

Mya, still on her knees, held Lucas's hand.

"Miss." The woman moved in closer. "Step. Aside."

Mya stared at him, unmoving, oblivious to anything around her. I rounded Lucas's still form, pulling her up and wrapping her in my arms. "They're going to take care of him," I whispered. "Come on." She finally moved, a marionette, each jerky step an effort.

Since arriving here, it was as if my sense of others' emotions had become submerged in a vat of mud, transmitting vague whisperings. In some ways, it was freeing not to work to block them, a constant necessity to avoid overwhelming myself. Only, now I wished I had a better gauge of Mya, Cate, and the healers who arrived. Were they worried? Confidant? Mya was easy to interpret—shock written all over her face. Cate held it together a few yards from me, her gaze never leaving Lucas. For once, no familiar jealousy bubbled, only the tug of desire for him to pull through.

The workers moved him to a board with handles, then picked him up to carry him to their van, blue lights affixed to thc top.

Cate followed behind them, the rest of us tagging along. "Which hospital?"

"St. Mary's," the man replied.

"How far is it? We're not… from here," she said.

"American, are ya?" he asked, noting her accent. "Couple of miles. East side of town."

Cate's head swiveled as if she had no idea which way was east.

While they loaded Lucas into the back, he asked, "His name?"

"Lucas. Lucas Bradbury," I answered.

"Address? ID?"

"Everything was stolen," Cate said. "We're kind of in a bind here."

The medic, a middle-aged man with a dragon tattoo crawling up his collar, nodded. The ink felt like a good omen that he'd watch over Lucas. "We'll take care of him." He eyed our outfits with curiosity, but didn't comment as he climbed in beside Lucas.

The back of the van held shelves and hooks of medical supplies. An IV bag hung from the bed in the center, the fluid clear instead of the typical blue in our world.

"The police will want a statement," he said. "They should be along soon."

Worry frissoned over our lack of identification. Nor did we want to report the supposed theft of all our possessions, and we somehow needed to avoid suspicion. The doors shut with a bang, and they were off, leaving Mya, Cate, and me standing alone in the street, an overhead lamp shining like a spotlight on our vulnerability.

Moments later, a police car pulled up behind us. Mya squeaked next to me.

"It's fine. We didn't do anything wrong." It didn't feel fine. The last thing we needed was to be carted off to jail.

"Officers," Cate said.

Two men had exited the sedan. "American?" one of them asked.

"I am, yes. Visiting. We were out in the park when a man robbed us. We didn't have money, so he tried to take her instead." She looped her arm through Mya's. "There was a struggle, and our friend, Lucas, was stabbed."

We proceeded to describe the guy as best we could, though it was so dark that none of us could provide many details.

"Curly-haired, wearing a navy jacket?" His bushy eyebrows descended. "You sure?"

"I'm sure." A flutter of nerves wafted from Cate. "We're worried about our friend. Can we go?"

Here's where we expected trouble, but Cate calmly gave her name and cell number, presumably her dead phone back in Caelum, told him our names, and that we could all be reached at the same number. She claimed we left our IDs back at the hotel. Her story didn't exactly explain why we were in the park in the middle of the night when we had a place to sleep, but they seemed to buy it, giving us directions to the hospital before retreating to their car. We watched them drive away as we sighed in relief. I wasn't sure if it was because it was late or because they were busy with other business, but we would take the stroke of good fortune.

"You were magnificent," I told Cate, wrapping an arm around her. "Let's go." I snaked my other arm over Mya, grim silence blanketing us, our thoughts returning to Lucas. I'd already grown accustomed to the four of us traveling together—the way he made Mya's smile light up her face, how he improved Cate's mood, even my mood when I tried not to laugh at his dumb jokes. And now, even with dampened powers, sorrow and anxiety emanated around us.

We finally reached the infirmary, which Cate reminded me was called a hospital, a blue cross symbol illuminating the three-story building. She directed us toward the lighted signs to the A&E. We entered a foyer with sickly yellow plastic chairs lining the walls, overflowing with a mixture of anxious or green faces, young and old.

Cate marched to the counter, which was behind a clear wall. "My brother was brought in by ambulance. Lucas Bradbury?"

A woman with cropped salt-and-pepper hair and deep brackets around her mouth checked her computer. "He's in the trauma bay. You're not allowed back there."

"But—" Cate started.

"Not until he's stable," the woman interrupted.

We took a seat on the hard chairs, squeezed between a woman holding a crying baby and a teenager with his head between his knees.

"Brother?" I whispered.

"In case they only let family see him."

We'd be lost without Cate and her knowledge. "So, what now?" Mya asked.

"We wait." Cate bit her lip. "I wish he wasn't alone in there."

"Who are *they* to keep *us* out?" Mya retorted. "I don't like this place." She sniffed, in full princess mode.

"They're trying to save his life. We'll just be in the way." She sent Mya a tiny reassuring smile. "I've seen it on TV."

Mya sighed. "I need to know what's going on. It's killing me."

"Mya." I shot her a warning look. "Let's follow the rules. Shall we? This isn't our kingdom."

She fidgeted next to me, her fingers tapping on her lap. An interminable two hours passed. Light cracked through the lone window as the sun rose.

"We're going to miss the train," Cate said, her tone flat.

At some point, she'd have to make the decision to leave Lucas and find our way to Oregon or stay here. Unless that wound was a lot less severe than I suspected, Lucas wouldn't be traveling anytime soon. "We'll catch another one," I said.

Each time the door leading to the back opened, our heads jerked up, only for someone else to be called. The room emptied until we were the only ones left except for a single teen who'd vomited twice, his head now bobbing in restless sleep.

Mya stood. "I can't stand this!"

The surly woman at the front also rose. I thought she might admonish Mya, but she called out to a person behind her and left the lobby unattended.

Mya slipped to the door and attempted to turn the knob. It held fast.

"Mya," I hissed.

"What? They could at least update us."

Without warning, the door swung open. Mya leapt back, narrowly avoiding being hit. Vomit-boy was called back. As the door closed, she caught it right before it clicked. She glanced at the still-empty counter, then back to us. "Now's our chance," she whispered.

Cate and I exchanged looks. "Okay. But just a quick peek."

Mya strode through the door and down the hall like she belonged, Cate and I more cautious. A sign labeled *trauma* lay ahead, the beige curtain open.

Inside, the floor was littered with used syringes, blood-soaked bandages, and disconnected wires strewn across a very empty bed, the sheets half-trailing on the ground. Trepidation skated down my spine.

"He's gone," Cate whispered.

CHAPTER 12
CATE

I couldn't tear my gaze away from the empty gurney. The abandoned bloody gauze, ruby drops staining the sheets, feathered brown at the edges. The red—my father's death crept into my vision until all I could see was pooling blood. Daniel's warm hand skimmed the small of my back, returning me temporarily to the here and now.

Why wouldn't they tell us if they moved him? Or worse, died? Something bad had happened here. I'd seen enough episodes of *Grey's Anatomy* to know that unless there was a true emergency, a room would not be left like this.

Daniel grabbed my hand, the gentle pressure of his fingers attempting to pull me from the haze. Mya stood beside me, her eyes wide and glassy.

A middle-aged woman, dressed in gray scrubs, wheeled an industrial-sized garbage can as she entered. "Excuse me. Housekeeping."

"Where is he?" Mya asked. "The person from this room."

"He was stabbed," I added.

"Emergency surgery." She pinched her lips. "But you didn't hear that from me. Privacy rules."

Tears of relief sprang. Alive—he was alive. "We're family," I assured her.

"Well then. The waiting room is upstairs. East wing."

"Is he okay?"

"No idea. I'm just the clean-up crew." She eyed the mess. "Worse than usual. They must have been in a hurry."

Dread crowded its way back into my chest as I surveyed every drop of blood, every red-soaked gauze.

"Right. Second floor, then." Daniel pointed to a sign for stairs. He broke me out of my trance, his no-nonsense tone a cover for his distress.

Each concrete step filled me with more trepidation, our situation crashing around me. We had very little money, no phones, no identification, and a deadline. Time kept creeping away. Time I needed to reach my family. I had no doubt that Rowan would carry out the deed. I could still picture his face when he killed Father: the glint of satisfaction at besting me, the relish at pulling the blade across his neck.

Lucas would not be in shape to travel. *I have to leave him.* The thought wedged its way in, wheedling deep until it forced me to accept my new reality. Tears blurred the yellow stripe on the edge of each step. My constant companion, guilt, roared to life. If I hadn't taken us through the portal, this never would have happened. We would have been prepared. Gone through properly. And now… My breath shuddered.

Once we reached the surgery waiting area, I checked in to let them know we were there, but the clerk refused to provide any further information. Mya and I sat in the padded vinyl chairs, an upgrade from the hard plastic downstairs.

"What now?" Mya slouched, at odds with her usual impeccable posture.

"We wait." Again. "And this time, there's no barging into the operating room."

She folded her arms. "We may be behind in Terra, but believe it or not, we do have surgeons. And yes, I'm familiar with germs."

Her haughty tone almost made me smile. Instead, I turned to Daniel. "We need a plan." I'd been subconsciously formulating one, but he wasn't going to like it.

"We do." He carefully took my hand as if I might break. Maybe I would. "Cate, we have to—"

"Leave Lucas and Mya. I know."

His jaw slackened. "Wait—what did you say?"

"Go without Lucas and Mya. It can't be helped."

Two lines shot together between his brows. "Mya's coming with us." He let go of my hand, punctuating his words. "She doesn't know anything about this world. She'd get lost—we'd never find her again."

Convincing him wasn't going to be easy. His voice was laced with fear rather than doubt for his sister. "Lucas needs someone here. Besides, Mya can take care of herself. She'll do great."

Daniel sent me an eye roll, one filled with brotherly over-protectiveness. "She didn't even want to try the chicken."

"Excuse me." Mya leaned over me. "I'm right here. How about asking me?"

"Because I'm in charge of you, that's why," Daniel snapped.

"Who says?"

"Your *older* brother. I outrank you." Daniel leaned over me to better glare at his sister.

I placed two fingers on his arm to hold him back. "Oh, he's trying that one again, is he?" I smirked at Mya, who stood, hand on hip.

"Yeah. Like my whole life. Who gets the last pastry? 'I do. I outrank you,'" she mimicked. "Who gets the room with the best view? 'I do—'"

"That's not true," Daniel snapped. "Your room has a lovely view of the forest."

"Really? This is what we're going to argue about?" I interrupted and looked to Mya. "Sorry to presume, but I thought you'd want to stay with Lucas."

"I do." Her chin tilted up.

"And," I swiveled my head to Daniel, "your sister will be safer here than with us. Look what we're walking into. You don't want Rowan to have access to both Terran heirs again, do you?"

"I presumed we would place her with our contacts near Staton," he said stiffly, raising his brows at her. "Where you'll be safe."

"But… Lucas can't wake up alone." Mya's hand slid from her hip, voice turning small. "Don't make me leave him. Daniel, if you ever cared about me—"

"Ah, don't pull that. You know I care about you. That's exactly why I'm trying to protect you."

As much as I wished not to be in the middle of this brother-sister argument, I *did* want someone here with Lucas. "Why don't we have your contacts travel up here and bring Mya a cell phone and money. She'll only be alone a couple of days at most. You think they'd be willing?"

"Probably? There's a whole community of them, some in London, although who knows where. We only met Brian and Lucy at Staton. Someone will likely help."

"Why did they stay here—the contacts?" I asked.

"Most of them liked it when they visited. Some fell in love. Others might not have been able to travel back. Who knows. There's been a society for as long as our worlds have been settled, and they take a strict oath of secrecy. When the portals were open, Brian and Lucy played a big part in acclimating those who came to spend a year at Staton. They missed Terra, but they felt needed. Like they were doing their part. You'll like them."

"We'll give Mya the money that was supposed to be for their tickets, so she won't be destitute. Hopefully, we can meet this Brian and Lucy soon," I said.

Daniel wanted so badly to protect everyone, but the stakes were too high to treat one of our numbers as a lame duck. Mya would have to pull her weight. "Let's put off leaving as long as we can. At least get an update on Lucas before we leave."

The helpless reality that it wouldn't change his outcome even if Daniel and I stayed at the hospital for Lucas, didn't help the guilt squirming in my stomach. Yet, delaying longer could be catastrophic for my family. Just the thought of Mom's warm touch and Dad's steadying presence brought stinging, unshed tears.

Daniel's fingers slid over mine. "I'm going to find a cup of water somewhere." I could tell he knew I was right about Mya. He just needed to fight his own demons and come to terms on his own. A few minutes of space from his sister would help him think more rationally.

"He's mad," Mya said after he'd left.

"You can feel his emotions?" My heart lurched in my chest. If

Mya's powers worked, it could prove useful. Maybe we *did* need her with us.

"Not really. It's like a vague sensation." A shoulder lifted. "I just know my brother."

"He'll come around."

She sighed. "He usually does."

"So, you and Lucas. How serious is it? Was being sucked into the portal with him good or bad? Barring the obvious." I gestured to the beige industrial tiles and filigree wallpaper border from 1992 lining the waiting room.

"Secret?" Mya lowered her voice.

"Of course." I leaned in instinctively.

"I had a crush the first time I met him at fifteen." Her cheeks flushed pink. "He'd come to Terra Castle for one of the council meetings. I'm not sure why King Aldridge brought him, but there he was—the cutest ambassador for Caelum ever, with that quick smile, even then. Maybe it was knowing my father would never approve—I'm a hopeless romantic for star-crossed love."

"And now?" I shifted in my seat to face her. "Is grown-up Lucas as enticing as teenage Lucas?"

Mya bit her lip. "I'm afraid so."

It would be a difficult path for them if they chose to stay together. "The fighting between the kingdoms is hard. So is dealing with your father. Daniel and I have already had some rough patches because of it."

"I'm hoping you guys are paving the way." She fiddled with the buttons on the cuff of her Terran-green gown. "And Lucas... I'm honestly not sure what he thinks of us together."

"He's smitten." I thought of the soft gazes he'd sent her way when she wasn't looking.

"But practical," she said. "He knows how hard a relationship between us will be. He also has..." Mya's gaze turned to the floor, "a strong allegiance to you."

Rather than deny it, I wanted to see how she'd react to Lucas's loyalty. "He's my knight. I'm his queen. I should hope so. Can you handle that?" I thought of the complications between Daniel and me, and how being on my side or Caelum's side didn't mean he was against Terra. Not only that, but Mya was used to being the center of attention. She probably *deserved* to be in the center. But I deserved loyalty from Lucas, too.

"I—" Her lashes fluttered. "I'll have to get used to it."

"He's not in servitude. He can stop being my knight whenever he chooses. I'm just hoping you're not going to force him into that decision."

She remained silent for a moment. "It's complicated, no?"

I gave her a sad smile. "More than a teenage crush. That's for sure."

All this time, we'd been discussing their relationship as if Lucas was around the corner searching for a cup of coffee instead of fighting for his life, with the two of us praying and hoping for his survival. Talking about a future forced us to believe he'd make it through.

Mya twirled the emerald ring on her finger. "I should have given it to him—the guy in the park. I hid it down the front of my dress. Maybe this wouldn't have happened. I'm just so stubborn and knew we needed every bit to get to America."

We all felt the guilt. Though mine trumped them all. None of us would be here if it weren't for me. "You partly did it for my family, and that's incredibly generous. We all feel helpless, and it adds to the guilt. Daniel wished he'd handed over the money. I'm the one who told the guy your earrings were fake." I rubbed my chest, knuckles scraping across breastbone. Scraping across a heart full of regrets. "We can't let it pull us under. Lucas wouldn't want it. He'll expect us to have a plan in place when he wakes, and that's exactly what we've done."

Mya slowly nodded. "He will, won't he? And thank you for sticking up for me with Daniel. He still sees me as a little girl."

"Oh, he'd cover me in bubble wrap and sit me in a throne room alone if he could." I almost laughed. "That sounds horrid, doesn't it? He's just so protective. He's been trained to be."

She raised a brow. "So has Lucas, but he's not that way. You have your hands full with my brother."

"Lucas has only known you as an adult; that's the difference. Daniel still thinks of you like you're ten."

She smirked. "He has no recollection of my early teenage mooning. Thank goodness for that."

The door opened, and a woman dressed in scrubs, mask dangling around her neck, appeared. "Lucas Bradbury family?"

We stood in unison, my stomach swooping. "That's us." We *were* his family. We felt it in our bones.

"I'm Dr. Hadley, the surgeon who operated on him."

At that moment, Daniel strode in, a water cup in each hand.

"Daniel. This is the surgeon," I said as he set down the paper glasses on a side table. "She was just about to update us on Lucas." My focus returned to the woman. She was around fifty, lines bracketing her mouth, mousy hair mixed with gray. The doctor's brown eyes held mine, steady but grave.

I swallowed hard. "Right, Doctor? You have news?"

CHAPTER 13
DANIEL

We'd said our goodbyes, the doctors informing us Lucas's condition was "touch and go." I had to force Cate to leave, her loyalties torn. The only way I'd convinced her was that Lucas wouldn't want her to stay. When he woke up, he'd never live with himself if anything happened to her parents and little brother. She usually responded to logic if her anxiety didn't take over.

Mya had pushed me out the door while I tried to impart more brotherly advice. It still bothered me to leave, but Cate assured me she would be fine as long as she didn't sleep on the street.

After the lengthy walk to the station, we barely caught the train to London, and now it was just pulling into King's Cross. Cate remembered changing trains here to go to Staton, so we'd chosen it as our destination.

"You ready?" I asked.

She tilted her head. "Are you? London's a big city, and you're more of a hang out in the forest kind of guy."

I straightened. "Excuse me? I handle myself just fine in social situations."

A smile tugged at her lips. "That broody prince thing might work in Terra, but here…"

"I am not *broody*. You make me sound like Mr. Rochester."

"Hmmm." She watched me with wide eyes. "I guess I'll have to reread Jane Eyre to decide."

I didn't mind her teasing *too* much. Anything to distract her. "And," I gave her my best smoldering gaze, "you like me broody."

She shook her head, holding in a laugh. Not exactly the reaction I was hoping for. "You're right. I do." She leaned over and kissed me softly on the cheek.

The train slowed. "First," she said, "the library."

"Yeah, I know. It's your answer to everything."

"Computers. We need them. And a pawn shop for Mya's earrings."

"Still can't believe we took them," I muttered.

"With the money we left with her, we barely had enough to make it to London. Besides, she still has the ring."

We exited the train into tunnels, people bustling in every direction, some openly staring or giving us double-takes at our appearance, while others couldn't be bothered to care. It's one of the things I enjoyed during my brief time at university here. No one knew I was a prince, anonymity turned addictive, and led me to delay telling Cate my identity far longer than I ever should have.

Cate found an attendant watching passengers in and out of the openings she called turnstiles, where people paid with phones or cards.

"Is there a library nearby?" she asked.

The guy, likely barely out of his teens, pulled out his cell. "About a ten to fifteen-minute walk to Camden." He showed her directions, Cate's hair shadowing her face as she leaned over the phone.

The cool air was a relief compared to the dank tunnels, and fortunately, it wasn't raining. After we arrived, I pulled up a chair beside Cate as she expertly navigated Google. I'd had a crash course from Brian and Lucy, enough to at least pretend I knew what I was doing at school.

"This one is well-rated." Cate pointed to a pawnshop. "Covent Garden. And ooh—look, an H&M is close. We can get out of these clothes."

She hunted for the easiest way to Staton, reiterating that we'd need money for a cab once we reached the train station. "Here's the map. Anything look familiar?"

My spotty memory searched for something I recognized. When we'd first arrived, Lucas and I walked to the safe house from the portal and stayed there for several days. Lucy had given us driving lessons, while Brian traveled to London and exchanged our jewels for money, visiting several locations, including an auction house. All the while, we'd learned about things like cell phones and computers. Now I wished we'd traveled with him.

"I'll find it," I said, more confidently than I felt.

We departed the library and found the pawnshop. Mya's earrings fetched what Cate thought was enough for plane tickets and a few other items, though it would be tight. Brian and Lucy didn't lead an extravagant life, but maybe they could pitch in, or knew someone who would.

Clothes came next. Lucas and I had driven to a local shop last time. I remember biting my tongue about the non-tailored clothing, so I wouldn't look like a spoiled prig and give Lucas more reason to hate me. This store was a new experience, with bright lights, crowded racks, and a moving staircase. Cate helped me pick, and I exited a dressing room in a T-shirt, zip-up jacket, and jeans. All items I'd worn as a college student, but Cate felt more at home in a similar outfit.

"Ready for college." Cate looped her arm in mine.

"Hmm?"

"Oh, sorry. We'll fit in at *university*. Uni, right? Whatever." At my confused expression, she poked me. "You don't know how people talk here better than I do. Get changed so we can buy them."

This seemed an unnecessary hassle, as we'd just have to put them back on again, but I did as I was told. The rules made me wonder why any Terrans ever decided to stay. Then I remembered the library, fried chicken, and the traveling speed, and could concede a few perks.

We arrived at Staton several hours later. Cate's anxiety ratcheted during the cab ride because of her near kidnapping the last time she took this route. She started spouting all kinds of strange statistics, like the number of people who die in car accidents each year, which changed my view of having cars in Terra, though I knew she also had a horse statistic in that brain of hers somewhere. Unlike her, the numbers stretched my nerves rather than calmed them, but I nodded and pretended to listen anyway.

We exited the taxi, the gray stone buildings of Staton sending a wave of memories and nostalgia: walking Cate to class, the early fall air, seeing her face light up with a smile. But it was her glare that caught me in the crosshairs initially. A chuckle escaped at the memory.

"What are you laughing at?"

"Just remembering how you hated me."

One side of her mouth tilted up. "Well, yeah. You were a jerk. Remember? What's so funny about that?"

Her offended expression widened my smile until I covered it with my fingers. "Because I deserved it. I was a total prat." I'd been so annoyed at my father for wanting me to woo Cate for Terra's advantage that I did the opposite. And it only frustrated me more when I saw her for the first time, my heart leaping out of my chest. Actually, she'd run into me and left her hands *on* my chest. I was sure she could feel my racing heartbeat.

Memories swam to the surface—this place—the musty new-rain smell, students rushing to class, Cate's hair curling in the breeze. She'd been eavesdropping on a conversation between Lucas and me, one green eye peeking through the door. I was so mad at Father and at my own unexpected feelings that I shouted at her. Even now, that instinct rose from back then—to protect her from myself.

"Come on." I turned on my heel. "It's this way." We headed in the opposite direction from the campus that held so many memories.

Brian and Lucy's house was south of the school in a neighborhood about a mile away; I remembered that much. Soon, we came upon a sea of row houses. Once we discovered the Embers stalking Cate, Lucas and I didn't visit them again, fearing the men would follow us, so I'd only made the trek a couple of times. Lucas sent a letter explaining what had happened before we left.

We wound through the maze of tightly packed brick homes, all similar in size and color, lined up like toys. "They had a flower box painted green." The detail flooded back. They were Terran, and Brian mentioned it was homage to their homeland.

"Did they care Lucas was from Caelum?"

"The society decided a long time ago to accept those from each kingdom. That they had more in common, especially here, than not. There used to be a pipeline to Staton if someone wanted to go to college, back when most of us came for a year before the portals were shut down."

"They work at the university?"

"Retired now, but they used to."

"There." Cate pointed to a house with a particularly large Terran-green flower box, out of proportion to the home's size. Unlike before, dead plants haphazardly sat inside, browned ivy straggling over one end. A prickle of unease grew. This didn't match Brian and Lucy's fastidious natures.

"Look, there's a For Sale sign." Cate gestured to a poster staked into the weed-filled grass.

"Doesn't look like anyone's at home."

We climbed the steps and rang the bell. No answer. A woman exited the home next door with a small, white dog. "Ma'am," I called. "Does anyone still live here?"

"That house? You don't want to buy that one. As much as I'd love a neighbor…"

"Why not?" Cate asked while we crossed the grass toward her.

"You from out of town, then. Didn't hear? They were murdered, those two. Lived there for what seems like forever—the sweetest couple. The place was a wreck, too. Someone upended everything. Emptied drawers. Cut open mattresses." She shook her head as if still disbelieving something like that could have happened one house over.

Grief hit me in waves. The woman continued to talk, her words blending together, a bee buzzing in the background. Lucy's laugh trilled in my head, bright and carefree, joking when we'd stumble over slang from this world. Brian and Lucy had been kind and loyal to both Terrans and Caelumites for years. They hadn't deserved this.

Cate and I exchanged glances, both of us thinking the same thing. *What do we do now?*

CHAPTER 14
CATE

We trudged toward Staton, both lost in thought. The Embers must have killed them while searching for information about me. Brian and Lucy might have had my home address if they'd worked for the school. Two more lives gone, with me the cause. The hollowness that comes with death left me cold, swallowing hope in its vast cavern. I shouldn't be so familiar with the feeling, yet these days, I carried it everywhere, a bottomless maw consuming me from the inside until one day, I'd disappear into nothingness. One by one, every piece taken by the Embers.

"We should check the registrar to make sure they didn't break in there, too," Daniel said, interrupting my morose thoughts. "At least one person from our world should be working to pull strings to let us into school."

"Even after all this time with the portals closed?"

Daniel shrugged. "I hope so."

His shoulders curled, jawline not quite as sharp. So much grief. It piled onto both of us. "I'm sorry about Brian and Lucy." I slid my hand along his bicep.

"I should have warned them myself. I—"

"You were trying to keep me alive. What else were you to do?"

"Something more, obviously." His voice was hoarse, raw. "They were nice people. It shouldn't have happened."

"No, it shouldn't have. The Embers are monsters. I don't know how many times we have to say it before they'll stop surprising us."

By the time we reached school, the sun had started to set. Students ambled along the paths, backpacks looped over one shoulder, focused on that math test or essay due the next day. A life I thought I wanted. Sometimes still did. I could picture Daniel and me strolling hand-in-hand here, meeting after class in the cafeteria for poorly made burgers and crinkle fries. We'd be happy, but only if we were blissfully unaware of our kingdoms' peril and our responsibilities back home. Funny, that's how I thought of it now. Oregon still pulled and tugged in that way childhood clings with nostalgia and longing, but I'd never truly belong there.

"It's almost dark. The office will be closed," Daniel said.

We desperately needed someone's help. Without fake passports, we'd never be able to board a plane. Plus, with Lucas and Mya still in Wales—his condition unknown—they counted on us, too. I halted on the sidewalk, my eyes squeezing shut. I would *not* spiral right now. I spotted the bench where I'd had a panic attack all those months ago, with Daniel nearby. What statistic had I spouted? Something about a bee? *Odds of dying by bee sting: 1 in 58,000.* That was it. My breathing regulated.

"Cate. You've gone pale."

I wrenched my lids open. "I'm okay. I—I have an idea where to go." I took his hand, brushing my thumb along his knuckles like a touchstone, and led him across campus.

I knocked on my old dorm room, crossing my fingers that Jenna would be there. The scent of lemon disinfectant and gym socks in the corridor brought another wave of nostalgia.

It opened. Jenna, her dark, curly hair pulled into a messy bun atop her head, stood with her mouth agape.

"Cate!" She moved in for a hug, halted, and stepped back, her brows raised. "This guy?" One hand went to her hip, further blocking the door. "You two together?"

I bit my lip. "We are?" For some reason, it came out more as a question than a statement. "Can we come in?"

She opened the door wider, her smile now a little too broad. "Of course." As I passed, she whispered in my ear, "I would've preferred the blond."

Jenna always did have her opinions, and she adored Lucas.

"I'm not sure we've officially met." Daniel moved in to take her hand.

"You're Daniel. Right. Cate might have mentioned you."

He tilted his head. "Did she now?"

Jenna sat on her twin bed, gesturing to my old one. A fresh blanket rested atop, one of those super-soft, fuzzy, synthetic kinds I hadn't realized how much I'd missed in Caelum until now. I brushed my fingers back and forth through the nap.

She cocked a half-smile. "Oh, nothing particularly flattering, mind you."

Sheesh. It was like introducing Daniel to a parent. "Anyway…" I drew out the word. "We're in town and found ourselves in a bit of a bind." I repeated the theft story and asked if we could stay the night. "We'll have it all figured out in the morning," I rushed to say.

"Of course. They never replaced you, so that bed's empty."

"And I'll take the floor," Daniel said hurriedly, attempting to get on Jenna's good side.

Jenna asked how I was doing back in Oregon. I had nearly forgotten I'd told her I'd left because of homesickness. Daniel smoothly deflected, lied when necessary, and gave an implausible story about how he'd always wanted to see America and sample the coffee in the northwest, so he visited… and the rest was history between us.

Jenna nodded, a bit confused, though she didn't challenge him. "I'll just pop down the hall, grab a few extra blankets and pillows from a friend, and let you get settled."

Jenna strode out the door, and I rolled my eyes at Daniel. "You wanted to sample the coffee?"

"Well, you're always going on about it. That's what popped into my head. You *did* name the bird Mocha."

He had a point—I *had* named my falcon after my favorite drink, though there were plenty of beautiful sights in Oregon other than coffee. Maybe after we save my family, I could show him. Silence settled as thoughts turned to Rowan.

"We'll rescue them. There's been some setbacks, but we'll get there. I promise." He kissed my forehead. A faint tingle of energy puffed around us.

"Do it again." I leaned toward him.

"What?" He smiled wolfishly. "This?" He feathered kisses along my cheek, moving ever so slowly to my lips. The energy pulsed. Impatient, I brought my mouth to his, savoring his touch and the power that came with it. I'd missed it. There had been so much grieving. So much pain. I hungrily pulled him to me, pressing close and deepening the kiss. He groaned, his fingers kneading into my shoulder blades. He retreated without warning, the space between us empty and gaping. I itched to reclose the void.

"I don't think Jenna likes me. Let's not make it worse." He stood. "I'm taking a shower. A cold one." He popped his head around the bathroom door. "Why doesn't she like me?"

"You were a jerk. Girls talk."

"Ah. I should have known."

The next morning, we headed to the registrar. Being back at Staton was surreal—the life I left behind. The bittersweet emotions of seeing Jenna again. A reminder of what could have been, especially since girlfriends were hard to find when one was the queen. Chatting about classes, boys, and the awful cafeteria food naturally tumbled out of her, sending pangs of jealousy. I *didn't* want this life. Or maybe I wanted both. But I could never give up my responsibilities and loyalty to our kingdoms.

"What?" Daniel asked, stepping over a sidewalk puddle from an earlier rain shower.

"Hmm?"

"You sighed."

"Did I? I guess I was just imagining what it would be like. Talking over lattes and complaining about my history professor." I squeezed his hand. "Life offers so many options. We can't choose every path—only the ones most important."

"I'm glad it led you to me." Daniel opened the door.

I nudged him as I passed, shooting him a flirty smile. "Same."

Light shone through the square glass window at the entrance to the office. "Good luck," I whispered. We had no idea if anyone was from Caelum or Terra, but we had to try.

A brunette in her twenties sat at the desk, a perky smile perched on her lips, hair curled in that perfect blowout look I'd never been able to achieve. "I'm afraid the time has passed for dropping classes. You'll have to stick it out and raise those grades, won't we?"

Her chipper demeanor, in contrast to her words, took me aback. "No—we're—"

"Not dropping classes," Daniel added. "We're looking for someone to help us. Someone from my hometown in Terra."

"Or mine in Neva." I provided our kingdom's capital city.

Twin crinkles knitted her brow. "I'm afraid I'm not familiar with those cities."

"Is there someone else we can speak to?" Daniel shot her a lazy smile. I'd actually never seen him try to charm a woman before, and the sight was a bit disconcerting.

Her sunniness faltered as she gazed up at Daniel, who'd moved closer to her desk. "I'm afraid we're short-staffed. I'm not sure you heard—there was a break-in a few months ago? Will—William Brody, my boss, was injured."

"That's who my mom told me to come see," I said. "I couldn't remember his name. Will, good old Will. When's he due in?"

Those crinkles returned. "I'm sorry, exactly why do you need to speak with him? I already explained you can't drop a class. We won't be able to pull any strings for you."

"Of course not." Daniel straightened from the desk. "Could we have his number?"

She ordered her papers and watched Daniel through her lashes. Her mouth pursed. "I'm not allowed to give out that information."

"But…" Daniel leaned closer. His flirting really was starting to annoy me.

She seemed to startle herself back to reality, scowling. "It's against policy. Off you go. Do some studying or something. Might help those grades." She fluttered a manicured hand in a shooing motion.

We trudged down the stairs. "That was an epic fail." Daniel's look of self-deprecation would have made me laugh if circumstances weren't so bleak. "Lucas probably would have been able to sweet-talk her."

My silence was telling.

"You're supposed to protest." He nudged my shoulder with his.

"You might need a little more practice... but I'm perfectly happy you're not an expert at flirting with women. You charmed me." I gave an exaggerated shrug. He'd had difficulty expressing his feelings when we first met. Okay, *still had* trouble. His inexpert moves endeared and softened my heart in ways a practiced flirt never could.

"What now?" I asked as we turned a corner, walking aimlessly. "You think this William Brody guy is from our world?"

"Seems suspicious. A break-in a few months ago? The timeline fits."

"Why else would they hurt him? Didn't find what they wanted from the registrar?" I stepped around a group of passing students.

"Who knows?"

"William Brody knows, and we need to find him." I didn't have to remind him of the clock ticking. Every moment here was another my family had to endure Rowan.

With nowhere else to go, we headed back to the dorms to regroup. Jenna, still in the room, greeted us with surprise. Books splayed across both desks, unruly hair secured in a bun with a number two pencil.

"Alright. Spill. What's really going on?" She eyed me critically, chewing the inside of her lip.

I studiously kept my gaze on her while I slumped on the bed, knowing if I glanced at Daniel, she would detect our guilty exchange. "We can't tell you everything. I know we didn't get much time together before I left, but if you could trust me..."

She nodded hesitantly, pulling out a desk chair and sitting. I didn't deserve her loyalty. We'd been roommates for less than two weeks before I'd abandoned her, yet she had opened herself up to us.

"You remember that mugging?" I asked.

"Of course. Freaked you out, then you went home."

I couldn't tell her the whole story, only nuggets of truth. "It has to do with that. This sounds weird, but I'm trying to track down someone who could help put that guy away. He works in the registrar's office—William Brody. Ever heard of him? He was injured in a robbery around the time I left."

"I remember that. Yeah, I did hear something. He was taking care of some grad application stuff for my friend Maggie—then *poof.* Disappeared. Word on the street is that he checked himself into one of those rest and recoup places for people who have breakdowns. The one in town. Pine Place? Peaceful Pines—that's it."

"Jenna. You're a genius! Thank you."

She held up her hands. "Hey. I'm good at listening to gossip, that's all. Was the guy who broke in the same one who attacked you?"

"We're hoping William Brody will help us answer that question." I patted Daniel's knee. "We'd better get going."

Jenna's expression clouded. "Wait—you're leaving already? Are you guys in trouble? Should I be worried?"

She had absolutely no idea how much trouble. I forced a smile. "We're fine. Don't worry about us."

She didn't return the smile. "So, what's all this cloak and dagger stuff?"

I wish I could tell her, I really did, but it would only make her worry. Or she'd believe we'd cracked up and belonged in Peaceful Pines, too. I stood, moving in to hug her. "You've been a lifesaver." I squeezed her a little too tightly. "We're fine," I whispered in her ear.

Her dark eyes reflected concern, and I hated that we couldn't be more convincing. I might never see her again, and she'd always wonder. I wanted to tell her I'd come back—check in on her one last time before we went through the portal. The realization that she'd worry even more if we never returned stopped me, sending goosebumps trailing over my arms. Because it would mean something had gone terribly wrong.

CHAPTER 15
DANIEL

After locating Peaceful Pines on the library computers—surprisingly, my login still worked—we trekked on foot several kilometers to reach a depressing gray building that appeared anything but peaceful. As we climbed the steps to the front door, signs of neglect with peeling paint, sagging eaves, and overgrown hedges gave it a tired, lonely impression. Though it was the iron bars on all the windows and the fence surrounding the property that sent Cate and me exchanging worried glances. Did Will Brody come here voluntarily? Or had he been committed?

The door wouldn't budge. "It's an intercom." Cate pointed to a black button next to it. "Probably cameras around here somewhere." She rang the bell.

A loud buzz, followed by a crackle, and a woman's voice, "Can I help you?"

"We're here to visit William Brody," Cate said into the speaker.

One pause led into minutes. I shifted my weight back and forth. Do we lie and say we're family? "Should we push the button again?" I whispered.

Cate's gaze circled the area as if the building held the answer. Before she could reply, the buzzing returned, and the door clicked open. Sterile tile floors and more gray paint on the walls greeted us.

We stepped into the entryway, turned a corner, and found a desk behind glass and iron. Apprehension curled in my stomach.

At the counter, a silver-haired woman sat in gray scrubs. It was as if someone whitewashed the color, including the workers. "Mr. Brody doesn't take visitors," the woman said after we asked, eyeing us skeptically.

"Are they allowed?" Cate asked.

"Of course," the woman replied, affronted, as if this place wasn't screaming modern-day dungeon.

"Then—" Cate leaned in.

"Mr. Brody doesn't take visitors," she repeated.

This was our last chance. If he didn't talk to us, I had no idea how we would ever find our contacts. And without them, getting passports, plane tickets… everything would be nearly impossible. At least for me. Cate might find a way since she was born here. But there'd be no record of me.

"How about a message?" I asked.

The woman tapped a pen on the painted gray desk, pursing her lips. "Go ahead." She slipped out a notepad and glanced up expectantly.

"Tell him Catherine from Caelum is here with Daniel." Cate leaned forward, speaking quietly.

"That's K-A-Y-L-U-M?"

"Sure. He'll know," I piped in.

The woman disappeared, leaving Cate and me once again waiting. I paced the small space, careful not to say anything that we didn't want overheard. If there were cameras outside, there were likely more in here. Two metal chairs sat against the wall, though neither Cate nor I moved to sit, too restless with everything riding on this one man. What if he'd lost his mind and was useless to us?

When she returned, the woman held a puzzled smile. "He agreed to see you."

She opened the door to a long corridor, the same depressing walls and scuffed tiles stretching beyond. Rooms stood on one side, mostly shut, with a few revealing a small bed and dresser with a view through barred windows. Halfway down, she disappeared through an already open doorway and gestured for us to follow. Inside, a man in rumpled pajamas, fine blond hair, and a lined face sat at a desk chair. He closed a worn paperback as we entered.

"I'll leave you to it." The woman left the door cracked.

"Mr. Brody?" Cate stepped forward to shake his hand. "I'm Catherine—Cate. And this is Prince Daniel." She tilted her head to me.

He searched her face. "Why are you here? I thought you left through the portal. I told them I didn't know anything. Only that you were gone."

"The Embers. They broke into the registrar's office, right?" I asked.

"They were searching for information on Catherine. I'd already destroyed it. They wouldn't let it go. One of them hit me, and I woke up the next day to the news that Brian and Lucy Sullivan were murdered."

My throat thickened at the thought of their brutal death. It must have been even harder on William.

"I ran." He watched the floor. "I'm not proud of it. But I checked myself in here, hoping it was safe, and they couldn't track me down. I haven't left since."

"We need your help," Cate told him. "We've come because an Ember has my family hostage in Oregon, and we have to get there. Do you know the society members in London? Our friend, Lucas, is in a hospital in Wales with Daniel's sister—long story—and they need help too." Cate's words rushed out in a flurry, her pent-up anxiety flying.

William's jaw hardened. "You haven't fulfilled the prophecy. You haven't destroyed them."

Cate froze, her eyes wide. She hadn't expected such a statement. She held the guilt of the people's expectations daily, wanting an end to the war as much as the rest of us. William's reminder hurt. Others often had trouble seeing the person behind the prophecy.

I moved forward. "The people believe in her. I believe in her. But the war isn't over, and we need help."

"So, why? Why come back when you're needed there?" His gray eyes didn't hold malice, only fear, and perhaps loyalty and concern for our world.

"The Ember's leader is holding her family hostage. We believe we have a chance to stop him here, where his powers don't work." It was the line we'd been telling to convince ourselves as much as them. Did we really believe we'd eliminate Rowan? I didn't want to think about our odds. *Couldn't* think about our odds. Supporting Cate was the only option. And if that meant lying to myself and others to get it done, so be it. "We need help with money and passports," I continued.

He narrowed his eyes in confusion. "You didn't bring gold?"

I explained the situation, but didn't fully divulge that we were worried about making it back across the portal. No reason to worry him more.

William turned to his desk. "I brought the contacts. Coded, of course, but I figured it would be safer here than anywhere." He pulled out a leather-bound blue notebook and a separate sheet of parchment. After a few minutes, he translated the code onto the paper. "The name at the top is most likely to have the money you need. He's in London. I have his address but no one else's."

"How many are here?" Cate asked.

"There used to be hundreds in the society. But I'm afraid we're all growing old. With the portals not working, we're a dying breed."

Cate put a hand on his shoulder. "It's because of me the portals closed. Thank you. For all you've done for our world, just by being willing to help. And for protecting me. What can we do for you? Will you…" she glanced around the room, "stay here?"

He didn't answer right away, circling the rim of his bottom lip with his index finger. "I'd like a message. When it's safe and they're gone."

"I promise." Her expression was so sincere, even though she couldn't promise such a thing. The logistics of the portal… would we even make it back from Oregon? Yet, she promised, anyway. And she'd meant it.

We had enough money to return to London to find the first person on the list, a Nigel Ballinger, located in a tall building—Cate called it a high-rise—on the top floor. She used a similar speaker system as Peaceful Pines. Thankfully, he was home and, after hearing Cate's name, let us into the building, much the same way as the "rest and recuperation" prison. This place was decidedly nicer. Sleek, smooth lines with whites and metals dominated, in stark contrast with Terra Castle, with its greenery flourishing in each room, stone floors, and warm rugs. We took the elevator up to what Cate called the penthouse and entered an expansive, high-ceilinged space with a view of the city. A slim man greeted us at the door with dark hair combed pin-straight.

He bowed, which took Cate aback, though I'd experienced it my entire life, so it didn't faze me in either world. "Prince. Princess. Please have a seat. May I get you anything?"

"We haven't eaten much." I stepped farther into the room. "Water would be lovely as well?"

Cate, likely too polite to ask for food, shot me a tiny smile. Her stomach growl on the train had sounded like an angry drundle, and I'd learned early on that a hungry Cate was a miserable Cate.

"Of course. I'm Nigel, as you probably guessed. Someone in the network sent you here?"

"William Brody. Do you know him?"

He shook his head. "Afraid we don't interact that much. For secrecy reasons. Heard the name, naturally."

I made a mental note to explain his plight before we left. William could use a friend.

We sat on a cognac-colored leather sofa with expansive windows overlooking the city. The amount of glass reminded me of Caelum Castle—I guessed him to be a Caelumite who found his own castle here. Nigel rummaged in the kitchen, while Cate tipped her head onto my shoulder, the emotional and physical toll setting in.

At last, he set a tray on the coffee table with sandwiches—a man after my own heart—a pitcher of water, some sort of yellow fruit cut into cubes, and a plate of what appeared to be shortbread cookies filled with jam.

Once we'd eaten, Cate began our story, catching him up on the results of the prophecy, including The Great Battle and her water powers. I stepped in and relayed King Aldridge's death and, ultimately, the note from Rowan regarding Cate's family. He absorbed our news until we finished nearly half an hour later. Assisting us would be burdensome from a time, financial, and legal standpoint, and he deserved an update on our world.

A full minute passed before he spoke, the faint sounds of cars moving below, my nerves tightening my shoulders into knots. Perhaps it was too much to ask. He might not feel loyalty to his old homeland anymore. His hands sat folded over his yellow jumper and brown slacks, a buttoned white-collared shirt beneath, spine barely touching the seat behind him. Even with my limited fashion knowledge, I could tell his tastes fell well outside the typical university student. Nigel's entire persona, from the sterile flat to the ruler-straight part in his dark hair, screamed uptight. Scrambling the routine of someone like that often led to resistance.

"You'll require more than just my help," he said. "I presume William sent you here because of my reputation for wealth." He inclined his head. "He presumed correctly. I can provide the money needed. Plane tickets, phones, fake passports…" he ticked them off his fingers, affect flat.

I could feel Cate's tension next to me as she stiffened her spine. He'd said he can… but would he?

"We'd be grateful for your help." I threaded my fingers with Cate's.

"We have a message system. A bit archaic, as no one has used it in twenty years. But I'll try. Doubt many are watching the newspapers. I've never met the forger. We'll have to rely on the network. In the meantime, you may stay with me, if that's to your liking." His focus bounced between us.

"How long will it take?"

"I'll make some calls now. I've some pull at the paper. Should be able to place it in the morning's news. We'll set a meetup tomorrow afternoon and see who comes."

More waiting. I counted the days we'd lost. We still had time to get to Oregon in the two-week timeframe. As long as someone shows up tomorrow.

CHAPTER 16
LUCAS

Chirp. Chirp.

A bird outside my window would not stop its incessant call. Over and over, as if marking time. It still wasn't enough to drag me from slumber, my limbs leaden. Returning to uninterrupted oblivion, my only desire.

If only the bird would stop.

A moan further marred my sleep. Unfortunately, it seemingly came from me. I cracked a lid. Bright lights shone overhead, the ceiling low and white. Not my room at home. So, where was I?

"Lucas," a voice called. Female. Familiar.

"Cate?" I croaked.

"It's Mya." The voice turned brittle. Dark hair floated into my blurry vision as my eyes slitted open a bit more.

"Hi." All I could manage was the one word, my throat parched and sore.

"You almost died, and all you'll say is *hi*?" she asked.

My body was curiously heavy, yet light at the same time, mind sluggish. The bird continued its racket. Did she say I almost died? Even in my best form, I often had difficulty parsing out whether Mya was joking. My brain refused to connect with my lips. I tried to reach out, but my limbs wouldn't cooperate. A single finger lifted.

Her expression softened, and this time I noticed the red rim around her blue eyes. "I—I'm so glad you're awake." Her cool hand encased mine. "Sorry, I've been overwhelmed. It's been… a tough few days."

Days?

She must have sensed my confusion, and continued, "The man in the park—he stabbed you. The doctors wanted to fly you to a bigger hospital, but you were too unstable, so they did surgery here."

"Cate—" I rasped.

"Cate and Daniel left me to look after you. They hooked you up to a machine, a tube in your throat."

Thoughts rolled through my brain as I tried to grasp hold of one. Mya was alone? How many days had passed? And Cate… she needed me too.

"They took your spleen out. Apparently, you were bleeding everywhere—both inside and out." A tear slid down her pale cheek, and she impatiently swiped it with her other hand. "But you've pulled through. Look—here you are. Everything is fine." She sounded like she was convincing herself rather than me. I wanted to wrap my arms around her. Feel her softness against me. Say I never meant to worry or leave her alone. My limbs wouldn't cooperate, so I brushed the pad of my finger along hers instead.

"How long?" I mumbled.

"Three days since you were stabbed. You'd lost so much blood, your other organs started to… not work right, I guess? Otherwise, you would have been awake before now."

The door swished open. A woman entered wearing matching tunic and trousers. "Our patient is awake, I see," she sing-songed. "I'm your nurse, Darlene, glad to meet you." She leaned over me, her short, dark hair coming into view with the no-nonsense expression I'd come to recognize from medics back home. "Any pain?"

Since Mya told me I'd nearly died, I would think everything would hurt, but surprisingly not. Mostly my throat, presumably from the tube. I shook my head slowly.

"Good." She turned to Mya. "He's on lots of painkillers. Probably isn't making much sense. You might have to repeat this conversation tomorrow. We'll wean him off the meds in a couple of days."

More *days*? But I needed to take care of Mya. And Cate.

If only I weren't so tired. *And that sound.* "Stop… the bird." My lips cracked with the words.

"See?" Darlene shook her head, a grim half-smile at Mya. "Not much sense. He could use some more rest. Why don't you get some too? Find that hotel I told you about?"

Mya's gaze hit the floor. "I'm fine, really. Can I just stay here? I'll be perfectly quiet. Silent as a mouse."

Unlike that bird.

"Okay, luv," she replied, disappointed. She pulled something out of her pocket. "Snuck you some crackers." The nurse handed them to Mya, then adjusted a few wires.

The door *thunked* closed just as my heavy lids couldn't hold any longer. The last thing I remembered was dreaming of the forest, Molly by my side, sparrows chattering. We were laughing, though I couldn't remember the joke. The thought of Molly sent me deeper into sleep, her comforting presence watching over me.

I woke to chirping. "Molls, make it stop."

"First, I'm Cate, now Molly?"

Mya's voice sent my dry lips tipping upward. At least I think I smiled—I meant to, anyway. "You're a better kisser." The frog in my throat was far from desirable, but I couldn't help teasing her. As I pulled myself from dreams, my head felt clearer, though a throbbing now ached through my right side. The bed dipped as she sat beside me.

"Better than who? Cate or Molly?"

Now, there was a trap even my groggy state recognized as dangerous. My mind flashed to that kiss on the road to Caelum Castle with Cate—her lips warm and soft beneath mine. Then I remembered how she'd flinched, covering her mouth in shock. I'd apologized. Of course, I'd apologized. She'd said it was a mistake. I would never forget her face—a mixture of surprise and guilt. Guilt over Daniel… who'd betrayed her.

"Lucas? You're frowning. Does it hurt?"

"Yes." I opened my lids to find Mya's worried expression. The truth was, it *had* hurt, but I rarely thought of it anymore. Even though I'd replayed that moment hundreds of times. The meds and fuzzy brain must have been to blame. A rush of affection washed through me for Mya, hovering over me. She was who I wanted. Today. Now.

"Should I call the nurse?"

"I don't want—I need my head clear. Help me sit up a little."

"Oh, you'll love this. It's a button!" Mya pressed an arrow on the side rail of my bed, and the top moved upward. Once sitting, I could see the room better. I was still attached to some kind of monitor. And with it—the bird noise.

She noticed me glaring at it. "It's monitoring your heart. That beeping is comforting, no? It means your heart is steady."

"The chirping. It's driving me…" I winced at the stabbing pain in my belly, "crazy."

"Ah, *that's* the bird you keep mumbling about. Hopefully, you'll be well enough to be disconnected soon."

Hopefully, very soon.

"Have you heard from them?" I asked.

"My brother and Cate? Not yet. They were supposed to find our contacts, then send someone back for us with money and one of those cell phone things. It's been three days, and I'm starting to worry. I haven't wanted to spend on a hotel. When the nurses kick me out of your room, I find a lobby somewhere else in the building." She fingered the buttons of her dress. "I'd love fresh clothes, though."

"You still look beautiful." I meant every word. She'd pulled her hair back since the last time I'd been awake, showing off pink cheeks. Dark-winged brows rose over her sparkling blue eyes that tilted upward ever so slightly, giving her a perpetual cat-in-cream expression. But the shadows beneath marked her fatigue.

"You should go. One night at an inn."

"A hotel," she amended.

I nodded. Speaking still hurt my throat, though her correction made me want to roll my eyes.

"What if the contacts come when I'm gone? Or the police. They've been here once already. I answered the best I could and told them I'd lost my ID. Not sure they believed me."

"If someone comes, they'll wake me." I glanced out the window, seeing the light outside. A clock on the wall indicated four. "Tell the nurses. You should go while there's daylight."

"Trying to get rid of me?" She stood and pursed her lips. There I went again, having a hard time deciding if she was hurt under all that teasing.

I patted the bed. "Mya," my throat was on fire, aching for water, "I've spent weeks locked in a prison cell with you, and it still wasn't enough. I find you endlessly fascinating, and selfishly, I would love for you to stay. But please. It hurts to see you so exhausted. I'll be fine."

Her shoulders slackened. "I've just been so… worried. About being stuck here, and Cate and Daniel, and you—you've been unconscious. You almost died. I'd like you to be around a while longer, you know?" Her voice cracked.

"I'll be here when you get back. You've done your job. Tomorrow we'll share the burden together. I promise." The responsibility had fallen solely on her, something that would weigh on anyone, not just a princess who hadn't been given duties her entire life. "It's close?" Escorting her wasn't an option—I hadn't even left the bed.

"Just down the street." She leaned over and kissed my forehead. "I'll miss you," she whispered, her words both feather-light and bound with the strength of forged steel.

She was gone before I could croak out an answer. I pushed the button on my bed with the picture of a nurse, hoping for water. The pain in my side had deepened, though I wouldn't take more medicine. Mya had watched over me, and it was time to be there for her, which meant a clear head.

I'd tried to pretend I wasn't worried to shield Mya, but something must have happened for a messenger not to have arrived from Cate and Daniel. Could they not find our contacts? Were they unwilling to help? Or had they run out of money, too? Perhaps we should be conserving instead of Mya using our coin on the inn. But she'd been here for days… she needed a bed. I thought about her figuring out how to use the shower. She'll love it. The best thing about this world, other than cereal, of course.

A sinking feeling grew in my stomach, unrelated to the surgery. Nothing about this mission was going according to plan. And unfortunately, the one thing I was never wrong about was my intuition when things were about to get worse.

Mya flounced in late the next morning in an ill-fitting pair of jeans, a flowered orange top three sizes too big, and a glow in her cheeks. "How's the patient?" She slid the blankets aside to sit next to me, planting a kiss on my forehead. "The nurses said you were doing great. Even got out of bed."

"They'll be moving me to another unit today." The doctor just informed me earlier. "I see you're all cleaned up with new clothes. I'm looking forward to a shower myself."

"I had the most terrible time at first. There was a man at the counter who handed me this thick card as my key to the room. I finally found it up four flights of stairs, and then there was no slot to put it. By this time, I was frazzled, exhausted, and ready to curl up in the hall outside the room."

"You didn't…" I eyed her clean, shiny hair, deciding she made it inside somehow.

"No. The last time we slept out in the open, you ended up in the hospital, so of course not. I'd never risk such a thing in Caelum either." Her pink cheeks flushed rosier. "It was really embarrassing, though. I forced myself back to the lobby and, thank goodness, a girl was working at the desk now. I explained I'd never stayed in a hotel before, so she walked me to my room and showed me the ropes—including the shower! I was in there for an entire hour. She also gave me directions to the thrift store a few blocks away." She stood up and twirled. "My first pair of jeans! Father would lock me up."

My grin couldn't be stifled at her enthusiasm. The trousers were above her ankles, sagging in the rear and somehow tight in the thighs. And that ghastly shirt… "You look gorgeous," I said. And she still did. Her long black hair hung shiny and sleek, her blue eyes wide, framed with sooty lashes, mouth stretched into an infectious smile. Though I wish she hadn't brought King Dryden into the conversation. Even the mention of him soured my mood.

Mya curtsied comically, then nestled against me again, her grin fading. "Any word?"

"Not yet. I'm sure it'll be soon." Truthfully, I wasn't sure. Neither of us was. "How much money do you have left?"

"Not enough for another night at the hotel." She bit the inside of her lip. "I feel like a new person, though. I can last a while now."

"You know…" I struggled to sit up, wincing at the pain in my side. "We can use this time to talk. Pretend we aren't worried about Cate and Daniel. We've certainly been in tougher spots before." I gestured around the room. "There're no metal bars. That's a win." In the Ember prison, every day we wondered if it would be our last, but at least here we were fairly confident tomorrow would come. At least the doctors seemed to think so.

She crossed the space to the single chair, curling up her feet beneath her. "Talk about what?"

I hesitated, various questions swimming to the surface before I settled on one. "What does peace between the kingdoms look like to you? If you could convince your father."

A crease pleated between her brows. "This? You start heavy like this?"

"Well, yeah." For a girl who wanted to be taken seriously, her objections surprised me.

"It's just… no one's ever asked me." She unwound her feet from beneath her.

"Exactly." I waited for her to begin. She was too smart to have never thought this through at some point. There was definitely more than gown swatches and gossip in that head of hers, and I wanted to be the one to pry it out.

"Trust," she finally replied. "I think it comes down to trust. If both sides continue to show goodwill, like in battle, then the tides will change. If—when we defeat the Embers, we need to intermingle more. Show we're not that different from one another. We both want the same things. Family. Love. Also," she let out a little breath, not quite a sigh, "we need my father to be on board. He has to be convinced we're allies."

I laced my fingers together. "And who's good at convincing people?"

She shot me a dubious look. "Yes, yes. Me. But you know how it works. Otherwise, we would have all walked out of that Ember jail unscathed without the tragedy."

That ache in my belly, which had nothing to do with the dagger recently passing through it, swelled at the thought of King Aldridge. "Wear your father down. Plus," I gave a half-hearted smile, "with me around, how could he not grow to love Caelumites? He'll be inviting me to family dinners, bestowing me with gifts—"

"Lucas. Stop." She covered a reluctant smile beneath three fingers. "Be serious."

"Oh, and she slays me while I'm wounded." My hands shot to my heart. "Alright. Think on it more. Because we're getting out of here somehow. When we finally make it through that portal, you and I," I pointed between us, "are going to help create this peace. The prophecy may say it's Cate, but she can't do it alone."

"Ah," she said lightly. "So, this is all about serving Cate?"

Her presence, that underlying tension which never quite left us, crept in. "No, it's about saving our kingdoms," I replied a little too sharply. "And she's my queen, is she not?"

Mya nodded slowly. "She is. Daniel told me he had some of these same issues. Figuring out which side he's on."

"He's on the side of peace. At least I hope." I smoothed back my blanket.

"That's pretty much what he said." She bit her lip as if holding back more of the story.

"Cate may be my queen, but you're the only princess I want in my life." I scooted over and gestured. "Come snuggle."

She slid into bed next to me, careful to avoid the surgery site, her cheek gently lying on my shoulder. She smelled of the inn's soap and her own special Mya blend of lavender and sweetness that followed her into both worlds. "Tell me about your cook's pastries," I whispered, suddenly growing drowsy. It'd been her favorite topic in jail, and we could both use a pleasant reminder of where we came from.

"I like the raspberry-filled ones best…" was the last thing I heard before sleep won out.

CHAPTER 17
CATE

Nigel's guestrooms were the same minimalist style as the rest of the penthouse, the kind of place where I felt like an interloper for even taking off my shoes. I slipped into bed and immediately changed my tune. The white sheets must have been a million-thread count, cool and sleek beneath my toes. The mattress contoured to my body in a way that only modern technology and money could provide. Certainly nicer than any at my home in Portland, and although the beds are quite comfortable at Caelum Castle, *this* was another level.

I used to flip through the fancy travel magazines at the public library and dream of fluffy cotton-white comforters and floor-to-ceiling windows with a city view like this. Dream of trips to London. Funny how, when dreams come true, they're never how you expect. There's always a catch. And in this case, one I couldn't bear to think about. Instead, I replayed every moment of this trip that should have been beautiful—my head on Daniel's shoulder on the train, the stroll to Camden library through the city, and this very comfortable pillow beneath my head as I drifted off to sleep.

The next morning, I woke to the blissful smell of coffee and bacon. Taking my time in the shower, I luxuriated in the rain-head faucet and fancy lavender body wash provided. Dressed in a spare outfit we bought at H&M, I headed out to the kitchen. A newspaper spread over the quartz countertop, with Daniel hunched over its pages, a dark lock of hair falling over his brow.

"So... that's a newspaper," I said, crossing the herringbone wood floor. "In case you didn't recognize it."

He barely glanced up as he shook his head. It was a low blow, reminding him that King Dryden banned them in Terra. An opportunity I couldn't pass. After he'd admitted that a drawing of himself in newspapers in Caelum allowed the farmers to recognize him that day after the avalanche, I used every chance to tease him.

"We're gathering in a pub at two." Daniel's finger slid over the classifieds.

I moved in next to him to read the advertisement. *T & C club long-awaited meeting. Be ready to work.* "That sounds like a good time," I snorted. "Come do some hard labor."

"It's a cry for help without saying it, and he doesn't want random people showing up." Daniel tilted his head to touch mine. "We can't mention the beautiful princess has arrived and come to save us all," he whispered. "Might be a bit distracting."

I leaned in closer. "You're distracting."

He smoothed my hair back to lean in and kiss my neck. "I try," he breathed into my ear, sending tingles along my scalp.

Nigel's shoes clicked across the floor, and I reluctantly pulled away. "You know what else is distracting? The smell of that coffee. I would love a cup." A pot sat behind me in an alcove next to the fridge. "Good morning, Nigel." I poured the rich, dark liquid into a white mug. Sugar and a little container of milk nestled by the coffeemaker, and I added generous amounts of both.

"I see you've found the advertisement," Nigel said. "I'm going out to pick up some phones for you, Princess Mya, and Lucas. And my personal shopper will drop by and take a few measurements. She's due here in around an hour." He donned a navy sport coat over his pinstriped button-down. "Make yourselves at home."

Once he left, I pounced on the bacon and toast sitting on the counter. I wished Jenna were here. She'd understand the eyebrow raise I gave Daniel when Nigel mentioned having a personal shopper. I covered a disbelieving grin. *I'm dating someone who thinks that's completely normal.* And admittedly, in Caelum, that would be normal for me, too. My other life—absolutely unexpected. Maybe one day I could actually enjoy the luxuries.

"At least we don't have money problems anymore." I took a sip of coffee, savoring the rich sweetness. "I'm sorry about your signet ring. We can try to get it back?"

"There's another in Terra. Not my first concern at the moment." He leaned against the island, eyes troubled.

I bit my lip. "What now?"

"Nothing more than what you already know. Will anyone show up at the pub is the first thing that comes to mind. Second…" He snatched a piece of toast from the silver rack. "You'll eat all my breakfast."

"*Your* breakfast, is it?" I took a step back with my slice of bacon and coffee, then sipped again, groaning with pleasure. "I have *got* to teach them how to make a proper brew in the castle kitchens."

Daniel wrinkled his nose. "You can have it."

"Lucas likes it," I teased.

He rolled his eyes. "Lucas likes my sister, too. His taste is questionable."

"Come on. You love Mya."

He sighed. "I do. I'm worried about her. It's easier to tease than remember I've left her up north alone."

I set down my drink and moved in to hug him. "She'll be okay. Give her more credit."

"Like Lucas is okay?"

"That's different."

"Is it?"

I dropped my cheek to his shoulder. Maybe it wasn't. Yet, the dangers of hanging out in a city sounded much less harrowing than the everyday trials of living with the Embers. No one knows she's there or that she's a princess. She *should* be safer than in Terra, where the threat of kidnapping loomed every day. Daniel wouldn't be convinced she was safe until he heard her voice. "You know," I looked up at him, "in the future, we're going to have to rely on your sister as an ally. It's time to start trusting her with responsibilities."

He took a plate and piled toast, bacon, and fruit in a precarious pile. I found the bread and slotted another couple of slices into the toaster while he sat on a stool by the island. "I'll work on it," he said between mouthfuls. "I promise."

After breakfast, we recharged on the leather sofa overlooking the city, me with a second cup of coffee in hand, Daniel watching me fondly. Would I get another chance to explore London? Did it really matter? No one here would ever experience Caelum Castle and its sparkling glass walls. They'd never feel the swooping in their stomachs from riding a dragon. Or the energy flow around them while holding the love of their life. With or without energy, love was the only real magic in both worlds. I slid closer to Daniel. You just had to fight for it.

Soon, the door sounded, and a woman called from the entry, "Knock, knock. Nigel buzzed me in."

Her heels *click-clacked* across the wood floors. A thirty-something with highlighted blonde chin-length hair strode in, a designer purse slung over one shoulder, red button-down silk blouse tucked into a belted slim-fit skirt, as if she just stepped off the runway. Exactly how much money did Nigel have if he kept this woman on speed dial?

"I'm Bri, nice to meet you both." We stood to greet her. "Just some quick measurements and I'll pop down to Harrods and get you all sorted." She pulled a measuring tape out of the oversized leather bag. "Shoe size?" She eyed me up and down, including the cheap canvas shoes I'd picked up at H&M.

"Something comfortable." I pointedly stared at her heels in return.

Daniel spoke up, "The goal is not to stand out. And some dark clothes would be appreciated."

Her pert nose raised. "I understand you have an important meeting this afternoon? Nigel informed me you needed to impress."

My shoulders collapsed in an exaggerated sigh. Of course. It didn't matter where I went; looking the part of royalty had its purposes. "One set of nice clothes. And a few comfortable items." I challenged her narrowing eyes. "Please."

She inclined her head. "As you wish."

Two hours later, Nigel hadn't come back, though Bri returned with a rolling suitcase, presumably to hold the items overflowing in bags from her arms when we traveled to Oregon. She pulled out piles of makeup, Nikes (oh-my blessed Nikes!), sweatpants—the kind you see celebrities wearing in the magazines, a few other comfy items, as well as chunky gold jewelry, a sweater set, trim pants, and heels. I stifled a grin at Daniel's "appropriate" outfit, which was a carbon copy of Nigel's from this morning, down to the pinstriped shirt and blazer.

I thanked Bri profusely, because in any other circumstance, I'd be over the moon to receive this kind of stash. Unfortunately, most of it would remain in this world, likely given to charity. When she left, I eyed the digital clock on the stove. Nearly noon, and no Nigel yet. Only two hours until we were to meet at the pub. Daniel raided the fridge while I stared out at the city, chewing on my thumbnail, stomach in knots. The couch sank beside me with Daniel's weight, though I remained deep in thought.

"Bite?" Spicy mustard wafted under my nose, a sandwich hovering.

"No thanks." I pulled back. "Wish Nigel would show."

"He'll make it." He took a giant bite. "He seems to be taking this seriously." He gestured to his clothes, leather wingtips now in place.

I huffed a small laugh. "You look as if you're ready for the British aristocracy."

He looked affronted. "Of course I do. Blood will out, and all that."

My brows went up. "You believe that?"

"I am the prince." He gave a self-deprecating shrug. "But could someone other than my relative take over and be perfectly capable of being king? Sure." He polished off his sandwich. "Just don't tell anyone I said that."

"It would solve the problem of your father."

"Mm… That it would." After a moment, he said, "It has its purposes. There isn't a power grab every time a ruler dies. It saves the kingdom from war."

"What about democracy? A vote. Maybe we should have council elections. Let the people choose."

He snorted. "You've met my father, right?"

"You've met *me*, right?" I shot him a look of determination. Though these were all problems for another day.

Nigel arrived a few minutes later, cell phone bags in hand. "I visited your embassy. I believe we can get the paperwork in time. But only yours. You'd have to go alone."

My heart stuttered. Facing Rowan by myself was a nightmare I couldn't think about right now. I rubbed the chills running up my arms.

"As a last resort." His buttoned-up nature cracked, just for a moment, with sympathy.

"Thank you," I forced out through a clogged throat. "You've done so much."

His head went back in offense. "Of course. It's the vow I took as part of the society. It may be my only opportunity to keep it."

After showing us our phones and me giving Daniel a tutorial, he stood. "Shall we?"

A riot of butterflies careened from my belly into my chest.

The Olive and Lamb had a back room, all dark wood and dim lights, much like the few pubs I'd visited in Caelum and Terra, though I'd been ferreted away from some of the seedier establishments. Nigel informed us that the society had been meeting here for well over a hundred years. A plaque hung at the door: *Established 1826*. The comfort of knowing that other Caelumites and Terrans had crossed this same threshold acted as a tiny candle of warmth and hope.

The reserved room sat empty. Daniel and I exchanged worried glances, the sound of Nigel's chair scraping across the wood floors jarring. Nigel ordered food and drinks while we waited. Daniel returned volleyed questions about our world while anxiety crawled up my chest, then began its vice-like pressure, cranking tighter every moment we waited for someone—anyone, to show.

I downloaded Instagram as a distraction, logging into my old account, scrolling through high school friends—more like acquaintances—with their selfies and group photos of college sorority parties. I never fit into that crowd, and honestly, really didn't miss trying. They looked happy. I found I *wanted* them to be happy. Wanted them free of the pressures I experienced. It weirdly calmed my anxiety.

A man and woman tromped in, dressed in bulky cable-knit sweaters and jeans. "T&C?" the woman asked breathlessly, pushing back curly silver hair, her cheeks flushed. "The train was delayed. Could have given us better notice." She huffed and planted herself onto a chair, pouring a glass of water from a pitcher on the table. A pint of untouched beer sat nearby. "We contacted a few others. Stanley should be along soon. You need his services?"

The man, presumably her husband, slid in next to her, his slim frame in contrast to her more robust, stocky shape. "Emmitt will be here. Just received a text," he said quietly.

"You're in contact with others?" Nigel gave her a disapproving look.

"Don't be such a stick-in-the-mud, Nigel," she said. "It's been years. We're not giving away any secrets by seeing each other every once in a while." She popped a pretzel from a bowl on the table into her mouth and sniffed.

"It's against our covenants," he replied stiffly.

"Saved your bacon today, though, didn't it?" She turned to me. "I'm Sarah, this is my husband, Bert. And who do I have the pleasure of meeting?"

Nigel answered for me, "She's the new queen of Caelum, Catherine. The Concealed. And the Terran Prince, Daniel." He nodded in a small bow.

"Oh! Well." She swallowed and sat up straighter. "I beg your pardon, Your Highness."

"The king?" Bert asked. He must have noticed my hesitation, and he quickly added, "I'm sorry for your loss." The deep brackets around his mouth were etched with sorrow. "I met your father once. He loved our kingdom."

Unexpected tears burned to life. He'd quickly surmised that me owning the title of queen meant my father was no longer king. "He did. Thank you."

Several others stepped into the room, introduced as Emmitt the forger and Stanley, an eager, short man with a quick smile. Daniel relayed our story, the space growing quiet and grave, particularly when they discovered Brian and Lucy's demise.

"How did we not know?" Sarah asked. "It had been a while since I heard from them... I should have checked in." She threw her fingers over her rosy cheeks. "See, Nigel? This is why we should be in contact. Isolating ourselves isn't helping anyone."

"Rules are there for a reason," Nigel replied stiffly from across the table.

Plans were set in motion. Sarah and Bert were to go to Lucas and Mya. Stanley's job was to watch for Ember activity around the penthouse. And Emmitt would construct the documents for us to travel.

"I'll need to get your photos," Emmitt said, dipping his balding head. "It's been a while since I've made a passport, but I think it'll get you through."

He thinks? I exchanged a look with Daniel. One more item to worry over.

"When are you leaving?" he asked.

"As soon as possible." Daniel took on an authoritative tone, sliding into prince mode.

A shiver climbed up my spine. We were so close. Warring thoughts swirled—seeing my family's faces again, the picture of Rowan with them forever tainting my memories. Their frightened expressions. The panic in Jack's eyes. They had no idea of the full extent of Rowan's evil. They *should* be afraid. So was I.

CHAPTER 18
DANIEL

Cate fidgeted while security inspected our documents at the airport. I wanted to remind her to act calm, but was too busy putting on a bored expression, an easy feat after years of masking emotions with my father. She was the one making me nervous, not the staff. The man returned our passports, Cate's United States and mine, emblazoned with the British crown. Emmitt performed his job well, and I silently thanked him.

I looped my arm in the crook of hers and pulled along our rolling case with the other, directing Cate and her too-wide eyes away from the man's hooded gaze. We reached our gate with Cate's guidance—I'd never been in an airport before—and found two spots together in an already crowded space.

"What's our seat number again?" She pointed to the bag where we'd stuffed our tickets, and I pulled them out and handed them to her.

She frowned. "These are near the front."

I peered over her shoulder at 10 A and B. I'd never flown before, even on a dragon, so I didn't know what it meant. "And…"

"They're business class." Her lips tilted up the barest bit, the first sign of anxiety easing I'd seen today.

"Nigel bought us good seats?"

"Very. You're going to be spoiled."

"I deserve it."

She elbowed me. Probably deserved that, too. "Well," she said, "if I'm going to fly to my death, it should be in style." The pinch of her smile stretched a little too tight.

We boarded the plane and found our seats. Cate called them pods, and they came with a toiletries kit, blanket, slippers, a sleep mask, and full recliners. She stuffed every item away as if they were the best Christmas presents she'd ever received. As if she didn't have luxury at her fingertips in the castle. My nose and eyes burned with tears, catching me off guard. I loved her so much. She taught me about gratefulness and loyalty, and pulled me out of the quagmire of moral gray Father dealt in daily. I couldn't believe she'd chosen me.

"Put these in your ears. Let's watch a movie." She handed me earphones, which I'd at least seen from my time at Staton. Lucas had taken to television, though I found it strange to view stories of other people's lives. But I'd humor her. She'd been in a better mood since talking to Lucas last night on the hospital phone, and to be honest, so had I. Knowing that Mya would soon be safe with Bert and Sarah and that Lucas was recovering was a huge weight lifted from both our shoulders.

"I love this one. It's old but good. Perfect for us." She snuggled in her blanket.

The title, *Kate and Leopold,* came onto the screen, and I settled deeper into my seat. The irony wasn't lost on me, as it was about an English duke from 1876 who was inadvertently dragged to modern-day New York. Cate laughed in all the places where Leopold didn't understand how this world worked, and I tried to pretend it was funny, even though the laughter jabbed a little too close to home.

Cate finally fell asleep, while I stared out at the blue sky, wondering how Terra was somehow connected to this world. Could a plane fly through a portal and end up on the other side? It had never happened before. There must be a better way to control them—portals, not planes. All that knowledge died with Alana. Because even if we freed Cate's family, the very real danger of returning to our realm still loomed.

We landed and headed to customs, where we separated into the foreigner and American citizen lines. Reaching the desk, I admitted to stashing a ham sandwich from the plane into my bag when asked by the officer about food in my luggage. They rather roughly pulled me aside and searched the rest of my baggage while further examining my passport. I feared Cate and I would forever be separated over a measly sandwich. Finally, they let me through with a warning. The rules baffled me.

I caught up with Cate, and we rushed to our next flight to Portland, barely making it. These were just regular seats, and by this time, I was more than ready to reach our destination. Admittedly, the movie helped my claustrophobia, but now, waiting to take off for yet another flight, it kicked into full force.

Cate laced her fingers in mine. "You'll be fine. This is the easy part."

I exhaled deeply. If anyone understood irrational spinning thoughts, it was Cate.

"You want a statistic?" she asked.

I hated those gruesome stats. "No, thank you. I assume you have one about planes?"

"I do. But I sense you'd like a different one better." She leaned over and whispered in my ear, "One hundred percent of the time, I want to kiss you."

"Then why don't you?"

Her hand flew to her chest in mock offense. "Because, Daniel. I'm a lady, and we're in public."

I cocked my head. "I seem to remember a certain road to Caelum… there were quite a few soldiers unsuccessfully looking the other way." I carefully failed to mention the panic attack that brought on said make-out session.

She rolled her eyes good-naturedly and rested her head on my shoulder, her answer drowned out by the sound of the engines at takeoff. As she traced the lines in my palm, we settled into the flight.

When we arrived, Cate rented a car, and we stepped out into a drizzly evening. The time change was strange—we'd left early in the afternoon and got here just a few hours later in Portland. Yet, my body felt every moment of the long journey. We planned to set up camp at an inn near Cate's house and then scout the area. The neighbor next door lived alone and worked nights—at least, he did when Cate lived there. We hoped to watch from his yard to see how many were with Rowan, when they took breaks, and plot the best chance to free her family.

"Is this the inn?" I squinted at the oversized, blindingly lit-up, blue-and-white sign.

"The motel, yes." She pulled into a parking space in front. "Wait here." She soon returned with a room number and key.

"How far are we from your house?"

"About a mile."

The room held two beds, navy, somewhat suspect carpet, an end table, a small fridge, a microwave, and a bathroom. The essentials. Well, according to Cate. I'd never used a microwave.

"I don't think Nigel would approve of this place." She wrinkled her nose at the patterned cover over one of the beds. "But it'll do. We can't all have thousand-thread-count sheets."

We changed into dark clothes, ate a few items we picked up, and piled into the sedan we'd rented. Cate drove the short distance, passing her home slowly.

"That's it. That's my house." Her eyes filled with tears as she pointed across the street to a yellow-painted single-story home with a steep roof and carefully trimmed hedges. An uneven concrete sidewalk led to a blue front door. The windows were dark, and unlike the houses on either side, the porch lights remained unlit. "I never thought I'd see it again."

She rolled the car forward until parking six houses down. Cate donned a dark baseball hat she'd picked up at a shop in the airport. "The last thing we need is someone recognizing me."

We waited until a man walking his dog passed, then exited the sedan, striding confidently, but quickly, our Nikes soft and quiet on the pavement. The neighbors' outside lights were on, windows dim. Cate beelined to the locked side gate, retrieved a key from under a loose stone, and slipped into the backyard.

"I used to help take care of Mr. Davis's dog," she whispered.

"Dog?" I listened for barking that might blow our cover.

"She died a while back. I don't think he planned to replace her. He works too many long hours."

A fence separated Cate's house from this one. The grassy yard was small, about the size of the castle dining room. Of course, everything felt small compared to the open spaces of Terra. A shed sat in the rear corner, and a concrete patio led to glass doors into the modest home. Cate stepped along the perimeter until halfway down, where the wood had rotted away, leaving a gap to peer through. "I can see the living room from here," she whispered. "There aren't curtains on the slider. I used to like to spy on my family to watch what they were up to while I waited for Roxy to do her business."

I huffed a laugh. "Were they ever up to anything?"

She pursed her mouth. "No. But it was fun to pretend sometimes."

Cate stepped up to the gap in the wood. A moment passed. Then another. A sharp intake of breath. "Daniel. Look." She made room for me, then leaned the back of her head against the fence, her lips parted in shock. "I—I can't believe it." Her voice shook.

I peered across Cate's backyard into her house, lamps illuminating the space, making it visible through the darkness. Rowan's silhouette faced away from us. Cate's brother perched on the floor, his hands and feet tied. And two women sat on the couch, their backs to me. *Two?* One of them turned, saying something to the other. Her profile was unmistakable. The second woman wasn't part of Cate's family, but someone from our world.

Someone back from the dead.

Alana.

Emotions bubbled. Confusion. Relief. Elation. Fear.

"How?" Cate's features, whitewashed in the moonlight, still hung in shock.

"I don't—" I exhaled, thoughts swirling. "But I'd like to know what she's doing with Rowan. And why she let us believe she was dead all this time."

CHAPTER 19
LUCAS

Another day passed. They moved me to a different floor, a space with a washroom, but I shared it with an old man who snored, with only a thin curtain between us. Torn between being eager to leave and grateful, it provided us shelter while we waited. The nurses looked the other way when she curled up in a chair in the corner and slept in the room. Maybe they suspected she had nowhere else to go. Or maybe some of her Terran persuasive powers still worked.

The man's presence left us with whispered snatches of conversations, and even those he probably heard. More often, we exchanged worried glances and, for the most part, remained silent, the tension building.

At the end of visiting hours, which they fortunately did not enforce, an older gentleman in a tweed jacket and a plump, rosy-cheeked woman entered the room. "Lucas?" the man asked, glancing at the curtain.

A jolt of excitement and nerves zipped through me.

Mya stood, shifting from foot to foot. "Yes, that's right. And I'm Mya." They'd passed our neighbor, my bed being the farther one from the door, so there was no need to warn them not to say anything they shouldn't.

The woman stepped forward as if to shake hands, then gave a

slight bow, indicating she knew of her princess status. "Sarah. And this is my husband, Bert. Your friends sent us."

"They're alright? Cate and Daniel?"

Bert nodded. "They left this morning for Oregon."

"Just today?" I worked to sit up, became frustrated with my weak abdominal muscles, then pushed the up button on the bed instead. "We still have time to join them." I glanced at Mya, who watched me stoically. "Right? We can go."

Bert and Sarah exchanged glances. "When will you be released?"

"Doesn't matter. I'll leave now." I could still help Cate. I knew more about Rowan than anyone after our time together in Ember City.

Mya's hand rested on my shoulder, stopping me from shifting my legs over the side of the bed. "Lucas." My name sounded soft, yet firm, with notes of sadness.

I gazed up at her, dark lashes shadowing her cheeks as she stared back. She couldn't stop me. This was my duty. Then I noticed the pain behind her eyes. Next, pity, because I wasn't fit to defend anyone. The realization came like a thief, stealing my worth. *I'd be a hindrance*. She didn't tell me not to go. But her quiet voice, speaking only my name, told me everything.

Cate and Daniel were on their own.

Now that I knew we had somewhere safe to stay, I couldn't wait to get out of this hospital bed. I walked on shaky legs for my nurse so she could report my progress to the doctor, sweet-talking to convince her I was ready to leave. My bravado backfired when my knees buckled, and I barely made it safely back to bed. "See? I'm all good." I plastered on a weak smile.

The nurse tipped down her chin and gave me one of those *I see right through you* looks. She really did. My side ached horribly, and my blood counts were low—fortunately rising—just not fast enough. My organs were supposedly mostly working again, albeit sluggish. Every time I stood, my head swam. Yet… I hated being useless.

The doctor strode in a few minutes later for her daily visit. "I hear you want to go home."

I nodded gravely. "I do. Friends have come to help."

She listened to my heart and lungs, then examined the wound, face stoic. "You're moving in the right direction. As long as you won't be alone, you're free to go."

"Really?" I hadn't expected this. The healers at home were much stricter.

An hour later, Mya, Bert, and Sarah arrived, and I told them the good news. Mya's dimples sprang to life. The thought of spending time outside these walls with her felt like I was being released from yet another jail. After Bert filled out paperwork, a car took us to the train station. I managed the short distance, and soon the four of us were on our way to London. I gave Mya the window seat so she could watch with sparkling eyes.

"You looking forward to seeing the city?" I asked.

"What's that saying Cate has about lemons?"

"You make lemonade. Right?"

"Something like that. I'm not supposed to be here. You should be in America helping my brother and Cate. I won't celebrate that. But…" One shoulder tipped up.

I nudged her. "You *are* happy about it. At least coming through the portal. Admit it."

She smirked. "A little."

"I'm glad you're here," I whispered in her ear, then turned to Sarah. "We're staying with this Nigel chap?"

"He has a flat big enough to fit Buckingham Palace, so, yes." Sarah's open countenance made me feel at home. "Though he's a bit stuffy. Doesn't approve of the society socializing except on official business. Well. There hadn't been much business since a couple of months ago—and we weren't even invited when you came around last time. We're a dying breed with the portals shut down."

Bert spoke up, rolling his eyes, "Hasn't stopped Sarah, though."

"Bert!"

"You're right. They should know, dear. Just don't tell Nigel."

"Sure," I agreed, especially having never met the man in question.

"Catherine and Daniel explained that this Rowan character has taken her parents hostage. Didn't think too much of him at the time, but Sarah and I got to talking," Bert said.

"Have you met him?" Sarah interjected.

"Who—Rowan?" I asked.

"We both have." Mya's flat tone spoke volumes. "What would you like to know?"

"Is he tall? Light brown hair?" Bert asked.

"Handsome." Sarah leaned forward.

Bert's features flickered in annoyance. "But with that creepy grin. Teeth too straight."

Something felt off. As if our two worlds were colliding, the air crackling with something—more than coincidence—the precipice of discovery. Mya's wide eyes turned to mine.

"How—" she began.

"How do you know that?" I asked slowly.

"He went to the same school as our kids. And… because his father tried to join our society," Bert explained.

"What?" Mya's slack jaw mirrored my own. "There are Embers here?"

"The society has been tracking Ember families for years. We weren't aware of Rowan's until his father approached us. Tried to pass himself off as a Terran."

"Bert figured it out." Sarah patted his knee. "His story didn't add up."

"So, what happened?" I asked. "Was he trying to destroy the group? A spy?"

"Of course, he was a spy," Sarah responded, her cheeks pinkening.

Bert stared at the floor. "I don't think so. He seemed to want community. Went away with his tail between his legs. Mighty awkward every time we saw him around our small town. But his son, Rowan, was angry. Used to bully our boy."

"Do their powers work?" When I straightened, the pain in my belly jolted straight through to my spine. The painkillers made me drowsy, and I wasn't going to bail on Mya again by conking out.

"We're not entirely sure. I believe Emmitt studied them—those Embers that traveled here. There are logs dating back hundreds of years."

This might be our only opportunity to understand our enemy better. It may never help us in the war—but every ounce of intel could prove important. "Can we talk to this Emmitt?"

They exchanged looks. "It can be arranged, yes. We might have to keep it from ol' Nigel. And we need him. He has more money than all of us combined."

I leaned my head back, suddenly exhausted, the realization hitting me. Rowan grew up in England. All at once, loose ends, things that never quite made sense, snapped into place. His speech patterns, his hygiene, his confidence. The way the other Embers looked up to him as if he knew more than they did. He'd had an education here—he *did* know more. Somehow, he'd made it to Ember City. And was out for revenge.

We arrived at Nigel's apartment, and I headed straight to bed, barely noticing my unfamiliar surroundings, exhausted from the trip. Mya joined the others for dinner after I assured them I'd be perfectly happy staying in the flat. When they had asked, the lift wall had been supporting a good part of my weight. I'd whispered to Mya to gather intel, telling her I trusted her to ferret out information. That mischievous sparkle lit up her face, as I knew it would.

A text came during the night that Cate and Daniel arrived safely, but nothing further. Our morning was their night, and they'd had a long trip, so who knew if they'd respond to my request to keep us posted. I checked the phone again in the morning. Three dots appeared. I sat up, wincing at the pain and the sunlight streaming through the windows.

We're safe. Found something unexpected.

More dots.

Alana's alive.

I nearly dropped my phone. "Mya!" I called. "My-a!"

She rushed in, pink robe tails flapping behind, while she fumbled to find the sash. I stared a moment too long at creamy white skin and a silky nightshirt. "What—what is it?" she huffed.

I held out the cell to her, speechless. She gingerly took it from me like it might explode any second and sank to the edge of the bed. "How can this be? You told me you saw her die."

I *had* seen it. During the failed peace treaty. I'd been tied up with the Embers as bait, watching the battle from the sidelines while Alana fought. A knife caught her in the back. She'd gone down and hadn't moved again. Mya and I never saw or heard any signs of her while we were prisoners in Ember City or on the long walk there.

I scrambled to take the phone from her, a million questions jumping into my mind, ready to type. The first: *where did you see her?*

She's with Rowan. In my house.

How? Why? Is she a prisoner? Or somehow… helping the Embers?

As I set down the phone, a strange mixture of surprise, relief, and curiosity permeated the room. I'd already grieved her. We all had. She'd been a cornerstone in both kingdoms and changed the course of my life by nominating me to go through the portal with Daniel to guard Cate those months ago.

"You don't seem happy." Mya sat beside me.

I ran fingers through my bedhead, trying not to wince at the pain the movement aggravated. "I'm just in shock."

"I didn't really know her. You were close?" Mya scooted nearer, our legs touching.

"She wasn't that friendly with anyone. But I respected her. Admired her—um, *admire*. I guess that should be present tense now." Unexpected tears burned behind my lids, and I couldn't tell if they were from happiness or dread now that Alana was with Rowan. Maybe a little of both.

CHAPTER 20
CATE

"You said she died," I repeated, as if Daniel might have a different answer. I plumped the pillow in my lap aggressively, the hotel bed springs squeaking. She'd been sitting next to my mom on our worn tufted couch. We couldn't see if they were tied up, but we presumed so because Jack's bindings were visible.

Daniel moved to sit beside me. "I know." He didn't bother explaining it again.

"Maybe Rowan had her prisoner this whole time. But why take her to my house?"

"He needed help with the portal. That's the only answer."

I shook my head. "It still doesn't make sense. She'd refuse. Right?" When Daniel didn't answer, I repeated myself in a whisper, "Right?"

"Of course. There has to be some explanation. We have to trust that we don't know what it is at the moment. Going in there to rescue your family and all the while worrying that she's a traitor won't help us."

And why… why would I even doubt her? Maybe because we hadn't heard anything from her in all this time, until there she was, calmly sitting on the couch, talking with my mom. *My mom!* She was there, too. Whole and alive. They both were. I should be rejoicing. And I was… the shock was just overwhelming. Both my stand-in mother and the one who raised me less than a mile from where I sat. I bit my lip, excitement welling up that I could have them both back in my life. We were so close.

I scooted over to face Daniel. "Let's go over the plan."

"We didn't see anyone else but Rowan, but that doesn't mean there aren't more Embers."

"Like someone watching my dad," I tamped down the panic swelling like an oversized balloon in my chest. Neither of us wanted to admit we might not have seen him because Dad wasn't alive. It would be easier to overtake the women without him around. I cleared my throat. "I'll keep watch through the neighbor's fence, my phone on vibrate, while you circle the house tomorrow night and look through the windows. You see any sign of danger, buzz me. I'll do the same."

I pulled out my cell and made sure he understood how to text. "How did you not learn this before?"

"Who was I texting—Lucas?"

"Maybe. You could have used it to tell him where the Embers were rather than leaving messages under each other's doors." Imagining them passing notes like schoolchildren nudged my mood up a smidgen. Lucas slid one into my dorm room once, too. It led to that day at the lake when Daniel and I first connected. Then the Embers tried to kidnap me… the beginning of my old life unraveling. The strangeness of both lives colliding left me unsettled, as if my brain couldn't quite figure out which reality was my own.

"We communicated plenty," Daniel said, reminding me of our conversation while my thoughts careened elsewhere.

"Don't start that rivalry again." They truly needed to get along better.

"Old habits die hard." He shifted. "Turn around. You're tense."

I scooted so my back faced him, and his strong hands glided along my shoulders, finding a knot. Traveling, even business class, left me rigid. Or more likely, the stress. He kneaded, easing some of my tension. The tingle of energy penetrated deep into my muscles, loosening them.

I leaned into him. His warm breath slid over my skin, lips hovering. I tilted so he could place a soft kiss where my neck meets my shoulder. Something crackled around us—energy, attraction… love. I turned to meet his mouth. Comfort mixed with desire surged through me, filling the gaps left by wounds. He patched the ragged holes, gaping with grief, even if only for a few moments of respite. The energy fused us together, sealed over the doubts, and arguments, and pain.

Something niggled at my brain. Suddenly alert, I pulled back.

Daniel searched my face. "You okay? We can stop."

"Do you feel it?" I caressed his jawline with the tips of my fingers. We weren't supposed to. Our connection was too strong to be dampened, even in this world. "The energy. It's here. Between us." Hot tears burned and spilled. Of course, it was here. We couldn't be separated from it. Our souls were melded.

He closed his eyes and kissed me softly. "Yes," he whispered. "It's here." He pulled my fingers to my heart, placing his on mine.

I hiccupped a laugh. "How are we going to use it to our advantage?"

His lips quirked. "Ah, there she is. Devious little queen. Those cogs always turning. Here I was just thinking about how much I loved you. And maybe how long you'd kiss me—"

I shoved him lightly. "You were not, Prince. You've been trained in battle strategy since you could walk."

"Ah, but this isn't a battle, though, is it?"

My hand dropped to my lap. "Close enough. When you used the energy in England at the lake months ago, you said you weren't sure how it happened. You thought it might be adrenaline. What if it was *us*? You amplify my powers back in Caelum and Terra. Maybe we do it for each other here."

We didn't think Rowan could make fire in this world, so there wasn't much reason to attempt rain. But speed and strength? Both could be crucial.

"Let's try it." Daniel sprang to his feet. "Throw that pen across the room. Hard." He pointed to the motel pen sitting alongside the phone.

I threw it in the opposite direction from Daniel. He bounded to it, catching it between his fingers.

I cocked my head. "That looked pretty fast to me?"

He handed me the pen. "Harder."

It torpedoed toward the bathroom. Daniel retrieved it just before it hit the tile. "I have to focus on the energy more than usual. But it's there. I just have to find it. Find *you*."

He was describing the exact feeling when I made rain. He was my center. My compass.

"I wonder what I can do." I stood.

His hand fell to my shoulder. "I don't recommend water in here."

I rolled my eyes at him. Even when using the Caelum and Terran energy, I'd never been fast. It wasn't my strength. Plus, most of my time had been invested in becoming the rainmaker. I focused on him first, like always, then the energy, and held it. Absorbed it. He lobbed the pen in the air, and I caught it easily. "That was a granny toss," I pursed my lips at him. "Give me more credit than that." It came quicker in succession until I could no longer catch it. Not nearly as fast as Daniel, though, pretty sure I could have been a star receiver on my high school football team, and I certainly couldn't have accomplished that on my own.

I yawned. The travel, stress, and adrenaline had caught up with me. "Let's try again in the morning." We had all day to kill because we didn't dare go to my house during daylight. We were still two days before the two-week deadline. I didn't want my family with Rowan a second longer than necessary, but it seemed foolish not to conduct surveillance.

The next day, we drove through for mochas. I wished we could sit and savor at my favorite indie coffee shop with an oversized ceramic cup, delicate feathering in the foam, but we couldn't risk being seen.

"Sweetener, milk, and chocolate make everything better," I told him as Daniel sniffed his to-go cup.

He took a skeptical sip. "It's dessert for breakfast."

"And those pastries of Hildy's aren't?"

"They have fruit." He leveled his gaze at me.

An unexpected homesickness ached in my chest at the mention of Hildy's tarts. I pushed it away, leaving our other problems—namely the portal—for tomorrow… or the next day. We drove through Portland so Daniel could see the sights, only exiting the safety of the vehicle to procure hunting knives. He loved the Willamette River snaking through the city, the arching bridges over the water, and snow-covered Mt. Hood in the background. I never thought I would see any of it again and tried to soak it in. Memorize every scene. It just all felt so hollow. Like that beautiful dessert that can't be resisted in the shop window that only ends up tasteless, my family's danger a constant strain.

After more skills practice in the room, a couple of TV shows, and a lot of pacing, it was late enough to leave. "Mr. Davis never parks in the garage. If we see his car, then we'll know he's there."

The driveway sat empty, an oil stain marking the center. We'd dressed head to toe in black—not suspicious at all—and acted casual, strolling hand-in-hand to the side yard after parking down the street. The gate opened soundlessly. We crept to the hole in the fence. My house was dark. Had they gone to bed? Maybe Jack, but it seemed too early for the others. A ribbon of fear wrapped around my middle. The home wasn't big. Both the kitchen and family room windows faced the backyard, as did my parents' bedroom. We hadn't seen light from the blinds of either. That left only the small basement. I'd drawn the entire layout for Daniel on a motel pad of paper earlier today.

"Basement or asleep," I whispered, trying to ignore the third option… they'd been… unalived. I couldn't even think the D word right now.

"Or not there?" he asked.

That thought stopped me cold. If Rowan took them somewhere else, he would have set a trap we couldn't win. "I guess we'd better find out. I'll keep watch from here."

Daniel pulled a patio chair over to the fence, used it as a step, and glided over, landing softly on the other side. I watched him creep along the edge between bushes to the other end of the house, where he could peer into my window. His plan was to retrieve the hidden key in the frog statue, so we'd have it when we were ready.

When he disappeared along the far side, I switched my view to the crack in the gate where I could see at least a part of the street. I tiptoed back and forth, keeping an eye on both the front and rear yards. The sound of car doors sent me racing to the gate. I froze before my heart stuttered into overdrive. Rowan was exiting my parents' SUV along with three more Embers. And instead of the front door, one of them headed to the side entrance. Straight toward Daniel.

CHAPTER 21
CATE

No, no, no. Panic crawled through my chest. The Ember, at least I assumed he was an Ember, paced steps from me, only the faded, slatted wood fence, a thin wall between us. I froze, not daring to pull out my phone to text Daniel. Small cracks separated each piece of lumber, and even though the lights were out, the moon shone bright enough for me to watch until he veered farther into the yard.

What was he doing there—patrolling? And if some were outside the house, who lurked inside? We'd only seen Rowan last night, but clearly, he'd brought reinforcements.

I snatched my phone from my back pocket once the man turned away. I'd have to take the chance that the vibration wasn't loud enough for him to hear it. Before I could hit send on my frantic text, a shout rang out.

"You there!"

I scrambled to peek through the hole. The Ember faced the other side of the house, where Daniel must be standing out of my line of vision. Were we too far from each other for him to feel the energy? My nails dug into the old wood as I blinked through the gap, paralyzed with indecision to stay hidden or help.

In a blur, Daniel tackled the man, coming into view from the opposite side of the yard. They toppled to the grass, rolling several times.

The Ember, larger than Daniel, ended on top. In the glow of the moonlight, the scene unfolded—two ghostly shadows fighting in the night. They grappled, shoving and blocking each other's swings. Daniel finally connected, still beneath his assailant. The man's head twisted with a snap before he collapsed.

Daniel rose, dropping a garden stone before creeping across the grass toward me. He was halfway when the living room light flipped on, partially illuminating the lawn. He launched himself over the back fence to the neighbors behind, still too far from me. I prayed the O'Sullivans weren't home. They were a nice older couple, but it would scare them to death to find Daniel.

Cold dread slithered down my neck as I debated whether to wait or meet him at the car. As soon as Rowan discovered his downed comrade, we would lose the element of surprise.

We'd have to go in now.

This is what we came for. Yet, it felt too soon. Rowan's sword, slicing through my father's throat, flooded my vision. The blood. Always the blood. In pools. In rivers. My cheeks tingled. Pressure built in my chest, heavy bricks stacking, piling, cementing, as the panic took hold.

The gate's latch clicked.

Daniel emerged. He rushed to me, sensing my frozen state. "Cate. Look at me."

His eyes, two roving shadows in the moonlight, raked across my face. A splash of blood crisscrossed his cheek. My stomach roiled.

"Cate," he whispered again. "Come back. Feel me. Feel the energy." His fingers slid along my temple to my neck, resting at the nape.

I snatched the familiar tingle like a lifeline. Traced the thin threads floating in the night air with my mind until they bloomed around us. I leaned into him, savoring the warmth, the steadiness. *Control. I am in control.*

I blew out a breath and stepped back, determined not to be the reason we don't rescue my family. "What did you find?" I asked.

"All the lights are off. I couldn't see anything."

Meaning we had no idea if my family was even in there. Despair flooded my thoughts, but I centered myself enough to tell Daniel what

I'd seen. "There are two more Embers, besides the guy you hit, plus Rowan. And maybe more inside. They drove up without giving me time to alert you. I'm sorry."

"It's okay. I managed." He brushed a cut I hadn't noticed on the side of his mouth.

If the Ember was on watch duty, the others might not expect to see him for hours. On the other hand, if he only stepped out for a quick walk-around, then they could come looking for him at any moment. The man lay in the shadows off the corner of the house, which was out of the line of sight from the living room windows. At least I hoped they couldn't see him.

"Did you get the key?" I asked.

Daniel held it up, the silver glinting in the moonlight. "Side entrance?"

I nodded. A door at the garage led to another into the house, which went to the laundry room. From there, we could enter the basement without being seen by anyone in the kitchen or living room. We weren't sure what or who we'd discover below, but it was our best shot to find out.

We crept out of the neighbor's yard and jogged around the block to reach my house from the opposite side without having to cross in front, in case someone watched from the windows inside. Every spare moment increased the chance they would uncover the unconscious member of their crew.

Daniel turned the knob to the side door into the garage. *Locked*. He inserted the key, which slid in easily. "Watch out for the bikes," I whispered. The single-car space never held a vehicle. Christmas decorations, bicycles, the lawnmower, and cleaning supplies cluttered the concrete, along with overflow stock from the family store. In other words, it was a hazard.

We stepped inside, waiting for our vision to adjust. The small glass window didn't allow enough moonlight to penetrate the darkness. I turned on my phone's flashlight. "Just for a second," I whispered.

We crept to the shelf of tools Dad always kept well organized, despite the rest of the space's disarray. A tire iron for me and a hammer for Daniel, in addition to our hunting knives. We reached the door to the laundry room, and I flipped off the light, making way for Daniel to enter first.

"Ready?" he asked.

I wanted to tell him no. Tell him we should call the FBI or raise our own army, as ridiculous as that sounded. But surprise was our best chance. Rowan wouldn't hesitate to kill his hostages. I'd already learned that lesson. "Let's go."

Daniel twisted the knob, darkness showing through the thin crack. Why were the lights off? Did they suspect we were here? We entered the house, the gloom as thick and heavy as paint. Daniel slid soundlessly through the basement door. My hand held the casing, ready to follow, when a deep voice rang out.

"Welcome, Cate."

A flashlight beam centered on my face, sending bright halos across my vision. I couldn't see him through the blinding light, but I knew. Knew his smooth, low voice anywhere because it echoed in my nightmares every night. It licked a trail of fear up my spine, and the room seemed to tilt, just for a moment.

"Hello, Rowan." I kept my tone steady, though I'm not sure how. "I came for my family." I squinted in the light, but he didn't lower it. Had he seen Daniel? All I could think of was to stall.

"Walk forward," he commanded.

I started to take a step, still blinded, when a voice cried out, high and shrill, "Cate? Is that you?"

"Mom!" The jump of my heart at hearing her was eerily similar to seeing my father in Rowan's hands in Ember City. Joy mixed with pain in discordant, haunting notes.

"Where are they?" The darkness left me unstable, off-balance.

"Let's go," Rowan said. He stood a couple of feet in front of me, judging by the sound.

I followed his footsteps until we entered the living room, stopping before the general vicinity of the coffee table.

"Mom?"

"I'm here, sweetie. Jack's in his bed."

"And Dad?"

"We're keeping your father somewhere safe to make sure you

behave," Rowan said. "Try to escape... well, you know how that ends."

Familiar thick panic fisted in my chest. The glinting sword. The crimson blood. My breath came in loud, jagged gulps.

"Cate." Mom's voice filtered as a lifeline. "How many birds die per year from airplanes?" She must have heard my breathing. I had come to save her, but here she was... saving me.

"Thirteen thousand," I whispered, shame now swirling with the anxiety. I wanted to see her eyes—coffee with a touch of cream. How often had she guided me through a panic attack? Or helped me avoid one altogether instead of spiraling? Before traveling to England, I'd been nervous about the flight and memorized all sorts of plane-related statistics. She'd gone over them with me. Dad was the even-keeled person in the family, but Mom—she knew when to be my rock as only a mother does.

"Exactly," she said calmly.

I focused on the squishy feel of the beige carpet beneath my shoes, how we always took them off at the back door, and the strangeness of having them on while inside. The familiar smell of home—paint, a touch of cinnamon, and Tide. Mom and Dad were forever washing clothes for the second-hand clothing store we owned. It permeated everything with a soapy, floral scent.

"How many more are with you?" Rowan asked. I wanted him to lower his still-blinding flashlight. Is this what it felt like to be interrogated?

"Why are the lights out?" I croaked out instead of answering his question, my throat thick.

"They blew a fuse," Mom said. "Using the knife sharpener and the microwave at the same time."

The house was notorious for its bad wiring. Our family had it down to a science; strangers wouldn't understand. Their trip in the car had probably been to the hardware store. Would they even know how to change one? The thought stopped me cold. The fuse box was in the basement. Exactly where Daniel just disappeared several moments earlier.

"Dempsey," Rowan barked.

Footsteps.

"Go check on Blaylock outside. But first, take all her weapons."

I dropped the tire iron with a thud onto the carpet. Rough hands inspected me—nothing like the gentle pat down at the airport. I held my breath. My entire body stiffened at the feel of this man's sausage fingers inside my bra. Hot tears burned. Inexplicable shame welled thick and bitter in my throat at being groped in front of both my deepest enemy and my mother. The spotlight, hazy and bright, shone as he continued to violate me. Dempsey, too, was illuminated—his eerie gray eyes salacious.

Those eyes.

They'd stared at me from the rearview mirror of a cab in England. Rowan had brought some old friends. I notched up my chin and clenched my teeth until he finally got around to checking my jacket pocket and easily found the small knife I'd stashed.

Dempsey handed Rowan the weapon and departed. He'd easily discover the man unconscious on the grass, likely wondering if I was capable of taking him out, then continue the search for Daniel.

"Let go of my family, and we can end this," I said. "You can have me." My primary goal was getting them out. And where was Alana?

"Somehow, I don't believe you've suddenly given up. I have more than enough reasons not to trust you."

"Me? What about you?"

His laugh in response grated, pilling the hairs up the back of my neck. "I've been perfectly honest. I said I would kill the king if you didn't stop the rain, and, as usual, you failed to listen. I've done exactly what I promised all along. It's the Terrans and Caelumites who are always going back on their word."

I took a deep breath, aware I'd never win a debate with him. "What is it you want, Rowan? To kill me, I presume. You're so big on honesty, promise me you'll let them go. Exchange them for me." If he releases them, then Daniel and I would have a better chance without the threat of their lives hanging over my head. Or at least I'd die knowing my family still lived.

"I'm waiting for my men to gather up anyone you have lurking outside. I can't imagine you came alone."

"I—you're right." I crossed my arms. "I wanted to bring a whole army, but I'm the only one who made it through the portal."

"Don't lie to me, Cate. I thought we were practicing honesty."

I was very aware that he didn't have to stand here and talk to me at all. While I stalled—at this point, I wasn't sure for what—for Daniel to incapacitate any Ember who might be in the basement? Rowan seemed confident. Too confident. How many Embers were here?

A door closed. Footsteps. Dempsey's voice rang out. "Blaylock is down."

"Dead?" Rowan asked.

"Not yet."

"Check on the others downstairs."

I desperately wanted to signal Daniel. Scream his name to warn him. But that would ruin the element of surprise. So, I waited. The mantle clock ticked. A bead of sweat trailed down my back. I wondered why Rowan didn't tie me up. His confidence troubled me.

"Mom?"

"Yes, honey."

"Has he hurt you?"

Silence. Then, "I'm okay. We're okay."

"And Dad?"

More silence. I wished Rowan would lower his light. I couldn't bear to have him watch the pain of worry cascade across my face.

"I don't know."

Her answer left me cold.

"Rowan," I said quietly. "Tell me. Is he dead?"

CHAPTER 22
DANIEL

Rowan's voice seeped through the door, low and menacing, while I hovered on the basement stairs. Cate's brave tone echoed. Instinct sent me lurching toward her before I caught myself. He hadn't hurt her yet. Rowan, the type to want to see her suffer, would make sure she knew what he'd done to her family or taunt her with what he might do. That would give me time to incapacitate anyone who lurked in the basement, using surprise as my best ally. The more Embers left in the house, the less our odds of survival. Yet with each step downward, my entire being craved to return to her side.

The space seemed even darker, if that were possible, the air turning colder as I descended. I trailed my fingers along the plaster wall to keep oriented. Why would an Ember be stationed down here in the pitch-black without a portable lantern or candle? It didn't feel right. Another step down… *squeak*. I froze, every muscle knotting and tensing.

"Who's there?" a gruff voice asked in an accent that definitely wasn't American. So, *not* Cate's father. I held my breath, motionless.

The distinct scrape of a match.

A light flickered, illuminating a man nearly twice my size, two steps below on the landing. I didn't hesitate and launched toward him, my hammer ready to strike. The connection to Cate's energy propelled me forward. With one lash, he tumbled to the concrete floor. The match snuffed, blanketing me in darkness again.

I stopped to listen.

Nothing but silence. I hadn't seen the entire space when the Ember lit the match. Cate had shown me how to use the flashlight on my phone in the motel, and I debated whether it was time. Should have practiced more. We hadn't predicted we'd be in the dark for this rescue mission. Each moment I hesitated was another Cate remained trapped with Rowan.

The scrape of a foot.

I strained to hear anything more.

Silence.

The hairs on my neck stood like rows of soldiers. I slipped the phone out of my pocket and tapped it. The home screen illuminated my face, a target for whoever was watching. I cast it outward, still not seeing anyone. Boxes piled in one corner that anyone could be hiding behind. I rushed to investigate, finding the space empty. Back to the wall, I fiddled with the phone's flashlight, finally found it, and shone it around the room.

There. On the other end, behind the stairs, stood a door. I unsheathed my knife as I crept across the basement and flung the door open. Inside was a tiny bathroom. And tied to the toilet, gag in place, was Cate's father. His eyes widened at the flash of my blade.

"I'm here to help," I whispered, lowering the weapon.

He must have noticed my accent because the fear in his eyes didn't lessen.

"I'm with Cate."

I pulled the gag from his mouth.

"Is she here?" I'd misread his fear. Instead of for himself, terror for his daughter crawled up the panicked question.

I nodded. "Carlos. I need you to trust me. Get out of the house. Go to the neighbor's yard, the one that used to have the dog. There's a shed. Hide inside. I'll get Cate out." I set the phone on the sink and cut his bonds. "I promise." I looked him in the eye. "Let's go."

He stumbled to his feet. How long had it been since Cate's father stood? After stabilizing himself on the towel bar, he moved forward.

We crept up the stairs. Softly opening the door a crack, voices became audible from the living room around the corner, faint light emanating. I gestured for Carlos to exit through the laundry into the garage, crossing my fingers he wouldn't run into any more Embers.

He slipped out—the knowledge of his own home guiding him in the dark. I still hadn't discovered why the lights were out. I edged closer to the entrance, where Rowan was speaking to another man, telling him to check out the basement.

Taking my chance, I hugged the wall and moved forward, hoping the shadows would cover me. A turn left me exposed for three large steps until I faced a closed door. According to Cate's drawings, it should be Jack's room. If he made a noise when I entered... I'd be caught. Cate's life balanced on the whim of a five-year-old.

I turned the knob. The door whispered open. A window set over the bed let in moonlight, illuminating a small figure. Another person sat in a chair nestled beside him.

"He's asleep, Daniel," she whispered.

Alana.

I hesitated. Was she still on our side? My nerves relaxed a fraction at seeing her hands tied to the rocking chair. I moved to cut through her bonds, trying to assess her condition in the dark. It wasn't that long ago when I'd seen her prone on a battlefield with a knife in her back. "Can you walk?" I whispered.

She nodded.

I gave her my extra blade to work on Jack's bonds, and told her where Cate's father waited. "Untie him when I leave, then sneak out during the scuffle."

In the pale light, I could see her eyebrows raise, and she said, "Do it right, and he won't know what hit him."

Sneaking up on Rowan would be easier if he didn't have that flashlight. I'd try, but just one step out the door, and I'd be visible from the living room. Taking my knife and hammer, I waited for Cate's energy to wash over me, praying she could feel mine too—tendrils connecting us, strengthening us.

One. Two... I charged at Rowan on three, aiming for the kill. He swung the light, blinding me, and I wielded the hammer. When it didn't connect, I barreled into him instead. Hitting his chest was like slamming into a crumbling brick wall, and we both toppled to the floor. The flashlight flickered out, cracked under my knee, and the hammer slid away.

The darkness disoriented, flying limbs and punches running wild between us as I rolled on top of him. A woman, likely Cate's mom, screamed. Every time I struck out with the knife, Rowan blocked the blow.

"Get out," I gasped to Cate.

Her mom whimpered somewhere in the room.

"What's going on?" a deep voice called.

"Catherine," Rowan ground out as he struggled to hold off my arm with the dagger. "Get her," he shouted to the man entering.

Pounding footsteps. A crash. Another scream.

This time, not her mom. *Cate.*

Rowan managed to shift the momentum, rolling atop me, his weight crushing. He wrestled my wrist to the floor in an attempt to disarm me, banging the back of my hand against the ground in forceful strikes.

More scuffling, heavy footsteps.

The sound of a match. Light flickered. Rowan's eyes locked on mine, a triumphant glint in the low orange glow. I stretched for Cate's energy and couldn't find it.

Nothing. There was nothing. Only my own escalating fear.

"Cate," I called, desperately trying to stave off Rowan, my head swiveling to see around his enormous frame.

The match petered out, and the man's footsteps approached.

The energy—where was it? "Cate!" I called, desperate.

Crash.

Someone heavy landed on top of us both, the air leaving my lungs in a rush. Had Carlos come back? Or was it another Ember?

Rowan lost his grip on my arm, and I struck with the knife, capitalizing on the pandemonium. I embedded the blade into tissue, then bone, connecting with his upper arm. He groaned, struggled to unseat the dead weight lying on top of him. I yanked out the knife and thrust again, aiming for what I thought to be his neck. The steel sank into flesh. Warm blood oozed over my hand.

He let out a roar and rolled from me, the other person thumping off him. I followed with my dagger, aiming for his now exposed heart. But the dark played tricks on my perception, and I struck air, then carpet.

"Find Cate," Rowan called, his words a gurgle above me. He'd managed to stand.

No one answered. Using the sound of his voice to track him, I caught his ankle, slicing again.

Another crash. He roared in pain but didn't fall. Someone had hit Rowan with something heavy. With a smack, he backhanded whoever attacked him—Cate?

I scrambled to my feet, wet blood soaking into my knees. Judging by the amount of blood, Rowan was severely injured. Uneven steps sounded as Rowan headed out the front door.

"Help me," a woman's voice called. "Cate—she needs help."

I stumbled to her, knocking into a coffee table.

"Lights?" I asked.

"Flashlights in the garage."

I'd hoped we could turn on the overhead house lights, but apparently, they weren't working. I pulled out my phone, using the dim home screen to guide my way. A woman with blood streaking down her face, whom I recognized from pictures as Cate's mother, Sofia, knelt over the prone form of her daughter.

"No," I called, hardly aware I was even saying it.

An Ember lay near us who might wake at any moment, but I couldn't bring myself to care. Or care that Rowan fled the house. Only Cate mattered. I searched for her energy as I rushed forward.

Nothing. I couldn't feel anything. Couldn't feel *her*.

CHAPTER 23
DANIEL

"Cate," I breathed her name, still not sensing the energy that tethered us. I reached for her. The home screen on my phone timed out, plunging us back into darkness. "Can you—" I fumbled with it, thrusting it toward Cate's mom. "Can you turn the light on?"

Cate's skin was warm beneath my blood-sticky fingers. The flashlight flicked on, illuminating the red streak I'd left branded across her neck from Rowan's blood staining my skin. I slid my fingers to find a pulse. *Please, please, please.* I'd never felt so out of control. My hands shook. Eyes burned. Breath locked in my lungs. It was déjà vu with Dev on the road back to Caelum; only it was the other half of my soul I might lose. Without her energy, her warmth, all hope was lost.

There.

Beneath the pads of my fingers. The bump of her heart. Life strumming through her. "She's alive," I gasped.

The flashlight wavered. Her mom's still-tied hands covered her mouth, her face crumpling.

Blood matted Cate's hair. She'd been hit on the head. I was no healer, but I'd seen enough skull injuries to know she wasn't out of the woods. Carefully, I moved her onto her back, examining her for other wounds. All the while, she remained motionless.

I turned to Sofia to cut her bindings. "I need more light. And rope. Do you have passports?" I peppered her with questions while I sawed.

"Y-Yes. We'd planned to visit Cate at school before…" She trailed off.

"Okay. Hurry. Jack and Alana should be out. So is your husband."

A sob escaped. "Thank you."

"Can you do it?" I needed her to focus.

She stood, her mouth held in a thin line. "I'll be right back."

I only hoped Rowan didn't lurk outside. Though, from the amount of blood spattering the carpet, he must be badly injured. The room was a complete disaster. A cast-iron pan sat upended near the man who'd fallen on Rowan. Who hit him remained unclear. I presumed Cate's mom. Maybe Alana?

Sofia returned with more portable lanterns and cord. "This okay?"

"Thank you." I gestured to the pan. "That you? You saved me."

She swallowed, her eyes turning away. "Yes."

A woman living in the suburbs of Portland had most likely never killed before, and I realized what she must be going through. I strode over and checked the man's pulse. Still alive. I recognized him as one of the men who attacked Cate and me in the woods in England. I started tying him up. If it were a battle, I likely would have finished him off. But Cate's mom had already suffered enough trauma.

"We have to leave," I said, tightening the knot. "You can't live here anymore."

There was no time to dispose of the bodies. Cate needed a healer, and Rowan could be regrouping. It would never be safe for them here again. The police would eventually investigate. I didn't know all the laws, but enough to understand that waiting for their justice system wouldn't work with Rowan on the loose. Plus, there would be questions. A lot of them. Nigel would help us with new IDs. In the meantime, we had to get out of here and to England as quickly as possible.

Our speed might depend on Cate's recovery. Last night, I'd been able to sense her energy while she slept—even in the next bed over. My gut curled and knotted with worry. It was as if her essence had disappeared.

I blew a shaky breath and finished tying the man, trying not to think about what might be damaged inside Cate's head. Rowan may not return here—meaning this guy might not have a pleasant death. It sent a twinge of guilt until Cate's mom returned with her purse, and I noticed the bruising on one side of her face. They didn't deserve my pity.

"We need to call 911," she said, rushing over to Cate.

"Sofia, listen to me. We have to get out. Rowan might return. You don't understand how much he wants Cate. He probably kept her alive only to take her back to Ember City."

I wasn't sure she'd heard me as she continued to stroke Cate's hair. "No. She needs an ambulance."

She didn't understand. "Rowan wants her execution to be a demonstration for our world. To prove he'd killed her. He's obsessed with your daughter, and he'll stop at nothing."

She bit her lip, hovering over Cate.

I checked the front door to be sure Rowan wasn't skulking outside. After seeing the street and yard empty, I lifted Cate, cradling her in my arms, then headed for the car parked down the road. "You have the passports?"

"I have them." Her voice sounded strained, almost angry. She hadn't accepted their fate yet.

I gently caressed Cate's temple after placing her in the rear seat. "Hold on. Come back to me soon." I gestured for her mom to get in. Cate's legs draped over her lap. It would be tight, but we'd all squeeze. "Be right back."

I jogged to the neighbor's, through the gate, and along the side yard to the shed, and swung open the door. They were all there, Jack asleep in his dad's arms. "Let's go," I whispered.

"Stop." The voice was like an icepick against my spine. *Rowan*.

I turned. The neighbor's backyard lights flipped on, illuminating the small, grassy space. One of his arms raised toward us. In it, aimed a gun. Blood soaked the side of his tan shirt from collar to mid-chest. Behind him, the glass door to the tidy house gaped and cracked in jagged edges. "Nice of Cate's mother to advertise that the neighbor owns a gun collection. She probably thought it was a threat." Rowan took another step forward.

"You don't even know how to use it."

"Don't I? I've spent a whole lot more time in this world than you have."

Had he?

"You're going to tell me where Cate is. Or I'll kill all of you. Starting with the boy."

Rowan's threats were never empty. Cate and her mom sat defenseless in the car. It would only be a matter of time before he found them parked four houses down. If I did nothing… I'd lose her. Forever.

My mind spun for solutions. Rowan stood roughly ten yards away and slowly paced forward.

No longer caring for my own safety, I jerked to one side, cocked my knife, and threw. It sang through the air, embedding in Rowan's shooting arm near the shoulder. I rolled, dodging the inevitable. The gun went off—the noise deafening.

Grass sprayed like confetti near my feet. I kept moving, channeling even the faintest hope of energy. The small yard left little maneuvering room. Whichever way I moved, it still placed me in firing range. I decided in an instant. I had to take him down.

Whether it was adrenaline or energy from Cate, an electric surge burst through my veins. I rushed forward and collided with Rowan.

Another shot boomed. *Please don't let it hit anyone.* Jack's form flashed in my mind's eye, cradled in his dad's arms. The shed stood in the corner of the small space, mere yards behind me.

I wrestled with Rowan's thick body, trying for the knife, which had dislodged from his shoulder and landed in the grass.

Out of reach.

I turned my focus to the gun, the earth's energy now flowing through me. Knocking Rowan's wrist to the ground, I forced his hand open and grabbed it. I scrambled off him, pointing the firearm at him. Now it was me who didn't know how to shoot. I'd never fired one.

Rowan rose and started to run back into the house. I pulled the trigger. It went wide. I tried again… only a click. Out of bullets? Did I need to press something?

Instead of chasing him, I turned to the others to ensure no one was hurt. Carlos shielded Jack while Alana hovered. I urged them to exit through the gate. Rowan would likely return with another gun if, according to Cate's mom, this neighbor collected them. We rushed down the street to the car. Alana squeezed into the back seat, cradling Cate's head, while Carlos and a now very much awake Jack climbed into the front. I wished Carlos would drive since he had more experience, but I was a stranger to the boy who watched me with a mixture of awe and distrust.

As we peeled away, I spotted Rowan in our rearview mirror as I turned at the block. "He's there," I said.

"He has a car," came Cate's voice from the backseat, slow and weak.

I reached out and felt our connection—two magnets locking together. My nose burned, unshed tears welling. I wanted to pull over. To hold her. To touch her and see that she was okay. I'd been so scared. But we couldn't stop. I aimlessly turned another corner to try to lose Rowan if he followed.

"Welcome back," I said, which felt completely inadequate. I wanted to tell her I couldn't live without her. To steal her away, just the two of us, and shield her from everything.

"Turn here," Carlos directed, interrupting my thoughts.

"This is Prince Daniel," Alana finally spoke. "I don't believe you've been introduced. He's in love with your daughter."

I huffed a laugh. Alana's signature bluntness. I was still reeling from finding out she was alive. "I am," I managed to say. "So much." A tear escaped. I couldn't believe I was crying. I hadn't cried in… I don't know when.

"I can see that," Sofia replied.

"I love my sister too," Jack said, his expression now less suspicious. "Is she okay? I missed her."

"I missed you, too," Cate said slowly.

After a circuitous route, we pulled into the motel. I quickly cleared out our things, leaving the others in the car, and we headed to a hotel farther from here, near the airport. We needed to book flights as soon as possible, but Alana informed me that Cate's scalp was bleeding everywhere. We couldn't risk the delay of finding her a healer with Rowan tracking us.

We checked into the new room to examine Cate and make a plan. I carried her to the bathroom to clean up, and Alana and her mom tended to her.

Sofia popped her head out. "We need bandages." One of the white hotel towels hung from her hand, a large crimson stain already blossomed across it.

"I'm trying to book flights." Carlos had borrowed my phone, having not made it out with his. "There's a pharmacy just down the road."

I didn't want to leave Cate, but everyone turned to me to run the errand. "I'll be back."

Carlos looked up from the phone. "You think he'll find us at the airport?"

I held up a finger to Carlos. "Alana?" I called. "Is there a portal around here?"

"It's how I came, yes. But it's unstable. I couldn't safely move all of us through."

We needed to get back to Lucas and Mya, not head to Caelum anyway. "How did Rowan get here?"

"By plane," she answered.

This led to more questions. I had a million for her… Like how she came to be captured in Cate's house, or how Rowan managed identification to travel.

"Is there another airport?"

"There's a flight in the morning out of Seattle. Less chance he'll track us there. We'll have to leave soon. It's about a four-hour drive."

"Let's do it." I handed him the credit card Nigel gave us. Jack moved in and snuggled closer to his dad.

"Would you like to see England, Jack?" He'd nearly been forgotten, quietly watching us from the corner chair. "It's a long flight, but there are movies on the plane."

He nodded shyly.

"Book it—what did Cate call it? Business class," I said.

Carlos's brows went up. "Okaaay."

"Daniel," Alana called. "I need you."

I rushed to the bathroom to find Cate slumped onto Alana.

Unconscious. Again.

CHAPTER 24 **LUCAS**

"How about some breakfast?" Mya asked. "There's coffee, and we can talk about it more if you'd like." She stood, squeezing my shoulder as I reeled through my emotions of Alana being alive.

"I think I need to process it a bit more." For some reason, talking about Alana felt too raw. Too new. The sheer wonder of someone returning from the dead took time for my brain to wrap around. "I'll get cleaned up and meet you in there."

When I stood, my head spun less than yesterday, and I didn't need the wall to hold me up. Slowly, I dressed in clothes Nigel provided me. Apparently, they were items that hadn't fit into Daniel's suitcase. We were roughly the same size, except I hadn't gained all my weight back from being a prisoner, so I notched the belt tight.

I entered the kitchen, doddering along like an octogenarian. Nigel, whom I briefly met the night before, greeted me dressed in a suit, on his way to work. Toast, eggs, and roasted tomatoes sat on platters on the counter. But behind… nestled beside a coffee maker, was a familiar-looking bag. "Is that granola? Cereal?"

"Oh, yes. Help yourself. Or—" He seemed to just now notice my slow speed. "I can get it for you."

"I'll make it. Milk in the fridge?"

He opened it for me and set the milk on the counter. "Okay then.

I'm off to work. See you two later. Sarah and Bert will come by and check on you."

I poured cereal and coffee, then gingerly sat on a barstool. My first spoonful sent me back to my dorm room, sitting cross-legged on the twin bed, shoveling mouthfuls before meeting Cate for class. This was chocolate-flavored with dried cherries, one of my favorites. How much could I stuff in my pockets when we returned across the portal?

Mya strolled in, dressed in an outfit that presumably was bought for Cate. She'd rolled the hem up on the jeans, but they still fit her ten times better than the second-hand store trousers she'd bought. A blue cable-knit sweater was oversized and adorable on her. She did a little twirl, her dark hair flying, clearly loving not wearing a multi-layered dress.

"Looks good." I gave her an approving nod.

Her hand went to her hip. "Just good?"

"Why don't you come here, and I'll show you?"

She sauntered over, and I placed a quick kiss on her cheek before I took another bite of cereal.

"That's it?" She nudged my shoulder. "That's less than good."

"You know what's amazing?" I asked with my mouth full. "This cereal. You're pretty fantastic too, but I don't want it to get soggy."

She rolled her eyes, but I knew she wasn't mad. Food was a major part of how we bonded. "Let me try it." She lurched toward my spoon, but I pulled it away.

"Get your own, Princess. Look," I gestured to the counter. "There's a bowl right next to the milk. Plus. I'm the patient." I gave her the saddest eyes I could muster.

She shook her head and fixed herself some. "You're feeling better this morning."

"It's the cereal. They should stop giving patients medicine in the hospital. Just feed them this. And coffee." I took a sip of the brew laced with just the right amount of cream and sugar.

"You're ridiculous." She took a dainty bite, unlike me, shoveling it in as if it was my last meal.

"Ah, one of the many reasons you love me." Did I say that out loud? I gulped another drink of coffee to cover the awkward silence.

Mya kept her eyes on her cereal, stirring counterclockwise. "You're right," she said softly.

I reached over and placed my hand on hers to stop the swirling. "It's going to get soggy that way." It's not what I wanted to say, but my tongue was tied in knots. Because, did I love her? The answer came as if someone whispered it in my ear. A soft, but insistent, *yes*. I loved that she teased me back, that she'd stay by my hospital bed for days, that she'd try cereal and fried chicken, and all the other new ideas opening in her life. That she cared about people. Not just her kingdom's citizens, but *all* people.

"I think I prefer pastries." Her gaze remained fixed on the bowl.

Oh, how I wanted to combat that statement with a rebuttal. Because clearly cereal… A debate wasn't what she needed right now. And I found nothing made me happier than to give it to her, whatever she wanted—needed.

"Mya." I waited until her lashes fluttered upward. "I love you." My fingers trailed up her arm, goosebumps pilling in their path. I leaned forward and kissed her cheek, then the corner of her mouth, then her lips.

"I love you too," she murmured into my ear, skin brushing across my neck and sending delicious shivers down my spine.

I pressed closer, deepening the kiss. She tasted of chocolate, and coffee, and promise, and I didn't want to let her go.

Finally, she broke apart. "Your cereal's getting soggy."

I pointed to hers. "So's yours."

A smile played on her thoroughly kissed lips. "Think I can have some of that toast and a nice cup of tea?"

I sighed noisily. "I must love you if you are going to disparage the cereal *and* the coffee."

I slid the plate of toast over to her. "But you liked the fried chicken, right? Can we agree on that one?"

She slathered berry preserves on her bread. "Definitely agree on the chicken." She took a bite of toast and chewed. "We're going to look at those archives today, right? And see what else we can discover about Rowan?"

"That's what Bert said. I think they'll be here soon. Better eat up." I poured another bowl.

"Knock, knock," Sarah called from the entry.

Mya and I rose, me slower than her, and met them at the door. My head swam more like a summer's lake rather than yesterday's ocean at high tide, still sloshing about until I gained my equilibrium.

"You ready?" Sarah asked brightly. "Bert's circling the block."

Mya's confused expression almost made me laugh aloud. "He's in the car, right?" I asked.

Sarah smiled indulgently. "No parking, yes. We enjoy visiting London, but it's much nicer a little farther out where we live, where there's space to breathe."

As soon as we reached the street, I understood. I hadn't paid much attention last night in my exhausted state, but Nigel's flat sat on a busy road with vehicles zooming in both directions. Mya's eyes darted in fascination. Bert stopped in front, much to the consternation of those behind him, and Sarah ushered us to enter the blue sedan. Horns blared, sending my nerves on edge while my side screamed for me to slow down as I slid into the backseat next to Mya.

"I don't think horses would take to that noise," I joked. "We'd have a stampede in Caelum."

"Maybe we replace them with cars," Mya replied.

It's not that we didn't have the know-how, but our lands lacked the petroleum products found here. The infrastructure to build vehicles in any quantity, not to mention roads, hadn't been developed.

In traffic, it took us around an hour to reach Emmitt's lodgings, located in a stone building not far from one of the palaces. "The society has owned it for a very long time," Sarah said. "We always have a caretaker assigned." A silver plaque next to the door read *Emmitt Walker, Solicitor*. "He runs his business from here as a cover. The records from the society are in the basement. He's also our forger."

A short balding man opened the door and welcomed us in after introductions. "Ah, Lucas. I remember your photos from the last time I made your documents."

Brian had taken our photos and delivered them. "Well done, they worked brilliantly last time." I shook his hand.

He ushered us toward an office lined with leather-bound books, various knick-knacks, including an ancient, weathered globe, and several leather chairs. "Tea?"

"No, thank you," Mya replied. "We were hoping to find information on the Embers. Specifically, a family—Bert, what did you say their last name was?"

"Valens." Bert stepped forward. "Remember the chap? Wanted to join the society, but we wouldn't let him?"

Emmitt snorted. "Of course. I'm surprised he managed to stay out of jail long enough to ask us."

Mya cocked her head.

"It's their impulsivity. They may not produce fire, but they're no better people here. I'm happy to let you review our archives—Bert told me that's why you were coming—but I doubt you'll find much useful. I have to admit, there's been little to document. I'm probably not the best curator, but we're getting few and far between, you see, with the portals shutting down." One corner of his mouth crept up in a deprecating smile. "I hope you'll forgive me for my lack of knowledge. I haven't reviewed many of the old books. Came into the position around ten years ago, and there hasn't been much activity."

I'd of course been hoping for someone more informed, but what could we do?

Mya interrupted my thoughts, "But you did know about Rowan and his father? We'd love more information on them."

"Oh, yes. Of course." He settled into one of the cognac-colored chairs. "I must apologize, I get little interaction from Terrans," his head tilted to Mya, "especially royalty."

Sarah spoke up, "We believe James Valens came through the portal with his wife thirty years ago, around the time she was pregnant. It's our understanding that most Embers don't know how to go through, or perhaps don't have access to a portal, even before Alana closed them."

"That makes sense. Otherwise, you'd have a ton of them crossing." Mya laced her fingers in her lap. "So, Rowan was born here?"

"That's what our records indicate. We weren't aware of the family until James came forward and expressed interest in joining the society. Once we investigated, we found he'd had a few run-ins with the law, as is typical. Trouble holding down a job. I believe the wife, Margery, ended up supporting the family."

Bert spoke up, "As you recall, Rowan went to school with my boy. He'd been a decent kid, flew under the radar, but once his father was rejected, the bullying started. He obsessed about his heritage. Asked my son all kinds of questions, and when he didn't answer, that's when things went south. Rowan was conniving and avoided getting caught. Occasionally, physical, but more often, little things, like a stolen lunch, vandalized car, that sort of thing."

"I'm glad he never found these records. From the sounds of things, he became obsessed with our world," Mya said.

"And he somehow traveled back through the portal. Maybe his parents helped him," I mused.

Bert traced the gray stubble on his chin. "It sounds as if Rowan became enraptured by the Embers, perhaps wanting to take on the mantle of their grievances with us. He likely saw their banishment as no different from the slight to his father."

"He went on to university," Emmitt added. "Then joined the Royal Navy. Must have learned about battle strategy there."

"Anything else? Do we know where his parents live now?" I asked.

"His father died," Sarah, previously propped against the doorframe, eased into the chair next to Mya. "Not long after the denial into the society. Drunk driving."

"Let me guess. Rowan blamed the society." The pieces fell into place. "And it only fueled his obsession for revenge."

CHAPTER 25 **LUCAS**

"Shall we go downstairs to examine the archives? See if there is anything else to learn?" Mya asked through the heavy silence of all of us processing the backstory of Rowan's deranged plans for revenge.

I slumped in my chair, no longer in the mood, but I wasn't much good for anything else at the moment. "Sure. Let's go." I feigned interest.

Bert and Sarah decided to run some errands and agreed to pick us up later. Emmitt snagged a few portable lanterns—he called them flashlights—and led us through a heavy, locked door and down a dank stairwell. "No electricity down here, I'm afraid. The place is too old, and no one wanted an electrician meddling near our papers."

There were no windows or even a crack in the door above that allowed light to penetrate the darkness, only the beam from our lanterns bouncing off the rough rock walls. At the bottom, I shone mine to illuminate rows of bookshelves, a heavy carved table with wooden chairs, and another larger lantern waiting for Emmitt to light.

"Better to read by." He backed toward the door. "I have work for clients. Londoners," he amended. "I'll leave you to it."

Mya strode toward a bookshelf, already browsing, while I leaned against the table, intimidated by the sheer number of tomes and ledgers. "Aren't you coming?" She sent me a pointed look. A chuckle escaped. Mya truly wasn't fazed by anything.

We both selected a stack and started flipping through pages. Several logs were filled with duplicate documents, presumably forged, from those who came from our world. Passports, fake birth certificates, and the like. No wonder Emmitt didn't want anyone pilfering through this stuff. We set them aside, as this wasn't the information we were looking for. After a few more tries, I found the material on Rowan and his family in one of the newer-looking leather-bound notebooks. Neat handwriting chronicled what we already heard from Bert and Emmitt.

"It's all the same stuff." I shut the book in frustration.

"Let's look at older volumes. If we don't learn anything more about Rowan, maybe there will be portal stuff." She stood. "Even if it's just useless history, it's still interesting."

"Is history ever useless?" I quipped.

"Only if it's lost I 'spose."

We shuffled between tight rows of bookcases until we reached the rear of the space. Some were books from Caelum and Terra. Which made sense, they would want to preserve the knowledge from the other side too. Mya piled volumes into my arms, and we headed back to the tables. Sweat beaded at the weight pulling on my still-healing scar. She'd likely been so engrossed in the project, she'd forgotten my condition. And I was too much of a soldier to remind her.

Stories chronicled how early settlers traveled back and forth for supplies and the necessity of keeping our kingdoms a secret. The monarchy at the time would have taken over, and we'd have been overrun if they found out about us. Grizzly tales of murder to keep the secret safe, and other lengths our ancestors undertook to avoid detection, kept us turning pages. The oldest accounts only documented Terrans. Another society was apparently located somewhere in Wales among the Caelumites, but they eventually merged. I found it interesting that we feuded at home, while here, there seemed to be relative peace. Terran and Caelum ledgers were separate, but as less came through the portal, they stopped distinguishing.

"It shows that peace is possible." Mya chewed on her lip. "Why can't we do it at home?"

"More's at stake, I guess. The land. Past grievances."

She let a finger glide along one of the leather spines. "My father."

"Baron Graftonberg," I shot back. "Hopefully, he's not doing too much damage while we're gone." Mya was right, of course. We needed King Dryden to actually want conciliation. And so far, there had been very little indication of him trying.

I stood. "Let's find another stack."

Finally, we'd found information about Embers from three hundred years ago. The first was a family that settled with two young children. The husband, as Emmitt alluded to, had difficulty with the law and was eventually hanged. The others went on to live productive lives. The boy became a shopkeeper, and the girl married. Their ancestors also smoothly fit into society.

"Look, this one's almost the same. The male Ember can't hold down a job, gets into trouble, but the kids seem okay. This family had five boys. Looks as if the oldest, a teen, had a bit of an issue, but the rest… nothing reported of consequence, anyway."

I sifted through mine. More commonly, they didn't travel in families, and it was mostly Ember men alone. It wasn't clear if the women who voyaged by themselves remained undetected or never traversed the portal without others.

"It seems like whatever causes their lack of conscience is triggered by being in our world." I flipped through the pages. "I've been wondering something, and this supports my theory."

Mya looked up from her book, giving me her full attention.

"The Embers have always shielded us from their women and children. Do females even have the gene to make fire? And if not, how had we never noticed? What'd you see when babysitting the kids?"

"The girls were better behaved, but not great. I never saw them start a fire. It's hard to know if they acted out because of the chaotic environment or because they were inherently…"

"Horrible?"

She cackled. "Yeah. Worst babysitting job ever."

"What about the grown women?"

"Honestly, I didn't have a lot of interaction with them, but they seemed…" Her thumb slid over her bottom lip absently, drawing my attention away from the topic at hand. "Fine? They weren't particularly mean. Just tired."

"Weren't we all. And hungry."

"Speaking of..." Mya patted her stomach.

We'd been in here for hours. "Time for cereal?"

Her expression read exasperation. "Always the cereal. We should have brought snacks. Bert and Sarah won't be here for a while."

I held in a sigh. "Let's get to work."

"You think this is helpful? I mean, it's kind of weird we're coming here to learn about our enemy, isn't it?"

I shrugged. "What else do we have to do?"

"Sightseeing. Have you seen that giant wheel?"

I gave her a dubious look. The huge contraption was visible from my bedroom window at Nigel's. "You've ridden a dragon. How could you think that thing remotely exciting after that?"

Her lips formed a cute pout. "We'll see."

I knew what that meant. Tomorrow we'd be viewing the city on top of that wheel. She was quite persuasive. Even without her powers.

"Poor Molly must be lonely." She sighed.

"Her favorite stable hand is taking care of her. It's the best I could do." I'd been trying not to think of her. Especially the problem of getting through the portal in the same century.

"I wonder what happened to her with the other dragons. If she would go back?"

Most of the time I'd been in the pit, Molly remained with the dragons in the Purple Mountains. "Since one of them nearly killed her, I assume she'd rather stay with me. I hope it's not just loyalty that's keeping her."

"Love, not loyalty."

My heart swelled. We'd been through so much together, and I couldn't imagine life in Caelum without Molly. "She does love me, you're right. Also, those dragons were eating rodents. She'd never agree to that long-term."

Mya chuckled. "She must have turned up her nose at that after the prime cuts you feed her."

My phone dinged. Daniel's text read: *Rescue complete. Everyone's alive.*

Elation raced through me in a shot of adrenaline. Mya jumped to her feet and laughed, reaching to hug me. They did it!

When we'd calmed our excitement, I texted back: *And Rowan?*

Escaped.

Our mood lowered.

Another text. My stomach dropped.

And Cate's unconscious.

CHAPTER 26
CATE

My eyes fluttered to bright fluorescent lights moving overhead.

"She wakes!" A middle-aged man with a cheerful smile and a thin, gold hoop earring in his brow hovered in my view. Navy scrubs and a yellow stethoscope with a badge labeled "Nick. RN." dangled above me. "We're on our way to CT to check out that head of yours."

The hospital. We were delayed. That meant… I reflexively searched for Rowan, swiveling my neck. A thick brace stopped my chin from moving far.

"Hey, hey," he said softly. "We don't want you to get hurt. Lie still. Plus, if you injure yourself in the hospital, there's a *ton* of paperwork." He tipped his head and gave me a look that said, *kidding, not kidding—behave.*

"My family?"

"In the waiting room."

More scrubs-clad men and a woman transferred me to the narrow table of the CT machine. "Just lie real still," the woman said.

"I—I want my—" Parents. Daniel. My brain was foggy, and pain pulsated like my head would explode into a million tiny pieces.

The table ran through the donut opening of the machine, then they wheeled me away. Dad met me in a curtained room. The space, though tidy, reminded me of Lucas's blood-strewn trauma bay.

"That was quite a fall you took down those stairs." He eyed me pointedly.

My mind functioned enough to understand we didn't want additional questions. When the nurse left, he sat next to me on the bed. "We drove as long as we could. Crossed the river into Washington. Doubt he'll come up here to get his wounds treated." He paused. "Or to look for you. Tickets are booked for the morning—only a day later than planned, but if we have to cancel, we will." He watched me anxiously.

"Will you tell everyone I'm awake? I'm okay. My head just hurts." Like a cross between a jackhammer and a vice, but I kept that part to myself. Once Dad left, my thoughts began to tumble. Where was Rowan? Was Dad wrong? Would he track us here? My skull pounded, but the medicine, or maybe the injury, pulled my lids downward, sinking into the swirl of questions.

"Hey, beautiful." At Daniel's voice, my eyes fluttered open. "You check out okay. No bleeding inside." He tapped his temple. "We've been spending too much time in hospitals this trip, don't you think? Ready to go?"

I must have fallen asleep. I reached for his hand. The familiar warmth and energy wrapped around us. "I'll send your mom in to help you dress."

I hadn't even noticed that I now wore a hospital gown.

They'd rescheduled the flight to a red-eye, and we set out to drive the four hours up to the Seattle airport. Jack chattered away, telling me all about kindergarten, the classroom fish he named Jim, and his best friend, Henry, who also loved soccer. My head ached, but I wouldn't trade his stories for anything.

"In England, they call soccer football. Maybe you'd like to play there—try it out and see if it's the same?"

He crinkled his nose. "Maybe. But it won't be the same without Henry."

No, it wouldn't, would it? Guilt gnawed, its little teeth grabbing hold. He'd likely never see his best friend again. They'd have new identities. All because of me.

"Alana," Daniel broke through Jack's chatter. "The last time I saw you was at the peace treaty." He minced his words due to small ears listening. He meant when he'd thought she was dead. "Can you catch us up?"

My attention flipped to Alana. I hadn't had time to adjust to her still being alive. "Were you there—in the city when it burned?" *When they killed my father.*

She shook her head. "I was left for dead and awoke among the other Caelum and Terran bodies on the battlefield."

Apparently, they didn't protect children from the brutality of war in my kingdom. Jack appeared unfazed, busily playing a game on my phone. My parents remained silent. I wasn't sure how much they knew, but they listened intently to anything that mentioned my other life.

Alana continued, "I thought a portal might be my best chance to survive, given the medicines here, but only as a last resort. There's one in Ember territory, close to the battlefield. I survived living on the land, but eventually, my wound became infected, and I had to pass through. I'd hoped to make it home to Caelum but was never well enough to travel that far. Unfortunately, I was seen by an Ember, and they reported it to Rowan." She seemed to grow smaller in her seat. "I'm sorry, Cate. About King Aldridge. I didn't know until Rowan told me." She focused on the scenery out the window. "I failed you."

"Rowan's fault. Not yours," I said automatically. She still hadn't explained the whole story. "How did you end up here?"

"I stabilized the portal, but didn't realize an Ember had seen me. Rowan followed a week after I crossed, likely not long after the king died. The healers—doctors in England—treated me, and I was on my way back when I spotted Rowan entering. I followed him. Did you know he has a mother who lives outside London? He grew up there."

"What?" I exclaimed. "Embers live here?"

"Apparently. I followed him to the airport and discovered he bought a ticket to Portland, and that's when I knew. He was after you, Cate. It's always been about you."

I wished she hadn't talked about it in front of my family. They didn't need to know the danger I dealt with every day. And now, I'd brought it on them as well. I returned to our conversation, ignoring her comment. "How did you get to my house?"

"The portal."

"But—it seems so unpredictable?"

She patted my knee. "There are many paths. You just have to know where to look."

All I remembered was nebulous space and tornado-like winds. "You'll help us get back?" The relief of realizing I would have someone to support me eased some of the pressure on my shoulders.

"I will. Daniel told me his sister and Lucas are still in England, so we have them as well."

A rush of affection ribboned around my heart. I'd been so focused on Rowan and saving everyone, I hadn't taken a moment to cherish her—my mentor, my mother figure. I tilted my head to her shoulder. "I'm so glad you're back. I missed you so much," I whispered.

"I missed you, too, dear Cate."

Mom interrupted our moment, "I'd like to go."

The car fell silent. My heart lurched at this new possibility, torn by the temptation to have her with me and the dangers she'd face. We were at war. Heading towards the Embers instead of away would catapult her into further risk.

"I mean," Mom continued. "*We'd* like to go. All of us. Right, Carlos?"

"Do they have soccer there?" Jack sat illegally on Mom's lap in our cramped rented sedan and looked up from his game. He'd had a haircut recently, a tuft refusing to lie flat in the back, and it bobbed when he spoke.

"We call it football, too," Daniel said. "And there's a lot of other fun games."

I jabbed him with my elbow. They couldn't come. As much as I wanted them, it wouldn't be safe. "Mom," I started.

"Please, Cate. Now that we've heard what's happening in your world, we'll go crazy with worry, not knowing. And you—you would never find out if anything happened to us. I can't live like that anymore. There's nothing for us here anymore. Nothing."

Mom was always the more emotional of the two, so it didn't surprise me she wanted to follow me through the portal, though it worried me that she'd risk Jack. "Dad?"

He remained ever steady and thoughtful. "Your mother's right. It would be better to travel with you."

"I'm uncertain you can cross," Alana spoke up. "You don't have any power."

"Oh." Mom bit her lip, and I could tell she was trying not to cry in front of Jack. "Are you sure?"

Alana sighed. "I would go to great lengths for your daughter. For her, we will try."

"What if they get stuck in there?" My voice cracked, memory of rushing winds echoing in my ears.

"I will be able to keep control. Either I have the energy to pull everyone, or they will be left behind. We'll have your contact, Nigel, with us, so your family can form an alternative life if it doesn't work."

An alternative life. It sounded so… unpleasant. Alana always did have a way with words.

I thought about what it would be like living in the castle with my family. Tea together. Someone else to argue with Graftonberg. Then I remembered when the Embers almost killed me in the forest outside Caelum Castle. They wouldn't be safe. Not until we were rid of them. "We'll have to hide you. Rowan can't know you're there. Otherwise, you'll be a constant target. That means we may not see each other often."

Dad nodded slowly. "It will be hard, no question. At least we'll know if you're okay."

"She's going to be queen," Daniel said. "Anything happens to her; it will be the only news in both kingdoms that anyone will talk about."

I wondered how many knew I wasn't at Caelum Castle. Were Graftonberg and Dryden covering for us, or had they sounded the alarm? Harlow probably told someone that we traveled unplanned through his portal. Otherwise, we would have left after breakfast and never returned, and they'd assume the Embers had us captive. I'd been so caught up in saving my parents and stressing about Lucas that I'd hardly had the time to be concerned about my own kingdom. Queen Lila was probably out of her mind with worry for Mya and Daniel. A burst of happiness surged at the thought of returning.

We'd done it. My family was here with me. Whole and safe. I should be celebrating, not letting anxiety take over. Suddenly, I couldn't wait to arrive at the portal and start putting the kingdom back in order. Show Graftonberg I was ready for him to hand over the reins, and then kick him to the curb where he belonged. Reunite with Lucas and Mya, and rebuild the blocks for peace in both kingdoms. Swinging the focus back home had a dizzying effect, as if the magnifying glass shifted without warning, and everything blurred into focus once more.

I reached over and took Daniel's hand, my heart brimming with hope. "We're going to do it," I whispered to him. "You and me. We're going to set things right. I know we will." I squeezed his fingers and said louder so the whole car could hear, "Next stop: the portal!"

CHAPTER 27
CATE

Nerves swirled, the butterflies arming themselves for battle in my stomach. We'd successfully dodged Rowan on our trip from Seattle to England and collected everyone for a mad dash to the portal in the forest outside the university. I'd been too distracted to realize Alana hadn't had a passport, but she'd known of another portal, and we dropped her off to meet her here. My time in the hospital delayed us, but Rowan wasn't without injury himself, and we hoped to beat him here.

We stood in a ring around the faint shimmer in the air in the woods outside Staton. Relief swelled at seeing Lucas's reassuring grin, standing across from me, holding Mya's hand. I could hardly wait to tackle Caelum's problems with him. I held Jack on one side, Daniel on the other. Cool air tousled my hair, which I should have remembered to pull back after the last tornado experience. The forest smell, the wet leaves beneath our feet, and the biting wind would soon be replaced with the dry, cracked earth near the most stable portal in our realms.

We all carried backpacks filled with essentials, even Jack. Daniel had to assure him there would be soccer balls, of a sort, in Caelum so that his entire kid-sized bag wouldn't be taken up by a ball. Nigel, Sarah, and Bert stood nearby, out of range of the portal, in case Alana and I couldn't pull everyone through, and my family was left behind.

When I'd explained what happened last time, the wrinkles in

Alana's brow deepened. "You were lucky to have made it. That entrance is incredibly unstable." She'd assured me that I'd been at least partly correct—not to fight it. Instead, use its strength with ours. The power of both Caelum and Terra. She'd coached everyone to feel one another's energy. My parents were interspersed, with Dad between Lucas and Alana and my mom sandwiched between Mya and Daniel, in hopes the energy would pass through a shorter distance rather than a stopgap with all three clumped together. It was risky, but Alana said she would halt the process if she didn't sense harmony before we passed through.

"Mom. Dad. Jack. I love you." There was a real possibility this would be goodbye. It would likely come down to my own strength—if I could amplify the circle of energy enough for Alana.

"Whatever happens," Dad said, "You know how proud we are of you. Of the woman you've become."

Tears burned, and I took a steadying breath. Controlling my emotions was imperative for this. I couldn't help thinking that the scene with my parents echoed the goodbye with King Aldridge in the stables before the peace treaty. I'd told him I loved him.

And now Father was dead.

Daniel's grip squeezed mine. He could likely feel my inner turmoil spilling over, and I focused once more on his steadying presence.

"Cate. Are you ready?" Alana asked. "First, we see if we can balance the energy."

I tore my eyes from my mom's worried gaze, closing myself off to her tension. I needed her to be reassuring, like Dad, but she wanted this too much, and it only added to the pressure. If I were being honest with myself, so did I.

The energy buzzed at a lower hum than back in Caelum, though still detectable. Daniel's overpowered the others, and I stretched my thoughts toward Alana in hopes hers would radiate. The tension grew as we waited and prayed for the power between us to escalate. I'd asked Alana if we could travel separately or in smaller groups. She'd said it was possible, but the portal wasn't as stable as it had been when we crossed last time. Alana previously spent days strengthening the path between here and there. I saved the "how did she do that" question for another time.

And then, I felt it. A surge. Mya's Terran energy and Lucas's Caelum joining Alana's and Daniel's. This was it. It was enough. It had to be.

The sounds of racing footsteps and cracking twigs startled my lids open. Nigel and the others were supposed to stay away from the circle. I swiveled to see better, my breath bottoming out.

Not Nigel or Sarah.

Rowan.

Rowan, with a small group of men, rushed our circle at breakneck speed. The dull black shine of Rowan's pistol sent everything into slow motion. A stone dropped into the hollow of my chest. Jack's cry echoed as he slipped his hand from mine to run to Mom before I even realized he'd broken the circle. Rage flashed on Rowan's face—iron-hard jaw, thunder rolling in his eyes.

A shot rang out.

Dad dropped Daniel's hand, red blooming across his chest.

"Cate, go," Alana commanded, her voice steel in the melee.

Before I could reset the energy and reach for Alana, she disappeared, along with Lucas, Mya, and my family. Jack had broken the chain by running to Mom. Only Daniel and I remained in the clearing with Rowan's murderous gaze upon us.

There was no time to think. Another shot fired. We rushed into the shimmering air of the portal, hands clasped. Tornado winds surged, and I tightened my grip on Daniel's. The last thing I saw before going through was the frightened eyes of Sarah, a bulky man holding her arms. Would she also die because of me? Would all our allies? Fear, panic, and excruciating grief built until my mind couldn't focus on anything else. Dad's dove-gray Henley, soaked crimson, morphed into my father's death in Ember territory, until only red clouded my vision. Oozing. Puddling. Splashing. The heaviness on my chest bludgeoned against my failing heart.

I was going to die.

The pummeling. The wind. My fluttering, weakening pulse. A snippet of consciousness buried deep bobbed to the surface, reminding me I'd felt this before. This pain. This impending doom. Red still swam through my vision, and I felt, rather than saw, the steady grip of Daniel's touch.

The brittle thought of grasping for a statistic seemed hollow. Childish after so many deaths. Grounding myself wouldn't work—there literally was no ground. But one thing did center me. *Daniel.*

I squeezed his hand, all the while gasping wheezing lungfuls of air. The pressure of his fingers tightened, and my surroundings focused. The wind threatened to tear us apart, and I'd been oblivious, fighting my own demons. I peered into the void, only the haze of fog before us, which, if this place made sense, should have been blown clear by the whirlwind.

I thought of the path to home. The exit into the northern wastelands, like we'd traveled those months ago. The energy tugged and pulled, beckoning me to release Daniel and float away. I remembered the need to work with the portal—to use the power, not fight it. I just couldn't seem to do it.

Daniel's hand jerked from mine, a strong gust ripping it from my grasp. We careened away from each other. For the first time, he came into focus. He was shouting my name, his lips forming the words in slow motion. Yet I couldn't hear anything but the rushing wind in my ears. His ice-blue eyes held mine, frightened and panic-stricken, a fear so sharp, I'd never seen him so terrified. His fingers stretched toward me, but the power of the tornado pulled me farther into the abyss.

I was losing him.

CHAPTER 28
LUCAS

My body bounced off the hard ground, scar screaming in protest. The sounds of others thudding and groaning sent me scrambling to see if Rowan or any of his crew followed us through the portal. Mya, Cate's parents, Jack, and Alana were all here. My gaze caught Mya's to ensure she was well, and she gave me a slight, reassuring nod. I scrambled to my feet, scanning for signs of danger, and slid the knife Nigel had given me from its sheath. Everyone was accounted for except Cate and Daniel. Unease stuttered across my clammy skin.

Cate's mom hovered over her husband. "Carlos," she cried, swiping hair from her face.

Red flashed at the corner of my vision. A chill swept down my spine. Blood covered Sofia's hand. Alana and I rushed over together. The bullet had found Carlos. My eyes fluttered closed for the barest of moments, remembering the feeling of my own recent wound. Cate had already lost one father. She couldn't lose another.

Alana crouched over Carlos. Blood soaked the right side of his chest. She pulled up the sticky shirt to find a bullet wound near his shoulder with more blood in his pectoral region. She wiped the area with fabric to find a shallow wound that skimmed across his chest, then entered and exited his upper arm.

I knelt next to her and examined the injury. "It's superficial."

"Unless it grazed an artery, he'll probably be okay," Alana said. "Bullets are not my expertise."

"Carlos? How are you feeling?" I worked to staunch the bleeding.

"Okay." The word came out in a rasp. He'd been silent until now, though the fear in his eyes told another story. "Where's Cate?" He tried to raise his head to peer around Alana and me.

Exactly. Where was Cate? Or the Embers? Renewed dread spilled, sticky and thick. What if Rowan wasn't here because he'd captured them? He didn't need to follow because he had his mark. Or perhaps… the next gunshot rang true to its target.

I stood abruptly. "I have to go back through," I told Alana. "To find Cate."

Her eyes met mine. "That would be a death sentence."

Mya gripped my arm, and I shook it off.

"So be it."

"Lucas." Mya's voice turned sharp. "You can't."

I avoided looking at her face, knowing it would be near impossible to turn away.

Alana still knelt next to Carlos. "Put pressure on it," she said to Cate's mom, and stood. "This way," she told me.

"What do you expect to do?" Mya asked. "You can't even run. You barely walk. Don't think I haven't noticed that your head spins whenever you stand up."

This time, I forced myself to turn to her. Her blue eyes flashed with anger. With fear. "It's my duty. And your brother is out there, too."

Her face crumpled at the words. "Lucas," she whispered, fat tears welling. "I'm so scared."

"So am I." If only I could draw her close, hold her to shut away the world for a few moments. We couldn't waste time. If there was a chance to save Cate, every moment counted. "Alana?"

We moved toward the portal, the glimmer in the air barely visible. I wondered if all that would remain of my life was a faint shimmer. Yet I had no choice. "Take care of them," I told Alana.

Alana closed her lids, holding her palms up. I wanted to bolt through it as I'd done months ago, but that had been when Alana reinforced the pathway with bolstering. With every second, my worry for

Cate deepened. It gave me time to think about what I'd be leaving here, too.

Mya. My mother. Molly.

My kingdom.

After an excruciating minute, Alana's arms dropped to her sides. "I can't settle it."

"Wait, what?" I had to go through. I moved forward anyway.

Alana grabbed my wrist. "Lucas Bradbury. Do not move," she commanded.

Her tone was enough to stop me short. I stepped back and exhaled, partly with relief, partly to settle my nerves. "Why? What's happened?"

We sat near Cate's family again, Jack huddled next to his mom, his eyes wide. Poor guy. It must be so confusing for him.

"The portal is a void," Alana said. "If one knows where to look, there are innumerable tunnels, but only if the energy cooperates. It naturally follows certain routes that strengthen with use, like a trail created in a forest over time."

"If this is the best entrance, why can't you use it?" Cate's mom asked.

Alana checked Carlos's wound while she spoke, "The energy feels as if it is being pulled in a different direction. We can hope that means Cate and Daniel will arrive another way. Or perhaps," she paused. "Perhaps it is Rowan who is pulling the energy. To the portal in Ember territory."

"How long before we can use it again?" I asked.

"Remember how you couldn't travel until the new moon when you were in England? That wasn't just my doing. The phases of the moon help. But also… it often reaches this state once too many people have used it. Cate and the prince missed the timing. For whatever reason, they weren't close enough behind us and… won't likely come through here anytime soon. Maybe in a month. Or perhaps they found another path." She examined Carlos's wound again, still oozing. "We need to get him care. Infection will be his greatest enemy. We don't have time to wait for them."

"But—" This was *Alana*. She returned from the dead, for heaven's sake. Surely, she could do something.

Mya took my hand, fresh tears for her brother and Cate tracking down her cheeks. "We'll have to have faith that they'll find a way home."

I glanced behind me at the shimmer in the air, hovering near the rim of the dormant volcano. I remembered the panic that day when we couldn't find Cate because she'd landed inside. How I'd joked with her even though I'd been sick with worry. And the look on her face when she'd collapsed into Daniel's arms when reaching the top. I scrambled up and peered over the edge. No sign of her.

"Cate," I yelled. "Cate!"

Mya came up beside me. "You think they're down there?" She didn't wait for my response. "Daniel!"

Our voices sounded through the cavern. Nothing else echoed back. We waited. Called again. Nothing. I scanned the mountain, and like déjà vu from when I stood in this exact spot with Cate, a dragon approached from the distance. After my last stent with the creatures, I had no intention of spending more time with any of them. Unless…

"It's Molly!" I yelled.

Mya squinted. "How can you tell? It's so far away."

Maybe it was the slightly asymmetric flap of the wing from when she'd broken it as a baby, maybe it was the angle of the spines trailing down her back, but it was her.

"Hey, Jack," I called. The little boy nestled next to his mom, shell-shocked. I knelt so we were eye to eye. Still a stranger to him, we'd been rushed in separate cars to the portal as soon as they'd arrived in London. "You want to meet a dragon? She's really nice."

"Is she real?" He studied my face as if trying to decide if I could be trusted.

"Absolutely. What do you think her name is?"

"Um, Thor?"

I cracked a grin. "For a girl? Her name is Molly."

Jack looked up at his mom. "Why is a dragon named Molly?"

Not this again. "Because she's a friendly dragon. Look. Here she comes." I pointed over Sofia's shoulder so he could watch her approach.

I jogged a few yards down the mountain to meet her. She must have been searching for us, hoping we'd come through the portal here. She gracefully landed, her gray-green scales shining in the sun, then bounded toward me. I threw my arms around her neck.

"Hey, Molls. You always know where to find me, don't you?" She nudged me with her head, her exuberance nearly toppling me backward onto my rear. "Whoa, now. Gentle." I soothed under her chin, finding something attached to a cord. A leather sheet unrolled, containing a letter.

Sir Lucas,

If you are reading this, I presume Molly has found you. Harlow Matthews reported your disappearance, along with our queen and the royals from Terra. I have dispatched a group of soldiers in the forest at the base of the mountain in the event you come through the portal. Mr. Matthews informed us that you might never return or be delayed for months or years. We will stay vigilant.

All the best,

General Dixon

My first reaction was relief. The second? Were we on the same timeline as when we'd left? With Alana's help, it hadn't been something I'd worried about. But the suggestion sent goosebumps crowding along my forearms, raising even more questions regarding Cate and Daniel's whereabouts.

After I showed the others the letter, we agreed it would be quickest for Mya and me to ride Molly to find the soldiers. She wouldn't be able to carry us all, and besides, we might have to dismount and hike through the forest. It should make it easier on Carlos if we found them first.

"You okay here?" I asked Alana. Although she hid her discomfort well, I knew she, too, was recovering from injuries. Daniel had briefly filled me in on how Alana had come back from the dead. I still hadn't adjusted to the idea.

"We'll be fine," she replied, her tone no-nonsense.

If Cate and Daniel couldn't travel through the portal, neither could Rowan, which made me feel better about leaving them.

A tug on my elbow caught my attention. Jack stood beside me. "Can I say hello?"

"Sure. She likes it when you stroke her chin." I placed a soothing hand on Molly's snout, so she'd bend low. "See? Right here, where she's orange." I indicated the patches on her throat.

Jack reached up and stroked Molly as if she might break. His expression filled with wonder, a tiny smile spreading into a wide grin, complete with a missing tooth.

"The princess and I are going for a ride to bring back help. We'll be back soon." I held out my hand to Mya, and Molly bobbed her head in greeting.

"Ah, you like her, don't you?" I leaned in. "I do, too," I whispered.

Mya and I soared down the mountain and circled the rim of the forest. A strip of blue cloth tied to a tree caught our attention. "There," I said, guiding Molly to land.

It wasn't long before we found them outside a makeshift hut built against a berm. The Caelum blue uniforms sent a familiar warmth in my chest. *Home*. I could have made a life with Mya in London with my cereal and an occasional hit of fried chicken, but until this moment, I hadn't realized how much I'd missed this land. These people.

Someone I recognized ducked his head out of the hut at the commotion of our arrival and jogged over. "Tim!"

"Lucas. Haven't seen you since that training last year."

"Quick, tell me. How long have we been gone?"

The pale skin beneath his freckles shaded pink. "Um… you don't know? Everything okay, Lucas?"

No time to explain the physics of portals. "Yes, fine. But how long?" I tried unsuccessfully to even out the desperation in my voice.

"Just under two weeks," he replied.

Mya and I exchanged relieved glances.

We arranged for the others to be retrieved, including a gurney, while I mounted Molly and scouted the area. I didn't trust them not to fall off my dragon, especially the wounded Carlos. No sign of the enemy from the air, and soon, Cate's family was safe inside the hut. Carlos's wound, cleaned and dressed, appeared non-life-threatening.

Alana took me aside that evening outside the ring of the crackling campfire. "I'll hide the family, as promised to Catherine. And I plan to stay with them and serve as their protection."

"You?" I didn't hide my surprise. "We'll need your leadership back home. Especially with Cate… missing. I'm not sure you're aware, but Baron Graftonberg—"

"You'll manage fine without me," she cut me off. "I gave my word to the queen. I know a safe place. And to be honest," her features sagged for a fleeting moment, "I need to rest and restore."

"Are you not healed?" I suspected, but was surprised she'd admit it.

"Mostly. Almost dying, especially with so little surrounding energy… is not good for someone my age. Or a young man like you, I suspect."

She must be truly ailing to remark on her age. She'd always come across invincible. A guiding force for our kingdoms. Though her words reminded me of just how tired my body truly was. How my side ached. How much I wanted to go home to my own bed.

"We'll instruct these men not to disclose that they've seen Cate's parents. I hope they can be trusted." She eyed the group, laughing and telling stories to Jack around the fire.

Tim would be a vault. The others seemed like a good lot—hand-chosen by General Dixon, not Graftonberg. "I'll take Molly at first light with Mya. The men will stay with you until you're ready."

"Take care of yourself, Lucas. Our kingdoms will need you and the princess."

"Same to you."

Worry sprouted that without Cate, we would need Alana. Graftonberg and Dryden were unlikely to be swayed by me. Perhaps with Mya's persuasive powers, we could plug enough holes to keep the dam from breaking. Our queen had better arrive soon, because I had a feeling we wouldn't be able to hold off disaster for long.

CHAPTER 29
LUCAS

Molly's sad golden eyes watched me slump in the corner of her barn, the structure built especially for her all those years ago. Honestly, if Graftonberg didn't enjoy the idea of having a dragon on our side so much, he likely would have kicked us both out for treasonous talk. Well, Molly wasn't doing the talking, but we came as a pair. Everyone knew that. She'd seen my discouragement morph into despair these last six months. My depression seeped into her as if she were a symbiotic creature, feeding off my emotions. Or maybe that's just what loved ones did for one another.

I rummaged through the sack next to me and pulled out a treat. A nut butter biscuit, one of her favorites, and I tossed it to her. She wasn't so depressed that she wouldn't eat, though she failed to catch it in the air, letting it drop to the floor where she stooped to scoop it up. Her enormous jaws chewed slowly as she watched me.

I'd come for privacy. To open the letter that burned a hole in my pocket, given to me earlier that day. My sentry duty finally complete, I'd rushed here to read it. My name written on the envelope in Mya's swirly handwriting almost made me smile. Until the bitterness of being barred from seeing her by King Dryden soured my mood.

Months back, Molly and I had visited Terra, not long after we returned from London, and Mya returned home with her father. We were lucky they didn't shoot us with arrows, because as soon as we landed, soldiers directed me back to Caelum. I wasn't allowed to speak to Mya. Later, I discovered she hadn't even known I'd arrived. Since then, we've been communicating with letters passed through her maid.

Lucas,

Not a day goes by that my father doesn't blame the rest of the world for Daniel's disappearance. Cate for dragging him there, Rowan and the Embers, of course, you for not protecting them both better—which somehow turned into all Caelumites—and last of all, me, for coming home safe while Daniel remains missing. He continues to propagate the lies against Cate that Graftonberg proliferated, taking them one step further in describing how she seduced his son into running away from all the problems in this realm and abandoning us. The Terrans are quick to believe such stories, and her name is now synonymous with traitor. My efforts at persuasion haven't worked on Father, but slowly, some of the advisors and soldiers have come around. Dev continues to be loyal, though I fear I'm losing Mother.

I presume things still aren't better in Caelum? Why anyone would believe anything the baron says is baffling. I'm sorry I don't have much news, especially since it's all poor. We must maintain faith that Cate and Daniel will return, while also gathering as many allies as possible. We'll need both of them, but especially Cate, as we have reports that the Embers are regrouping. With all these rumors, surely Rowan heard that Cate never returned, making us all the more vulnerable. It's only a matter of time before the Embers strike again. Father won't hear this argument and continues to rail against her. In a strange way, it's his form of grief. Blame and anger are his only method of coping.

Give Molly a hug for me. But maybe not a kiss since you declared her a better kisser while in hospital. You were pretty out of it. Do you remember? I'm a bit jealous, you know. I miss you terribly. Don't give up hope that one day we can be together once more.

Sending my love,

Mya

She hadn't lost hope. Not in us. Not in Cate. Her words bolstered my resolve to do the same. Perhaps we were the only ones able to buoy the other. To keep the underground support for Caelum's rightful queen alive. More and more, I'd noticed how the other soldiers turned away when I arrived. How their gaze hit the ground when I mentioned she would return. The longer Cate remained missing, the harder it became.

After saying goodbye to Molly, I headed to the guardhouse to retrieve my jacket, rubbing my arms in the late-night air, or actually, early morning. My shift ended at midnight. A line of carriages snaked from the front circular drive of the castle. Graftonberg and one of his opulent parties, no doubt. I ducked my head and quickened my pace, eager to gather my things and return to a pot of leftover stew in the small quarters I called home, followed closely by bed. My cooking wouldn't compare to Mum's, but I did all right for myself.

"Yoo-hoo," a woman called. "Sir Lucas!"

I ignored the voice coming from one of the carriages. No longer a distinguished guest at such events, demoted to the tasks reserved for first-year soldiers, I didn't particularly want to talk to the crowd I'd been displaced from. General Dixon remained my ally, but the order had come straight from Graftonberg. At first, I'd been vocal about what happened when we went to London. How Cate almost killed Rowan, bravely saving her family. This directly contradicted Graftonberg's story, and he did whatever he could to silence me. The general had taken me aside, informing me we'd have to work in secret for the queen or face banishment. Or worse, treason charges and risk hanging from a rope.

"Lucas, dear! Don't think I can't see you running away," the woman's shrill voice called.

My shoulders sagged. All I wanted was to mind my own business, eat dinner, and sleep. It had been a long fifteen-hour shift on my feet. All the sentry men were working overtime at Graftonberg's orders to stretch our resources. It led to exhaustion and low morale. Still, none of us were willing to give up our jobs that paid in actual coin. He'd started moving to reimbursing the laborers in room and board rather than money, the first steps toward indentured servitude. "For the good of the kingdom," of course. Thinking about it further lowered my mood.

I turned toward the carriage with a purple fleur-de-lis insignia to find Dame Hemlock waving a lace-trimmed handkerchief out the window. I'd enjoyed speaking with her at King Aldridge's funeral dinner, especially her take on dragons. 'Spose it wouldn't be the worst thing in the world to talk to her.

"Young man, may I drive you home? I would enjoy the company," she said once I'd reached the carriage. Her gray brows raised in such a way that it was clear she wanted more than a companion, piquing my interest. Yet anyone who overheard would believe her to be just a lonely old woman.

"That would be lovely, ma'am." I climbed in, jacket forgotten. My cottage wasn't far, in a series of small houses built for castle workers and soldiers down the slope on the edge of the forest. But it was the gleam in her eye that interested me, not the drive.

"What information do you have on our queen?" she asked as soon as I'd shut the door.

The use of "our queen" made me believe she remained on Cate's side, though months of experience showed me that most believed Graftonberg's slander. "What would you like to know?" I asked carefully.

"You were there. What happened? I can't believe she ran away. Not after risking her life for the kingdoms."

I thought of the gunshot ringing out and Carlos's injury. How we'd been swept away by Alana, leaving Cate behind. And the very real possibility that Rowan fired again and hit his mark. "Cate was on her way back here," I said. "She was standing across from me, but we didn't all make it through the portal."

"You don't think she chose to stay?" She leaned in. "With the prince?"

I shook my head. "I believe the best option is to have faith that she'll return. I'm confident that she very much wants to be here for this kingdom. And I would like it to still be hers when she returns."

She straightened her skirt and looked away, making me wonder if she really was on Cate's side. I waited until she finished fiddling, having enough sense to know she was stalling. She stared out her window and said, "Have you heard about the announcement at tonight's dinner?" She sniffed and turned to me again. "Well, it will only be a matter of time. You see…" The moonlight glimmered across her troubled gray eyes. "Graftonberg has set a time for his coronation. He's declared that Catherine will not be returning, and he will be taking the throne instead."

Her words sat like soured drundle pie in my stomach. Of course, I knew this might happen. I'd been in denial, aching for Cate to return. Once Graftonberg becomes king, there may be little she can do without an all-out civil war. There was no way that man would step down on his own. And Graftonberg was correct about one thing. Resources were slim. We couldn't afford to lose more soldiers in battle because it would only weaken our position with the Embers.

"What are we going to do?" I whispered, more to myself than to her.

She answered me anyway, "Pray Queen Catherine returns. And quick. The coronation is set for two weeks."

CHAPTER 30
LUCAS

Mya's dress, a shimmering wave of greens and aquas, sparkled in the sun as she walked up the aisle. She projected her political stance on coronation day through fashion, blending our two kingdoms as a sign of peace and unity. My feet nearly left their post before I caught myself from running to her. *I love her with my whole being*. I stood guard by the podium, and her gaze found me, illuminating her features before she fixed her attention forward to find her seat next to King Dryden.

They'd arrived last night, though I hadn't been allowed anywhere near her. We'd planned a meeting location for later when she could more easily slip away after this charade of a coronation. I longed to speak freely with someone again, instead of constantly guarding my words, and to hold her… I tried not to think about that part. Not in front of thousands of people.

At first, I was surprised to be placed near the podium in a location with high visibility. Then I realized Graftonberg carefully crafted the decision so that others could witness my support of his ascent to the throne. Which I didn't, but what choice did I have? As much as I'd hoped and prayed, Cate hadn't arrived. I still remained on high alert, fantasizing that she would waltz down the center aisle and take her rightful place. This… couldn't happen. Graftonberg as king. It just couldn't.

Instead of Cate, the baron tottered up the Caelum blue center carpet, jewels glittering in the sun. They must have raided every fabric shop in the kingdom to source the amount of gold braid that trimmed his clothes. *Understated* wasn't a word he'd recognize.

The trumpets blared as he strode up the steps, his son, Roy, already waiting to stand at his right side. Was this the future of our monarchy? Of our kingdom? Too many supported Graftonberg because he rewarded those who showed unwavering loyalty. And those who crossed him faced never-before-seen taxes for new and ever more preposterous reasons. Yet, nobody figured out how to oppose him. Anyone who did was punished, either financially or publicly. We'd had more hangings in Caelum over the past six months than in the last hundred years. Some of his claims, I'd credit as truth. Constant battles *had* drained our resources, first with the Terrans and then with the Embers. We did need to raise funds, just not through immoral tactics. No one truly knew how empty the coffers had become, but I couldn't believe it was that bad, considering the parties thrown at the castle for him and his sycophants.

One such crony, another aristocrat with lands bordering the baron's, had been droning on these last few minutes, extolling his praises. All too soon, it was time for Graftonberg's crowning. I searched the audience for any signs of unrest. For someone to put a stop to this madness. Graftonberg climbed the steps to the throne, the ornate chair from the castle brought out to the same spot where King Aldridge's funeral had been months ago.

The gold crown held above the baron's head hovered. A pause. The man's gaze fell on the crowd.

Had something happened? I craned my neck, hope surging.

The man's eyes fell, returning to his duty.

Graftonberg's worm-like lips puffed into a smug smile as the heavy crown was placed on his balding head.

It was done.

No Cate running down the aisle. No Ember attack to halt the proceedings. Not even a single protest. Had they all just been craving a leader to step up for our kingdom? Any leader? Or was it fear?

"Long live the king!" It echoed in sickening clarity. As a knight of the realm, my duty was to my king. To Graftonberg.

I stooped to one knee, hand fisted over my heart in an act of deference on autopilot, following the other soldiers. I couldn't feel my legs. Actually, my whole body turned numb. I'd been in denial, and it came crashing down in vivid reality.

Graftonberg spoke, but I barely listened. "I'm honored to take on this role for Caelum. Your queen-in-waiting abandoned you. But I give you this promise. I will always stand with Caelum!"

Applause rang out. Perhaps some gave him the benefit of the doubt. But many felt bitterness toward Cate, and with all the lies being spread, I didn't blame them. Even the truth wasn't particularly flattering. She'd known the risks to save her family and taken them. Now, a power-hungry monarch reigned over us.

The rest of the ceremony flew by in a blur. If an Ember raid came upon us, I would have been the last to know, my mind abandoning sentry duty in a haze of disbelief. The crowd stood as our new king retreated down the aisle. I caught Mya's gaze, a wrinkle visible between her brows, even at this distance.

"Are you okay?" she mouthed.

I straightened. Was it that obvious? After a quick, reassuring nod, I headed to my mount to follow Graftonberg to the castle with the rest of the guards. I spotted Dame Hemlock watching with somber gray eyes, and in my horrible mood, I didn't acknowledge her. Guilt led me to turn back, but she'd already disappeared. The only thing propelling me forward was seeing Mya after the coronation festivities.

Six hours later, I paced Molly's barn, our designated meeting location. No one came here in the evening but me, unless I asked them to check on Molly.

"Where is she, Mol?"

She snorted, steam releasing from her nostrils.

"Careful, there. You know better than to do that in here."

She'd learned not to produce fire in the barn, lest she set her own house ablaze. She usually had more control than that, and I blamed my own agitation as much as hers. I placed my hand on her snout, leaning in so our foreheads touched, her smooth scales cool against me. It calmed us both, a lone comfort these past months. There had been so many times I fought the urge to just fly away with her. To become a deserter and end up like the man in the woods we'd met all that time ago, the one who'd poisoned Molly. Banished from Mya, too, it'd been difficult to keep up hope.

The door creaked open, and Mya stepped in, still in her gown, glittering in the lantern light. "There you are, kissing the dragon again." She grinned, that dimple showing itself. "Should I be jealous of you, Molly?" She bypassed me and placed her hand under the dragon's chin. Molly tilted into the touch, ever a fan of the princess.

"What about me?" It was my turn for jealousy.

She stepped into my arms and exhaled slowly against my chest, her shoulders dropping. "How does this feel so much more like home than anywhere else?" she murmured.

This was the reminder I needed. I could never run away with Molly because I'd be deserting Mya. Deserting the hope we had of one day being together. Deserting the dream of peace for our kingdoms.

I kissed her.

Not just because I wanted to feel her skin beneath mine, because I did, but we needed that connection. The reminder that we weren't alone, even when the distance stretched a kingdom away in Terra Castle. An invisible tether held us together no matter how far. The time we'd spent hadn't been long, yet we'd been through an eternity—a lifetime of near-escapes. She'd always been there. A quiet—and sometimes not so quiet—comfort.

Finally, I pulled my lips from hers. "How did it go tonight?" With me being relegated to the lowliest of soldier duties, we were relying on Mya's spying prowess. The question contained a dozen unsaid problems: Did King Dryden make nice with Graftonberg, or would there be a battle between Terra and Caelum? Did she ferret out any supporters for Cate? Is her father softening to the idea of the two of us?

"Father is not happy about dealing with Graftonberg. There were a few insults, but no all-out war declared. With Alana not here and the Embers relatively quiet, it's as if everyone has forgotten the real enemy."

"It's easier to ignore it. They're both more worried about posturing for the other."

"Father is out of sorts with Daniel gone. He cares more about his son than even he realized. He isn't admitting it, but he seems off. Volatile."

A more temperamental King Dryden. *That sounds enjoyable.*

"I've been collecting people." Mya's lips tilted in a small smile, despite our circumstances. "You know, flipping my fan and getting results."

I chuckled at her reference to ballroom flirting code, then sobered, hoping there hadn't been any actual flirting going on. "What kind of people?"

The door to the barn swung open. Even though we had been standing several feet apart, we both instinctively took a step back. A reflex, somehow attempting to make this clandestine meeting seem more proper, but our startled movement only made us appear guiltier.

Dev strode in, a slight limp still evident from his injury in Ember City. Although I didn't know him well, Cate and Mya both trusted him, which was good enough for me.

"Nothing like setting up a meeting where one of the members can roast you alive," Dev joked, edging toward the side of the enclosure.

"Don't say anything to upset her." I crossed my arms, unsure why I felt the need to be antagonistic. Probably because his distrust of Molly automatically raised my hackles.

"Me? Never. Sorry, mate. I had an unfortunate experience with a dragon years back. I'm glad this one's on our side, that's all."

"She's a sweetheart. Don't worry." Mya punched Dev in the shoulder. "Who else did you get?"

"I'm working on it. For discretion, I only invited one more."

"Working on what?" I asked.

"The underground movement," Mya replied. "For when Daniel and Cate return."

Graftonberg's coronation had deflated my hope. Seeing that crown placed on his head was as if the final hammer dropped. "Maybe…" I watched both their faces. "Maybe we need an underground for peace. Caelum and Terrans who believe that's the best way forward. A group to fight for equality. Like our own alliance." I warmed to the idea. "We can share news with each other. Build trust." Glancing at Mya, I continued, "Your father still doesn't allow newspapers? We can make our own. Quietly distribute them and pass on information."

Dev's eyes shifted uneasily to Mya's before he spoke, "Not to knock any of your ideas, but I thought this movement was for Cate."

Guilt swirled at his response. Practicality still won out. "Can't it be both?" I'd grown weary of the avoidance of those who'd lost faith, but how could I expect others to believe she'd return when even my belief flagged?

Before I could answer, General Dixon joined us. "Is this everyone?" I noted that he'd asked Mya, not me.

"For now, yes," she replied. "The four of us will be the key contacts. Dev hasn't had much trouble convincing his troops that Cate's no traitor. Many saw firsthand how she hadn't stopped the rain so she could save the soldiers, sacrificing King Aldridge. But I've had more difficulty with the gentry. The ones that hold the purse strings. They want to stay in my father's good graces."

"Same trouble here," I replied. "Except Dame Hemlock… I think." The older woman hadn't come out and said that she believed in Cate, though her feelings on Graftonberg were pretty clear.

The general nodded. "The soldiers here feel betrayed. They'd put their trust in Cate. They loved Aldridge, too, so there were already mixed feelings about how he died."

"I can't believe I'm saying this, but Cate's support is coming from Terra, not Caelum?" The signs had been there, though it was hard to swallow. I loved my kingdom. Seeing them flip their allegiance so easily brought a wave of shame. With it, shame that I'd lost my own faith that she'd return.

"I'll go back to Dame Hemlock. We'll need funds to distribute our messaging," I said. "Money she definitely has."

"And what will that message be?" Dev raised his brows. It was his turn not to trust me.

"We have two goals," I replied. "To change the narrative on why Cate's missing—she's no traitor—and promote peace between the kingdoms." Mya slipped her hand in mine. "Agree?"

Both men nodded. "Now that Graftonberg is king, there will be even less tolerance." The general's gaze fell to me. "We have one more goal. Don't end up swinging from the end of a rope."

CHAPTER 31
CATE

"Daniel!" I screamed. I was losing him.

I was losing everyone, and it was no one's fault but my own. I did the only thing I could think of, and it might turn out to be the biggest mistake of my life.

I let him go.

He drifted out of reach, and I turned from those panicked, pleading eyes. Airplane safety, with the smiling attendants demonstrating the aircraft, jumped into my head. *Place your own mask on first before helping others.* I had to save myself before I could rescue anyone else.

Reaching for the whirling energy, I focused on what I'd done the first time when we'd traveled to England. *Don't fight it.* My mind cleared. The pain in my chest from my panic attack faded. Everything fell away except taming the chaotic power. No, taming wasn't correct. Finding a rhythm and coaxing it.

The energy formed a tunnel I could feel, but not see. *This way,* I asked it. It propelled me toward the opening. Daniel floated near, pitched in the same direction. In my excitement, the power wavered, the tunnel disappearing.

I blew out a breath, aligning my thoughts. This was it. The winds still rushed around us, but in concert toward one goal.

I landed on my backside, the sun shining through trees above, Daniel grimacing next to me. One day, I'd learn the art of a soft landing, though at this moment, the earth never felt so good. But where was everyone else?

Wait. Trees… the portal is in a wasteland. Are we back in England? I scrambled up, preparing to find Rowan's calculating stare and knowing smirk. The only sound, the breeze rustling the surrounding leaves. I recognized this place.

Harlow's.

We must have gone through a different portal than the others. Daniel's slurred voice cut through my scattered thoughts, "Are you hurt?" He listed to one side, as if he couldn't quite catch his balance. He squinted. "Blood…" His arm raised slowly to me.

I rushed to examine myself, and sure enough, part of a sleeve was blood-stained. I tugged down the loose-knit collar to inspect my shoulder. A long scratch, already mostly closed, barely registered. I could feel the sting now that we were back on land.

"A bullet grazed you." He rubbed his arm. "I thought maybe that's why things went…"

"Awry?"

He took a step forward, swayed, then leaned on me.

"Still finding your sea-legs?" The hairs on my arms rose. "Or are you hurt?"

Daniel sank to the ground. Something was very wrong. I knelt next to him, watching.

His eyes wandered, unfocused now that he'd discovered I was unharmed. "Don't you feel…?"

"What? Feel what?" When he didn't answer, I asked, "Do I need to fetch Harlow?"

He cocked his head slowly, as if he couldn't remember who Harlow was. "Like I'm underwater," he slurred. "Everything is moving in slow motion. My mind and my body are at different speeds. And you… you're lightning fast."

"Me?" Compared to Daniel, I was the sluggish one. I scooted next to him so that our legs touched, ignoring the dampness beneath. "Hey." I waited for him to look at me. "Put your hands in the dirt." I guided his fingers to the soil, tufts of grass poking between them. "We're home. Can you feel the energy? Focus on it."

We sat there, listening to the birds, the way the leaves created a song of their own in the breeze—gentle, as if the tornado we'd just experienced never existed. Daniel dug into the earth, burying them until we both lay down next to each other, heads touching. If I listened carefully, I could hear the portal calling. Beckoning us. Yet nothing felt as good as Caelum soil.

It wasn't long before, sunk in the quiet, that I began to worry about my family. Alana had more control than me. Surely, she guided them safely through the other portal? I glanced at the blood on my clothes. The worries swirled again, the peacefulness evaporating with the wind. Dad was out there somewhere, wounded.

I turned on my side to face Daniel. "Are you ready?"

"I think so. Thanks for taking care of me."

"I didn't do anything." I brushed a lock of hair and traced one dark eyebrow with my fingertip.

"Being there is enough." He attempted a smile, lips tugging upward, long, black lashes framing his searching blue eyes.

I let the words soak into my battered soul, lacing my fingers through his dirt-covered ones. Even if my dad was hurt somewhere, he would be with Alana and Lucas. I had to put my trust in them. Because that was my only choice.

Daniel sat up, and we trudged to Harlow's cabin. Flowers bloomed near the porch, new since we left. I glanced up at the sun. Must be due to a few unusually sunny days in autumn. I still didn't have a handle on the weather or vegetation patterns here in Caelum. Daniel knocked. We waited long moments before movement shuffled on the other side of the door.

Harlow arrived, disheveled as usual, with his collar undone and gray hair uncombed. His eyes rounded, and he took an unsteady step forward. "Has anyone seen you?" he asked, his tone urgent.

"N-No," I answered.

"Get in. Now."

Daniel was feeling well enough to raise his brows at the old man's impertinence, though he gestured for me to enter first, anyway. The inside was as I remembered it. Books haphazardly scattered, worn furniture, a sweater hanging over a chair in the corner. Somehow, it put me at ease. Maybe because I'd like a cottage in the woods filled to the brim with books, too. For now, I'd make do with a castle. I smirked at my internal joke, though it quickly faded at the sight of Harlow straightening his jacket in that nervous habit of his.

"You sure no one saw you?" he asked.

"We're sure." Daniel crossed his arms. "What's this all about?"

"How long did you travel?"

He acted as if we'd been on a sightseeing tour. As if we hadn't been fighting for my family's life and trying to eliminate Rowan in the process. As if we weren't even royalty.

"Ten days," I answered.

Harlow sank into one of the tufted chairs, not bothering to move the leather-bound tome in the seat. "Please. Sit."

He didn't help us stack books off the sofa either, though he appeared more dazed than rude. We sat, unease growing with each beat of silence. He hadn't even asked if I was alright, ignoring the blood on my shirt.

He fiddled with a bookmark in his lap, turning it over and over in his hands. "Ten months have passed since you left."

My heart sank through my stomach, straight into the floorboards creaking beneath my feet. What happened while we were away? The Embers. Have they taken over?

"Graftonberg is king. And he has named you a traitor."

My heart dropped the rest of the way—below the floor, somewhere into the abyss below. Fingernails dug into wool couch cushions. Daniel blew out a tiny breath. Time stopped, even as the mantel clock ticked.

"You," he pursed his lips, "are now the enemy."

CHAPTER 32
DANIEL

Ten months. No wonder disorientation and sluggishness plagued my body. It was trying to catch up with the time jump we'd apparently encountered. And this… this dilemma was worse than any of us conjured when we'd brainstormed worst-case scenarios. How could her people forget? They had been shouting, *long live the queen* mere weeks ago. She was their hero. Only, for them, it'd been close to a year. A year without a single sighting of their queen.

"And what of Daniel?" Cate asked Harlow. "Is he an enemy too?"

"You must escape to Terra," he replied, leaning forward, ignoring her question. "They watch the house. I'm surprised you missed them. They're slacking in their duties, growing tired of waiting. Difficult to hide you, but we will. I have contacts, and I'll start the chain."

"The chain?" I asked.

"There is an underground movement for our rightful queen, in the event you returned. Though I must warn you, do not put your trust in just anyone. You'll find the kingdom changed. For the worse, in my opinion, but others will disagree. Lies have been spread. Your people are not yours anymore. And the prince?" he turned to me. "They believe you complicit in the betrayal. I've been told the Terrans are more mixed in their views. Your father will take you back, but it wouldn't surprise me if he turns on Catherine. We'll get you to Terra, and you must hide the queen."

One moment, we were propelled through the portal, gunshots firing; the next, we're being told she's the new enemy, and nothing is as it was when we left. "I won't abandon Cate to align with my father."

Harlow stood. "That's your choice. I'll meet my contact. It may be several hours." He started closing curtains. "Do not leave this house."

"Wait," Cate called. "The others. My family. Lucas. Mya." I started toward him. "Alana? Are they safe?"

"Alana is with your family as she promised. They are well. In hiding. No one knows any of them are here. Lucas informed me, aware you'd want to be told if you returned through this portal. Princess Mya is at Terra Castle."

I blew out a breath. Cate's tight expression loosened at the news, fresh tears of relief brimming. Our world had turned in an instant, but knowing Mya was safe at home made it tolerable. As if the most important things hadn't changed, and it was still possible to erase whatever had happened these last months.

When the old man left the house and the door locked behind him, Cate whispered, "Can we trust him? What if he's fetching the guard to take me to the baron while we wait here?"

"Why would he warn us then? He could have taken us to Graftonberg himself."

Cate collapsed against the cushions. "You're right."

I leaned in next to her. "He'll find Lucas." But Cate's words had planted a seed of doubt.

"What are we going to do?" Her head fell to my shoulder.

"Whatever else is happening in the kingdom isn't our priority. We keep you safe until we can figure out how to fix things. It's still my job." I traced her kneecap with my finger. "My forever job."

"There you go again, calling me work."

"Isn't that a saying? Love what you do?"

"In my world. How'd you hear that one?" She elbowed me before settling. "I love you, too. And I'm so glad our families are safe. Let's rest. I have a feeling we won't get much for a while."

Harlow returned four hours later. "It's in motion. Now we wait."

Like we hadn't already been waiting anxiously this whole time. When he shuffled into the kitchen, I followed. "Can you elaborate? I'll protect her with my life, and I want to be more involved in this plan."

He removed a glass from the cupboard, poured himself water from a pitcher, and drank. I almost felt sorry for ambushing him. His journey had left a pallor clinging to his skin that hadn't previously been there.

"What would you like to know?" He set down his cup.

"Where's Lucas, for one?"

"Doing his duty somewhere. He'll be informed. We've established a messaging system of trusted people. I couldn't go to Lucas because it would be too suspicious. Nor will he come here. I've asked for a distraction so you two can move past the cottage's surveillance. At eight o'clock tonight, someone will meet you at the bridge a mile west of here. Now, if you don't mind," he brushed by me, "I would like to sit down. It was a long walk for these old bones."

"Harlow," I grabbed him by the arm, "one question. When we first met, you at least tried to give us deference for being royal. What's changed? Have you turned us in?" I said, softly, so Cate wouldn't hear us.

"I suppose I'm tired. Sorry, Your Highness. Would you like me to bow?"

Maybe I was being overly suspicious, hearing that no one could be trusted. But his behavior unnerved me.

Harlow went to lie down, leaving Cate and me alone once more in the small living room.

"I heard what you said. You're not a very quiet whisperer." She crossed her arms.

"Or this cottage is tiny." I rolled my eyes. "So, you think he's telling the truth?"

"Weren't you the one reassuring me earlier?"

"True. I can't put my finger on it. Something doesn't sit right."

"After he got over the bowing last time, he was awfully stubborn. I think he's just a grumpy old man who's been living alone too long. If what he says is true, he's risking his neck to be part of this underground organization. We should be grateful."

"Fine. But I'm staying on high alert."

We left several hours later under the cover of darkness through a back window. Whatever the supposed diversion for Graftonberg's soldiers was, we never discovered it. Perhaps they were late, or maybe it was as simple as someone bringing them dinner, neglecting their duty for a few minutes to eat. We followed Harlow's directions through the woods, the night air cool against our skin. We still had our backpacks, though there was only a change of clothes from Cate's world. Our original traveling garments had long since been discarded. We wouldn't be able to stay undetected for long, dressed like this in daylight. I tripped over a stump and regained my balance.

"Are you all better? From… the time travel thing?" Cate whispered.

Ordinarily, I would have sensed the obstacle and stepped right over it, but my slow reflexes hadn't triggered. At least my brain seemed to work again. "Mostly," I replied, not willing to worry her. Though it certainly troubled me. I alone protected Cate, and if we were walking into a trap, I would need all my senses intact. The energy felt… off. Muffled, like I was buried in cotton.

A branch snapped nearby. I froze, snagging Cate's arm to stop her advance. We were still half a kilometer from the bridge. Suddenly, I very much wished we'd been sure the guards were distracted. Cate's shallow breathing sounded next to me, but little else. We both held daggers, procured from Nigel before we left England.

"An animal?" she asked under her breath.

Maybe, I thought, but didn't say it aloud. I squeezed her hand, wanting her to understand the message: remain quiet. After a time of only silence, we proceeded at a snail's pace, every step slow and calculated. My body screamed on high alert, while my brain reminded me I wasn't in fighting shape. Especially if I was up against Caelumites who could use the energy for speed as I normally would.

After a few minutes, we sped up so we wouldn't arrive at the meeting point late.

"We okay?" Cate whispered.

"Yeah," I reassured her. "Just stay ready," I couldn't help adding. Cate had trained enough for combat that she would be useful, though a Caelum soldier would have years of battle-readiness under their belt.

As we cautiously crossed through a wall of brush, we found three men. Dressed in typical civilian clothes from our kingdoms, they put me at ease, as we expected soldiers under Graftonberg's command to be our enemy. When they stepped forward, moonlight glimmered off weaponry. Two held swords, and a third brandished a dagger.

"It's them," one of them said.

"Told you I saw someone crawl out that window," another replied.

"No one said you didn't."

I took advantage of their argument and lunged. He easily sidestepped me.

"Ho-ho. Come on, Prince. I've heard you're better than that. Or you can join us without all this ruckus. The king just wants to talk."

"Which king?" Cate asked, her knife held at the ready.

The shortest man stepped forward, lean but small, and I imagined he'd be the quickest of the three. "Don't even know what kingdom you're in?"

Valid question. As much as my father caused problems, I'd willingly return to Terra to speak to him.

"The false king?" Cate's voice rang steady. "Graftonberg?"

"She's making this treason charge easier and easier." The short guy smirked.

Cate held her ground. "You're from Caelum, right? I don't want to hurt you. The last thing I want is civil war."

"You're an enemy of the kingdom now. The king knew you'd fight for the crown if you ever came back. It's too late. It isn't yours anymore. Not after you left and gave it up. Just because you decide you want to live in your pretty little castle again, doesn't mean you can." The man's features twisted with bitterness, demonstrating how deeply the lies had rooted.

"What about the Embers? You don't need me?" Cate replied.

"We *can't* need you. Because no one trusts that you'll stick around. We rely on ourselves." The other two nodded in confirmation behind the first.

I started believing that trying to convince these men of anything would be fruitless, when I realized what Cate was doing. *Stalling*. Had she heard someone else here? Or did she believe our contacts would wonder why we hadn't arrived at the bridge and come looking for us?

She probably thought she needed to handle this herself because she knew I couldn't physically defend her. The shame of failure prickled across my skin, sinking deep into my chest. I vaguely *felt* the energy, though it was like I was still stuck in England, or worse. My body hadn't caught up. Yet even there, I'd been able to use at least some power in Cate's presence. I switched tactics, barely listening to their conversation, focusing on my connection with her. Electricity buzzed between us, yet it refused to sink in, bouncing and fizzing away like bubbles.

"That's enough." The biggest guy stepped in. A burn scar climbed up his neck, a sign of a prior run-in with an Ember, reminding me he was someone who'd once upon a time fought by my side. "Let's go. Both of you."

I lunged forward. My dagger clanged against another's sword, sliding along its length until it reached the hilt. The other man's weapon was no match for mine. I tried to step back, but he raised it again. It swung at alarming speed. I dove, rolling and reaching for an ankle to bring him down, but missed. He stood above me, steel hovering.

At that moment, five masked men crashed through the brush. I rolled away, using the distraction to create distance. Within minutes, our attackers were disarmed and being tied up by the new arrivals.

"Don't hurt them. Just bind their arms. Loop all of them together. They can walk home like that," one of the disguised men said. He'd lowered his voice, but it still sounded like Lucas. He leaned in and whispered something to Cate. My skin flared hot. *Definitely Lucas.*

We jogged in the opposite direction, leaving Graftonberg's men behind. When we came close to the bridge, we veered deeper into the forest to a tiny, one-room cabin. More like a shack. Nearby, a long rope tethered four horses.

"Inside," the Lucas-figure commanded.

We followed him in, and he shut the door behind us, just the three of us. A few candles burned in the space. He pulled the stocking mask off, revealing familiar blond hair. Instead of his usual jovial expression, his pained features brought me up short. He had a hollowness about him, reminding me of when I'd seen him captured by the Embers. He reached out, running his hands along Cate's shoulders. "Did they hurt you?"

"I'm fine. We're okay." She searched his face, seeing the same pain I'd detected. "We only just arrived through the portal. What's going on?"

"I'm sorry, Cate. I'm so sorry I couldn't hold the kingdom together for you." His voice raked gravely with anguish. "Graftonberg. He's turned… turned everyone against you. He hopes to see you hanged." Lucas scrubbed his face with his hands. "There have been so many deaths. Hangings. Anyone who disagrees with him. He claims it's for the kingdom's peace, but he's turned us into sheep. Only allowed to parrot what he wants said."

Cate wrapped her arms around him, holding tight, her cheek against his chest. "It's not your fault. It's mine. I'm the one who couldn't navigate the portal. I'm the one who had a panic attack. Now, Daniel can't use his power. Everyone wants me dead. The kingdom in ruins." She stepped away, tears careening down her cheeks.

Lucas pulled her in, stroking her hair. "I'm so glad you're alive." His voice broke. "We—we didn't know."

She sobbed against him while I looked on, helpless. I hadn't realized how much she'd been holding herself together for me. The old burn of jealousy was only a dim flame. Relief that Lucas was alive and well doused the fire. She obviously needed someone else to lean on. She'd been shielding me. Until now, I hadn't fully realized I barely felt her emotions. I'd been so used to them being dampened on the other side of the portal. Based on her tears, I should be drenched in her pain, yet I only detected mild sadness. It left me off-balance, wondering if I'd ever regain my powers.

Cate's tears began to dry, and she stepped away from Lucas. "Tell me about my family. Can I see them?"

The lines forming around Lucas's eyes spoke volumes. "There's more support for you in Terra. Alana is watching them like she promised, but you'd have to cross the entirety of Caelum to reach them. Plus, no one knows they're here. No one except Harlow and General Dixon, and a handful of Dixon's men. At least that part of the plan worked. If anyone tracks you, you'll lead them there."

"My dad? He's alright?"

"He's fine. The bullet didn't hit anything vital."

Cate gave him a watery smile. "Just like me. We're lucky Rowan doesn't have better aim."

"And Mya?" I asked. "How is she?"

A pause. "She's fine. We're communicating with letters. Your father won't let me see her."

I snorted. "Some things never change."

"Dev and Mya are leading the underground on your side. Our goal is to get you to him. Probably should have killed those men, then no one would know you two are back. I just…"

"Couldn't kill your own people," Cate finished for him. "You did the right thing. If there's a movement to put me back on the throne, the people will have to find out I'm here, eventually. I can't be in hiding forever."

Lucas's voice turned sharp. "We're not ready. Stay hidden for now. It's not safe."

He turned to a knapsack leaning against the rough-hewn wooden wall. "Disguises for you." He patted the pack. "Your cover is that you're a married couple traveling to meet Daniel's brother. No inns. Tim will escort you to safe locations. You can trust him. We can't spare anyone else."

"You're not going with us?" Cate's voice cracked.

"I'm already on thin ice. Graftonberg keeps me alive because I'm famous." A glimmer of the old Lucas appeared. "Too scandalous to off me. Plus, Molly would leave, and he loves the idea of having her. Doesn't know what to do with her, but it feeds his ego to have us in his pocket."

"And his ego runs the kingdom, I imagine," I said.

"Exactly." Lucas placed his hand on my arm. "I'm glad you're okay, and I hate to say it, but we're going to require your father's protection at some point. If we're ever going to defeat the Embers, we'll need him then, too. Because… I have a bad feeling about what Graftonberg has planned."

CHAPTER 33
CATE

Mere hours had passed, at least for me, since we'd escaped from England, all of us in a circle, hands interlocked. Everyone I loved together, brimming with hope. How had it gone so wrong?

I wanted to stay and hug Lucas, ask him a million questions, but he reminded us that our assailants from earlier had likely sounded the alarm. Soon, both kingdoms would know the disgraced, dethroned queen had returned.

Before he could rush out the door, I wrapped my arms around him one more time. "Be safe," I whispered. "I've just gotten you back, and now…" I couldn't finish. Would I even see him again? Leading the underground movement while serving Graftonberg treaded on dangerous ground.

He held tight, then broke away. "Always worried about everyone else, Princess. Or I should say, Queen. Take care of yourself. The rest of us are expendable."

Tears smarted, welling up again like a bubbling fountain. "You are *not*. I need you. Mya needs you. Hold on to that."

As we rode away, his haunted eyes burned through me. These had been dark days for Caelum. Days that turned into weeks and months where I'd been absent. The truth: I'd deserted him, and he'd lost hope. The most painful part? Graftonberg's claim rang true. I *did* abandon them. I knew the risks and took them anyway. And Lucas had been left with the consequences.

"Cate." Daniel's voice interrupted my thoughts. "Where'd you go? I've been calling your name."

More guilt. He'd stand with me forever. I had no doubt. And I'd led him into this mess. "I'm… processing."

"It's a lot. I was—" His breath whooshed out in an exhale. "I was surprised how much you've been holding inside."

I reached for his hand across our mounts, reminding me of the last battle and how he'd been my touchstone for creating rain. "You are my compass. My everything." I squeezed his fingers. "I'm sorry I didn't share. I've been confused. It's all happening so fast."

"And?" He could tell I wasn't telling him the whole truth.

"And the guilt." My nose tingled with another round of tears. "The guilt is crippling."

His sigh was audible. "Cate. We all agreed. If things had gone differently, you would have come home a hero."

"You all said yes because you knew I'd do it with or without you. I was too stubborn."

Daniel remained quiet, the only sound the *clip-clopping* of horses' hooves, matching my aching heartbeat. Tim rode ahead, out of earshot of our soft voices, his red hair gleaming in the moonlight. "Let's look at what you did accomplish. You saved four lives. Alana and your family. Rowan wouldn't have hesitated to kill them. Then what kind of guilt would you be living with? Put the blame at the feet of where it belongs —with Rowan and the Embers. We are at war. It's messy and there are horrible consequences no matter the choices."

At first, his words bounced off the armor I'd erected. Then, gradually, they hit their mark. What if I hadn't gone? I'd have to live with both my fathers' deaths. My mom's. Jack's. "We have to stop the madness. Get rid of the Embers once and for all." It was just so *hard*. A road filled with obstacles, with bitterness for Graftonberg adding to an already near-impossible situation.

Daniel's soft expression, visible in the moonlight, nearly broke me. "We keep looking forward, not back. Deal?"

I nodded, trying to convince myself as much as him. "Deal."

The next five days consisted of ferreting us into supporters' homes under the guise of a married couple visiting friends. We traveled in the dark, though not too late as to draw suspicion from anyone by arriving in the dead of the night. We stayed with all sorts: single men, alone in a stocked cabin in the woods, and with families with small children who'd wake sleepy-eyed in the morning to strangers. One boy reminded me so much of Jack that I choked back tears. He disappeared, only to return with a wildflower to cheer me. Bittersweet feelings settled as we rode away from this brave family, who risked their livelihood to support the dethroned queen.

The limited travel hours led to slow progress toward our ultimate goal of Dev's family's hunting cabin in the woods, about a two-hour ride from Terra Castle. When I quizzed Tim about whether there was any chance of meeting up with the Duke of Earlington or his daughter, Emily, he merely shrugged. "Dev said it was safe."

We'd learned my underground movement's four initiators and leaders were Lucas, Dev, General Dixon, and, to my surprise, Mya. She'd been instrumental from the Terran side, both with funding and discovering supporters. Her desire for peace and belief in the prophecy, coupled with her persuasive powers, proved instrumental in turning the tide of support in Terra. Apparently, her organizational skills rivaled the general's. Daniel initially scoffed at hearing this, yet a tiny smile played on his lips.

When we finally arrived at the Earlingtons' hunting cabin, it lay empty. White sheets covered the furniture. A thin coat of dust layered everything else, which, although we'd have to clean in the morning, helped convince me that the duke wouldn't come strolling in.

Tim packed up his horse the next day, his freckles standing out against his pale skin in the soft-yellow light of dawn. "There's some flour and a few other things in the pantry. Someone will be along later today. I have to head home. 'Sposed to be visiting my sick mother, but they only give you so much leave, ya know?" He dipped his chin in deference. "It's been an honor."

After he left, Daniel turned to me. "You know how to cook, Your Highness? Because I'm hungry."

"You know how to hunt, Prince?" I shot back.

He smirked. "Who's going to clean the carcass?"

Not me, obviously. I didn't bother answering and headed toward the tiny kitchen. Cupboards revealed flour, something unlabeled that resembled baking soda, salt, and a few glass jars of preserved vegetables. I could handle Bisquick, or even a simple recipe, but this? Hopefully, someone will arrive soon with more supplies. Although I *did* believe Daniel knew how to prepare game. But actual cooking? Hildy would shoo him out of the castle kitchen every chance she could. No wonder he couldn't bake. Now, to impress him.

Tink, Tink. Daniel tapped the top of the biscuit with his knife. I slid over the jar of preserves I'd found to cover the hockey puck texture.

"Be liberal with the jam." I sliced—more like sawed—into my piece.

"Too bad we ran out of cereal."

I slathered a chunk with unidentifiable red jelly. Lucas had brought us items to put in our packs when he'd met us at the portal in England. I'd saved one package to give back to him. It didn't matter how bad my cooking might taste or how long it took to reunite; that cereal would not be eaten.

Daniel stretched his legs out in front of him. "I guess there's nothing to do but wait. Hopefully, Dev doesn't take too long."

"I could think of worse things than being stuck out in the middle of nowhere with you," I crossed the room and sat on the arm of his chair, leaning close.

"Mmm. So could I." He grinned lazily and played with a strand of my hair. "Care to pass the time?" He leaned forward to kiss me, then pulled me into his lap.

I squawked at the sudden movement and laughed, then kissed him lightly on the nose. "Later, Romeo. Let's fix this place up first, shall we?"

After a day of cleaning, we both collapsed to sleep that night. The next day and the one after that led to more of the same, with Daniel providing rabbit for dinner, along with a green veggie someone had once preserved. The jar was suspiciously dusty, the contents barely edible. A modest library helped pass the hours, the only positive point I'd give the duke and duchess.

Dev strolled through the door as if he'd been caught in a time warp, acting like only minutes had passed since we arrived. "The rumors are incorrect. You two aren't ghosts at all. Even if you did return from the dead." He grinned and pulled me, then Daniel, in for hugs.

"Good to see you, too, Dev," I said.

"So, what's the plan?" Daniel immediately settled down to business, restless from our time on the couch.

"I had to wait until the excitement of your arrival died down. The chain passed the news, but so did those Caelum soldiers you guys let go. Now everyone in both kingdoms will be watching." Dev sat in a chair near the stone fireplace, and we followed. "Your father," he said to Daniel, "would like to see you."

"What does that mean?" I asked, tamping down my horror that King Dryden was in on the plan. "Does he know where we are?" Reflexively, I glanced at the door.

Dev hid a smile. "Dryden part of The Concealed underground? Ah, no. Definitely not. He does, however, miss Daniel. And… Graftonberg can't resist being a pompous blowhard, which the king has had to tolerate if he doesn't want all-out war. The Embers are relatively quiet, but we all know they're regrouping. Waiting for the right time."

I bit my thumbnail, nervous as the next steps unraveled.

Dev continued, "The king asked to see me when he heard the news. He wanted to confirm the rumor and figured you might come to me. I, of course, lied and told him I knew nothing. Not sure he believed me."

Daniel and I exchanged glances. With King Dryden's ability to read emotions, he essentially acted as a human lie detector. He absolutely knew Dev was lying.

"Were you followed?" I peered out a curtained window.

"No," he said quickly. Too quickly. "I had to come up with a plan to get away. And the king was watching. I found someone to help. Somebody the king would never suspect of being on Cate's side, so he wouldn't bother following me."

"*Is* this person on Cate's side?" Daniel asked.

Dev bit his lip. "They can be trusted. I promise." He stood. "I'll be right back. They're taking care of the horses."

"I don't like this," I said after he left.

He leaned back in his chair. "We trust Dev, so I'm sure whoever it is will be fine."

The door swung open. Standing in the entry, dressed in a raspberry-pink riding habit, her hair curled into an elaborate up-do, was my nemesis.

Emily.

CHAPTER 34
DANIEL

"Daniel!" Emily sauntered over, smugness stretching her pink lips. "I'm so happy you're okay." I stood out of politeness, and she moved in for a hug and cheek kiss. "I've missed you," she whispered in my ear, lingering there.

It took so long to detach, it felt like she had four arms. I caught Cate's eye from behind a mountain of blonde hair. If I weren't so uncomfortable in Emily's embrace, I might have laughed, because Cate's disgusted glare was absolutely priceless.

"And Cate." Emily gave the once-over, examining her well-worn traveling outfit meant to portray her as a humble farmer's wife. "I brought a trunk full of clothes. You may borrow if you wish. Although they're probably a bit small for you."

The curve of Emily's lips even seemed to annoy Dev, who stepped in. "Looks like I have some explaining to do. And you," he glared at his sister. "Behave."

Emily's false surprise sent my eyes rolling. *What's her angle?* The thing about Emily is that she's not dumb. She's quite aware of the act she's putting on, and I wasn't sure what she hoped to gain.

When we were all seated, Dev began his story, "Both my parents and King Dryden were on high alert, knowing I'd be the first to help you two. And Emily had a feeling I wanted to be out from under their thumb."

"I knew exactly what was happening," Emily cut in. "I concocted a tale that I couldn't bear to hear all the chatter about Daniel because I was too heartbroken to listen anymore, and that I wanted peace and quiet." She shot a triumphant look in my direction. "Don't get a big head. Anyway, I even got Mother to suggest the cabin, though she'd never let me come out here alone. She *made* Dev escort me."

"You sure they weren't playing you?" Cate asked, her voice laced with skepticism.

"Mother didn't suspect," Dev answered. "Emily is—"

"The favorite," Emily supplied. "She also hates gossip, and she didn't want those old stories about how the prince jilted me to circulate again."

"People said that?" I certainly didn't hear any of that. Of course, I'd spent most of my time in Caelum during those months.

"No," Dev responded automatically to his sister. "They were *afraid* that's what people were saying." He sent Emily a judgment-filled look. "Then you told everyone that *you* dumped Daniel. Remember?"

Emily's chin inched up. "No one was brave enough to say it in front of you, that's all."

"Fine. Whatever," Cate jumped in. I didn't need my power, which still hadn't shown itself, to understand her annoyance and impatience. "Can we get to the plan, Dev?" she said. "I hope it isn't me hiding in the woods until I'm old and gray with your sister. I have a kingdom to run."

"You don't," Emily replied smugly. "That's the problem."

Cate exhaled slowly. "Dev." She inclined her head. "The floor is yours."

He laced his fingers together. "I've brought a wagon of supplies with a couple of trusted men from the underground as guards. I'll drive to the castle with Daniel hidden in the back and sneak him in." Dev turned to me. "You need to reestablish yourself as the prince. Staying hidden won't help our cause. I don't trust that your father might turn over Cate to Graftonberg, at least yet. Lucas is working on a coup from the Caelum side. Once the people know she's alive and well, it'll be easier."

"If I'm hiding, how will they?" Cate asked.

"Once Lucas and the general have changed enough minds, at some point, you'll have to risk it and show yourself. First to the underground, then the citizens. Right now… it's too risky."

"I'm not leaving Cate," I said.

Dev raised his brows. "You will if that's what's best for her. Cowering together won't help. Your father is a hairsbreadth away from supporting her. He *really* doesn't like Graftonberg."

"Who does?" I muttered.

"Exactly. But the king will never support Cate if you two remain hidden together. He wants his son back."

I watched Cate, seated across the room, gaze fixed on the floor, the muscles in her neck working to swallow past the lump that must reside there.

Her eyes flicked up to mine and held. "You should go. I'll be fine. It won't be forever. Lucas will work his magic. Maybe then we can travel to Caelum together."

I found myself chewing the inside of my lip, an old nervous habit I'd broken years ago. "When do we leave?"

"When you're ready."

That's what I loved about Dev. He understood when to push and when to give space. We spent the next hour helping with Emily's trunks, enjoying the fresh food Hildy packed from the castle kitchens, and catching up, studiously avoiding heavy topics. The cupboards were now well stocked, so no one would be forced to eat Cate's terrible bread. Though, to be fair, she lacked butter, which even I knew would have made them better.

Finally, I pulled her aside out in the yard. "Are you sure about this?" The soft breeze blew a strand of hair into her eyes, and I tucked it behind her ear.

"Dev's right. Your people need you. And… I need you. Not just as the love of my life, but the power you'll gain if you have your father's support."

"What if I said I wanted to stay? That I'm not sure my heart will beat the same when I'm not with you?" The tips of my ears turned warm at my words. I still struggled to tell her all the things she deserves to hear.

Her fingertips reached up and covered my lips. We were so close, even with my stunted powers, I could feel the buzz of energy. I relished the sensation, tilting into her hand. She rose on her toes and kissed me. The longing to stay together pulsed between us as I drew her closer. Ever closer.

Love.

It held us no matter the distance. She had my heart in her hands, and hers in mine. And we wouldn't have it any other way.

After an uneventful trip in the back of Dev's wagon under a blanket, I hid for another few hours where he'd parked it behind bushes near the castle so we didn't arrive simultaneously. I finally snuck out and entered through the kitchen. Hildy's eyes lit up when she saw me, but she quickly recovered her usual stony face for appearances.

"'Bout time you showed up," she said.

I put a finger over my lips, snagged a tart cooling on the rack, and bounded up the rear stairs. Hildy wouldn't tell, but the half-dozen other kitchen staff would spread the news like wildfire. I quickly changed in my room, then headed to my father's office. The servants did a poor job of hiding their surprise with whispers behind hand-covered mouths. Many of them furtively, or not so furtively, glanced around for signs of Cate. *She's not here, everyone. It's just me.*

When I entered his office, King Dryden rose from his desk and walked past me, his expression neutral. I thought he might continue right out the door, but instead, he closed it, then wrapped his arms around me. I couldn't remember the last time he'd hugged me. I must have been small, maybe ten years old? So surprising, I almost forgot to hug him in return. He smelled of shaving soap and the wax he used to keep his well-trimmed beard in order. A smell I hadn't even realized I'd missed, clouded in nostalgia, sending me back to childhood sword lessons beneath the bake of the Terran summer sun.

Father broke our embrace and led me to the sitting area in his office. He usually kept the massive desk between us. This new arrangement made me feel more like an equal. "Are you unharmed?" he asked.

This question took me aback. I figured there would be the obligatory lecture, followed by pointed questions and derogatory remarks. "Yes," I said automatically, but I found myself continuing. "My powers have diminished." I paused, unsure I should share my weaknesses with him, but then I blurted, "almost completely."

With his encouragement, I unwound the entire story, how it'd felt like days had passed since my time in England, when in reality it had been months. How I'd come so close to killing Rowan. "I assume it's because my body is still catching up," I said, returning to the current issue. "Have you heard of this before?"

Father shook his head. "We'll investigate. Track down anyone who went through the unstable portals. I'll put my best men on it."

I swallowed the lump forming in my throat. He was treating me like a human… no, more than human. Like a son. Had he actually missed me this much? Was it the wake-up call he needed to reprioritize his life?

"And Catherine?" he asked.

This was the question I'd been waiting for. He hadn't buttered me up enough to disclose her location. "Somewhere safe. I came back to reestablish myself as the Terran prince, to help out where I can, and to represent this kingdom. I want to see Cate returned to the throne. In the past, you've promoted war and unrest with the Caelumites, but now that they have an unreasonable king, I was hoping you'd see it isn't in either of our kingdoms' interests to support Graftonberg. It's what the Embers want—fighting between us. And Graftonberg makes it pretty tough not to deteriorate into an all-out war."

"I'm no fan of Princess Catherine. She stole you from me. Bewitched you."

A ghost of a smile flickered at his fitting choice of words. "No stealing involved."

He stood and strode to the window, which overlooked the lawns. "I will think on it. I've been angry. Angry at her, mostly. She was supposed to be the savior. Bring power to our kingdom, and instead, we are only weaker." He turned back to me. "*You* are weaker."

"Funny, I feel stronger. You've always wanted me to follow your every direction, and now… I'm able to think for myself. She's made me believe in my own thoughts and opinions. Made me feel like I mattered."

"What for? I am king. Following my command isn't a choice." His hand sliced through the air in emphasis.

I no longer felt his anger. Didn't anticipate his every mood based on his emotions. That build-up to his next explosion didn't exist. It loosened my tongue and granted confidence.

"And what will happen when you aren't king one day?" I asked. "Shouldn't I learn to make my own decisions, so I'll be ready for the throne? You haven't taught me how to become the next ruler, nor is it a meaningful father-son relationship. You're the dictator, and I'm your subject. You rule through fear, and I'm not interested in that anymore. Do whatever you want to me, but understand, you've lost me once," I leveled him a sobering look, "don't let it happen again."

His fist clenched. The vein on his forehead bubbled. I couldn't feel the thick bitterness of anger, though from experience, I knew he fought through it. "Every interaction with you *is* a lesson," he ground out. "I teach by example, as my father did before me. If you do something wrong, I correct you."

"And what about when I do something right?" I said softly. "What about then?"

"You can assume if you aren't told differently, then I'm pleased with you."

I huffed a laugh. "Pleased?" This conversation was almost like an out-of-body experience. All the things I'd wanted to say, suddenly out in the open without the guilt of his hurt or anger pressured upon me. My power may never return, and if it didn't, I would not be sorry if this part were gone forever.

Suspecting the conversation had run its course, I changed the subject back to the real reason I'd come, "How can we overthrow Graftonberg and put Cate back on the throne?"

"That depends," he crossed his arms, "on whether I'd rather have the false king or the girl who has caused me nothing but problems."

CHAPTER 35
CATE

I flipped another page of my book, studiously ignoring Emily's third sigh in the last ten minutes. She hadn't thought through her plan. Daniel left mere hours after she arrived, leaving her alone. With me. After Daniel and I kissed, I caught her watching our goodbye from the window, one narrowed blue eye visible before the striped curtain dropped back into place. Daniel must have presumed my satisfied smile was because of him. It was… but I also enjoyed the voyeur getting what came to her.

"Is that what you plan to do all day?" Emily finally spoke.

I closed my book and gave her an amused expression. "It's your family's cabin. What do you normally do?"

She sighed for the fourth time. "I've actually never been here. Just Daddy and Dev."

I smirked at hearing the Duke of Earlington being called Daddy. "So, why'd you do it? Why help me? Is it a trap, and Graftonberg's soldiers will break the door down any minute?"

Her mouth pulled into a frown. "Of course not. I did it because… because everyone is *doing* something. Mya's running this underground movement—don't think I haven't figured that out—Dev is loyal to Daniel, and by proxy, helping you. I thought I'd find out what all the fuss was about."

I chuckled. "The fuss?"

One shoulder tilted up. "You know, 'The Concealed,' the one who came to save us all. I wanted to decide for myself."

I set the book on the end table. "And if you don't like what you find?"

"I guess you'll see, won't you?"

Her coy smile irritated like a fly that kept dive-bombing the family picnic. Even though Daniel left only an hour ago, I was already considering announcing my presence to the world just to get away from her. I picked up my book and resumed reading. It was a dry tome about survival in the wilderness with various tips, including how to skin a rabbit and forage for mushrooms, but it was still better than talking to her.

Several days passed, all the while spent trying to avoid Emily, only for her to annoy me anyway. Apparently, she'd never set foot in a kitchen, so I prepared the meals with the supplies she provided. Tempted to feed her the hockey puck biscuits, but then I'd have to eat them too. Over dinner one night, while twisting a lock of golden hair around a finger, unimpressed with my cooking skills, she asked, "Why do you care so much about the Terrans and Caelumites getting along? You're not even from here. What does it matter?"

Annoyance morphed into hurt. I debated whether to bother defending myself, then remembered I had to convince an entire kingdom I should be their queen. May as well start here. "I loved my family in America," I began, "but something always seemed missing. My life was like a set of too-tight shoes. I tried pair after pair, but they never felt right. Not until I came here. Has it been easy? No." I almost laughed at how far from "easy" going through that portal made things. "I can make a difference here. I can render the Embers' power useless." I took a breath. "Honestly? The weight of expectation to save everyone has been crushing. Yet, what if? What if the prophecy is true? The number of lives I would save from this horrible war…"

I pushed away my plate, no longer hungry. "So, why do I care? Because one person's life in this realm is as important as someone's in my world. The same is true for Terrans and Caelumites. We're all just people. With hopes and dreams, who want to fall in love, live happily ever after, and have the opportunity to pursue anything we wish."

Emily tapped her fork absently on her plate, seemingly unimpressed with my proclamation. "*You* get the opportunity to go after your dreams. You've had the chance to try on those shoes. Me? Along with most women here? Those dancing slippers had better fit because they're the only ones I'll ever get. Daniel was my chance to make a difference. To one day be queen. Now… I don't know what will happen to me. My father is talking about marrying me off to an ally." She looked up from her food, her eyes boring into mine. "He's twice my age. And doesn't believe in brushing his teeth. Says it feels weird." She made a face.

"Weird how?" I wanted to laugh, though once it sank in, I realized there wasn't anything funny about it.

She shrugged. "Seems like missing a few teeth would feel worse, but I wouldn't know."

A snag of guilt for judging her so harshly bit my conscience. I knew these stories of women being used as bargaining chips. Most of my world had lived through and moved past them, something we so easily took for granted. "Things are changing," I said. "Look at Mya. She's taking charge of the underground—demanding to be more involved in running the kingdom. And me… if my throne is returned, I'll continue to fight for women. You deserve boots, and high heels, and bunny slippers—whatever you want."

"Bunny slippers?"

"They're comfortable." I picked up my plate and brought it to the sink. "I'll take some food to the guards. Be right back." I sliced sandwiches in half, wrapped them in parchment paper, then stepped out the kitchen door toward the small barn on the property. One of the men was usually in there, and if not, they'd discover the meal soon enough.

A horse whinnied, followed by nervous hooves tattering the wood floor. A river of goosebumps rose down the back of my neck. Ever since I'd returned from the portal, I'd been more aware of the energy. As if being without made it much more noticeable. And now… it felt wrong. Broken.

Instead of heading to the entrance, I crept to a small rectangular side window. As I grew closer, horror sliced through me. Red streaked the glass, as if a bloody hand had brushed up against it. The sandwiches dropped into the soft grass, abandoned.

Everything slowed—my breathing, my steps, my thoughts—all except my heart. It pounded in my ears, urging me forward to see what deep down I already knew.

I peeked through the window. Both guards lay on the floor. Red blood everywhere—staining the hay, darkening the floorboards, streaking across the stalls. Bile gorged my throat. The memories, the nightmares, roared to life. I leaned against the rough barn wall, nearly collapsing.

Emily. I had to reach her. The front door of the cabin banged shut. I'd left her in the kitchen, at the rear of the small house. I gauged the distance. Too far.

I could leave her.

Grab a horse and save myself.

The decision came in an instant. I'd never live with the guilt. I sprinted toward the kitchen and burst through the back door.

A swarthy man held Emily, her arm wrenched behind her back. The steel of a knife gleamed at her throat. Flashbacks of Rowan. My father. The dagger against Jack's neck.

"No!" I screamed, snatched up the blade still lying on the counter next to the bread, and launched toward them both.

My knife connected with the man's shoulder. He'd been unprepared for the attack, with his grip focused on Emily. He shoved her away, and she tumbled to the floor, knocking hard against a cabinet. His clothes were indistinct, though not the typical coarse brown cloth of the Embers. Three-day-old dark stubble added to the scruffiness.

"You Caelum?" I sidestepped closer to the door, keeping laser-focused on his movements. "We're supposed to be on the same side. Can we talk?"

"Aren't you talkin' now?" He spoke in the accent I'd come to recognize as Northern Caelumites.

"I want what's best for our kingdom. Graftonberg has turned everyone against me for power." I edged closer to the door while Emily slowly stood. "What about the Embers? Might be hard to get rid of them without me."

"The king has a plan. Besides, I need the money, and he's offering."

"A ransom?" I prayed the stipulations were to keep me alive.

"A pretty little pot. So, no offense, Your Highness, but I'm taking you in."

I bolted toward the door, shouting, "Run!" hoping Emily was right behind me. I burst through, only to find two more of them.

"Cate!" Emily cried.

I glanced backward. The first man had Emily's arm in a tight grip, leaving me with no option but to abandon her. She wasn't their target —all I could hope was that they would let her go. Out of the corner of my eye, the barn flicked into view. The bloody guards. What if they did the same to me? I lurched left, but one of them was too fast. He had me in a chokehold before I could take another step.

I was caught.

CHAPTER 36
DANIEL

A few days after my talk with Father, I sat at my desk in my suite, rifling through papers from the underground. Mya handed me more documents. "This is who I have so far."

Three pages filled with lists of names offering to support Cate. Numbers nestled next to some, which I assumed were pledged funds. Notes in the margins, scrawled in Mya's neat script, such as *bring back more of Hildy's tarts* and *his daughter loves archery*. Others were more practical, like *distributor* or *runner*. The names surmised the entire underground: a safe place to stay, a printer to help us set the record straight, or those with the means to back our cause.

Stars denoted a more ominous group willing to invade Caelum to upend the monarchy for Cate. This was dangerous territory, and I didn't want to pursue it. For one, Cate would hate it. Too hazardous, and would completely abandon her goal for peace. Two, power was difficult to relinquish once won. Would these Terrans give back what they took and put Cate on the throne, or would it be an excuse to start an invasion? Or a better question: would my father return the crown to her?

"Well?" Mya said, chewing her lip. "It's not much. But I had to do something. Not just for Cate. For you, too. I couldn't let the entire kingdom hate you."

I looked up at my baby sister, hovering next to me, a silk-slippered foot nervously shifting, waiting for my answer.

"I know it's not enough," she blurted, taking my silence as my answer.

"Enough?" She'd done this on her own, and I couldn't be prouder. The transformation from ballroom princess to commander of an underground unit was nothing less than incredible. "It's amazing. All these people? *You* are amazing."

A tiny smile played on her lips. "I kinda started a newspaper here in Caelum by accident, too. Father doesn't know."

He banned them around ten years back, something I hadn't thought much of until a few months ago, when I found out Caelum didn't have such restrictions.

"I thought publishing our story would be the easiest way for people to see it. So, I tracked down the printing machines—they were hard to find, and many weren't working—but I did it. Once we started distributing flyers, people wanted more. They craved news. Even if it was just which crops were growing best in the next town over." She ducked her head. "It kind of took a life of its own."

"I'm so proud of you. Father really doesn't know?"

She gave a sardonic laugh. "He knows about a secret newspaper but can't seem to catch who's printing it. Helps when someone from the castle knows to tip our guys when there's a raid. I've collected enough friends here that even if I don't get wind of it, someone else always does."

I shook my head in disbelief. "He thinks you're just planning parties? No idea his daughter is defying him?"

"Nope. When you can't open your eyes to see what's underneath a person's skin, then you'll never see what's inside."

A strum of guilt played through my gut. Is that what I'd done? She'd proven herself more than capable if given the chance. No one ever bothered to give it to her before.

A knock at the door.

"Got it," Mya said, already standing.

Dev stood in the hall, his collar undone, a dark smear of something on his shirt. "Isn't it time to dress for dinner?" I asked, glancing at the silver clock on the wall. When he strode into the room, his mouth held a thin line, eyes red-rimmed, halting my jovial expression. "What's wrong?"

"They're gone. Cate and Emily."

"What do you mean, gone?" I barked. His Adam's apple bobbed with a thick swallow. "Gone where?" Dev had been so careful. No one had seen us. Had they? "Did they wander off and get lost in the woods or something?" Cate was known to lose her sense of direction a time or two.

"I went to check on them and bring them more supplies. The guards," his gaze hit the floor, "I found them dead in the barn. There was blood in the kitchen, too."

No. This can't be happening. "Was it Embers or Graftonberg's men?"

"No sign of fire," Dev said.

"The underground reported something to me they'd discovered. I —I wasn't sure how to say it." Mya bit her lip.

"Tell me. Now." My words came out too sharp, but I couldn't force myself to care.

"I only just found out. Graftonberg has put a price on Cate's head. It's enough to make anyone in either kingdom as rich as a duke."

"Last I heard, Caelum was having money problems."

No one knew the answer.

Whether or not Graftonberg had the funds, he was still offering. "What are the stipulations? They'll take her to Caelum Castle, and then we fight to get her back. Right?"

"That's just it. My sources say…" She looked between Dev and me, realizing this applied to Emily as well. "They get the money either way. Dead or alive."

CHAPTER 37
CATE

"Let me go!" I fought against the hard chest at my back and fingers digging into my biceps. There were four of them in all. One was tying Emily up, each knot easing my fears that her fate wouldn't be the same as the guards in the barn. Why tie us up just to slaughter us? Following her fate, my arms were bound and ankles secure. They took turns carrying Emily and me into the woods where a wagon waited, then tossed us in the back, covering us with a blanket, including our faces.

"You okay?" I whispered once the wagon's rhythmic movement started.

"Wait until my father hears about this," Emily hissed.

If the circumstances were better, I might have laughed. She was fine. I pictured the duke's spluttering face at his baby being captured to de-escalate my panic. I strongly disliked the man, and his wife was even worse, but if he helped in our rescue? I'd give him a medal.

"We have to escape before we reach the castle." I tested my bonds. My wrists didn't move at all. If Graftonberg was willing to pay a huge ransom, his intentions included something worse than letting me hang out in my old room. He had bigger plans, and if I were to guess, those plans involved elimination. Now that he was king, he wouldn't let anyone strip him of that power. Leaving me alive would always be a risk. I could hardly believe he once called my father a friend. It felt like weeks since I'd talked with him in the library. He'd almost been tolerable. It reminded me that even a villain was unlikely to be wholly evil or good. My thoughts drifted to the blood in the barn, and that sick feeling resurfaced. "Emily, are you listening? We have to escape."

"I'm trying to stay calm, Catherine. Unlike *someone*. I wouldn't have taken you for a panicker."

Every ounce of the brief goodwill I'd shared with her evaporated. Now I had two reasons to find my way out of this wagon: getting away from Emily and saving my own life. "You do realize they'll kill me if we make it to the castle."

The filtered light through the wool blanket allowed a peek at her skeptical expression. "Not if the people get wind of it. They might be mad at you for leaving, but most are superstitious enough not to want The Concealed killed off. After all, they know your power. This will blow over, and you'll be on the throne again. Far as I'm concerned, this speeds up the process."

"That's what Graftonberg is afraid of. If he's smart..." my stomach swooped, "we'll never make it that far. They'll kill us in the woods before anyone finds out." The more I thought about it, the more I believed this made the most sense. My breathing bottomed out. My thoughts started to turn over themselves until they tumbled out of control.

It was Emily's annoying comment that pulled me out of it, "Speak for yourself." She sniffed. "There's no reason to kill *me*. If they're smart, they'll wait for a ransom from my father, then get paid twice."

"So, you're not going to help me escape?"

"Out in the middle of nowhere? My odds are better right here." She grimaced as we drove over a pothole, our heads knocking against the bed of the wooden cart.

She hadn't seen the splattered, smeared blood, way more than necessary for a simple kill. These men couldn't be trusted. Though maybe she was right. Maybe I was the only one who should be worried. If I died, Daniel would be free, and she'd be able to live out her dream of being queen. Surely, she wasn't that callous?

Emily took that moment to turn away from me, scooting on the dusty floor until she faced the opposite wall. "I'm going to get some sleep. Good luck with your escape plan."

If she wasn't that heartless, she sure did a great imitation.

Days passed. Hunger gnawed at my belly. The kind that toyed with thoughts and played with emotions in a way that only someone who'd always had food on the table can experience. I cursed my weakness and reminded myself over and over that millions of people experienced worse daily. The men would pull the blanket back a few times for gulps of water and a few bites of bread, then would cover our faces, the scratchy wool now feeling like a death shroud. They hadn't let us out of the wagon, leaving us to soil ourselves, the smell of our own bodies trapped beneath the fabric.

Emily cried softly next to me. I'd tried to convince her to work on each other's bonds, yet she had no appetite for escape, firmly in denial, insisting things would improve once we arrived at the castle. I started to wonder if we were going there at all.

Something hard poked me in the flank—a stick or some sort of spear. "You alive in there?" one man asked. I'd grown accustomed to the sound of their voices, sometimes as a steady hum of conversation, the occasional guffaw of laughter while they ate around a campfire, the smell of roasting meat causing my belly to ache, or the sharp tang when they argued, which was more often than not.

I chose not to answer, hoping for the sweet fresh air that wafted in when they pulled the blanket away.

"Check on her," someone else said. "'Bout time for the muzzle, anyway. May as well put it on."

"What if she's dead?" The movement of the wagon stopped with a lurch.

"Better hope she's not."

Feet scuffled. "We didn't sign up for this to be babysitters. He changed that order after we took the job."

"Stop complainin'. Now you've got one less death on your conscience."

Another snorted. "He doesn't have one."

Despite the humidity under the blanket, gooseflesh rose at their prior intent to kill on sight rather than turn me in to Graftonberg. Which made me wonder. Had the baron gained the conscience that apparently these men lacked?

Cool, fresh air kissed my cheeks, so good it brought back memories of that first breeze at the Oregon coast when I'd pull open the car door after the winding ride from Portland. I gulped the air, my eyes watering from both tears of relief and the contrast with the stale wool blanket.

"She's alive. Lookin' at me."

His glare showed annoyance at my lack of answer, forcing him to stop our progress. I didn't much care.

Emily shifted beside me. "Has anyone contacted my father?"

The man's dark stubble had grown into a patchy beard, which twitched. "Why'd we keep her again?"

"She'll be worth something. Look at that dress." The youngest one said, still on his horse.

Emily's outfit had been "casual wear" at the cabin, yet the intricate stitching and tailoring couldn't be replicated without money. Even in its wilted form, she exuded more royalty than I probably ever would. I'd be more comfortable in athleisure than in gowns until the day I die. One didn't forget how great moisture-wicking spandex and sneakers could feel.

He thrust a waterskin into my mouth, and I choked on the cool liquid that sloshed down the wrong pipe. When I coughed, he switched to Emily.

"Please?" I asked through chapped lips, wanting just a few sips more. Okay, if given the chance, I would have gulped down the whole thing.

Instead of water, he shoved a cloth that smelled and tasted of sweat into my mouth, pushing aside my tongue, then tied another around my head to hold it steady. I gagged at the pressure on the back of my throat, grunting and shaking. He rounded the wagon to properly gag

Emily, too. *Still glad you wouldn't try to escape, Emily?* I'd read that survival book. Surely, I could find some mushrooms. Maybe even berries.

The bearded man shot me a warning glance. "We're going through town. Keep it quiet. I have no problem killing your friend as punishment."

His companions already mentioned he had no conscience. Emily managed to elbow me in warning. I turned from them, mind spinning. Maybe she was right. Our best chance was the castle and Graftonberg. At least we'd be away from these thugs. A tear slid down my cheek as the blanket pressed over my face again.

Suffocating. I was suffocating. The gag in my mouth, the thick wool, the girl next to me who wouldn't help. *How many people are murdered by asphyxiation in the U.S. each year?* The statistic raced through my head. *Ninety-four.* But I wouldn't be counted in that number, would I? My once-soothing statistics had run stale. All those numbers applied to another world. Another time.

It wasn't long before the sounds of town filtered over the creaking wagon wheels and through the blanket. A laughing child. More horses' hooves, voices crescendoing and fading away as they moved past. What would happen if I struggled? They'd already tied me to the bars, making it impossible to sit up. If I wiggled and squirmed and moaned through the gag, would they think me an animal being transported to the next farm or a person? Would anyone notice? My captors surely would. Emily's form next to me was a constant reminder. As much as I didn't like her, she didn't deserve to die. Another death on my conscience. I wouldn't survive it.

So, I stayed silent and listened to the town, wondering if it was Bandit's Hole, and picturing the last time I'd been there with Daniel. Date night on our way to Terra, complete with a candlelit dinner. Things had been dire: Lucas, my father, and Mya all captured by the Embers. It had been a final reprieve before King Dryden's betrayal, my father's death, and Rowan's kidnapping of my family. A tiny, cherished moment in time, and I clung to it, staving off threatening tears. What I wouldn't give to be sitting in that inn's restaurant with Daniel. To forget our problems for a few hours.

The wagon's rocking and exhaustion took over, and I fell into a restless sleep, with dreams of blood, rain washing it pink until it pooled crimson again. When I woke, darkness had settled, light no longer filtering through the blanket. The motion had stopped. No one came for what felt like hours, until finally, the cover lifted. All four men hovered over us. We were in a barn somewhere, several small lanterns now lighting the space.

"Don't struggle." The bearded man's bushy brows lowered. "Unless you want someone to get hurt." His head jerked toward Emily, dark eyes glittering in the light.

This time, I didn't listen. I squirmed and screamed through the rags stuffed down my throat. All four descended, gripping me with granite holds. They lifted me from the cart, bent me in half, and shoved my body into a wooden crate. For good measure, they tossed the putrid wool blanket on top to muffle the sound. The hammering of nails sealing the lid echoed, sending chills shuddering along my spine. Mob movies played in my mind like a flickering reel in black and white—a box thrown into the river, slowly sinking, bubbles rising to the surface as it vanished into the depths. But why bring me all this way just to get rid of me here?

The coffin-like crate lurched to the side, jamming my shoulder against the rough boards. They'd lifted it, the box swaying and jostling. As soon as I sensed we were far enough from Emily, I started kicking and moaning through my gag, hoping someone would hear and realize there was a person inside. Honestly, I wasn't sure if Emily was right behind me in another container, but our situation was so desperate that I was willing to risk it. The image of the wood sinking underwater, with only the *glug-glug* of bubbles to show I'd ever been there, pushed me to kick harder. If I tilted my hips in the cramped space and pulled my knees to my chest, I could rock the crate, even with my ankles tied.

The swooping sensation of falling jolted my stomach before I crashed to the ground with a *bang*. I ignored the reverberating pain, kicked again, and pressed with my head against the blanket-covered lid, hoping it had come loose. It held.

A low growl of frustration sounded through the planks, sending shivers sliding across my forearms. "You *will not* do that again," he hissed in a low voice. "Or I will smash this box with you inside into so many pieces it won't be fit for kindling. Then I'll do the same to your friend. You're about to have new jailers, and you'll never have to see me again if you behave. Got it?"

I didn't doubt him. He'd wanted me dead three days ago. I responded with silence, the gag still in place. They lifted the box, like pallbearers carrying me to my grave.

Or to the next ring of hell.

The crate tipped, my abs screaming to hold myself to prevent my neck from being bent in two. The cadence continued until down, down, down, we went, each step jabbing my spine. Once we reached one landing, another set of stairs appeared. And another. Finally, we leveled out. The clang of metal. A squeal of a door. A few steps, then shooting pain as they dropped me onto a hard surface.

Someone used a crowbar to pry the lid open, and I stared at Roy's doughy features. Graftonberg's weaselly son gave me the heebies in the best of times. I involuntarily recoiled at his amused perusal. The bearded man removed my gag, breath rushing through my lungs. I'd like to spit at Roy, but my saliva had dried hours ago. I settled for glaring daggers.

Emily was deposited next to me while Roy watched, arms folded. One of my captors shook hands with Roy before filing out of the space. Stone walls surrounded me. Metal bars. Caelum guards avoided my pleading stare. These were my new jailers.

CHAPTER 38
LUCAS

It had spread like dandelion seeds in the wind. A soft whisper, then roots forming an incestuous weed, impossible to extricate. Graftonberg had captured Cate and charged her with treason. He'd laid the groundwork by inflating her abandonment of the kingdom into betrayal, then fanned the flames, claiming she returned with a plot to dethrone him by any means necessary. Enough rumors of the underground existed that the story hadn't been that far-fetched. She supposedly planned a coup, and now everyone, especially me, was under even tighter surveillance, if that was possible. She was locked in the castle dungeon, yet I couldn't get any closer than Molly's barn without sounding an alarm. The ever-pressing ache in my chest grew. She would think I abandoned her.

I had to find a way to break her out. If only I knew who to trust. Even the underground had gone dark.

A carriage rolled down the drive, a purple fleur-de-lis insignia on the door. *Dame Hemlock.* She'd kept her cards close that night after the party when she'd informed me of the coronation, yet something told me she could be trusted. She had money. A way into the castle. But I was forgetting one important thing: her age. She wouldn't be able to fight off a guard if it came to that. My need for an ally outweighed my reservations.

I knocked on her door an hour later, after discreetly following the carriage by horse. Ivy climbed the massive glass windows and stone walls of the expansive home. The residence was one of the oldest in Caelum, and I'd never had a chance to visit. Generations of Hemlocks had tended to these lands, becoming wealthy off the rich soil, then later from the dame's great-grandfather's inventions, including a fleet of ships and half the electricity in Caelum from power sourced from the river rushing through their property.

Arriving on the front step probably wasn't the best for a covert mission, but sneaking in didn't make me appear any more innocent. At least it was mid-afternoon rather than the middle of the night. I'd simply pretend this was a social call.

"May I help you?" a thin man answered, dressed as one would expect a servant in a fancy house like this—wearing a tunic-style uniform adorned with braided cord—and he was so tall he nearly brushed the doorframe. I wasn't short myself and wondered if he had giant blood. They were the stuff of fairytales, of course, but I liked to believe they were real.

"Yes?" The man's bushy brows grew together.

Lost in my own thoughts, I hadn't realized I'd been staring. "Dame Hemlock? I was hoping to meet her for tea? I'm Sir Lucas Bradbury." It might be a bit presumptuous to include tea, but it was that time of day, and my stomach had relentlessly growled on the way here. My fourteen-hour shift with a measly small sandwich at break left an empty cavern in my belly.

The room off the entry included spindly legged, stuffy brocade chairs and a dizzying wallpaper pattern. It didn't take long before the tall man ushered me into another space. My shoulders relaxed at the contrast between the two rooms. The sitting area where I'd originally waited was clearly for people who hadn't passed muster. This room, however, matched Dame Hemlock's personality. Still fastidious, the seating was oversized, a soft palate of welcoming blue, a tea tray piled with scones, cakes, and sandwiches.

"Leave us," she commanded. "And please close the door, Adams." She gave a meaningful look over her wire-rimmed glasses at the steward, then turned her gray eyes onto me.

"It's simple enough to deduce why you are here. I have too many servants to trust them all. I'll have to come up with a story for Adams to spread below to the staff." Her tone more than hinted at disapproval.

She must have noticed me eyeing the tea tray. "Maybe I'm mistaken. My cook is renowned, and perhaps you just wanted my hospitality and to keep a little old lady company." Her hand fluttered. "Go on. It'll be suspicious if no one eats."

The guilt at wanting to fill my stomach while Cate sat in a dungeon sank in at the same moment my teeth dug into an egg and cress sandwich. I chewed, hardly noticing the pop of mustard seeds and creamy egg. And… what was that spice? Okay. Yes, I did notice. And it was delicious. Those novels that always described food as becoming tasteless in times of stress remained a mystery.

"Who can you trust?" she asked after I'd swallowed.

No one was my first thought. I sent her a charming grin. "You, of course." I snuck the rest of the sandwich into my mouth and reached for a pink cake striped with white frosting. Perhaps a bit of sugar would untangle my thoughts. I hadn't the slightest idea how we'd go about breaking Cate out of jail. I'd followed the dame to her house in desperation without clear foresight.

"We need more than that. We need someone on the inside. Someone Graftonberg trusts."

I searched my memory. "The guards rotate. Assignments aren't posted for the dungeon until the same day. There's General Dixon, of course. But I don't think he qualifies. The king sent him to the border for security."

"Hmmm. Yes. I had heard that. What about Brandon Hanson?"

He'd been a prominent landowner for years, with close access to Graftonberg. An ally of King Aldridge, I'd been surprised when he aligned with the baron even before he'd become king. I'd wondered where his allegiance lay, though I hadn't seen any signs of defection. Instead of answering, I volleyed back, "What about him?"

"That young man practically grew up in this house, did you know that?" She didn't wait for me to answer, but it was news to me. "His late mother and I were the best of friends. She'd spend summers here with Brandon to be closer to the city."

Another sandwich slid down, this one tastier than the last. Not that I noticed. "Let's invite him to tea," I said between swallows. I still had questions about whether we could truly use Hanson or anyone close to Graftonberg. He'd be risking more than just his lands. He'd be risking hanging from the gallows, so might the dame.

"Ma'am? Can I ask you a question?" I pressed on without waiting for an answer. "I realize that I'm the one who showed up at your doorstep asking for help, but I'm wondering, why would you give it to me?"

"You notice anything different about me, young man?"

I noticed quite a lot, her no-nonsense attitude. Her sharp tongue. That I was faintly frightened of an old lady. None of these likely the answer. "How do you mean?"

"I am both a woman and dark-skinned." Her gray eyes leveled a stare. "I didn't get where I am today, quadrupling my family's assets since I've taken the helm, without effort and ingenuity. You've met Graftonberg. And his son. How long do you think it will take before they trump up a charge to steal my power and wealth?" She stood. "I'm with the queen. I'd much rather work with someone than against them. Enough said."

Fortune provided the same shift the next day, a midnight to two in the afternoon, a painful fourteen hours standing alert at the outskirts of the castle. The lack of sleep left me irritable, yet a spring still bounced in my step at the thought of coming up with a plan for Cate. No one knew Graftonberg's timeline, but he wouldn't hold her there forever. As soon as he decided enough people had turned against her, she would be sacrificed to preserve his power.

Adams, the giant of a steward, greeted me, and this time led me to Dame Hemlock's comfortable sitting room. Brandon Hanson, a bland man with pale skin that matched his pale hair, was already seated inside. We exchanged pleasantries until a silence fell over the space. I slathered jam and clotted cream onto a scone and waited for the dame to make the first move in this game of chess.

"I trust you won't turn in your auntie, Brandon," she finally said.

His eyes darted around the room. "Turn in to who?"

"The baron, of course." She smiled sweetly.

His mouth was a thin line as he set down his teacup. "The king, you mean."

"I believe I had his title quite correct. Now," she sat up straighter, "other than your mother, I'm the one who knows you better than anyone in this world."

A nervous chuckle escaped him. "My wife might disagree."

"Ah, but I'm right. I know the boy you used to be before the man you've become. Loyal. Willing to stick up for others. Brave." She leveled what I now recognized as her signature stare over her glasses at that last word. "Tell me about Graftonberg and how you've managed to stay in his inner circle. Especially with morals like yours."

He took a deep breath. "It started with support of Aldridge. He'd chosen Graftonberg, for unknown reasons, I might add. I wanted to understand what the king had seen."

I interrupted, "Aldridge? He told me before…" my voice faltered, "before he died, that he didn't believe Graftonberg would come save him if things went poorly at the peace treaty. He hoped to prevent Cate from coming. His main goal for her was to ascend the throne safely, out of the hands of the Embers."

"So, his trust was actually in Graftonberg's cowardice?" Hanson asked.

"Exactly."

"That does make more sense. At any rate, it all sort of snowballed. I thought I'd be Catherine's eyes and ears, then he became more and more ruthless to anyone who crossed him. I didn't—didn't know how to get out from under his thumb." He bit his lip. "You're wrong about something, though. I'm still the same boy—the same man. I've been waiting for the right opportunity. And…" he looked between us, "I'm guessing it's arrived?"

"He trusts you?" I asked, leaning forward.

"He only truly believes in Roy, though I'm ashamed to say I've given him no reason not to."

"Here's what we're going to do," I said. "First, we have to start planting the seeds of doubt. Give him false reports that his soldiers are turning against him."

He nodded. "I can do that."

"Good. Because after that, things will start to be tricky."

CHAPTER 39
DANIEL

Mya handed me a letter from Lucas and sat on the couch next to me. "We can stop searching for them."

I scanned the words, glossing over the lovey-dovey parts to my sister until I found that Cate and Emily were locked in the Caelum Castle dungeons for treason. "Does Dev know?"

"Know what?" Dev strode into the yellow sitting room.

I handed him the paper and watched his emotions change as he read it. "How can Emily be held for treason? She's Terran."

"He's probably calling her an accomplice of Cate. Claiming she's helping overthrow Graftonberg," I said.

Dev sank into the chaise. "How serious is this? They wouldn't dare hang her, right? It would start a war."

"A war Graftonberg can't afford to start, so I'm not sure of his motive." Though with someone as power crazy as the baron, he might not need another reason.

Mya turned up her nose. "I say we use his stupidity to our advantage. Let's stir the hornet's nest and tell Father and the duke. We'll demand that Emily be released, along with Cate."

I'd once explored the dungeons when I lived there. The smell of dank mildew, wine, and damp stone floors floated in my memory like yesterday. And now Cate was being held there. How had it come to this?

"I'm sorry, mate," Dev slumped. "I've been focusing on Emily—it's hard not to worry about her. I can't imagine she'll fare well in jail, but we have to focus on Cate. I wouldn't be alive if it weren't for her." He scraped his forehead with his palm, an unusual sign of despair from Dev. "If we can't save her, I'm afraid we're all doomed."

The prophecy was vague, but surely it didn't imply that Cate would become a martyr. She's not meant to die hanging from a rope. She couldn't be. Anger flared. Anger at Rowan and the portal. At the citizens for believing their savior abandoned them. And at Graftonberg. For his insatiable desire for power. "We have to get her out," I said more to myself than them.

Mya's hand was on my arm. I hadn't noticed until I saw it there, grip tightening. "Let's be strategic. We tell Father and Dev's dad. Convince them that a peace envoy would be best. We'll demand Graftonberg hand over both Cate and Emily, warning him there will be war if he doesn't. We already know the Caelum army is struggling to retain soldiers. He won't have much choice. We just have to make it there before he…"

She trailed off, unwilling to say what we were all thinking.

"Who's going?" I ask. "Me, of course."

Her attention bounced between us. "All three of us. I can be convincing."

Dev still wasn't aware of her specialized power of persuasion. One more thing to feel guilty about, and wasting time explaining wouldn't help. The fewer people who knew, the better.

"I'll find Father. We'll meet in his office in fifteen." Mya started for the door.

A sinking reminder of my new reality sprouted. Before she crossed the threshold, I blurted, "I still don't have my powers. Since the portal…" Fear choked the rest of my words out. Cate could be executed at any moment, and I didn't know how to help her. I *couldn't* help her. "We need you. Convince Father. Do whatever you have to do." My voice echoed my desperation. Somehow, we had to make this plan work.

Two hours later, the three of us were on the road with ten trusted soldiers, all from the underground. We left a scared, angry Duke of Earlington behind, who demanded military retaliation for his daughter. My father, for once, kept a cool head. Or Mya's persuasiveness convinced him not to fly off the handle. It helped he wasn't fond of Cate. He liked Emily, though not enough to start a war over. Come to think of it, he wouldn't start one for his own daughter when Mya was kidnapped by the Embers.

I'd barely had time to reunite with Mother, and now I was putting myself in peril again. She held herself together, but even without sensing her emotions, I knew she broke inside.

Overall, the underground in Terra supported Cate. They wanted her back on the throne, so any discussion of treason against Graftonberg led to support rather than anger. Once we crossed into Caelum territory, according to Lucas, the story would change.

"Think your father is going to raise an army of his own?" I asked Dev.

He huffed a sarcastic laugh. "Wouldn't put it past him. He'd be on the road with us if we hadn't lied and told him we were leaving tomorrow."

Mya and I exchanged wry glances. No one wanted a three-plus day ride with the duke. The only one who might be more annoying was his wife. Funny enough, I hadn't felt that way until meeting Cate. The duchess's condescending remarks toward Cate allowed me to see her in a different light. Mya, however, had always seen right through the Earlingtons, Dev the obvious exception.

We rode hard, exchanging horses several times, and listened for any news of Cate, which was very little—hushed whispers of how she planned to overthrow the king. Some would turn their eyes away, quietly supporting their queen, yet not brave enough to speak up. Others gleefully passed the gossip, never accepting a woman as their leader, or perhaps believing the prophecy had been too good to be true. Some felt betrayed by her absence—those who yearned for the Embers to be gone once and for all.

I kept a low profile, focusing on avoiding recognition, though a few times I was met with inevitable jeers. Cate and I had thought we'd been close to peace between the two kingdoms, and in a few short months, a single man, Graftonberg, tore apart everything we'd accomplished, seeking doubt and hate. Trust took time to build. Peace was a project Cate and I were passionate about, pouring the foundation, molding the bricks, stacking them higher and higher each day. Yet, with one swoop, it'd had all been toppled. The animosity toward Terrans was greater than I'd seen in my lifetime.

We finally arrived at Caelum Castle, the guards halting us for nearly an hour before letting us through. I spotted Lucas near the gate. Stoic, standing erect on duty, unable to help. He'd descended from trusted confidant and agent for his kingdom to the lowest of duties. It was almost as if Graftonberg kept him here, at the entrance, as a trophy, an emblem of his power. For me, the castle had been nearly a second home, living here for over two months. I used to have my own room for heaven's sake. Being treated as anything but a welcome guest was strange and left me uneasy.

Roy met us in the courtyard. His thinning blond hair ruffled in the breeze, face sour, not bothering to attempt a diplomatic smile. "Prince. What brings you here?"

"I'm quite certain you know why I've come. We'd like to speak to your father."

He adjusted the cuffs of his too-tight jacket, his gold rings glittering in the sun. I'd never liked the man. Smarmy, a ladder climber who'd step on anyone to reach the top. And Cate hated him. Toward me, I'd always detected notes of smugness mixed with pure hatred. Though currently, I felt nothing at all. I'd be relying on Mya for her dissection of the mood.

Mya spoke up, "We are the heirs to the Terran crown and a duke's son. You'd best let us in and treat us with respect unless you want an even greater incident on your hands."

"I'm sorry." Roy's mouth curved into a falsely coy smile. "I don't believe we've been introduced. You were in an Ember prison last time I heard?"

Mya crossed her arms, her anger radiating so strongly that faint pulsations washed over me. Hope buoyed at sensing the emotion. At least Roy might be good for something—helping me regain my power.

"I happen to be second in charge," Roy said. "You *are* being treated with the utmost respect. Otherwise, I wouldn't be here."

"Can we talk to your father, or not?" I asked.

"He's indisposed. Perhaps come back tomorrow. Neva has a few lovely inns. I'm sure you'll be quite comfortable."

I took another step forward, towering over the man. His cheeks reddened. "I believe my quarters here in the castle will be adequate."

He sneered. "They're currently occupied. And your… *things* were disposed of after you failed to return from your little adventure, while my father ran this kingdom without the help of your girlfriend and Terran meddling. Do you need an escort out?" He puffed his chest like a preening bird. If I weren't so frustrated, I'd laugh.

"We'll be back," I said. "Tell your father he doesn't want another war. I know he's short on soldiers. Remind him that Terra is not. The only thing keeping us from invading your kingdom is me. You'd best remember that." I turned on my heel and remounted my horse, Mya and Dev close behind.

As we passed Lucas at the gate, I said louder than necessary, "Since they don't have the class to let us stay, we'll go to the Willow Inn instead."

"The Willow Inn?" Mya scrunched her nose, putting on a show. "Don't they know I'm a princess?"

"Come on, Princess." Dev spurred his horse on. "I have a feeling it's going to be a long night."

CHAPTER 40
LUCAS

The jump of excitement beneath my ribs at seeing Mya, Daniel, and Dev made it nearly impossible to finish my shift. My first impulse was to take Mya into my arms and swirl her until we were both dizzy. I'd expected the prince, but this was better in so many ways. With Mya here, we'd have to find a way to enhance the operation using her persuasiveness.

After work, I checked on Molly and the established location of communication—a small box at the rear of Molly's pen. I'd given my cologne to Hanson and instructed him to dab a bit onto a message, which would allow the courier safe passage through Molly. I scanned the letter, and my stomach tumbled.

Something is amiss. Changing to tonight. Have the three Terrans meet me at Dame Hemlock's at six. The rest of the plan is as we discussed.

Everything would go down this evening under the cover of darkness. The scheme toppled into motion, and it hinged on execution with precision and stealth. But what was amiss? Graftonberg had to be up to something nefarious to speed up our timeline by three days. If Hanson hadn't done his part, I would be walking into a dicey situation. One that would be difficult to explain my way out of.

The Willow Inn stood in the center of Neva, a landmark in the small city that maintained a reputation for serving the wealthy on their business trips or as overflow for castle events. Sparkling chandeliers in the lobby were a far cry from the tidy, but austere locations I frequented when traveling. I'd changed out of my uniform and donned a low-brimmed hat to avoid drawing attention. On more than one occasion, I'd served as guard for high-ranking noblemen, escorting them to the largest suite. If available, it should house the trio. I knocked softly.

Dev answered and ushered me inside.

"What took you so long?" Daniel stood from a navy-padded chair nestled around a gleaming wood table.

"I can't leave my post without drawing suspicion." I suppressed an eye roll. The guy had obviously never held down a real job in his life.

I took a seat next to Mya. Her hand went to my leg, tracing little circles on the kneecap. Just as gorgeous as ever, her entire being seemed to sparkle at my arrival. I couldn't wait to be with her. Alone. But tonight, we had bigger problems than my suppressed desire to kiss her silly.

I pulled out the note from Brandon Hanson and read it aloud.

"Wait, who's Hanson? Start from the beginning, mate." Dev said.

I explained my friendship with Dame Hemlock, her connections, the money she funneled into the underground, and her involvement with Brandon. "Our plan was for Hanson to plant the idea in Graftonberg's head that the men guarding Cate couldn't be trusted. Hanson spread the lie that there were too many who believed in Cate, making it a ticking time bomb if one or more of his soldiers betrayed him and broke her out. Hanson would exploit this mistrust and offer his own personal guards. It's a tremendous risk, because after tonight, Graftonberg might never trust him again. If we do it right and stage injuries for the new security, we might get away with it. But Graftonberg will always wonder about Hanson's loyalty, of course."

"Wait, let me get this straight. Cate's guards will be on our side... then what?" Daniel asked.

"Because I'm familiar with the castle, my job is to sneak in and lead the girls out."

"I know the castle as well. I'll go with you," Daniel said.

I shot him a skeptical look. "*You* know the dungeons?"

Daniel didn't even bother appearing embarrassed. "I explored when I lived here."

"Spying for Terra?" I couldn't believe his audacity in sneaking around when he'd been a guest.

Daniel crossed his arms and leaned into his seat. "Curiosity."

"Can we get back to business?" Mya interrupted. "Why does Hanson want us to meet him at this dame's house?"

"Don't know. I guess we'll find out."

Adams ushered us inside without fanfare, bypassing the uncomfortable sitting area. Hanson already paced the blue room, the dame perched on the edge of her seat. I'd never seen her keyed up before—her normally smoothly arranged gray hair held a few sagging wisps from its bun.

After quick introductions, Hanson spoke, "I'd like you to come to the castle with me tonight as my guests."

Daniel's eyes narrowed. "Roy already kicked us out earlier today."

"Did he?" Hanson smirked, indicating he was well aware of what happened.

"Your note said something was amiss. Care to enlighten us?" Dev asked.

"Graftonberg has asked his closest advisors to the castle tonight. I suspect he plans to discuss how to get rid of Cate. Some have shown squeamishness when the topic of a hanging comes up. Those members aren't invited."

"So why bring us? Won't he kick us out?" Mya asked.

"I'll say you were my guests, and I thought Graftonberg would want to hear what you're offering for Lady Emily before we make any decisions." He shook his head. "Honestly? I'm not sure what he's up to other than I have a bad feeling. I'd be more comfortable if I weren't the only one in the castle on the queen's side tonight. My guards are in place, although Graftonberg insisted on keeping two of his own." He turned to me. "Mine will have a small cross drawn on their index finger. You'll have to take out the other two. I'm sorry."

"What time?" I asked.

Hanson snapped open his pocket watch and flipped it closed again. "In two hours."

"I'm in." I popped a bit of cake into my mouth from the dame's ever-present excellent tea tray.

"I wouldn't miss it," Mya piped up.

Dev and Daniel also agreed, all of us falling into silence, reflecting the grim reality that we might only have this one chance to save Cate.

The front cliff below Caelum Castle held a hidden tunnel that King Aldridge constructed so our soldiers wouldn't be vulnerable if the lift system broke or was destroyed by Embers in battle. The back side of the mountain sloped gently, allowing horses and carriages through. Sheer rock rose up to the castle here but was closer to Neva. The secret tunnel became not so secret during The Great Battle when the Ember spies discovered it and wound their way into the castle. The entrance remained well hidden and guarded. Hanson assured me they would allow me to enter. Dug deep into the hillside, the passage skirted alongside the entry to the dungeons.

I entered the opening, raising my arms above my head. "I'm alone," I called. The air turned cooler, a few flickering sconces emitting an eerie glow, the flames bouncing off the uneven dark stone.

Two Caelum soldiers stepped into the light. "This isn't a pass-through. Go around," one said.

I checked their fingers. My breath skipped. No inked cross. Had something gone wrong? These weren't Hanson's men. Which meant I should either turn back and abandon the mission or disable two Caelum guards. Men who should be fighting on the same side as me. Yet our new king had turned us against one another.

"Will you let me pass, no questions asked?" I tested.

One grunted. "Not if we don't want to lose our jobs, or worse. Leave, and we won't report you."

"And if I don't?" I edged forward.

"Expect the gallows."

Inside, I withered. I didn't want to hurt them. Nor did I want *them* to hurt me. I rushed ahead, using the energy to slam into the smaller of the two. I scooped up a stone and struck him on the skull, praying the impact would knock him out and not cause permanent damage.

With a shuddering sideswipe, the other tackled me. I rolled, escaped his grip, and popped to my feet. We circled, stepping over the downed man. My first blow to his jaw careened him into the rock wall. I hit his belly next, connecting with hard muscle, though it still doubled him over. Finally, a strike to the back of his head dropped him to the ground, motionless. Not wasting time to restrain them, I sped toward the dungeon, readying myself for another fight.

A guard met me at the heavy wooden door to the prison, the iron ring clanging as he opened it. My muscles relaxed a fraction at the small cross inked on his index finger.

"She's gone," he whispered.

Panic raced. I was too late.

CHAPTER 41
DANIEL

Hanson, Mya, Dev, and I crossed the castle threshold. I'd become accustomed to using the back door near the stables. The formality of the towering glass ceiling, lit with glittering lights in the foyer solidified the fact that I no longer came and went as I pleased. Cate's presence had left an indefinable vibrance the structure now lacked. Hanson escorted us to a sitting room on the second floor, well known to be Graftonberg's favorite.

Count what's-his-name, as Cate liked to call him, because his name always eluded her, stood huddled with Roy, the top of his bald head visible as he bent in low conversation. No sign of Graftonberg yet.

Roy's face flashed crimson at our arrival. "What is the meaning of this? You shouldn't be here."

Hanson intercepted. "I brought them. They have an interesting offer on the table, and I thought we should consider it before making decisions."

"You mean before *I* make the decision?" Graftonberg entered behind us, his jowls shaking in anger. Cate had been so furious with him she hadn't called him Jowly in some time, deciding it felt too familial, and usually spat his name out like a curse instead. "Guards," he shouted.

Two Caelum soldiers flanked him immediately. King Aldridge had never required bodyguards inside his own castle. The baron—I still couldn't think of him as king—glared. "I'd like to have a private meeting with my counselors. There's another deal on the table. You three…" he attempted to stand straighter to seem taller, though he couldn't measure up to anyone in the room, including Mya, "wait here. I trust I won't need to hold you in a cell?" He glanced at his guards.

I chuckled. "I'm more used to being offered a brandy than iron bars, Graftonberg. We'll be here. Go off and do your business." I waved a hand dismissively.

His ruddy cheeks deepened pink. He turned on his heel and marched out of the room, the rest of his entourage following behind, including Hanson.

I crossed the space, picked up the heavy brandy snifter with a flicker of a glance to catch Dev's eye. My back to the guards, I said, "I left a few items in my room. Wouldn't mind retrieving them." Never mind that Roy already told me they tossed all my belongings. "Think one of you gentlemen would escort me?" I strode toward them at their post near the doorway, heavy crystal decanter in hand. Dev shifted behind me.

"Our orders are for you to stay here, Your Highness," one said.

"Bonus points for the honorific. Sorry about this," I replied.

The guard on the right's brown eyes barely had time to register confusion before the crystal container knocked him over the head, brandy splashing both of us. Dev took care of the other man, moving quicker than I, his powers still intact.

"Pity to waste it." Dev eyed the decanter.

I half smiled. "Worth it."

Mya stepped next to me. "Well done, boys. So, where to? The conference room or Aldridge's office?"

"Both are on the first floor," I replied. "Let's go."

Ordinarily, I'd worry about taking Mya with us, but I didn't want to leave her alone. Besides, somewhere along the way, I started trusting her. "The back stairs," I whispered.

We crept down the servant's stairs and froze at the unmistakable sounds of footsteps rising below. Dev and I blocked Mya, preparing to fight. Emma, Cate's maid, startled at the three of us looming over her.

"Oh! Your Highness," she said. "I'm so glad to see you." Her expression always hovered between *the world is ending* and *something terrible is about to happen*. "The queen is in trouble."

"We're aware. Do you know where Graftonberg is?"

She shook her head, pale wisps of hair that had escaped her ponytail shifting back and forth. Emma wasn't known for her talkativeness.

"Have you seen her?" I asked.

She bit her lip and shook her head again. "I wasn't allowed. I'm sorry." Her light eyes filled with tears.

"It's not your fault." I squeezed her arm. "Don't tell anyone you saw us." We stepped down to pass her.

"Wait. Your Highness." She paused.

She was often a useful source of information because she blended so well into the background. But hesitancy wasn't what I needed tonight. I took a breath to calm my nerves.

"Yes, Emma?"

"I heard they were taking Cate out of the dungeon. And that…" her eyes shifted downward, "she wouldn't be coming back." The ponytail swished again. "I'm worried—worried she's headed for the gallows as we speak."

Everything tilted, my entire world off-kilter. Beats of silence dragged, words frozen somewhere between my brain and mouth.

"We'd best be on our way then. Take care, Emma," Dev managed to spit out.

I passed her, each step wooden, an unknown force propelling me forward. When I peered back, she watched us with her terrified, wide eyes.

Regaining our composure, we strode down the hallway as if we belonged, our nonchalance serving as our armor. We encountered a few servants along the way. Our ruse wasn't working—we were far too recognizable. Raised eyebrows and furtive glances showed surprise, though no one stopped us, and a few even bowed or curtsied in respect. It seemed Graftonberg required guards in the castle because his own household wasn't loyal.

The conference room stood empty, so we continued to King Aldridge's office. I couldn't shake the feeling that Graftonberg taking over Aldridge's desk would somehow disturb his soul in the afterlife. We crept to the closed door, listening.

"Take or leave the deal, Graftonberg, but decide quickly," a deep voice said.

"No! He can't be trusted." *Cate.* What was she doing here? Lucas was supposed to be rescuing her. Emma was right. She'd already been taken.

"He'll just kill her," another said. "Do you want her blood on your hands?"

Who? Who will kill her? I strained to hear more.

"The prophecy will be fulfilled," came Graftonberg's voice. "Don't you see? It's part of the plan. She's the sacrifice for the rest of us."

"Rowan is a liar," Cate spat.

"Don't listen to the girl. I can be trusted."

I can be trusted? *Rowan was in the room.* I exchanged frantic glances with Mya and Dev. "He's bargaining for her," I whispered.

Mya nodded slowly, and before I could stop her, she opened the door.

All eyes turned to our group. Cate stood in the center, her arms shackled, dressed in a sack-like tunic someone must have provided her while in jail. Her beautiful face flickered from surprise, to relief, to terror at seeing us. "Go," she mouthed.

Guards stepped forward, ones I hadn't noticed initially, flanking the perimeter, converging on us as a wall of blue.

"You don't want to do this," Mya said, advancing with her head high. "This isn't right." Her stare penetrated each person in the room, including a small group of Graftonberg cronies, alongside Hanson, Roy, Cate, and Rowan, all held captive by her gaze. "Your Highness," she addressed Graftonberg. "Wouldn't you rather secure peace with the Terrans? We'll offer Caelum protection in your hour of need."

Jowly swallowed, taken aback by this new development.

"My plans are not to kill Catherine." Rowan's voice boomed. "She'll help feed our lands with water. Control our fires and allow us to live in peace. We won't need to invade your kingdom if we have workable ground of our own."

"She'll be your prisoner," I shot back. "And your lot are never satisfied. You'll invade soon enough."

"How many times do I have to tell you, Prince. I always keep my word." Rowan edged toward Cate.

Graftonberg stood next to them, his gaze volleying between us. He finally landed on the count. "It's the fulfillment of the prophecy. I'm sure of it."

"I agree," Roy chimed in. "Let him take her."

Hanson sidled beside the count, speaking low and calm, his words indistinguishable. For a few moments, we were all locked in a state of indecision—the Caelum guards ready to drag Mya, Dev, and me out, Rowan, waiting to abscond Cate, and Graftonberg's advisors deciding who they'll support. The baron must have brought them here as witnesses so they could report Rowan's lie and tell the people Cate left alive. Graftonberg wanted them to proclaim him a hero, repeating his lies, instead of being marked as the villain he'd become.

"No," Hanson said. "This isn't the way."

"I agree," the count stood a little straighter.

Then everything happened at once. Rowan grabbed Cate, his other hand raising in some sort of signal. Graftonberg blustered and shifted toward Cate and Rowan. I lurched forward while the guards closed in on us.

That's when the windows broke, and a group of Embers burst through Aldridge's office.

Rowan gave a curt nod to his men, pulling at Cate, while another Ember snatched her other arm. Lucas burst into the room through the castle entrance behind us, dagger poised to launch. I'd seen Lucas throw knives before. With his Caelum powers directing the air, he never missed.

Cate struggled to fight her way out of Rowan's grasp. A Caelum guard caught me by the shoulder. Dev brandished his weapon, sending more Embers in motion toward us, shoving Graftonberg in the process.

At that moment, Lucas's knife soared.

It connected at the chest. Blood bloomed. Only it wasn't Rowan's.

Lucas's knife landed right through Graftonberg's heart.

CHAPTER 42
CATE

Pandemonium. Graftonberg fell at my feet, blood oozing from his chest, the embedded dagger gleaming in the sconce's yellow light. The inevitable flashbacks of my father came next, his wound inflicted by the man who held me in a vice grip, each finger bruising.

My heart pounded in my ears, panic racing. I couldn't get away from it—the blood. It surrounded my dreams, intertwining with every reality. I couldn't hide from it. Was I destined to see crimson forever? I cried out in agony, like a wounded animal. No more. The madness had to stop.

"The king's down!" someone shouted.

Lucas stood planted across the room, skin pallid, eyes two shocked orbs. Caelum guards, advisors, and my allies were all in various states of motion or shock. Soldiers rushed to Graftonberg's side.

For the first time, I looked at the baron's face. Jowls sagging, wide lips slack, pupils unregistered. A guard reached for a pulse, but I already knew the result. Another gestured to seize the person who had thrown the knife.

"Lucas, run!" I screamed, just as Rowan and the Ember dragged me to the broken windows.

Rowan lifted me onto his shoulder, allowing a dizzying view of those in the room. Dev zoomed toward me. An Ember blocked my vision, and I heard the contact of bodies slamming together, followed by Dev's grunt.

"Stop!" Mya's voice rang out. "She's your queen! Don't you all remember? Save her. Save *her*!" Even I could feel the power of her persuasiveness behind her words. Commanding. Beguiling. Her message just *felt right*. Maybe that's because I was the rightful queen, and I felt that too.

I started resisting. Kicking, squirming, even with my shackles attached to my hands. The cool night air hit my face, and below the floor turned from warm rugs to landscaped grass and shrubs as he exited through the shattered window. "No!" I yelled, helpless to Rowan's tight grip.

Flames erupted from the other Embers, and fighting ensued as they battled Caelum soldiers. Despite my position, a warmth of gratitude flashed. They'd come. The Caelum men had turned against me, but they still came to save me.

Instinctively, I forced the water molecules together. They coalesced, collecting at landmark speeds. Rain gushed, drenching us all in seconds, extinguishing the fires and protecting my soldiers.

I'd gone slack against Rowan, all my focus on the rain. "Let go," I hissed in his ear. "You won't stand a chance carrying me. You'll never make it."

"Or I could kill you now." His voice was low and huffed with exertion.

The speeding ground beneath me grew wet and muddy. "Then you'd be breaking a promise," I said between jostling teeth. "A promise that you're trustworthy."

Shouts rang out close behind us.

"Help," Rowan called.

He hoisted me toward another Ember, but I fought, kicking out, my foot connecting to his face with a satisfying crunch. He bellowed, dropping back. Caelum soldiers in hand-to-hand combat with Embers moved like shadows in the moonlight. "Fight!" I called. "Fight!" Dev's blond hair shone in the low light, advancing to us. I searched for Daniel but couldn't find him.

"Give up," I said to Rowan. "You've lost this time."

His grip tightened. "I'm coming for you. With an entire army. Caelum doesn't have the numbers to win. I'll thank Graftonberg for that info. Your kingdom is falling apart." His smile flashed out of the corner of my eye. "Don't worry. I'll be here to pick up the pieces."

My breath shuddered at the naivety of Graftonberg divulging that information. Jowly truly was an idiot. Without warning, he dropped me into the mud, turning on Dev with a gun. He must have carried it from the other side. Dev obviously knew what it was, because he raised his hands. Caelumites could change the bullet's trajectory by manipulating the air, but the other soldiers were oblivious, locked in their own battles.

"Just go," I told Rowan. "There's no reason to kill him."

"Except to torture you." His words sent prickles sliding down my spine, and I knew he meant every word.

"You're wasting time." I wiped sluicing rain from my face. "And if you really want my help one day, how would killing people I love make me more willing?"

"Fear," he replied, turning and splashing into the night.

Dev bent to help me up, first focused on my bindings. "Let him go," I said. "It's too dangerous with that gun."

"Agreed."

"Where's Daniel?"

"Fighting some Embers near the castle. He'll be okay."

I held out my wrists, and he slashed through my shackles with his sword and I took his hand. He lifted me upright out of the mud. When I drew close, I whispered, ensuring no one would hear, "He doesn't have his powers. Did you know?"

He nodded. "We'll find him. But do you want to go back? They might throw you in jail again."

"I don't care." I didn't hesitate. A pivotal moment was at stake in our kingdom, and I had to be here. "Let's look for Lucas, too. Where's Mya?"

"I left her inside the castle. Everyone poured out to chase the Embers, so she should be fine."

We started walking. The Embers and soldiers seemed to have all disappeared, the garden eerily quiet. "And my sister? How's Emily?"

Dev's voice sounded strained, and I immediately felt bad for not updating him sooner.

"In a cell, but fine. She's enjoyed torturing me just as much as Roy. In the annoying sense. Not physically, thankfully."

"Sounds about right. I wouldn't want to be locked up with my sister either."

After a few moments, I added, "Emily has some good points. I'm grateful not to have been alone. She needs… a hobby, maybe. And not to marry that old dude in your neighborhood. Now that Graftonberg is probably dead, they'll hopefully let her out. And not put me back in." I held up crossed fingers. "She always presumed your father would pay a ransom, and she'd be released. I didn't understand why they brought her, but I'm glad they did. The men who took us wouldn't blink twice at killing her. We're lucky they were greedy."

"Thanks for being there for her. She might act strong, but I'm sure she was grateful to have you with her."

I was less sure. The longer we were locked up, the more bitter Emily became, blaming me for her plight. These past two weeks in the cell had been filled with insults and vile abuse. Then Roy would come down, taunting me. Warning that at any moment I could be hanging from the gallows. I wondered every day if it would be my last. Weirdly, Graftonberg never faced me. Perhaps the connection he'd had with my father gave him a twinge of conscience. Roy's hatred ran deeper—the kind that erupts after being spurned. The kid on the playground who never found friends and finally seized the opportunity to be the bully. The boy who didn't get the girl.

The rain continued to pour as we trudged. A few Ember bodies lay on the muddy grounds, but the rest appeared to have followed Rowan. With the clouds blocking the moonlight, it was difficult to see, castle lights in the distance guiding our way like hazy, floating beacons.

Someone moved toward us, their footsteps squishing in the mud. Dev and I froze. "Who's there?" he said.

"Dev?"

Daniel's voice brought hot tears burning behind my eyes in relief. "It's us," I said softly.

His arms circled me in the darkness, steady and strong. "You're safe," he whispered. "I don't—I don't know what I'd do without you." His voice broke.

We stood, water dripping between us, both soaked to the skin and shivering, savoring each other's warmth. His lips found mine, and I sank into him, knowing Dev would watch for attackers for this short reunion. He tasted of new rain and brandy, something I didn't usually associate with him. The longing, the despair, the hope swirled together as we clung to each other.

He cupped the back of my neck, pulling me closer, and I let him, wanting to crawl into his skin. The cold, stone cell had seeped into every crevice. I'd lost hope in the dark hours in the blackness of night, wondering if I'd ever see him again. Ever hold him.

"I missed you so much," he whispered.

"It's been no picnic for me either." My voice held a bite of sarcasm. "I wasn't served cocktails in the dungeon, unlike whatever you've been drinking."

He chuckled. "I used the brandy snifter as a weapon earlier and had to make it believable."

I stepped from him, my grip still tight on his forearms as reality crashed. "Daniel? What's going to happen? Because I'm not sure I can handle any more days in that prison, and I don't want to hide anymore."

"Graftonberg's advisors might support you. If we go back now, we'll find out. Plus," he leaned in and whispered in my ear, "Mya's there to sway them. It might be our best chance."

"I, for one," Dev interrupted, "will be returning. If I don't show up in Terra with Emily, there'll be war. My father will make sure of it."

"Here's an easy decision." Daniel brushed a lock of hair plastered to my face, rivulets streaming between us. "I think it's okay to stop the rain."

I laughed. It turned hysterical, deep in my belly, strung with the tension of these last weeks, before morphing into tears. "I barely know I'm doing it," I said after gaining control, both boys staring at me like I'd lost my mind. Maybe I had. "The time away from the energy helped me understand it better. The *only* thing good to come of this disaster." It felt a little guilty saying it out loud since Daniel's experience had been the opposite. I pulled at his hand. "Let's go face the music."

"I don't know that one." Daniel shook his head at my colloquialism. "You mean find out if you're still considered a traitor?"

"Exactly."

The scene through the window of my father's office was grim. The medics carried Graftonberg on a stretcher, every expression downturned. Mya didn't notice our arrival while she watched the baron's departure. Hanson saw us first and ushered us inside through the broken glass with a quick gesture.

"Is he?" Daniel whispered to Hanson when we reached his side. The metallic smell of blood still hung in the air, the dark stain an irregular marker on the patterned woven rug.

"May he rest in peace," he replied.

Roy trailed after the stretcher, glassy-eyed and shell-shocked. A rush of sympathy for him washed over me. I knew what it was like to watch my father be killed. Knew the sick ache in my stomach and the nightmares that followed.

I caught Daniel's eye. "Once he recovers, he'll want revenge. Is Lucas…"

The count, who I hadn't even noticed standing next to us, replied, "Gone."

He might be with Molly. If he flew away, it would be difficult to find him.

The count continued, "No one needs to share that the king tried to sell out The Concealed. We'll say Graftonberg died a hero."

Hanson stepped forward. "We need to unite in this time of need. Unite with the Terrans." He nodded to Daniel, Mya, and Dev. "And restore the rightful heir to her throne. Roy will be unable to cope through his grief, and I suspect Catherine is correct. He'll be consumed by revenge and thus unfit to rule us. Catherine has already proven herself."

One of the landowners wearing a garish orange waistcoat narrowed his eyes. "Has she? Catherine left when things became too hard."

"I *left* to hunt down Rowan," I replied, venom in my tone. "The portal had…" I began to lose steam, "other ideas about our return. Daniel and I never wanted to abandon anyone." I lifted my chin, my voice carrying. "Caelum is my home. I will fulfill the prophecy. Which will not involve helping the Embers, our enemy, flourish. They've killed without remorse and taken over our lands. We'll fight to get them back. And my powers? I'm stronger than ever."

Mya spoke up, "Call a meeting with your aristocracy with every voting member. Make sure your stories are straight about what happened today. Cate is your savior. Cate is *Terra's* savior. I'm sure of it. Daniel and I vow to work tirelessly for peace between our kingdoms, and that can't happen if Roy is on the throne."

"And what about Dryden?" the landowner in orange asked.

"We'll manage him," Mya's voice rang with confidence. With persuasion. If I didn't know King Dryden well, I might even believe her.

Daniel edged next to Mya in support. "Print your newspapers. Convince the citizens that Cate was never a traitor. She only wanted what was best for her people and to stop Rowan. Tell them that. He's your enemy, not her."

"I agree," Hanson said. "If carefully managed, we can pull this off." He glanced around the room to a mixture of nods and skeptical shifting glances. "Who's with me?"

CHAPTER 43
LUCAS

What had I done? Bile churned, bubbling into my throat. I killed the King of Caelum. I'd pledged allegiance to him. Vowed to serve my kingdom and sovereign. I stumbled out of the castle, half out of my mind, and found myself at Molly's barn, then scribbled a note and placed it in our secret hiding place.

I'm sorry. Tell them I'm sorry.

Them. A million faces flashed through my head. Cate, for failing her. My mother, who, as a fugitive, I'd likely never see again. The citizens of Caelum—those I'd promised to serve. And Mya. I could see her dark lashes fluttering away tears. Blinking back the hurt of abandonment. Now we could never be together.

Molly felt my pain, the enclosure filling with steam before I opened the doors, and we escaped. I didn't know where to go. Maybe Quorum, the border town where Grace lived. I couldn't stay long, but at least it would be a direction to head, my brain unable to contrive a better plan.

I tried to work out exactly what had happened. I'd listened at the partly open door for several moments, catching on quickly. Graftonberg was selling Cate out. Claiming that by helping our enemy, she'd be fulfilling the prophecy. Had he really believed his own nonsense? Or was it just a way to keep himself in power? When I entered, dagger ready to strike, I'd seen my exposed target. I finally had my chance to rid us of Rowan, to save Cate, and all my senses zoned in. I'd let the blade fly, singing through the air. Yet somehow, Graftonberg crossed into its path. He must have been shoved. Purposely? Perhaps an Ember had seen me cock the knife and pushed the king to protect Rowan. Or maybe it had just been bad luck.

With sickening clarity, I watched my target become obscured by the gold-trimmed, blue waistcoat of the king. Too late. I couldn't take the blade back, flying end over end. The steel met its mark. And now, I'd be banished from my kingdom forever.

Several days passed in a blur until we reached Quorum. When I stepped up to the gates, I handed over paperwork denoting my Caelum army status, and they let me in without difficulty, marking my name in the roster. No sign of the big-nosed guard I'd had trouble with last time. I left Molly in the woods to not be recognized by the townspeople. If they issued a warrant for my arrest, we would be faster than a courier, so I should be safe for a day or two. Unless… they used falcons. If they wanted me badly enough, they'd employ messenger birds to pass the word.

A wash of hot, then cold, spread over my body. *I killed the king*. Of course, I would be the most wanted man in Caelum. I'd been riding for three days. Why didn't I think of this earlier? Truthfully, I *hadn't* been thinking. I'd been feeling. Grace was a friend. Someone far away who felt safe. I'd panicked, and now my name was scrawled in a book at the gate. Could I steal it? Sneak away before anyone noticed?

"Lucas!" a voice called out.

John, Grace's father, stood across the street, juggling an armful of bags containing fresh vegetables for his tavern. My heart sank even further, somewhere near my toes. No escaping now.

His curly blond hair was shorter than the last time I'd seen him, and I jogged over. A smile widened his round face, easing my fears a bit. If he'd heard of my plight, I wouldn't expect him to be grinning from ear to ear.

"Grace will be pleased to see you. What brings you to town?" He switched his bag to his left arm so he could shake my hand.

"How is Grace?" I dodged the question.

"She's doing well." He lowered his voice, "There are some who don't want to associate with her anymore after being in the Ember camp all that time. But we've found out who our real friends are. And most eventually show their faces, tail between their legs because they can't resist my wumbeast pie." He chuckled and clapped me on the back.

I'd only seen two sides of John: irritable at me for accidentally clearing out his tavern, or heartbroken from losing Grace. He'd been so overcome with emotion when we returned, I'd never witnessed this good-natured version. I debated divulging my secret, ultimately deciding I shouldn't share my soul on the sidewalk in town.

"I'd love to see her. Is she free?" Now that I was here, I couldn't leave without saying hello.

"In the tavern." John started walking and waved me on to follow. We entered the dim pub together, the door swinging shut behind us. Still morning, the place hadn't opened yet.

"Grace," he called. "Surprise for you." He left to empty his bags in the kitchen, leaving me alone in the familiar dim room, dark wood, and slightly sticky floors.

She bounded out in a pink dress that actually fit, blonde hair neatly pulled into a braid. Her feet skidded when she halted, her expression morphing from open-mouthed shock to wide smile. As soon as she recovered, she scurried to me, arms outstretched for a hug.

"Lucas! I was worried when I hadn't heard from you."

Worried? What did she know?

"When Cate disappeared, I wasn't sure if you were with her or not."

Ah. She's behind the news. "Let's sit. I'll tell you all about it. And I'm sorry. I should have written."

Talking to Grace was like speaking to a confidante and friend well beyond her years. Our shared experiences at the Ember camp cultivated a bond that couldn't be replicated. My story spilled out. England and the hospital, the discovery that Rowan grew up outside of London, and how we'd almost been shot as we passed through the portal, followed by Cate's time warp. Grace listened intently, chewing her lip.

"Now she's a wanted criminal," she said. "The king says she's trying to usurp the crown."

"Her own crown?" I tipped my head.

She gave me a half-smile. "I'm still on her side. Just stating the problem she's up against. Graftonberg will never give her back the throne."

I hadn't thought I'd tell her I was a fugitive until that moment. It all came tumbling out. The knife. How the moment it left my hand, I wanted to recall it. That Graftonberg was dead, and it was only a matter of time before someone came after me.

She set her jaw. "We've faced worse. We'll figure it out."

"We?" I shot her a skeptical look, a cross between half-friend, half-older brother.

"Da!" she yelled before I could stop her.

John lumbered in while Grace relayed my story at lightning speed. He sat heavily on the wooden chair next to me. "Well," he said. "Jones probably took your name at the gate," he spoke slowly. Or, maybe it just seemed slow after Grace's rapid-fire explanation. "He's a buddy of mine. Imagine I can convince him to switch out those books and keep quiet. In the meantime, there's a couch upstairs you're welcome to. At least until we figure this out."

There was that "we" again. "I don't want to risk getting you two in trouble. If you can cover my tracks, I'd be grateful. Otherwise, a meal and a few supplies, and I'll be off on Molly."

A flicker of a smile flashed on Grace's lips. "Molly's here?"

She finally called her by her name. Things must be serious.

"What if..." Grace started. She fiddled with the ends of the apron that overlaid her pink dress. "What if Cate is put back on the throne? Then she would pardon you, wouldn't she? Why don't you wait here until we hear the news? Silly for you to wander off in the wilderness and never know."

I hesitated. She had a point. But Cate being crowned was a big if.

"I'll take care of Molly for you," she sing-songed.

"Just for a couple of days." I shifted in my seat, the guilt piling up. Kindness remaining in this world humbled me. "I'm sorry I haven't checked on you. Things have been… busy," I finished lamely. "Are the Embers still kidnapping girls?" I'd been so caught up in my own problems, I hadn't even attempted to address the issues up north. Not to mention the horrific things going on in Ember City. We'd all vowed to return. To free the girls from the baby factory. And we'd accomplished none of it. If Graftonberg didn't help, Roy certainly wouldn't either. I clenched and unclenched my fingers, leaving crescent impressions in my palms. The thought of Roy on the throne filled me with anger, with disgust… with despair.

"No one's been kidnapped in the last few months," Grace said, interrupting my thoughts. "Rowan might have been occupied elsewhere."

I wondered if he, too, had been stuck in the wormhole that held Cate and Daniel, or if he'd been plotting and building his army while he waited for her to return. "I guess there's nothing to do but hide and wait. Thank you. Thank you both." I shook John's hand and wished I had something more to offer them other than the risk of harboring a fugitive.

CHAPTER 44
DANIEL

The room turned eerily quiet when Hanson asked who would support Cate. Even without powers, I sensed their uncertainty. If they did believe in her, could they convince the people? Another hitch—she didn't actually qualify to become their queen based on Caelum law because she hadn't spent enough time in the kingdom. That's how she ended up with Graftonberg as her regent. She needed a vote from the rest of the aristocracy, not only to choose her as queen, but to change the laws approving her to lead. Fear of Roy prevailing and not backing the winning horse, so to speak, would play a factor. Because everyone knew Roy would want revenge on anyone who wasn't loyal to him.

"Let's call the meeting," the count said. "We'll see what the others say."

"How long will that take?" Mya asked.

"A few weeks, I imagine."

Dev spoke up, "Can we agree to let my sister out of your dungeons? My father won't wait weeks before he either convinces King Dryden to attack or creates an army with his own men."

Hanson caught the attention of one of the Caelum guards still present. "Take the duke's son to his sister and tell the steward to find them rooms for the night. Same for Prince Daniel." He turned to Cate. "I believe your room has been left untouched. You may return there."

"I think it's best she remains in the castle." The count's chin ticked up. "To make sure she doesn't stir up trouble and take the crown by force."

"My father was King Aldridge. Do any of you remember that?" Cate burst out. "There was never any intention that the Graftonbergs were next in line to the throne." She threw up her hands.

"Guards," Hanson said. "Please give us some privacy."

They filed out of the room, leaving Mya, Cate, Hanson, the count, and several landowners. "Graftonberg has given out favors to many. Including," he glanced around the room, "some of us here. They know Roy will provide for them, likely illegally, with bribes. And some," this time he avoided the gaze of the others, "enjoy his take on indentured servitude. They don't want to pay their workers."

"Slavery." Mya's hard-lined mouth matched her tone.

One of the landowners, a tanned man with a hawkish nose, spoke, "They are well provided for."

"Every person deserves the opportunity to work hard and move up in life," Mya responded. "You're taking that away from them, and in the process, removing innovation that a farmer might create, because why would they bother now? All they have is their homes, the clothes on their backs, and food. People want more. They want to make a difference." Her voice wobbled at this, and I could tell the argument had become personal. "In the long run, Caelum will suffer. They will only fight for a kingdom they feel a part of. And from where I'm standing? Caelum is fractured, and you need as many loyal countrymen as you can find." She blew out a breath, unused to holding the room's attention.

Pride for my sister filled my chest. Her ideals and talents had been hidden too long. Suppressed by an overbearing father and a brother who didn't take her seriously. As a Terran, she wouldn't be invited to the vote in two weeks, and she used every ounce of persuasion she could muster here and now.

"Who will bring you together?" she continued. "Certainly not Roy. It's the prophecy. The people will unite around Cate. Anyone notice how she's standing there absolutely soaking wet? She made it rain. She just escaped Rowan for the umpteenth time and saved those Caelum soldiers—the same ones who held her captive—by bringing a downpour. Get your heads out of your—" she swallowed, composing herself, "get your heads on straight and support her. For Caelum."

As Cate watched Mya, her eyes misted at my sister's allegiance. She had no idea Mya felt so passionately about her. Neither did I. "Thank you. What she said." Cate smiled weakly. The adrenaline from the fight with Rowan, her kidnapping, and the two weeks in the dungeon had drained her energy. She could barely stand upright. "While you're at it," she continued, "Lucas should be pardoned. He's served Caelum tirelessly and should not be repaid with treason charges for attempting to save me. He had no ill intent."

"Roy will want revenge. We might need to concede something," the count replied.

I crossed my arms. "Cate can deal with Roy. I wouldn't worry about him."

The count and Hanson exchanged glances but said nothing.

"Well," Hanson clapped his hands together. "I imagine you would like some dry clothes and rest. Let's adjourn, gentlemen."

Everyone left but Cate and me, both dripping on the carpet. I shut the door, locked it, and took her in my arms. We'd had a brief reunion out in the rain with Dev, though not nearly long enough. I rested my forehead on hers. "Was it truly awful?"

"What, being locked up with Emily?" she murmured.

"You don't have to pretend with me." She joked to protect me from the horrors. I gazed into her green eyes. "My brave Cate. You amaze me."

"I'll tell you one day." She touched her fingers to my lips. "I'm not ready to relive it," she whispered. She kissed me lightly. "Hanson's right. I would love dry clothes. And you know what would be even better? A hot meal. With dessert. You'll be my hero if you find me real food."

What had they been feeding her? I ran my hand down her sides, feeling the bump of each rib. Not enough. "I'll be your knight in shining armor."

A soft smile crossed her pale lips. "Just being my prince is enough."

I located a servant to search for Emma, who appeared after hovering nearby.

"I saved some of your clothes, Your Highness," she told me.

"Thank you." It was kind of her to think of it, and I'd be happy to regain some of my things I'd left. "Will you take care of Cate first? Bring her a feast."

She curtsied. "Of course."

They retreated down the hall toward Cate's tower suite. "Don't forget something sweet," I called. "Two somethings. Or maybe three."

Cate shot me a half-grateful, half-exasperated look, then blew me a kiss goodnight.

After donning dry clothes and grabbing a tray of food, I pulled a chair outside the door to the lift leading to Cate's rooms. There was only one way in and out, and I intended to make sure no one bothered her. I trusted only a handful in the castle, Emma included, and planned to spend every moment I could, including sleeping in the chair to keep her safe. She'd never allow me to hover, so I'd watch over her in secret.

A week passed. I'd turned irritable from trying to sleep in that blasted chair every night. No sign of Lucas. Cate and Mya bonded over his absence, their eyes watering whenever his name was mentioned. With Molly missing too, he could be anywhere. Dev returned to Terra with Emily and spread the word to the underground that Cate was safe. We didn't wait for Caelum's newspaper reporting. We wanted to control the narrative and provide Cate's side of the story.

Dev had our printers in Terra working around the clock with runners passing out copies all over Caelum. Mya wrote the stories from here, with Mocha delivering to Dev. We had no idea whether her persuasiveness would hold up on paper; I doubted it would. We did know, however, that she'd made a powerful speech to the advisors of Caelum. She had a way with words, and it helped her feel useful while waiting for Lucas.

Roy ordered funeral arrangements, demanded the entire household wear black, but for once, stayed out of sight, either grieving or plotting. My bet was both. Perhaps Lucas's absence was for the best. At least until we confirmed Cate's ascension to the throne.

She would have liked to travel the kingdom giving speeches and answering questions, but the advisors kept her under house arrest. A cage more gilded than her last.

Finally, after another week, the funeral arrived. The aristocracy, in town to pay their respects, would meet the next day. It had been less than a year since King Aldridge's funeral, which seemed like a handful of weeks for Cate and me.

Cate, Mya, and I waited outside the castle entrance for transportation. A navy-colored veil half covered Cate's face. "You going to make it through?" The raw emotions stirred up for her father today would be difficult. Even though Graftonberg turned into her enemy, she would grieve for the kingdom over the loss of another king, which would lead to further instability. The carriage arrived, one of many in a long procession to the funeral. Mya entered first.

"What are you doing here?" a voice called behind us. I turned to see the ruddy-faced Roy striding jerkily toward us. "You're supposed to be confined to the castle."

Cate straightened. "I'm paying respects to your father."

His sausage finger pointed at her face, dangerously close to her eye. "You're making this about you. That's what's happening. I will not have my father's funeral become a spectacle for you."

The finger sent me over the edge. I grabbed his arm, digging into his fleshy bicep. "Kindly lower your hand." I kept my voice low and menacing.

He glared and slumped his arm to his side, rubbing the spot where I'd gripped.

Hope I left a bruise.

He returned his attention to Cate. "I see through your plans. Attempting to become the sympathetic daughter of the former king by pretending to grieve my father and win over the crowd."

Cate took a step forward. "Only you would think I would have such machinations." She gestured toward the carriage, Mya watching wide-eyed through the door. "Prince Daniel and I are leaving."

"You take one more step, and I'll throw you back in your cell." The beginnings of jowls wobbled in fury.

She ignored him, turning away, and entered the carriage.

"Guards!" Roy yelled, throwing a hand up, his cheeks mottling into patches of beet purple.

A swarm of blue-clad Caelum soldiers was upon us in moments.

"Throw her in the dungeon," Roy commanded. "Now."

CHAPTER 45
CATE

A guard—a man built like a bus—pulled me out of the carriage. I struggled, angling my weight backward, but I was no match. The horses whinnied and stamped their feet, unhappy with the commotion and the surrounding herd of soldiers.

"I'm not going back to that prison." I gazed at each of them. Baby faces, beards, graying temples, all with one thing in common: uncertainty in their eyes. "King Aldridge was my father. Maybe you're unsure about me, maybe you aren't. But most of you respected him and his wishes. Would he have wanted me thrown into a dungeon for the second time? In his own castle, no less?"

"She's trying to make you feel guilty. Who's in charge here? You're trained to follow orders, nothing more."

I huffed a laugh. "Exactly. Who's in charge?" I eyed Roy skeptically.

I took pity on the guards, their faces, a collage of downturned mouths, shifting eyes, and blushing cheeks. "Fine. I won't attend the funeral."

"Are you sure?" Daniel asked. "Because I think you should be there."

"Is King Dryden coming?" I'd been so wrapped up in everything else, this hadn't occurred to me before.

Daniel's hand slid to my back. "He went to your father's out of respect. I don't believe that's the case today." He flashed a glance at Roy, then turned his attention to me. "Stay or go?"

On the one hand, the proper thing would be to attend the funeral. It's what my conscience tells me is right. Yet, the faces standing before me tell a different story. These guards didn't want confrontation, and Roy wanted to remember his father with a proper ceremony without having me, someone he despises, present. I just put my own father's casket in the ground. The day had been horrible, and I didn't relish reliving it.

"I'm sorry for your loss," I told Roy, softening. "People will be telling you that nonstop. I had to block it out and focus on getting through it. Today is for the public and your father. Tomorrow is for grieving." I don't know why I said it. He'd just tried to put me in jail. Again. He'd taunted me daily when behind bars. But maybe he needed someone to treat him like a human. "And for the record," I started for the castle, "I *am* sorry for your loss."

The relief of not having to be reminded of another king's death the whole day slackened my shoulders. In truth, Roy had given me an out. I was tired of fighting. Tired of doing what was right.

"Your Highness," someone called. Brandon Hanson rushed toward me in his funeral finery, a silvery-blue cravat tucked under his neck. "You're leaving? The people need you. To ease their fears of a civil war."

"I—" My gaze shifted between Hanson and Roy.

"Come." Roy clenched his jaw before his features softened. "You might not believe it, but I think he'd want you there."

The ache in my chest returned. I'd braced myself to attend, and now that I'd let down my guard, I'd have to face it anyway. A nod was all I could muster. I half-stepped, half-crawled into the carriage across from Mya in my full skirt.

We watched the scenery march by. There were a few people observing the procession, some throwing flowers, but mostly, the road outside Neva lay empty, unlike the crowd-filled path before my father's funeral or one of my speeches. I didn't have it in me to feel satisfaction. The reality of more death was nothing to celebrate.

Daniel stretched out his legs in the carriage, letting out a small sigh. He'd been sleeping outside my elevator to stop anyone from coming up, and his exhaustion showed. Emma had told me the first night. I had her warn him before I went down so he could keep his secret, knowing he wouldn't listen if I told him to go to his own bed. And honestly, the comfort of someone I trusted guarding me while I slept—well, attempted to sleep—I didn't have the strength to give it up. The fatigue of restless nightmares left me emotional, raw, and on edge.

We arrived and were escorted to special seating in the front row, likely as much for Daniel and Mya, representing the Terran crown, as for me. Faces I recognized from fancy parties sprinkled the crowd. Those dinners my father had held to introduce me to the aristocracy, and to practice, often unsuccessfully, my social skills. I winced, remembering how many times I'd stuck my foot in my mouth, used the wrong fork, or failed polite conversation. If these were the people who were voting tomorrow, my odds just became slimmer.

An older woman sat next to me. I'd seen her before, though I couldn't remember her name. Daniel leaned over, a genuine smile crossing his lips, not the political fake one he often used. "Dame Hemlock. It's so good to see you."

So, *this* was the famous dame who'd been on my side this whole time. Daniel told me how she'd helped provide funds for the underground. It was humbling that she'd been my advocate for so long when I hadn't even remembered her name. Before I could greet her, the ceremony began.

The crowd was about a third the size of King Aldridge's funeral. I wondered how many truly supported Graftonberg. As the ceremony dragged on, appointed speakers extolled his good points. Like most villains, Graftonberg hadn't started or perhaps hadn't even ended entirely evil. He loved the kingdom, and he'd stood by my father. Beneath the power grab, the thread of wanting Caelum's success still wove its way into the fabric of his brief reign. This played out in the faulty belief that converting workers into unpaid servants to fill our coffers would help fight the Embers. He'd convinced himself that handing me over to Rowan was best for Caelum. He hadn't thought a teenage girl from America capable of running the realm, and he'd tried to prevent it the best way he knew how. Of course, this also meant he could continue as king.

The comparisons to my father's funeral ached like a never-healing wound. That day returned in flashes—the empty coffin lowered into the ground, the buzzing in my ears, the ice shell I'd constructed around myself to cope. I'd been up on the dais looking down at the people, at *my* people, the weight of their expectations chipping away at my confidence. Today, I was a spectator. In less than a year, Rowan had partially succeeded. The Concealed wasn't on the throne and may never be.

Once it ended, the pallbearers lifted the coffin onto the ceremonial carriage. I wished… I'm not sure what I wished. That he hadn't died, for one. That we'd been able to agree and work together. But it didn't matter what I wanted, because if I started down that path, I'd never return. I began to stand, but the count strode up the stairs of the dais, and simultaneously the dame placed a wrinkled hand on my knee.

"Thank you all for coming," he said. "The voting members of the aristocracy met early this morning. We know your hearts are heavy, and you, the people, are also concerned. Concerned who will lead us. Who will fight for our kingdom and protect us from the Embers?"

"They're announcing it now, not tomorrow," Daniel whispered, his breath hot in my ear against the icy chill that snaked across the rest of my body.

A stone the size of a bowling ball lodged in my windpipe. I would either need to flee from a newly appointed Graftonberg monarchy or take the helm. The dichotomy flip-flopped through my thoughts. How would I get out through all these people? The pressure built, my invisible bricklayer mounting cement onto my chest. I searched for the easiest exit, finding guards posted everywhere.

My fingers dug into Daniel's leg. "We need to be ready to run." Then I leaned in toward Dame Hemlock. "Will you help me? Help me escape?" Suddenly, I couldn't see any other path. Why else would they announce the successor after a love-fest for Graftonberg? They were setting the people up for Roy. I glanced across the aisle. His normally ruddy cheeks had turned the color of soured milk.

"We've weighed our decision for two candidates, both heirs to the crown." The count's voice echoed.

Roy was only an heir because Graftonberg stole the crown, but whatever.

"The great King Aldridge led us, as did his father before him, and so on. We believe that Princess Catherine is the rightful successor to the throne."

The crowd broke out in whispers, spreading like a game of telephone on the playground.

"I trust you, dear." Dame Hemlock patted my knee again. "Now go up there and convince everyone else."

Up there? As in give a speech, unprepared? I turned to Daniel, my heart ping-ponging beneath my ribs. His expression tamped my fear—pride and relief etching every feature, his eyes watery with unshed tears.

"You'll be amazing," he whispered.

I didn't have time to spiral. I climbed the steps as the count called my name. Deliberately, I avoided looking toward Roy. An irrational panic that this was all a trick and the guards would collect me for the dungeon, kicking and screaming in front of all these people, erupted. I swallowed down the fear and faced them.

The citizens watched expectantly, the atmosphere different from my father's funeral. There were no shouts of *long live the queen,* only uncertainty mixed with fear. Graftonberg hadn't treated them well, and I'd abandoned them.

"First," I said, projecting with the Caelum amplifying device, "I would like to make sure every one of you knows I will not disappear again. Caelum is my home. You've heard a lot of stories about me. Some of them are true, some are not. I did travel through the portal to save my adoptive family. We almost killed Rowan, but failed. In turn, he nearly murdered me in the seconds before I passed back through." I wanted to be truthful, but to keep my family safe, I kept their presence a secret.

"The portals are unstable. I was scared, lost control, and ultimately lost time. In your reality, I stood up on this dais nearly a year ago. But for me, it feels like a little over six weeks. My heart is still raw from my father's death. A wound scars my ankle that hasn't completely healed from an Ember's sword when I fought in Ember City. I didn't plan to abandon my people, yet I disappointed you. You counted on me, and I wasn't there. But I promise." I placed my hand on my chest. "I promise it was not intentional."

My thoughts tumbled out of my mouth before I could catch them, "So, what can you expect moving forward? I will rule as my father taught me. Every Caelum citizen will be paid what they've earned. Every person in this kingdom matters, and it's our loyalty and love for Caelum that will make us stronger. And you know what else will help? Peace. Not with the Embers, but with the Terrans. Our kingdoms will join forces to rid us of the true enemy." I swallowed, taking a moment before my closing remarks, when the sounds of whispers rippled through the crowd.

I searched the horizon to find a sea of Caelum soldiers approaching on horseback. Not just an ordinary scouting group. An organized battalion. In the next few seconds, I needed to know… whose side they were on… mine? Or Roy's.

CHAPTER 46
LUCAS

Seven days ago…

I scraped the last of the rich eggs and sausage from the ceramic plate and scooped them into my mouth. Living secretly above a tavern had its perks. John kept me well fed. The only problem? I'd need new clothes at this rate. Nothing to do but eat. I paced the small, tidy room. The blankets I'd used were already folded and stacked at the end of the too-short tweed sofa that left my neck in a crick every morning. The only whiff of the outside I'd experienced in four days was the small vase of wildflowers on the table Grace arranged, as if I were an honored guest. Every moment, I wondered if today would be the day I'd leave for the wilderness with Molly and never return. Yet Grace continued to plead for me to wait for news, and John plied me with delicious offerings, making it too easy to delay my departure.

The only portal to the outside was the small, curtain-clad window overlooking the northwest area of town, which I kept cracked to hear and smell whatever I could. Anything to make me feel a part of something other than these four walls.

The street below typically bustled with store owners opening their businesses and early-bird shoppers preparing to gather their day's supplies. Most had a spring in their step, rushing to complete their tasks, yet still taking the time to smile and chat with their neighbor. Quorum still had plenty of problems, but this border town appeared happier than southern Caelum near the capital, under Graftonberg's iron fist. His edicts hadn't yet trickled here, or perhaps the townspeople just ignored him. They had a tight-knit sense of preserving their own that came from living this long close to Ember territory.

Today, however, something rang different. Men and women still hurried through the streets, their movements deflated. They talked periodically, sometimes pointing, then skittered off to the next person. Closed signs hanging in windows didn't turn to *Open*. No jaunty tinkle of bells from customers opening the doors to shop. My breakfast turned over in my stomach. Something was afoot. I paced the room, peeking out the window with every lap of the cramped space. Down, back, curtain, repeat. With each circle, I became more and more convinced something was wrong, yet I didn't dare leave in daylight, so as to protect John and Grace from others discovering they harbored a criminal.

Just when I was ready to throw out caution and creep down the stairs, Grace came barreling up, wisps of pale hair escaping her braid, sticking to a damp forehead.

"Lucas," she huffed. "I was out near the gate buying onions when I heard the news. Ran…" she doubled over to catch her breath, "here."

I waited, dread oozing down my middle.

"There's an army. About five minutes outside the city. And they're coming this way."

Instinctively, I glanced across the room at my weapons still sitting on the coffee table. "Embers?"

"No, that's just it. They're Caelum soldiers. I climbed the steps up the wall to see."

Why would they send an army just for me? My brain flitted through options: sneak out and head toward Molly while I still could or stand my ground and face the consequences. Yet… Roy would be a fool to waste this many resources. It had to be something else. Didn't it?

"Stay here," Grace said, deciding for me. "Pack your stuff up just in case." She too glanced at my weapons. "We'll wait here. Da's heading to see what's going on." She bit her lip, spotting my empty plate. "You want more breakfast? I can whip up—"

"No." A nervous chuckle escaped. "I'm full. Too full." I patted my belly. "Gotta keep this figure up, ya know?" My joking fell flat, the room descending into silence. Truthfully, the breakfast sat like an enormous cement block in my stomach.

Grace played with the strings of her flowered apron she'd looped and tied in front. I idly wondered if the ill-fitting garment had been her mother's.

"I'll just… clean the tables downstairs and wait for Da." She jogged down the steps, unwilling to stare at the walls with me, nervous energy trailing behind.

There wasn't much to pack. I'd left in a hurry, snatching up a few things I'd stored in Molly's barn. This left me pacing until, finally, John called up the stairs to have me come down.

Were they turning me in? That first panicked thought filled me with shame. I trusted John and Grace. I grabbed my bag and joined the two of them in the restaurant. The place still sat empty except for them. Neither cracked a smile at my appearance.

John tapped his fingers nervously on the table. "General Dixon is taking his regiment along the border towns and gathering soldiers."

Dixon was an ally. Good news for me, not for Caelum. He could need that army only for one thing.

War.

But with who? Civil War? Terrans? Or Embers?

"The Embers are coming," Grace answered my unspoken question.

"What? Why now? I thought they were playing the long game." I exchanged perplexed looks with Grace, both of us thinking of the baby factory we'd witnessed in The Camp. How they were raising an army.

Grace scrunched her brow. "I don't know?"

"Rowan's struck a deal with Roy, Graftonberg's son," I sounded out. "That snake can't be trusted." It was the only thing that made sense.

John slumped into a chair, rubbing his forehead with three fingers. "Lucas. I think you should meet with the general. Caelum's going to need you for… whatever this is."

"But, Da! What if he's arrested?"

Dueling thoughts of duty versus self-preservation swirled like a stirred pot of overdone wumbeast stew. I hesitated, digesting my options, knowing that abandoning my kingdom turned my stomach more than fear for my life. I was a soldier. I'd given my word, and I'd keep it. Until they no longer wanted me. Which could be sooner rather than later, but there was only one way to find out.

Grace held back tears admirably—she always was stronger than me. I stepped outside for the first time in four days. The smells of nervous bodies, baking bread from the bakery next door, and horses filled my lungs, reminding me what I'd be missing if Molly and I disappeared forever.

I headed to the gate and found a group of Caelum soldiers just inside. Presumably, the rest of the battalion waited elsewhere. Among them, General Dixon spoke to one of the guards.

"Lucas!" he called, catching sight of me. A lopsided smile stretched, the scar from Ember flames permanently marring one side of his face.

At least *he* didn't want to arrest me. Dixon would never appear this happy to see me hanged, I was sure of that much.

"What are you doing here?" he asked. The unspoken question lay heavy between us: *why are you not helping the underground at Caelum Castle?* There were too many people around to explain. Too many questions my explanation would raise.

"What about you?" I asked instead. "What's going on?"

A flash of humanity struck his features—the downturned mouth, the sheen of worry crossing his eyes—concern poking through the usual mask. "The Embers. They're preparing for war. Our spies have seen it." His gaze locked on a weed sprouting through the cracks of the dusty path. "I'm glad you're here." He nodded more to himself than to me. "Molly?"

"Out in the woods. Not far. You need us to carry a message?"

"I've sent multiple messengers. Men. Falcons. Graftonberg should have received them."

He doesn't know. No one bothered to send word this far north. Or had he survived? A chill climbed my scalp. "General." I pulled him away from the men nearby and lowered my voice. "I believe Graftonberg to be dead. Have you not heard?" I shuffled my feet. "Or at least gravely injured?" That last bit was laced with hope. I had no desire to be the man who killed Caelum's king. Even if I lamented his placement on the throne.

His salt-and-pepper bushy brows raised. "Been on the move. I've heard nothing."

"We need some privacy. Can you spare a few minutes?"

He directed soldiers to continue their work, which involved collecting every able-bodied man and asking them to fight. A hard sell for the remaining people of Quorum, who'd lost so many in The Great Battle. "Evacuate everyone," he called, more a warning than a new instruction.

"What?" I asked.

"The border towns. They aren't safe. And every village south of here. Their plans are not to travel through the forests. They want to raze the kingdom."

The town teemed with people, weaving and darting, gathering supplies, finding their families, and spreading the news. The general agreed to head to the tavern with me for privacy. "Rowan tried to make a deal, and it didn't go his way. He's out for revenge." I dodged a young boy dashing in my path before opening the door to the pub.

"Grace. John. Pack your things. We're all going," I called out as soon as we entered. It took a moment for my eyes to adjust to the dimness. John poked his head out from the kitchen.

"The town is evacuating." I turned to the general. "How long?"

"We need to be out in two hours." He swiveled. "May I form a headquarters for my officers and me here?" He tilted his head toward me. "Lucas, too."

John still worked to digest Dixon's words. "Uh, yeah. Yes. Of course you can," he said, his voice growing firmer.

John brought the general food when he should have been packing, as I unwound my tale.

"So, you don't actually know he's dead."

I shrugged. "No. But…" The glassy look in his eyes. The puddle of blood. His barrel chest motionless. I'd seen plenty of dead men before. "I'm pretty sure."

"And who will succeed him?"

I tilted my head toward the beamed ceiling. "I wish I knew. Depends on how much dirt Roy can hold over people's heads, likely."

The general leaned forward, a shock of gray hair falling over his brow. "We could use you in this fight, Lucas. You and Molly."

He didn't ask it, though I knew what he meant. He wanted to know whether I planned to desert. Like that guy in the woods who poisoned Molly. For a fleeting second, I imagined myself growing a long beard and trading wild game for food. My decision had already been made. The general didn't have to convince me.

"I'm with you," I said. "What can I do?"

"There are a few more border towns west of here. You and Molly can warn them. Instruct the townspeople to evacuate to the capital and meet us on the road to Neva in a couple days." He took another bite and chewed. "Would you rather stay low profile?"

"No," I assured him. "I'll come." I didn't know what we'd be marching to, but I was certain it needed to be faced.

CHAPTER 47 **DANIEL**

My chest filled with so many emotions that I could hardly listen to Cate's speech. Relief for her safety. For Caelum. Pride for facing her fears and climbing those steps. She addressed the crowd like a queen. She'd be up against enormous obstacles: the promise of peace between two kingdoms that were bent on finding fault with their neighbor, Rowan, and his threat to come for her again, and me left without my powers to protect her.

Cate, up on the dais, saw them first. Her eyes fixed on the horizon. I, too, craned my neck to take in a sea of Caelum blue soldiers, interspersed with villagers. As they came closer, women and children became apparent, families clustered together, all marching toward us. Mya's breath caught beside me.

"Look." She pointed to the sky in the distance.

Molly. And if I squinted, Lucas could be seen riding her.

"He's come back." She turned to me, tears tracking her cheeks. "He's back," she repeated. Her love reflected in every tear. I'd known her feelings were strong, and she'd been struggling without him, but it wasn't until this moment, the sheer joy so evident, that I understood how deep they ran.

She loved him. She loved him as much as I loved Cate. I squeezed her arm, fighting back my tumultuous emotions of this day. Two Terran heirs had completely fallen for the enemy's finest. I caught myself. They weren't the enemy. Not anymore. And Mya and I must do everything we could to make sure it stayed that way.

General Dixon greeted Cate and announced that a massive number of Embers marched this way. The crowd erupted in murmurs, the sound growing like an ocean's wave until the group shouted and talked over themselves in alarm. When Cate finally persuaded them to quiet, Dixon continued, explaining that one of our men had escaped The Camp and divulged the Embers' plans. Additional spies confirmed the invasion.

He'd dispatched messengers to King Dryden and hoped the Terrans would join the fight. I wished there was time for Mya or me to convince Father ourselves. We'd need to assemble quickly and meet for battle as far north as we could, because each town the Embers traveled through, they intended to torch. Ember City had been emptied of every male fighter and marched our way.

The crowd dispersed, and the carriage ride was surprisingly quiet, our internal thoughts and fears dominating the ride back to the castle.

"Will you check on Lucas?" Cate asked. "He should be at the meeting." We'd planned to convene with General Dixon in one hour.

I glanced around for Roy and watched him enter the castle, suspicious that he might track down Lucas first. "I'll find him."

Mya arrived in the carriage behind us, accompanied by the dame, and I strode toward her, whispering, "Let's find Lucas."

We scurried toward Molly's enclosure on the outskirts of the castle grounds. Lucas hadn't landed at the funeral, though we both watched him fly in this direction.

"He may not even know Cate is queen," Mya said.

Lucas had come to fight the Embers, knowing he might have to turn himself in. Once, I considered him an enemy. Then my opinion changed to simply *thorn in my side*. Somewhere along the way, I'd grown to respect him. My pace quickened at the unease growing in my belly.

The door to Molly's enclosure stood partway open, and Mya rushed in. I peeked inside, finding them embracing, Molly resting in the back. Giving them a moment or two, my thoughts turned to battle, body sagging against the barn. We'd just been through this. *Twice* in the last few months. It must feel longer to everyone else, but surely not long enough. We had to get rid of them once and for all.

The sounds and smells of war infused my head. The fallen men, the panic in their eyes, right before I killed them, the acrid stench of smoke. I'd be putting myself in peril to fight with almost no power. But Cate needed me. Didn't she? I'd been ignoring my problem, hoping it would go away, and the energy would return before I truly required it.

Unfortunately, I just ran out of time.

The door creaked open. "Daniel?" Mya asked. "You coming?"

I followed her into the dim space. I clapped Lucas on the back. "Thought you needed a whole army for your return to civilization, did you?"

He grinned. "Nothing but the best. Cate's been promising me a parade for way too long." He held his palms up in a what's-a-guy-to-do gesture.

He sobered and explained he'd been hiding out in Quorum and delivering evacuation warnings to towns that would be in the Embers' path. "And…" he watched our faces. "You guys know I never meant to kill Graftonberg. I would nev—"

"Of course you wouldn't," Mya interrupted. "Anyone who's ever met you knows that."

"I don't want Cate to pardon me if it's going to make people question her decisions. I shouldn't get special treatment."

I had started to like the guy, but he was being a bit of an idiot. "You had a clear shot of Rowan. It's not your fault someone shoved Graftonberg. I would have taken it too." I placed a hand on his shoulder and smirked. "I'd tell you otherwise."

He laughed. "You would."

"Come on," Mya dragged Lucas toward the door. "We don't want to be late for the meeting."

"What meeting?"

"We'll fill you in on the way."

When we arrived at the conference room, General Dixon, Cate, and Hanson were already seated. The expansive space with the enormous round table wasn't one of Cate's favorites, but it was likely chosen for privacy and to convey a sense of formality in her role. She'd posted two guards outside, instructing them not to let anyone in without her permission. Ironically, those same soldiers had first been under Graftonberg's and then Roy's command just an hour earlier. She'd have to ferret out loyalty, though for now, her primary worry remained the Embers.

"We need a battle plan," Cate said as we took seats around the table. "Daniel, the general has sent word to King Dryden. Would you write a letter to your father as well? Send it through Mocha. We don't have time to travel ourselves."

"Of course," I replied. "And Mya can pen something too."

Cate shifted her attention to the general. "I assume you've come up with an idea?"

He kept his face neutral. "What kind of range do you have these days?" he asked Cate, referring to her rainmaking abilities.

"It's good. Natural," she said.

He tilted his head. "And the prince?"

She placed her hand on my knee under the table. "I haven't tested it, but since the portal, the energy feels different. More accessible."

My leg tensed under her fingers. I wanted to contribute. The impotence of losing my powers, the implication that Cate didn't need me, felt unbalanced. Like I was missing a part of myself. My worth. And I wasn't sure how to move forward. "I have the opposite problem," I said, striving to keep the hollowness out of my voice. "I might not have a role in this battle, because at least for now, my powers are essentially gone."

Dixon's steady expression helped ease some of the emptiness. "We'll use you in an advisory position, then."

I leaned forward. "I still need to be there. At minimum, to meet the Terran soldiers when they arrive."

"Fine. Anything else?" He looked around the room.

"It all seems so fast," Lucas said. "Mya and I thought he was raising an army… and now this?"

Cate sighed heavily. "Graftonberg informed him how far the Caelum military has dwindled. He's also seen us arguing with the Terrans. He probably believes now is his best chance while we're unorganized. I don't know… Rowan's hard to figure out."

Mya and Lucas exchanged glances. "We discovered Rowan grew up in England," Mya blurted.

"We heard," I said. Alana had told us.

Mya continued explaining to the general. I wasn't sure where she was heading with this. "His parents were Embers that crossed through the portal," she said. "The archives back in England had a lot of information."

"I think his hatred started with his father being snubbed by the society there, then dying not long after," Lucas added. "Rowan connected the two. Sounds as if he became obsessed with the Ember culture."

"And proving that the Embers were worthy," Mya said. "That's why he's always saying he's a man of his word. It's not about a lack of impulse for him. Or inherent evil. In his own sick way, he wants to help build a society for them."

"And he hates the Caelumites and Terrans because he blames them for his father's death."

"The villain origin story." Cate tapped her lip. "No time to do anything about it now." She turned to Dixon. "General? One more thing. Alana's alive. Here."

I'd almost never seen the man surprised, but Alana returning from the dead would drop anyone's jaw.

"She's guarding my family," Cate said.

Lucas piped up, "Alana's still healing. I'm not sure she's able to battle."

"At this point," Dixon said, recovering from his shock, "let's keep gathering fighters. We may have to go forward without Alana. And a plan won't be definitive until we find out if the Terrans show." The general laced his fingers together on the table. "I'd like to meet the Embers at the border near Quorum. If we make it that far north and avoid clashing with them, I have some ideas. We'll have to be fluid, ready to adapt to how quickly the Terrans and the Embers march. The meeting point will be crucial." He stood. "We leave tomorrow, if that's alright with you, Your Highness."

Cate swallowed. "Tomorrow. We'll be ready."

CHAPTER 48
CATE

Once again, my world tilted on its axis. I'd seesawed between nearly being thrown in prison this morning and becoming the queen of Caelum. It wouldn't be official until after the coronation, which still remained in peril. We'd have to survive the Embers. This may be the last time I sat at this conference table with these friends.

"We need every able person," Lucas's voice strummed with tension, breaking me out of my spiral. "I'm going to pass the word with the underground."

"Not just the underground," I responded. "We don't have to hide anymore. I'll craft a plea to the people." I turned to Mya. "Will you help me write it?"

"And we'll get it to Terra too," she replied.

"Send as many birds and messengers out to every printer in the kingdom. We'll have to hope people show. Last time we said it was the final battle. We can't keep crying wolf. This has to be it."

"Will you be okay?" Daniel asked quietly.

The undercurrent of unspoken words rattled beneath my ribcage. What he really meant to say was, *Can you make it rain without killing yourself?* The energy pulsed under my skin, ready to be harnessed. The feeling so different than before, I almost wondered if some of Daniel's powers had transferred to me. Yet I couldn't detect others' emotions, so that didn't make sense either.

"I think so," I replied. But I didn't know for certain. As strong as I felt, when the time came, everyone around the table knew I'd sacrifice myself by using my own energy—my lifeblood—to stop the Embers, and none of them could stop me.

"Lucas," I said, changing the subject. "I haven't had a chance to tell you how glad I am to see you. We all are."

"I didn't mean to," he blurted, blond head ducking.

He didn't have to say it. I knew he'd never intentionally kill Graftonberg. "We know."

When we all stood, I squeezed him tight. "Thank you." I smiled into the wool of his uniform, my cheek squished against his chest. "Seems like we've been here before," I murmured. I'd thanked Lucas more times than I can count, and it would never be enough. His loyalty couldn't be matched.

He pulled back. "Let's get to work. We have two kingdoms to rally."

It was strange to be astride North again, traveling toward Ember territory. For one, my body had turned soft being out of the saddle for so long, and I'd be sore. Two, the last time I'd done this, we'd been going to rescue King Aldridge, Lucas, and Mya. I tried to shift my focus to the good times Father and I shared together rather than his death. The lessons he'd imparted on how to be a monarch and lead the realm. We'd pored over maps, he'd described areas in such detail, with a gentle smile, it I almost seemed as if I'd been there myself. I loved my kingdom, and gratitude spilled over for those who supported me—Daniel, Lucas, Mya, and Dev. And new advocates, like the dame or Hanson.

The Caelumites had come in full force. Anyone old enough to fight within riding distance had shown. They believed us. Nobody wanted our kingdom razed to the ground, decimated by our enemy. Shopkeepers, businessmen, cooks, and stable hands emptied from Neva. Even some women who claimed to be adept with knives and pitchforks answered the call, preparing in their own way behind the scenes. No one stopped them. We welcomed everyone with open arms.

The atmosphere buzzed with both tension and a proud sense of duty. Chills rippled up my scalp at the sight. They believed in this kingdom. They believed in me. I blew out a shaky breath. Now I had to deliver.

I glanced over at Daniel, riding beside me on Raven. He'd erected a wall between us. Still flimsy, as if I could break through it with effort, but I sensed he needed more time. The constant worry in his expression, the desperate, wide pupils I'd catch for a moment before they shifted away, stirred an ache in my chest. He knew the foolish risk of going into battle without his powers.

Yet he would not abandon me.

I wanted to lock him up in my former cell. Wrap him in tissue paper and keep him safe forever. We'd fought about this before, and if nothing else, I wanted to learn from my mistakes. He'd never settle for advising from afar. I hated him for it. I loved him for it. My stomach protested its contents because of it.

I racked my brain to formulate a plan, one that would make him feel useful and keep him out of danger. None had materialized. I'd tried to send him to Terra with Mya, who traveled to rally troops and persuade King Dryden, if he hadn't already mobilized their army. We ignored the uncomfortable reality that a late Terran presence might just be *too* late. I couldn't dwell on those circumstances—being woefully undermanned even with every able Caelumite in my midst.

Mya had worked with me to write a plea for help, addressed to both kingdoms. The two militaries' paths wouldn't cross for days, both heading north, which meant we had no idea if Caelum would make this stand without Terran backing.

Mya and Lucas had said their goodbyes not long after our meeting yesterday. Their passionate kiss heated my cheeks before I turned away, pulling Daniel's stare from them and prying his clenched fingers into mine. "They're good together," I'd whispered in his ear.

He'd nodded distractedly, the idea still growing on him.

"What's going on in that brain of yours?" I asked once we had a bit of space between us and the other riders. His dark hair hid part of his face, flopping over the brow of his slumped head.

"What if I never get it back?" he asked quietly. "A king should be able to lead his kingdom in battle. Be able to use the power unique to their people." He kept his gaze on Raven's mane.

How has life flipped on end so quickly? The irony of our switched roles sat bitter and sour on my tongue. The number of obstacles to our happiness continued to pile. Once we solved one problem, another arose. Would it always be this way? After his words floated between us with no answer, I asked, "Is it better when we're close? Does it help like back in Oregon?"

"I—I don't know. We can try." The pain in his voice reverberated through me, a mournful echo in a lonely tunnel. "Later. Tonight, at camp." After a moment, he whispered, "Maybe I shouldn't be king."

"Hey." My tone turned sharp, and he finally looked up, eyes the color of a smoky sky, and so uncertain I could almost see the storm brewing beneath them. "It's about what's in here." My free hand clutched my chest. "You have the hugest heart of anyone I know. It will lead you and Terra, no matter your powers."

"I've never felt worthy." He bit his lip and looked how I imagined a boy-Daniel appeared ten years ago. Lashes shadowed his cheeks, the pain and doubt brought on by a father who never approved.

"That's King Dryden talking. Not you," I shot back.

His hair drooped forward again, his gaze returning to Raven. "I can't tell the difference anymore," he mumbled. "Between what I want, what I should want, and what I'm capable of. It's all muddled." He straightened. "Doesn't matter. Let's just ride." Raven trotted forward at his urging. I let the space remain between us, the gap widening. A chasm only he could fix.

CHAPTER 49
LUCAS

"Time to go again, Mols." I hefted my tired body onto her back. "One more stop before we meet up with the others."

We had flown for days, zigzagging across the kingdom until we'd reached Graftonberg's funeral, Cate's ascension to the throne, and the relief of receiving my freedom in the form of a pardon. Though it hadn't freed me from the guilt.

Molly and I traveled a serpentine route north, warning and spreading the word of battle and of our new queen. With my saddlebag full of Cate's written plea, I relayed the news. The reactions were almost all the same. Fear. Panic. Resoluteness. They'd been too scared to speak out about Graftonberg, but belief in the prophecy, and ultimately Cate, created an undercurrent of strength. They'd fight with her because they believed in the prophecy. Deep-seated in their makeup, it had been part of bedtime stories, passed from adult to child, and on to the next generation. I'd memorized a portion of Cate's letter to the people, read over and over in those quiet moments at night by the fire, or aloud to a crowd in a town square.

The time is now.

If you've ever believed in the prophecy, take up your mantle and fight. Fight for your kingdom, because if we don't come together, there will be no kingdom to fight for. You have created this place full of heart, and resilience, and magic, and hope. A place I've fallen in love with and call home. We cannot hand it to the Embers.

I will be with you. In the rain, we will save ourselves.

Together, we stand stronger.

Villages and towns packed up supplies. They took the grandparents' swords from their honored places, proud above the mantle, sharpened their knives, and headed toward Quorum. I'd grown fond of the little town and hoped the Embers were slow to gather and slower to march. Because if they moved quickly, I feared there would be nothing left of the Four Horseshoes Tavern and the Royal Inn, or the ice cream shop I'd yet to sample.

Molly dipped in the sky and shook her head. "That's right," I told her, "there aren't any towns this way." In another hour, I estimated we'd be there. "You can rest for a bit when we get there." Her wings flagged. We'd flown too many days, her fatigue showing at each slow flap, along with our loss of altitude. I'd pushed hard. Every citizen I reached was another who might help save our kingdom, the fire in my belly fueling me to keep going. One more village. One more person.

We landed outside a cottage in the woods, Molly's talons shifting with renewed energy once she realized where we were. A boy ran toward us first, his dark hair growing over his ears.

"Molly," he cried, cheeks appled into a wide grin.

I slid off and knelt to him. "Hey, Jack. How are you?"

Cate's little brother ignored me, arrowing straight to Molly's head, which had bent to greet him.

Cate's mom emerged next, with a surprised expression that morphed into a huge smile. "He's been bored out here in the woods with no one to play with." As she came closer, she asked, her grin fading, "Cate?"

"She's good."

Tears of relief rimmed her eyes, and I gave her arm a squeeze. "A lot has happened. Can you find the others?" I glanced back to see Jack running his hands down Molly's seal-skin orange neck. "Mols? Keep an eye on Jack?" If she weren't so tired, I might worry she'd hurt him in her exuberance, but it wouldn't surprise me if she curled up and watched with one golden eye open, allowing him to stroke her spine.

We found Carlos cutting wood behind the house. Alana sat on the porch, her gaze calculating. I eased my muscles into a wooden rocker next to her, staring out at the forest beyond. "It's time," I said.

We sat there, her rocking back and forth, me waiting for her response. She'd know what I meant. Carlos and Sofia sensed we needed a moment, though their tension at discovering more about Cate was evident in their whispered exchanges.

"I'm enjoying this life," Alana finally replied. "No politics, no fighting. Just the peace of this forest."

"Good for your recovery," I replied, implying that I hoped she was well enough to join us. Alana was renowned for her stubbornness, and even with my subtle jabs, it would be difficult to convince her to do anything she didn't want.

The rocking stopped. "I've done my part."

I retrieved Cate's letter from my satchel and handed it to her. "You need to finish."

I stood and pulled Cate's parents aside, giving Alana time to process. They peppered me with questions, some of which were easy to answer, while others were more difficult. Because I didn't know if Cate would survive. If *any* of us would survive. Taking Alana from them might prove dangerous, but we needed her. Tim and another soldier I trusted were traveling behind and would be here in several days. They were all we could spare, but at least Cate's family wouldn't be completely alone out here in the wilderness. Someone had been bringing them supplies every two weeks, though they could have joined the rest of the army. Cate had approved of the plan to provide them with guards, her green eyes filling with longing to see her family, creases forming in her brow with worry over their safety.

"Can we stop it? The battle?" Sofia asked, her voice strung with panic. I could tell Cate's mom struggled to understand how this could be happening. Her teenage daughter, who used to have trouble cleaning her room and finishing her homework on time, now led an army. They hadn't had the opportunity to see who she'd become. A leader I trusted. She had more to learn, but we all did.

"I hope—I believe this is our chance to end the war," I said. "If all goes as planned, you won't have to hide. Jack can go to school, live a normal life here." It all hinged on Alana's prophecy and whether it would be fulfilled.

"I want to see her," Sofia demanded. "Just in case..." Her words deflated, her features collapsing.

She doesn't make it, I finished in my head. "There's no time. I'm sorry. She wanted to visit, but it was too dangerous. Rowan still doesn't know you're here. And if... if things don't go as planned, you'll still be able to have a life. In time, integrate with society." I didn't want to give them false hope. If Rowan succeeded, there might not be anything left. Guilt led me to add, "One day, you may need to travel to Terra." If the Terrans didn't join us, they had a chance to survive. At least longer than Caelum did.

Alana stood, joining us. "Will I finally get a chance to ride that dragon of yours?"

A laugh burst out of my chest, full of pent-up nerves and relief. "No time like the present."

Alana gathered a few belongings, and we left Cate's family, teary and confused at the sudden change of events. I didn't blame them. In the span of an hour, their lives had once again been upended.

We soared closer to Quorum, a day's dragon ride from the secret cabin in the forest. Below, the Caelum army marched. The front, a sea of cerulean uniforms, and pulling up the rear were villagers dressed in a patchwork of colors, mostly blue, as they had been instructed to avoid brown to prevent being mistaken for Embers. I circled the area, flying south to see the people of Caelum in varying-sized groups. If I flew far enough, I'd likely find more several days behind our soldiers, either delayed or simply not receiving the message in time. I just hoped the battle wouldn't be over when they reached it.

And somewhere out east, I prayed the Terran military marched this way.

We swooped over a knot of soldiers, searching for Cate or the general. We found them in the center, surrounded on all sides. Flying low, I shouted, "Make way!" They created space while Molly hovered and dropped into a small patch of grass.

Cate rushed forward, embracing Alana, then me. "I knew she'd come," she whispered in my ear.

More optimistic than I, she hadn't been there to see the weariness beneath the deepening wrinkles when I'd left her those months ago. I hoped she'd healed enough to fight. I hadn't asked, only assumed she would refuse to come if she wasn't fit. Seeing her next to Cate now, she seemed small, almost frail. A creep of doubt slithered its way in.

"I need you to find the Embers," Cate told me, the abrupt subject change catching me off guard. Her mouth was taut, the strain evident around her eyes. "Is Molly okay to keep going?"

"A little food, then she'll manage," I said with a stab of guilt. I'd rather she curled up for a nap, but she'd be willing to do whatever we needed.

She leaned in. "Any news of the Terrans?"

I shook my head.

"I'm trying to convince Daniel to go. He keeps telling me they'll be here or they won't. Nothing will change either way."

"He still doesn't have his powers?"

"No. And I'm out of my mind worried about him. I've discreetly instructed at least twenty soldiers to guard him. It's just…"

"If we're outnumbered, it might not matter."

"Exactly." Her gaze raked across me. "You think you can convince him?"

I huffed a laugh. "Me?"

A smile crept onto her lips. "Believe it or not, he respects you."

"Impossible," I volleyed back, trying to keep a straight face. Truthfully, the feeling was mutual. Daniel had proven himself. Plus, being Mya's brother helped. I couldn't hate him forever while loving Mya. Thinking of her, even for a moment, veered my focus elsewhere—to Terra. She buffeted my will to win this war. Because if we did… nothing would stop me from pounding down the Terran castle door to be with her, no matter what King Dryden said.

Daniel stood a few yards away, speaking to Alana. I rolled my neck, stiff from days of riding, as if preparing for battle, and strolled over.

"Hey." I punched him lightly on the arm.

He raised his dark brows.

Maybe we weren't at the arm-punching stage. While Alana moved to speak to General Dixon, who just arrived, I leaned in. "The best way to help Cate is to fall back and join the Terran army."

His eyes narrowed. "She put you up to this?"

"Of course she did. Doesn't mean I'm not right."

"She might need me. I strengthen her abilities, you know." He crossed his arms, widening his stance.

My turn to raise my brows. "Is that still true? She thinks she has it under control. And worrying about every step you take will distract her."

His gaze shifted away. "I promised I would never abandon her."

"It's not abandoning if she *asks* you to leave."

The hurt crossing his features came as a surprise. I'd always thought the guy was as cold as ice. Looked as though I'd hit too low with that one.

"I..." A pause. A heavy breath. "I don't know how to do this, Lucas. Leave her and not be a part of this battle."

"If you stay, you may unintentionally leave her." This time, I spoke softly, his vulnerability pulling on my conscience, "The Embers—"

"Might kill me, yes, I get it," he interrupted irritably.

"So?"

"I still think I can help her with the energy, especially if she weakens."

He was so stubborn. I shook my head. "I'll tell her I tried. Just be sure you're making this decision for her and the kingdoms, not your own ego." Again, with the below-the-belt shots. This conversation made me feel worse and worse. Even if I was right. "Think on it. I'm going to take Molly to find the Embers and hope I don't run into any dragons."

The farther north we flew, the greater the possibility. In my last foray with them, I'd learned they had no interest in helping us, though I did discover their desire for freedom from humans. Hopefully, that included the Embers. Because if they came in full force, we didn't stand a chance.

CHAPTER 50 **CATE**

I watched Lucas and Molly until they were specks on the horizon. My chest brimmed with gratitude for my supporters. Lucas. Alana. The people of Caelum. And Daniel. My heart felt fragile and stretched, as if any loss could tear it and cause it to burst. I worried over them. Loved them. Feared for them.

If only we had time to strategize and allow the kingdom to strengthen its bonds with me as their queen, but Rowan had seen Caelum's vulnerability in our chaos and knew he should strike. Speed was his ally, and I could only hope he struggled to organize his own men enough to delay a battle. The more we fell back, the deeper he'd invade Caelum's lands. More towns and villages would be decimated. At The Great Battle, they'd committed mild damage on their way south, but their main objective was to fight on Caelum Castle grounds. They'd discovered the underground tunnel beneath the castle and sprung a trap. This time, they were after revenge.

We arrived at Quorum and made camp in the woods outside the walls, the red sun setting on the horizon, glowing through the trees. Lucas still had not returned, and I kept glancing to the sky.

General Dixon settled next to Daniel and me on a log outside my tent. "There's a clearing nearby where we'll meet for battle if all goes according to plan. We'll avoid the forest, so they can't hide from the rain under the boughs. Or light it on fire, of course."

I nodded slowly, preoccupied with thoughts of the fight tomorrow. Worry for Daniel, who stuck next to me like glue, stirred deep, dominating my attention. I'd need to assign more men to watch him. I wasn't playing favorites; he was the Terran prince, after all. King Dryden would blame both Caelum and me if anything happened to him. That is, if Caelum still existed.

Before I could answer, Lucas strode up, saluting the general. He must have landed Molly in a nearby field. "Still here, are ya?" he greeted Daniel, crossing his arms.

"What did you find out?" Daniel asked, ignoring his comment.

"I waited to see if they were bedding down for the night or marching straight through. That's what took me so long."

"And?" the general asked.

"They're making camp. Expect them early in the morning. They aren't far, and they know we're here. I saw a few of their scouts heading back to the rest of the army."

I swallowed through a tight throat, my stomach now rolling with nausea. "How many?" The words came out raspy.

"They must have emptied out Ember City and all their small villages in the north. It's," his voice lowered, "not good."

Lucas and Dixon left to update the soldiers, leaving Daniel and me alone. Or as alone as two people could be surrounded by an army. I set my cheek on his shoulder. "You think your father is coming?"

"Maybe we should find out."

I lifted my head to watch his expression. "I wanted to send Lucas and Molly, but if they're going to help us with the Embers tomorrow, they need to rest."

He kept his attention on his feet, a sure sign of his discomfort. "What would you say if I left tonight? To look for them."

For once, I was glad Daniel didn't have his powers and couldn't sense my relief at hearing his words. Anything to get him away from the battle. "I'd say it would be useful. You direct them to our location. Let everyone you pass know how close the Embers are. And then lead the Terran army, with plenty of guards, of course." I left out the part how I worried they weren't coming, and he'd be on a wild goose chase. "At least inform the other Caelumites who haven't caught up to us yet."

"I don't want to leave you," he whispered. "I promised I never would. Last time I did, you ended up in the castle dungeon."

Unshed tears burned. "You're helping. Not abandoning."

He finally focused on me, his blue eyes as damp as mine. "I'm terrified something will happen to you, and I won't be there."

"And I'm scared something will happen to you because you are. Can I ask you to do something?"

He didn't answer, waiting to hear my request.

I powered on, "Promise me you'll always keep your assigned bodyguards and stay out of the main battle. You're too important. And too—"

"Much of a failure right now?"

"No—too vulnerable."

He looked away. "Not better."

"Hey." I tilted his chin toward me and studied his beautiful features—almost too perfect—the way his dark brows winged over the bluest of irises, the full, soft lips contrasting with his chiseled jaw. Yet none of those things were what drew me to him anymore. "You once told me you'd love me no matter the outcome of the prophecy. Even if I never gained my powers. Let me have the same feelings. Your powers don't define you, and my love isn't restrained by those borders. My soul still jumps at the sight of you, aches when it's not with you, and maybe you don't feel it right now, but the energy ignites when you're with me. Our connection is as strong as it ever was, and I need you just as much. Need you to come out of this alive. Please." Those unshed tears spilled, hot and wet, across my flushed cheeks.

He kissed me. The chatter and bustle of soldiers around us melted away. I kissed him back, shifting closer so I could feel his warmth. Feel his strength that he didn't believe in anymore. And feel the intoxicating energy encircling us. He pulled me in, as if desperate for those things too.

"I love you, Queen Catherine of Caelum."

I let my fingers trail down his jaw. "I'm just Cate. And you're just Daniel." I kissed him softly. "And we belong together."

He still felt it. Felt *something*. Because the light in his eyes told me he believed it too.

"Be safe." I lightly pushed against his chest. I wanted to stay like this forever, but the longer he waited, the harder it would be to leave. "And come back to me," I whispered.

"Always." He softly kissed me one last time.

I watched him mount Raven and ride away, weaving through soldiers, townspeople, and trees until he disappeared behind the foliage. "Please come back to me," I whispered again. But this time, no one was listening. My words lost.

The next morning, after tossing and turning nearly all night, the sounds of men packing, sharpening swords, and finding their breakfast woke me. I exited the tent to find General Dixon speaking with a group of soldiers, including Lucas, who sent me a distracted half-smile at my appearance.

"They're not quite on the move," the general said. "Slower to rouse than Rowan probably liked."

At my questioning look, Lucas replied, "I did a flyover."

"You didn't get much sleep last night." I sipped on a cup of tea a soldier handed me.

He ran a finger under his eye. "Neither did you, from the looks of it."

"I'm not here for a beauty contest," I shot back, enjoying the distraction of banter with Lucas. "How long do we have?" I asked, my tone lowering.

"Midday at the latest." Dixon eyed the sky as if judging the time of day.

"And the Terran army? Did you look?" I asked Lucas.

"I didn't have the chance to go far. A quick sweep showed more townspeople on the move. Could be untrained Caelumites or Terrans. No one in uniform."

There's not enough time for the Terran army to come to our rescue. I didn't say it aloud, though we all thought it.

"You ready?" the general asked.

"For rain? Yes," I answered more confidently than I felt. I wondered how far it would reach. The energy buzzed at my fingertips, but I could never be sure if it would give out on me or if I'd start using my own internal sources. Would it have been better if Daniel stayed? My stomach dipped at my decision.

Dixon gave a single nod of approval. "You'll be well protected in the center. I'm assigning a squad to watch you."

I patted my sword. "I've been practicing."

In truth, my time in the dungeon had weakened my muscles from the confined space and limited meals. I'd have to rely on the energy to propel me faster than the Embers. I wasn't sure why I couldn't speak the hard things out loud. Probably because I wanted to project strength and confidence. No one needed to hear my inner demons.

The general departed, leaving me with Lucas. "You'll be on Molly?"

He planted his feet. "I'll be with you."

"What? No, we need you in the air." This constant push to protect me was destined to get everyone I love killed.

"Molly's never fought in battle. Besides, the Embers are fire-resistant, and I'm afraid she might accidentally hurt one of ours. I'm sticking with you for now."

He could lead a battalion elsewhere. Make more of a difference in this conflict than being my bodyguard, but I didn't have it in me to send someone else away. His familiar presence eased some of the pressure. "It'll be nice to have you here," I replied, not sure how to adequately thank him.

"It'll be nice to be with you without the annoying prince." He grinned, dimples flashing.

"We're not going there again, are we?" I crossed my arms in mock sternness.

He put his hand on his heart. "Me? Stir up trouble? Never."

"Well, you'd better be kind. He's Mya's brother, after all."

He sobered. "Don't I know it. Honestly, I'm glad he's gone, because the last thing we need is an Ember striking him down. Knowing King Dryden, there's no Terran army coming, and we've sent him on a fool's errand."

"Won't that mean we're the fools? For fighting the Embers without enough soldiers?"

He attempted another smile. This time, the edges of his mouth barely curled, his eyes missing that sparkle. "Maybe. But I'd rather die a fool than a coward."

I forced a smile, more of a grimace, really. "And with those inspiring words, let's get ready to meet our doom."

CHAPTER 51
DANIEL

Raven and I rode all night, Caelum guards flanking me, warning camps of villagers armed with a collection of pitchforks, family heirloom swords, and the odd bayonet. I was like the old American stories of Paul Revere shouting, "The British are coming," to everyone who would listen. Though Cate informed me that bit of historical fact wasn't quite accurate. One day, I'll tell my history teacher. I never understood why we had to study American history while living here, but they always told us we should learn from it so we wouldn't repeat the same mistakes.

And here we were.

Anxiousness to find the Terran army kept me alert, even though it was well past three in the morning. I held a portable lantern in my outstretched hand, the crescent moon providing little light between the trees. Over and over, I asked if anyone had seen Terran soldiers, but the answer was always no, my hopes plummeting with each response.

The underground had succeeded in gathering Terran citizens, and the farther I traveled, the more Terrans I found. They, too, believed in the prophecy. One of them told me Mya's words had convinced them, and I secretly smiled. She'd gained respect from many over these last months, working tirelessly for Cate's cause. Concern about my position as the Terran prince had been an afterthought. I turned that over in my mind. Mya probably hadn't seen it that way, but I had. The truth that my role as heir mattered little unsettled me.

Before I could explore the idea further, I came upon another group sleeping by a fire, with one rather small man keeping watch. He scrambled to his feet.

"Any Terran soldiers?" I asked.

The man grinned, a gap hollowed between his front teeth. "On the way. Feels good to have 'em at our back."

I smiled at him, the first genuine one in days. "Yes, it does."

After he pointed me in the right direction, we continued south. Even Raven had more of a spring in his step. Finally, I saw them. Campfires dotted the landscape in the valley, stretching below like a swarm of fireflies lighting up the sky. It wasn't just a few Terran soldiers. This was the entire army. The first signs of dawn lightened the blackened sky to velvety navy. The birds had started their songs, as if sounding the alarm that too much time had passed. If the battle truly started in the morning as Lucas suspected, it might be over before we arrived. But we'd try, anyway.

Raven cantered down the hill, my Caelum guards holding at the outskirts to wait. I stopped at the first watchman. "Who's in charge here?"

When he squinted in the darkness and failed to answer, I held the lantern closer to my face. "I'm the prince. Quickly, now."

He blinked in surprise. "You don't know? Your father is here, Your Highness."

"The king is *here*?" I blurted. Father hadn't joined a battle in… actually, I don't remember him ever joining one.

"That way, sir." The guard pointed then stood at attention once again.

We picked our way through resting men until I found a large tent near the center. Of course, Father would be resting in the only shelter with green braiding and tassels swooping along the sides. Sure enough, Dev had spread his bedroll by the fire. He jerked upright at my approach, hair standing in a multitude of directions.

A slow grin crossed his features. "If it isn't the prodigal son."

I slid off Raven. "It wasn't that long ago you were recovering in a hospital bed. You sure you're okay to fight?"

"Me? Miss this? And don't forget you had that little time skip. I've had longer to recover than you think."

I would have loved to sit and chat with Dev by the fire, but we had no time to lose. "The Embers are coming. The battle is about five hours north and will happen…" I glanced at the horizon, "in about an hour. Two if we're lucky."

"Why didn't you say so?" Dev launched out of bed. "Your Highness?" he called toward the tent.

"Father," I said, hoping he'd respond better to me, though no promises on that front. "We have to go. Now."

The canvas flapped open, and the king emerged, buttoning the gold fasteners of his uniform. "I heard the two of you." His gaze fell over my shoulder. "Is Cate with the Caelum army?"

"I left her to fetch you."

"She'll produce the water?" His keen stare bored into me. Would he turn the Terrans around if she couldn't?

"Yes," I answered.

He nodded curtly. "Sound the alarm," he told Dev before striding off to his horse.

Dev grabbed a metal pot and started banging on it, awakening the neighbors and spreading the word. Finally, a lieutenant with a horn blew it, the blast echoing in the crisp air. I gave Dev a wry smile. "I'll have to remember to carry a pot next time."

He shrugged and started gathering his things. "I never could blow that thing. Pawned the job off to someone else a long time ago."

Another soldier started to disassemble the tent. "Leave it," I said. We needed to travel as light as possible; we certainly wouldn't need it in battle.

Dev dumped half his saddlebag onto his bedroll. "It'll be here when I get back. Or an Ember might enjoy that hand mirror and silk cravat."

I rolled my eyes. "You brought a silk—"

"Wanted to, of course. But sadly, no. Wasn't lying about the mirror though." He ran a comb through his messy hair before tossing it with the rest of the stuff. "Okay, ready."

"I'm sure the Embers will appreciate your blond locks right before you run them through."

"You understand me so well." Dev tightened the saddle on his horse and mounted, and I followed.

Father rode up beside me. "Are the numbers as bad as the early reports?" he murmured.

"Affirmative."

He sat tall on his stallion, dark beard neatly trimmed, only a few wrinkles feathering at the edges of his eyes. Not for the first time, I wondered why he hadn't fought in years, and why he chose now, when our odds were at their worst. Tossing out caution, I asked, "Why'd you come?"

"If the Embers are successful today against Caelum, it won't be long until Terra is next. Joining forces was a tactical move."

Of course, he wouldn't support anything that wasn't beneficial to Terra, though he'd dodged my question. "No, *you*," I clarified. "Why are *you* here?

"If this is to be Terra's downfall, I should witness it first hand to see if I have a kingdom left. And do everything in my power to keep it." His horse sidestepped, nervous from the ruckus of soldiers preparing to fight.

I scanned the valley. He'd done well collecting every able-bodied soldier in the realm, with a smattering of civilians lacking uniforms. Mobilizing this many took effort, like a lumbering herd waking up from a nap. "We need to hurry," I said.

"Let's go, then. They'll catch up soon enough when they see the king has left without them. You know the way. Lead us off, son."

A strangeness settled at being comrades with my father. We'd always supposedly been on the same side, yet somehow, it never seemed as if we had. Galloping off to battle next to him, where the fate of the kingdoms would be decided, gave me hope that this could repair some of those old wounds between us. Knit the chasm that had developed in what could be our last hours together. I had no business riding into this war, handicapped as I was. Yet, I'd never felt surer that this was exactly where I was supposed to be.

CHAPTER 52
LUCAS

Molly soared above as we traveled to the field. I rode next to Cate, her white knuckles gripping North's reins, reminding me to loosen my own hold. The anxiety of war touched all, even seasoned soldiers.

"I wish we'd heard from Daniel," she said for the fifth time today. "We can't delay any longer?"

"It's better to fight them in the open. If they catch us in the forest, it would mean disaster. He'll be here," I replied with more conviction than I felt.

While riding Molly this morning, surveying the ocean of Embers stretching north, I'd broken out in sweats, a wave of dizziness so powerful I'd nearly toppled. She'd trembled beneath me, feeding off my mood, the fear taking over both of us. We would have made it to camp sooner if we hadn't taken an extra loop south to calm my nerves before reporting to Cate and the general. I'd told myself it was to search for the Terrans, but truthfully, I'd needed the time to lower my racing heart.

Despite not waiting for the kids from the baby factory to be old enough to fight, the Embers massively outnumbered us, even with the addition of the Terran army. Cate's rain would be the key to saving us. Which meant they would have one goal: find the Caelum queen and stop her.

Murmurs traveled from those in front as they reached the field. They were already assembling, and from the sounds of their frightened whispers and warnings, others were discovering that we were way over our heads.

"Now?" Cate asked.

"Now would be good." I hoped she'd been telling the truth when she said she'd manage rain without Daniel. My neck warmed with shame to even think she might place Daniel before the kingdom, though there might be a part of her that protects him subconsciously. The two of them were like a pendulum; one moved, and the other followed, as if sharing the same energy.

I'm not sure why I'd had trouble seeing it before. I'd been blinded by my own affection for her. Had it been love? Maybe. The relief at losing that intense feeling for her unbound my heart and left it free for Mya. I would always be fiercely protective of Cate, and yes, love her. How I loved my kingdom. We shared a deep connection, but with Mya, it ran deeper in that intangible way when you can't live without the other person. Our separation these past months highlighted the emptiness that ate me from the inside without her.

Drops of rain interrupted my thoughts. We had come prepared with drundle coats to keep us dry and protected from fire, and I hastened to fasten the oblong buttons trailing down the front. Not every farmer and townsperson owned drundle, due to price. I worried for them, yet was grateful for each person who loved our land enough to protect it and stand with Cate.

The downpour commenced as soon as our mounts stepped through the trees and onto the field. My cold sweat returned beneath the cloak's stuffiness. Cate gasped at the sight of them. We'd thought they'd come with huge numbers at The Great Battle. But this… it was a feat only Rowan could have accomplished. No ordinary Ember could mobilize this many and organize what we'd thought was an unteachable group. Since we'd learned he'd received training from the British Royal Army, it made sense that he'd be the leader they needed. What I couldn't understand was why he didn't see them for what they were: unredeemable.

The field wasn't the ideal meadow one usually pictured with

rolling green hills dotted with wildflowers. Instead, scraggly grass grew between what was once cracked, dry earth, now muddy, with charred tree stumps creating tripping hazards. It opened onto a vast chasm of wasteland to the north. Another fire-induced border inadvertently created by the Embers long ago, an old forest burned to cinders. Our enemy continued to file in, a great moving mass like ants marching to a feast. We'd delay as long as possible and wait until they made the first move.

"You think Rowan will want to talk?" Cate asked.

"Don't do it," I replied, my voice sharper than intended. "Don't trust him. He'll do anything to capture you—he's proven it over and over."

"I just want to stop the killing." She swiped droplets from her brow, and I wondered if Rowan was delaying his attack to exhaust her.

"You should take a break." I pointed upward. "Everything's good and wet. Don't tire yourself out. It might be his plan."

She nodded, drops cascading from her hood. "Send a message to the general that I'll start again when needed."

It wasn't long before Rowan's voice boomed. He'd stolen one of our speech amplifiers, the sound echoing through the air, eerily quiet with the rain pattering gone. "Everyone should know that I did not want this war," he shouted, his tone commanding. "I believe the prophecy is for Catherine to help the Embers with our water supply and quell the fires to allow us to grow enough crops for our lands. We can all live in peace. King Graftonberg agreed. But before Catherine was transferred to me, your king was murdered. I saw it with my own eyes."

The hair on the back of my neck prickled. Rowan was trying to control the narrative by turning Cate's people against her. And against me. I glanced around warily, now wondering how easily friend could turn foe.

"Catherine could fulfill the prophecy by helping us. She could create peace and prosperity for us all. But she's too selfish. She wants to be queen. To lead you into a war you can't win in hopes of holding on to the throne. Her comrade, who still stands with her, murdered Graftonberg unpunished. She had the opportunity to save her own father, but wouldn't do it, knowing she was next in the royal line. Hand her over to me, and we can all go home. Is this what you want? For your children to lose their fathers here on the battleground? To have no one left to work the land or guard what remains of it?"

"Don't listen to him," the general shouted, barely audible over the murmurings of the soldiers.

"Someone get him an amplifier," I yelled.

Everyone started talking over one another. Cate's head swiveled, scrambling to evaluate if the people would once again turn on her.

"He can't be trusted," Dixon's voice boomed, now amplified and carried in the air by Caelum soldiers. "His claim is false. His plan is to slaughter our queen so that the prophecy can never be fulfilled."

"I've had opportunity to kill her," Rowan shot back. "Yet she's still alive, here in our midst. Graftonberg was smart enough to believe me. But she silenced him."

I swallowed thickly, my throat feeling as if it might close with panic. Or was it guilt? Instead of helping Cate, I was a liability. Soon, fingers would point.

The assassin. The queen's right-hand man.

"Stop!" Cate yelled. "Listen to me."

A hush fell over the crowd. Caelumites passed her words through the wind.

"Rowan murdered King Aldridge, not me. I was forced to choose between saving thousands of our soldiers and one king. My father made the choice, and I carried it out. Don't let Rowan distort the truth." Her green eyes flashed with anger. "Graftonberg was killed by a rogue knife because, in this supposed peaceful transfer of me to the Embers, he ambushed the castle. Graftonberg's death was an accident. Do not believe Rowan's lies. The Embers will keep taking and taking until there's nothing left. We must fight for our kingdom. For Caelum!"

The words had barely left her lips when the roar of our army erupted in a battle cry. At the tide's changing, Rowan gave the signal, sending a wall of Embers rushing in our direction. Orange fireballs launched into the air, crashing among us. The horse next to me reared and unseated its rider, flames erupting.

"Now, Cate. The rain," I yelled, unsheathing my sword.

The Embers had prepared stone-filled rags soaked in tree sap. Slingshots or larger launchers sent fireballs showering toward us, leading to pandemonium. Heavy enough, when they hit their target, they could kill a man or leave them unconscious. Both North and my mount were well-trained and accustomed to flames, yet many of the horses balked and reared, inciting further chaos.

The air filled with smoke, shouts, and screaming horses. Our well-organized army moved in a state of confusion, trampling one another. Rowan discovered Cate's location by the sound of her voice, and they concentrated their ammunition on us, which could have been his plan all along. As the fire fell, Cate struggled to keep her focus on the rain. The clash of men and swords at the front of the line further fueled the frenzy.

"Lucas!" She jerked North's reins to dodge another fireball. "I don't know how to do this!"

"Dismount. Come up behind me."

She slid off North and climbed onto my horse. He was sturdy and reliable and would easily carry the two of us. I tied a rope to North to keep her near, ensuring she had enough lead to dodge any incoming fire.

"Just focus. I'll take care of everything else." Cate's arms wrapped around my waist, the weight of her head pressed against my shoulder. Her breathing slowed, and water droplets began to fall. The rain didn't completely extinguish the sap-soaked rags' flames, though it helped.

The Embers tunneled into the fray, fighting toward Cate. Blood spilled, mixing with the puddles, and soon the Embers stumbled over bodies—both their own and Caelumites.

"Pull back," I called. "We need to hide the queen." Cate's guards were under my command and obeyed, edging away from the center of the fight. "We're going to dismount to make it harder to find you," I told her.

I looped my leg over the horse's neck and hopped to the soggy ground, helping Cate down. She watched me with strangely contemplative eyes for being in the middle of war as I adjusted her drundle cloak over her head.

"Have you ever wondered," she said softly, so that only I could hear. "That maybe he's right?"

"Who's right?" Now was not the time for heartfelt conversations.

"Rowan."

"What?" Her answer genuinely confused me. She'd just given a speech to rally every Caelum member in the kingdom, and she didn't believe it? "Never. You're not a sacrifice."

She looked so lost, her lips parted, eyes wide.

"Listen to me." I pulled her close, whispering harshly in her ear. "You were meant for more. You were meant to lead. Don't let him get into your head."

The soft exhale against my cheek was filled with pain and uncertainty, and perhaps a hint of relief that I still believed in her.

"Come on." We weaved through the soldiers, heading for the rear, the guards helping secure passage. Alana commanded a battalion on the other side of the field. She turned as if feeling my eyes on her and pointed toward the woods. She too knew it was time to get Cate out.

"It's harder to look for Daniel down here." Cate reached up and patted North's neck, craning her own, as I returned to leading her through the crowd.

There had been no sign of the prince or the Terran military, and if they didn't show soon, this might turn into a mission to save our queen. And ourselves. I eyed Molly overhead. She'd be our last resort. The two of us would fly her to Cate's parents. Then we'd try to get her through the portal. Because if we lost today, there would be no kingdom left. Though convincing Cate to leave without Daniel would be… impossible. Frustration bubbled at the prince. Cate had wanted him out of the way and safe, but I hadn't thought about the ramifications if he never returned.

Molly swooped lower to catch my attention. Something else caught my eye. Déjà vu from The Great Battle. On the horizon.

Dragons.

CHAPTER 53
CATE

I tugged Lucas's arm, trying to thread through the teeming men, but he stood still as a stone. "Lucas, what's—" I followed his gaze north. At least ten dragons flew toward us. I dropped his hand, my whole body freezing. "No," I whispered. "I thought they didn't want to get involved with humans anymore."

"So did I."

"They're not coming to help us, are they?" A gossamer thread of hope wound around my heart. Lucas had told me what happened when he'd visited the dragons, which led him to being thrown in the Embers' infamous pit. Molly had spent some time with them, but she either left of her own free will or escaped.

"No." Lucas's flat tone allowed no room for question. A bad situation just became worse. Much, much worse.

"Go with Molly," I said. "You convinced them once before. You can do it again."

"I know you think I walk on water." His lips curved in a half-hearted smile, providing a poor cover for his reluctance. "It won't work this time. You weren't there. You didn't see how much they hated me. Hated us."

"Maybe they're different dragons from the ones you and Molly met." I grabbed both of his arms so we faced each other. Water clung to his lashes, and his coffee-colored eyes mirrored my own fear. "You have to try." If he couldn't lure them away… I let out a short, heavy breath, one step from a sob. Who was I kidding? It was too late anyway. "Should we retreat?" I asked softly.

Lucas shook his head, wordlessly handling my feelings with care. "I'm sorry, Cate. We've run out of options. The Embers will chase us down and burn the entire kingdom in the process. We have to take our stand."

A crash near us startled me back into my surroundings. If we didn't hurry, they'd find me. The noise of combat—men grunting, swords clashing, and bodies falling—surrounded us. The rain fell, though it had lightened considerably. I returned my focus to maintaining the downpour.

"I'll go," Lucas said abruptly. "I don't like leaving you, but I will." He turned to the nearest guard, a dark-haired man with lines feathering around his eyes, presumably the lead. "Timmley. Take her somewhere safe. Make sure the Embers don't find her. And always," he held up a finger, "Always stay with the rest of the guard. She needs protection."

And he was gone, sprinting through the battlefield, dodging and weaving while signaling Molly to pick him up in the nearest space large enough for her to land. I watched him disappear, wishing I could at least give him fair weather to ride. "Be safe, Lucas," I whispered, before turning to Timmley. "Should we head to the rear?"

I searched the back line, the muddy ribbon of clear earth speckled with roots stretching into the forest with its scraggly trees and bushes. I wanted to show the citizens that I stood with them in battle, yet if the Embers' primary goal was to find me, staying in the thick of it was foolish.

"This way," he called. The group, numbering around twenty, followed suit, reforming a protective circle. We headed to the forest while I kept up the water. The energy had started to waver, growing harder to bend to my will. I took a steadying breath. It was too early to pour myself into the rain. I wouldn't be able to hold out. Again, I wondered if it had been the right thing to send Daniel away.

We reached the trees safely, heading southwest through the bramble. "Not too far," I called. "I need to be sure my rain covers the battle."

Timmley only nodded and continued deeper. I strained to balloon the energy north. Without seeing the fight, it became more difficult to direct the water, yet we continued on. "Stop," I commanded. "This is far enough."

He glanced back. "Just a little farther. I scouted out a place, ma'am."

My nerves wound tighter as my worry grew that the rain wouldn't sufficiently shield our men. Every step left me more uneasy, hairs standing along my forearms in waves. The brush rustled ahead. My hand shot to the sword at my waist, still sheathed, heart thumping deep in my ears.

The edge of a blue uniform came into view, a Caelum soldier emerging from the thicket, the emblems on his chest demonstrating his high rank. "There you are," he said. "We can take it from here." Around ten more Caelum soldiers came up behind him, poking around trees and brush.

"See, Your Highness," Timmley said. "Reinforcements." He pointed to about half of my guards, including a baby-faced blond who reminded me of a young Lucas. "You can return to fight. The rest of us have the queen."

Something didn't sit right. "No. Stay," I blurted, my sixth sense blaring like a fire bell.

The new soldier approached and saluted me. "Cranston, Your Highness. I'm afraid we need every man at that battle. The soldiers with me know the forest around these parts in case you need a getaway." One of the men I recognized from the castle, but he could have grown up near here.

Half of my guard filed out, their shoulders drooping. The knots in my belly doubled at their departure, and I wished Lucas were here, the uneasy sensation persisting.

"There's shelter. Up ahead." Cranston started deeper into the woods.

I kept my head low to shield my face from the droplets and to watch my footing on the slippery terrain. A shelter from the rain did sound appealing.

"Finally," someone called.

At the voice, my heart skipped like stones across a stormy lake. I forced myself to keep my tone steady. "What are you doing way out here, Roy? I thought you might be safe and sound at home in your manor?"

His cheeks flushed. "Caelum Castle is my home."

I pretended to act curious. "Huh. That's not how the vote played out, is it? It's a big place, but I don't think there's space for both of us."

"They wouldn't have voted that way if they understood Rowan's plan. I'll be the hero, along with these boys," he gestured to the soldiers near him, "for ending this battle and saving Caelum peacefully."

I flashed cold at the confirmation that Roy intended to turn me over to Rowan. My mind raced for a solution. Could the guards be convinced Roy was wrong? "You're committing treason," I said calmly, catching the eye of any soldier who dared return my gaze. "Sending me to my death."

Timmley spoke up, "Depends on your point of view. We don't accept you as our queen. You're more American than Caelumite."

"Your life for many. Isn't that what your father did?" another spoke up. "You aren't fit to wipe Aldridge's shoes."

The realization that I wouldn't be able to talk myself out of this situation seeped under my skin, leaching out the hope. The belief that I was fit to lead the kingdom dissolved with their words. Yet… I didn't want my life to end like my father's.

"Help!" I screamed. A shred of tattered hope that one of my old guards would hear propelled my voice.

"Quiet," Timmley commanded. He lurched forward, grabbing hold of my upper arm, fingers digging deep into the tender undersurface.

"Help me!" I yelled again.

A hand clamped around my mouth. I struggled free and bit down hard, soft flesh sinking beneath my teeth.

"You—" his angry voice started.

Something solid connected with my skull. Bright spots spun in a kaleidoscope before blackness slid further and further until… nothing.

CHAPTER 54
LUCAS

Cate disappeared into the forest, and the feeling of despair wove inside like poison ivy as I watched the sheer number of Embers now visible from the air. I'd seen where they'd camped the night before, yet hadn't passed directly over them. The dragons circled, almost as if they waited for something. The signal to attack? I wavered, wondering if I should double back to find out if the Terran army was on the way, though it would only ease my depression rather than provide any true tactical help at this point. My job was to lead the dragons away, and until I'd accomplished it, there was little use in doing anything else.

"You alright, Mol?"

Sometimes she'd give me a nod or a snort, but today, she stayed focused as we raced toward the beasts.

"Okay, fine. Keep me on track. You can be the responsible one this time." A part of me wished she'd balk, and we could turn with our tails between our legs. Was there any hope of winning? The Caelumites made progress, fighting through the masses. If only there weren't twenty of the enemy to replace each fallen. The Embers had spread, no longer solely focusing on the area Cate had ridden near the center of our troops. At least that portion of our plan worked; they hadn't figured out where she'd gone. As long as the rain still fell, I knew she was safe, and I attempted to focus on that small token of comfort. The lines held, with the combat not yet making it to the rear, where the field turned to forest.

We crossed over waves of Embers until the dragons started to take shape and become more than toy-sized figures in the distance. I squinted. *Could it be?* A red dragon with spikes protruding from its face and laddering down its spine flew in front, gliding side-by-side with a smooth-scaled behemoth. Clammy sweat broke out. "Molly, is that Big Momma and Leo?"

Again, with the lack of answer. You'd think my dragon had a teenage attitude. There were eight more besides the two I recognized from my short time with the dragons months ago. Leo had speared Molly in the side, then deposited me in the Ember Camp, leading to my imprisonment. But if she planned to let bygones be bygones, who was I to interfere?

Okay, I was totally interfering. This was crazy. I pulled on Molly's neck, hoping to at least swing around and talk this over first. She shook her head and kept moving. Resigned, I let her take over. Delaying my death wouldn't help much, anyway.

By now, we'd flown over the conflict and all the Embers. The dragons had slowed their progression, flapping their wings to maintain a hover. Molly still sped headlong toward them. Leo dipped in greeting.

A glimmer of hope. Maybe she'd parted on good terms when she'd escaped their lair.

The dragons parted as if making room for Molly. She swooped between them, and they bobbed, several gliding alongside. They were... playing. These were her *friends*. The other dragons' size indicated they were likely adolescents like Molly. Leo and Big Momma watched on as if proud parents. *Wait, were they the parents?* Leo gave me a disapproving glare, as if I were the rebel kid dating his daughter. *Molly is too good for you,* he seemed to say. *She doesn't belong with your kind.*

Not for the first time, I wondered the same. I let them have their reunion, holding on for dear life as they played, oblivious of the rain as we barrel rolled and nosedived, ducking when dragon wings came too close. "Molly," I finally said. "They're not going to join the Embers, are they?"

She shook her head and made an arc in the air until we faced the dragons.

"We should go. Say your goodbyes." I stroked her neck, sad that she'd have to leave her friends, yet content that someone would be there for her if something happened to me. I twisted to watch the battle behind us. Still no sign of the Terrans.

That's when it happened. The rain dried up. Bursts of flames from Embers came to life. Which could only mean one thing.

Cate was in trouble.

Molly sensed my fear, muscles rippling beneath me. She sped toward the fight. My kingdom didn't stand a chance without Cate's rain. Something red caught my peripheral vision. Leo flew beside us, the other dragons following suit. When we reached the rear of the battle, comprised mostly of a sea of Embers, Leo dove toward them, his great tail catching several and throwing them meters in the air. One of the smaller dragons picked up an Ember, flapped its wings until it flew next to us, then dropped him onto his comrades. The terror on the man's face almost made me sorry for him. Almost.

They already knew their fire wouldn't work against the Embers, but did they understand not to hurt the Caelumites? A brutal tail swing by Leo left me wincing. If we traveled back over the main fight, I worried too many of ours would be injured. I was torn. Stay and whittle down their men, or search for Cate?

She was my priority. She had to be.

I directed Molly southward, and the dragons followed. My heart sank. They'd go where we went. Still no rain. The worry grew heavy. Something was wrong. But if Cate was… dead—I swallowed down the thought through a clogging throat—we'd only be hurting the army by not fighting. "What should we do, Mols?" As the words left my mouth, I knew she wouldn't have a good answer either.

Higher and higher we climbed until the fighters appeared as tiny toy soldiers below. Several of her dragon friends followed, including an electric blue one who shadowed her every move. I tugged on her spines. "Too high, Mols. Where are you going?"

I scanned the landscape, hoping to see some sign of Cate now that we had a better view. It hadn't been a bad idea, and I patted her neck to tell her so, when, in the distance, through a break in the trees, I saw them. The Terran army. My shoulders sagged in relief. Daniel should be with them, and they were nearly here. He wouldn't rest until he found her. He, too, would understand something had happened. All I could hope was that she really did need him after all, for the rain, and with his presence, they could start the flow of water again. Because thinking of Cate as anything but alive… well, I couldn't just now. *I wouldn't.*

"We have backup coming. Let's fight," I called. For the first time, I thought we might stand a chance. For now, I'd support the kingdom from the air. The advantage of eleven dragons, counting Molly, was too much to waste.

We dive-bombed the Embers, sending them screaming and scattering as the dragons plucked them, one by one, letting them fall to their deaths. Molly had never participated in battle before, and her movements were uncertain and timid. Well… timid for a dragon. She'd daintily swipe up an Ember, careful not to injure him, only to drop him from fifty meters onto his comrades.

"Only from behind!" I called as Molly grasped one who faced toward her. I leaned over her neck, craning to see. The Ember raised his sword, slashing forward, straight through her leg. Dragon blood ribboned across his face and tunic. She screeched, the heart-wrenching sound renting the air. "Mollls!"

CHAPTER 55
DANIEL

Mobilizing the Terran army took far too long. Every second felt like it marked another death. Another moment Cate might need saving. I set the pace at a slow canter—slow enough so those on mounts that weren't as strong as Raven could follow, instructing several to lag and guide those on foot. Anyone not astride might be too far behind to be of any use to us. I swallowed back the fear that we would be too late.

Hugo rode up beside Dev and me, his expression stoic, showing his quiet support. I felt equal parts sad that my usually gregarious friend wasn't safe at home, and grateful to have him by my side.

"Thanks for coming," I said.

"Same, Prince. Same. It means a lot to the Terrans that you're with us."

He didn't intend to incite guilt with the comment, but it held the same effect, nonetheless. Being torn between the two kingdoms and supporting Cate always left one side with less of me. My father overheard Hugo, because, of course, he did.

"Listen to your friend, Daniel. They want you with us."

Irritation sparked. "Honestly, Father. I'm not focused on that right now. Real end-of-the-world problems are happening. No one cares if I made it to the last family dinner." I wanted to steal the words back as soon as I released them. Now wasn't the time to argue. Nor was it the moment to be ungrateful about people wanting me near. And it certainly wasn't a time to be taking relationships for granted. Death loomed in the balance, both mine and theirs. "Sorry." I loosened my grip on the reins. "I'm glad I'm here, too."

I tried not to seethe on the inside at Father's smug expression at my apology.

Hugo shot me a grin that soothed over the annoyance. "How's Cate doing?" he asked.

"She's stronger than before. I suspect we'll run into some rain soon." I left out the part about how we'd switched roles. She'd gained strength while I'd lost it. Becoming a burden wasn't in my nature, so I let the thought pass unspoken.

"She doesn't need you?" Dev asked.

The words stung more than they should have. "She always needs me," I deflected. "Just not for making rain." I hoped both parts of that sentence were true, and we'd ride into a torrential downpour soon.

We stumbled upon an injured Caelum soldier lying in a mound of leaves, shivering, blood weeping from a nasty leg wound. Hugo hopped off his horse to help him. "Medic!" he cried.

"Is it over?" I asked, fear fluttering anew in my chest. "Are we too late?"

The man grimaced. "I—I don't think so. Just had to get away. No good… like this." His words came out in breathy starts and stops.

"How far to the battle?" I asked.

"It's just up that way." He pointed northeast. The medic settled next to him with bandages.

If we were close then—

My father finished my thought, "Where's the rain?"

The soldier gasped at something the healer applied to his wound. "It stopped. A few minutes ago."

Sure enough, the ground was wet. But the sky… the sky was clear. Every muscle tensed, feeling like my body might snap in half. Scenarios spun through my head: Cate used her own energy and her heart gave out, they'd captured her, the Embers struck her down.

"Son." Father positioned his horse next to me. He must sense my despair, and if his power worked as mine had, it would nearly overwhelm him. "Let's find her."

For the first time since I'd returned from the portal, I felt more than just a hint of emotion. From the king of all people. Empathy and worry projected. My eyes stung with sudden, unshed tears at the momentary return of my power mixed with the surprise of Father's feelings. I dug my heels into Raven, hoping to hide my vulnerability.

The energy dispersed as quickly as it came, though it didn't matter, because I became consumed with finding Cate.

We rode into the battle's clearing. I halted to survey the situation and let the rest of the army catch up. An ocean of Embers spanned north as far as I could see. The Caelum soldiers and citizens fought alongside one another, each swinging their weapon as if it might be their last. For every Ember that fell, there were twenty to replace them. Some had sheathed their weapons and started using Fireballs, which erupted from their hands in great streaks of orange and red, yielding the Caelum swords nearly useless.

Hugo pointed at something off in the distance. "Dragons."

A grouping of them flew together, impossible to tell if they intended harm from this far away. Everything snapped into place. "Lucas left Cate to take Molly to meet the dragons. Her other guards must have failed."

"How do you know?" Father asked.

"Trust me. But look who came." I spotted Alana a few hundred meters away.

"I'll lead the men," Father said. "Dev and Hugo, stay with Daniel. He's not in fighting shape. Take a few more with you, but not so many that they slow you down. Find Catherine."

We started in Alana's direction, my nerves vibrating the closer we came to combat.

"Prince?" Hugo rode closer. "What did the king mean by that?"

"He lost most of his powers," Dev replied for me. "Along with those months in the portal."

Hugo swung his horse around, glaring. "Then what are you doing out here, mate?" he yelled over the sounds of battle, his expression a mixture of incredulity and anger.

"Where else would I be?" The words were calming, reminding me of what was important. I might not have all my abilities, but I couldn't imagine being anywhere else. I looked him in the eye, clenching my jaw. "Let's find Cate."

He watched me in return. "I won't be looking for *her*. I'll be watching you." He fisted his chest in a sign of deference before turning back toward the fighters.

I exchanged looks with Dev, who sent me a tiny smile. If today were my last, I'd die knowing I possessed the loyalty of my friends. We tightened our fireproof drundle cloaks and raced to Alana together, swords aloft, dodging fireballs and anyone who came in our path. Alana had cleared an area with her Caelum and Terran powers, forming a cyclone around her, earth spraying. It reminded me of the day we'd thought she'd died. A knife had miraculously passed through her tornado, connecting squarely with her back. Worry frissoned at the memory.

"Alana," I yelled. "Where's Cate?"

The wind ceased, and debris dropped to the muddy earth. Terran soldiers moved in to protect us. I dismounted, and she said in a low voice near my ear, "She headed to the woods to hide for safety." She gestured behind us. "Every Ember here targeted her. The battle became more about them finding Catherine than anything else. Her guards were with her."

"Something happened," I said.

Alana nodded, holding up her palm indicating the lack of rain. "I've sent a group to search. They haven't returned."

"How long ago did the rain stop?"

"Less than an hour, around twenty minutes after she entered the forest."

"I'll find her," I said with more confidence than I felt.

She yanked me to one side, a fireball narrowly missing me. "You're slow today, Prince."

"Yes." There was no time to explain. "Be safe." I squeezed her shoulder, then gestured to Dev and Hugo toward the tree line, back in the direction we'd come.

I relayed the information once we fought through the chaos. My only saving grace was that Embers didn't possess the power of speed, and I'd had more practice with a sword than most due to Father and his endless expectations. For once, I was thankful for every exhausting hour I'd spent training.

"Which way?" Hugo turned his horse in a circle, the foliage thick and enveloping.

"Southwest. Avoid where the Terrans came through," Dev said. "We would have seen her."

Five additional soldiers accompanied us, and we spread out, ten meters apart, searching for signs of life through the trees. Broken branches, footprints, and scattered items littered the area, which the Caelumites likely left behind as they traipsed through on the way to war.

"This is hopeless." I thrashed my sword through a low overhanging branch, annoyed I couldn't just make it move out of my way with my powers like usual. The blade failed to cut through, sending it flailing into my face. Just before it bounced back, a flash of blue caught my eye.

"That way," I pointed. "Someone moving through the bushes. Caelum colors." I urged Raven forward, racing to where I saw the figure. It could simply be a late arrival or a deserter. My instincts propelled me, the others at my heels. I caught sight of a blond man on horseback in the Caelum uniform. His head shifted, and a ruddy cheek came into view.

Unease scraped across my skin. "Roy!" I called. Even from behind, his soft figure was unmistakable. He certainly wasn't in fighting shape. Why had he come?

Roy noticed us approaching fast, glancing back several times before pulling his horse to a stop and facing us. His gaze bounced around our small group.

"What are you doing out here?" I asked.

"I could ask the same of you," he blustered.

"We're searching for Cate," I said evenly.

His horse danced nervously. "I was on a scouting mission. Just catching up to the others."

He showed no surprise that Cate was missing. Anger bubbled. Dev and I exchanged looks. "Roy?" I struggled to keep my voice even. "What have you done with Cate?"

His already bulbous eyes widened. "Done with? Nothing."

I was off Raven in a flash, dragging Roy from his gelding. Pretty sure I used some powers based on the speed I reached him, purely fueled by rage. He unceremoniously tumbled to the dirt, and I yanked him up by the front of his shirt. It was a disgrace that he even owned a Caelum uniform. The man hadn't trained a day in his life. "Tell me what you've done." I could hear myself. I sounded unhinged and didn't much care.

His baby jowls wobbled and flushed. "I—I don't know where she is."

I pulled his wool jacket tighter, so his fleshy neck squeezed between the folds. His fish-mouth dropped open from shock at my manhandling. Or maybe because I'd cut off his air. *Good.* I hope he suffered. He and his father deserved it after what they did to Cate. No one would question it if he were found dead out here alone. Everyone would assume an Ember killed him. The thought took over, spinning on repeat in my head. Roy knew where she was. He was lying. I tightened my grip.

A hand fell on my shoulder, gently prodding me back. "Daniel." Dev's voice was low.

I resisted, squeezing tighter. "Tell me," I hissed.

Hugo and Dev forcibly pulled me away from Roy while our men circled him, ensuring he wouldn't escape. "What'd you do that for?" My hot anger spilled over onto my friends. Spilled over everything. My lack of powers. The Embers. Cate's disappearance. And most of all, this snivelly man who wanted so desperately to win back his throne, he'd throw away an entire kingdom to get it.

"Take a breather." Dev's brows elevated in warning.

I tried. I really tried. But when Roy smirked at me, straightening his coat, I lunged, knocking him into the mud. My knee rested on his windpipe. "Tell. Me. Where she is."

CHAPTER 56
CATE

The only thing I could see was a brown blur. I blinked, trying to clear my hazy vision. My fingers dug into the earth for traction, but they met only smooth, well-worn wooden planks. A foot shuffled. My foggy brain sifted through events. I remembered the battle was about to start. The Embers were coming… then it clicked, the horrific day tumbling into place.

I blinked again, gradually bringing things into focus. A wall stood a few feet before me, made of logs, like in a cabin or shed. The front part of my hip bone throbbed against the hard, wooden floor where someone had likely dropped me unceremoniously. Someone who was here with me, and I had a terrible feeling it wasn't one of my guards.

Slowly, I inched a hand down my leg for the place my dagger should be strapped.

"Don't bother. I won't make that same mistake twice. You've been disarmed. I checked… everywhere." Rowan's low voice vibrated across my skin and curdled my stomach. The innuendo? Enough to push me into a spiral.

I am not that girl. That girl who lets the bad guy send her whimpering into the corner. I am not that girl, I chanted to myself. The tiny bit of willpower pulled me to sit up. The rest of my soul desperately wanted to be her, the one in the fetal position. I scooted until my back rested against the wall for support, my head swimming from the knock it received.

"Why am I alive?" I croaked. "What do you want from me?" Even as I asked, I scanned the space to see if it was only the two of us. The cabin was more of an old shed. One room. A small table, chair, and a single window. I presumed his lackeys were guarding the door outside. Rowan leaned against the other wall, confident in his position. He wore a brown, fitted jacket trimmed with gold buttons, boots he likely traveled with through the portal based on their rubber waffle soles, and a bemused expression.

"You just don't listen, do you, Cate?" He crossed his arms.

"You really believe I'm the key to the Embers' happiness? That a bit of rain will solve all your problems?" My head pounded, but my thoughts turned clearer. "I know about your family. How you grew up in England, and your dad was snubbed because he didn't get into some club."

His lips curled. "That society was the only thing that would have held my father together. He needed a reminder of home because he regretted going through that portal every day of his life."

I huffed a sarcastic laugh. "Why, because he couldn't stand abiding by the rule of law? Don't you get it? There's something wrong with them. They can't distinguish right from wrong."

Rowan's face mottled with anger. He crossed the room in several strides, now looming over me. "I turned my life's mission into finding a way back for him. Only… I was too late. He didn't belong there. And neither did I." He took a step back, working to collect himself. "You can't see them as I can. There's good in there. They just have to be treated with respect."

"You are kidnapping young girls, raping them, and trying to create an army!" My voice shook with anger. "There *is* no good."

"Those girls hate us. They spread the lies their parents tell them. They deserve it."

His words hit like a slap, hot and startling, bringing color to my cheeks. I took a shaky breath. It didn't even seem worth trying. I suspected his origin story was a tale repeated countless times throughout history. "Back in England, did you ever hear about breaking the cycle? How, when a kid is abused, they are six times more likely to become like their abuser. Your dad… he hit you, didn't he? He called you names. Told you that you were worthless." Based on what I knew of the Embers and his bullying tendencies, this wasn't a far-fetched guess.

His gaze shifted away, just for a flicker, and I knew. Knew all this was about proving to his father that he had worth.

"He never hit me," Rowan defended, not correcting the remainder.

"You can be whoever you want to be," I whispered. "You don't have to do this for him. You couldn't save your dad, and I'm sorry for that. I really am. And you can't save the rest of the Embers either."

He shook his head. "No." His voice came out hoarse. "No." He strengthened it. "You're the key. I found the solution." He pointed at me. "You'll save us."

"I won't." I slowly stood while he watched me. "I'm just a girl who can make rain. I can't be their missing piece—their conscience. I can't be the one to break the abuse cycle. They have to decide for themselves." It was freeing to say it. To release the part of me that felt responsible for them. The tiny corner that believed maybe, just maybe, the prophecy was about me saving them. I let that possibility fly away with my words, and even though my head swam as I leaned heavily against the rough-hewn wall, and Rowan might run his knife through me at any moment, I felt lighter.

He took another menacing step forward, pinning me. "I can make you."

I lifted my chin, both to look him in the eye and show defiance, despite my heart fluttering like a bird in a cage. "You cannot."

He raised a brow, his handsome face showing a flicker of enjoyment. "I'm quite adept at torture. Fire isn't a comfortable way to die, and I'll make it slow."

I marveled at how this boy who'd grown up in London had turned so evil. Unlike the Embers, he'd had a choice. Whatever tripped the genes for males in this world that left them without conscience shouldn't have affected him. He'd been born in England. My mind went to Daniel. How he'd helped me gain my powers. How *love* triggered the energy. Goosebumps spread along my arms like ripe wheat across rolling hills at realizing Rowan's powers.

All was not lost.

Think, Cate.

A sheath at his side held his dagger. Rowan stood a foot in front of me, obscuring my view of most of the room. Part of the dust-covered table was visible, with the hilt of a sword peeking over the edge. "You won't hurt me," I stalled.

"I will if you won't cooperate."

"I know you can't make fire." I forced my voice to sound confident. "It's hard to gain your powers if you didn't grow up here, isn't it? You don't just want me for the Embers. You want me for yourself. To teach you." I had to be correct. I'd *never* seen him use fire.

My mind spun as I thought about those outside these walls battling. Of Lucas and Molly. Of Daniel, who, like Rowan, was struggling without his powers. Without me—without my rain—they wouldn't survive.

He watched me, the muscles in his jaw tightening with anger.

"How did you do it?" he burst out. "How?"

"I know what it's like for everyone to have expectations and not be able to deliver. It's hard."

He blinked a few times, both of us locked in a staring contest. "You couldn't do it either?" His words came out soft. Vulnerable.

I shook my head slowly, the throbbing reverberating with the motion. "I'll teach you. Let me go, and I'll teach you."

His jaw tightened, and he tutted, "We both know that won't happen."

I forced myself to move off the wall, standing straight. He shifted on his heels, only an inch or two, but allowed me the space. I ignored the pain in my left temple, driving deep into my skull.

"You must feel the energy first." I stretched out my arms. He took another step back. I shuffled, closing my eyes and folding my hands forward, palms up. I felt the energy. Weaker than before, like me, wavering, heavy with concussion. Another arm movement, wider this time. Another sidestep.

"Nothing," Rowan said, frustration ringing in his voice. "It's always nothing."

My lids flipped open. I'd maneuvered nearly to the center. Three sidesteps and I'd be at the table with the sword, but I didn't dare take my attention off Rowan. "Try again. This time, imagine your happy place." I closed my eyes again, hoping he would do the same. Displaying my vulnerability might lead him to let down his guard. Or there'd be no warning when he sliced open my neck as he had my father's.

"Mine is the forest outside Caelum Castle. The smell of pine. I can feel the needles beneath my feet. What's yours?"

A long moment of silence. "My mother. We'd sit together on the couch when my dad worked late and eat dinner together. I liked her shepherd's pie best."

My throat tightened at his words. I thought of my mom, too. Her spaghetti. The soft way she spoke to everyone.

"I left her," he whispered. "I left her to be here. I tried to get her to come back, but she wouldn't. Said she had escaped once, and that was enough for her."

I could sense renewed agitation. "Tell me about the pie," I said.

I ignored his discussion of fluffy mashed potatoes and thought about rain, and about the men in battle and how they needed me. How my mom needed me to survive. My strength grew as the energy absorbed into my fingers and deep into my bones, at first a tingling sensation, then a throbbing. A longing to be released. I hadn't practiced starting storms from inside, not wanting to ruin the castle. But this time, I directed my thoughts to the battlefield. To the dragons far off at the edge. Imagined a great shield for our men. I let go, and somehow, I knew the clouds formed. They coalesced and crashed together in black, dark, angry formations.

And the rain came.

Not inside, but out there. I miscalculated my reach, and thick, fat, drops pounded the little shed's roof. As soon as I heard it, I knew Rowan must realize that I wasn't teaching him at all. I was helping our army. Our eyes locked, and in one swift motion, I lunged for the sword. His longer arms snatched it before me. My dagger was still left on the surface, and I swiped it up, angling the table between us.

He flipped it end to end and roared, sending me scrambling backward. I bumped against the far wall, dodging the swipe of his steel. With his free hand, he grabbed a table leg and threw the whole thing at me. A corner of it knocked against my thigh, ricocheting in a blaze of pain that ripped through my leg. Rowan might not be able to produce fire, but his strength couldn't be denied. I refocused on harnessing the energy to increase my speed. I'd need it if I hoped to exit alive. Not my talent, especially when practicing against experienced Caelumites or Terrans, but it didn't matter.

I only had to be faster than him.

With a dodge and parry, I ducked past, heading for the door.

"You'll only be greeted by my men out there. It's no use, Catherine. Agree to fulfill the prophecy by helping the Embers. Or die."

He didn't want to kill me. That had to be the only reason I still lived. Maybe he believed in his version of the prophecy so badly he couldn't let go, or maybe he'd found a glimmer of empathy after spending time with my family in Oregon. He'd seen my pink-ruffled bed. Met my baby brother. Maybe even monsters had limits. At least enough to hesitate.

He was right about something. If I opened that door, I would only meet more of his supporters. Probably someone else to take up the mantle of his false prophecy. I remembered how I'd fought the Ember in the woods outside Caelum Castle who'd tried to kidnap me. There would only be one chance for this to work.

I dropped to the floor, rolling forward instead of heading for the exit, taking him by surprise. Before he could lower his sword, I angled my dagger upward, catching him in the groin. I dug my knife and twisted, warm red blood spewing over my hand. I veered before his sword could catch me.

But the sword never came.

He stood in shock, weapon clattering to the floorboards, turning sticky with blood. I'd learned enough anatomy in school to know I'd caught a major artery. His hand went to cover the wound, to apply pressure, but it pumped through his fingers in bubbling spurts. My stomach roiled at the memory of my father dying much the same way.

"Help!" he called, but it only came out as a croak. "Help me!"

The rain continued to pound outside, drowning out his voice.

Rowan collapsed to his knees, eyes wide in horror, before sinking onto his side. "I knew it would be you," he whispered. "You'd either join me or kill me." His words were slow, labored. "The prophecy. I hoped… I hoped I was right."

Tears burned. I'd killed before, but watching someone slowly die was a different experience—knowing I could put pressure on the wound, at least attempt to help, but my feet remained still, concreted to the floor. I thought of his mom sitting on their couch back in England. How she'd never see her son again.

But this was war. He killed my father. I should be happy. I should want revenge. All I really wanted was for it to end.

"There is good in them," he ground out.

It took me a moment to realize he was talking about the Embers.

"Save them. Find a way." His voice weakened, barely above a whisper.

"I will," I found myself whispering back, a tear careening down my cheek. "I will."

CHAPTER 57
DANIEL

"Tell me," I snarled, knee digging into Roy's throat. His eyes bulged, and I let up just a bit, enough to hear him wheeze. His hand went up, pointing southwest. I released a little more.

"Half a mile that way," he croaked. "An old shed."

I caught Dev's eye. "Let's go." As the words left my mouth, it began to rain. Sheets of water fell from the sky, and I'd never been so happy to be drenched. I jabbed my shin into Roy's chest as I stood, a crackle of broken ribs sounding. He deserved to die, but the least I could do was give him a little pain. "I'm feeling generous," I told him, catching drops in my upturned palm.

We left, not giving him a backward glance.

Hugo jostled me before I mounted Raven, a huge grin splitting his face. "She's alive."

Those words became my mantra as we raced through the forest. A log cabin came into view, not quite a shed, not quite a house, with about fifteen guardsmen visible, an unknown number hidden in the back. Our smaller group would have their work cut out for them, because not only were there Embers, but about half were Caelumite military. One pounded on the door but turned when we approached. The rest held their swords at the ready.

"There are more soldiers behind us," I called, forceful in my lie. "Surrender now, and you won't be hurt."

A dark-haired man with graying temples stepped forward. Rows of brightly colored patches on his chest displayed his rank and achievements in the Caelum army. He gave a brief bow, more of a nod, to acknowledge my royal status. "We desire peace as well, Your Highness. The prophecy foretold it. We believe the Embers will let us alone if Catherine's with them."

"Peace for how long?" I asked. "What happens when she dies? Tonight. Tomorrow. A hundred years from now. What then? Your solution is a patch in the overflowing dam, one that won't last."

"She'll grow back their lands. Rowan will teach them how to take care of it and preserve the forest. Then they won't need to invade ours," the Caelumite leader replied.

"They'll never learn. That's a fool's errand."

The soldiers behind the older man shuffled, a few stealing glances at one another, the stormy expressions of Embers circling the second row, not appreciating my insinuations that they'll lose control.

"We'd like to find out." The soldier lifted his weapon.

"You're willing to strike down the Prince of Terra?" I asked. "You'll have a bigger problem if you do." I unsheathed my sword. The ring sounded in the air, the sharp metallic song of age-old battles, the chorus echoing with my comrades' weapons.

"Not if they don't know who did it." He raised his brows.

Only a few moments before, I'd been thinking the same about Roy. All too often, the difference between good and evil balanced unsteadily on the tip of a sword.

"We aren't going to talk our way out of this," Dev said under his breath.

We both knew it. I could see it in the determined set of the man's jaw the minute we approached, the straight line of his shoulders, the solidness of his wide stance on the muddy ground. Fallacy or not, he believed Rowan's version of the prophecy and would fight to the bitter end to preserve it.

"You're wrong. And the punishment for treason is death." I raised my free arm in a battle cry filled with frustration, hope, and desperation.

Dev and Hugo raced forward, blocking me from the first line of men. The others weren't aware that my powers had left me like wisps of smoke through a chimney. An Ember, rounded on foot, while my friends' swords clashed with two Caelumites. Adrenaline surged—every man an obstacle to my goal.

To Cate.

My energy burned to life like a wick, not an explosive, but a candle, flickering and growing inside. Raven and I dodged the oncoming man while I swung my sword, slicing through until it thudded against hard collarbone. He collapsed, and we raced on, vision tunneling to the single door hanging slightly askew on the old shack. A cry sounded beside me. One of my men doubled over, a sword protruding from his belly, blood welling. The Caelum soldier pulled it loose, knocking the Terran to the ground.

The sharp tang of blood filled my nostrils, swirled my stomach, curled my insides. The Caelumite urged his horse forward, straight toward me. A flick of a glance showed the others thick in their own combat, Dev's blade swinging. Another flick to the door. To Cate.

Focus.

Killing a Caelumite would prove much harder than killing an Ember. He thrust his sword. I ducked, and Raven maneuvered to better position my steel. We clashed again, locked, horse flesh bumping, eyes staring into one another. His, brown and wide, ringed in green, lashes wet from the rain. I recognized that face. He'd been my guard on occasion when staying at the castle. A memory wafted to the surface. He stood at attention while Cate and I enjoyed tea, exchanging whispered secrets in between bites of scone piled with juneberry jam and mounds of clotted cream. Cate saved him a plate, and his cheek flickered in the barest of smiles, pretending not to notice while on duty.

Anger flared. How could he take her offerings, take her kindness, and repay her like this? My strength built with fury. I shoved, nearly unseating him. "You know her," I said through gritted teeth. "Benefited from her generosity."

His mouth gaped. Cheeks, splotchy and red. "I—" Suddenly, he appeared lost. As if he didn't know whose side he was on.

"Help me get her," I pleaded. "We're almost there." The door stood twenty yards beyond us, with only a single Ember between it and me, the others locked in combat.

He wavered in indecision, those eyes flashing more green than brown as they flickered from his commander to me.

"Are there more? Out back?" I whispered.

He shook his head.

"What if we killed him?" I tipped my chin to the leader of the pack. "Would the rest surrender?"

"Cranston? Maybe, but..." A shoulder tilt. Another glance. This time to the cabin. "Rowan," was all he said in return.

Fear crawled into my throat. I'd known. I'd already known Cate shared the tiny space with that monster. Yet the confirmation struck with surprising force. What was happening inside, and why hadn't Rowan come out? Surely, he'd heard us.

He's obsessed with her. The thought popped so clearly into my head it wouldn't shake free. Rowan would never leave Cate. Never stop tracking her. His death was our only solution, but first, I had to get through his men.

The Embers wouldn't surrender, but perhaps the others would. Slowly, I lowered my sword. "You can help by staying out of the way," I reassured him, hoping to make the decision easier for him. I sensed he didn't want to kill me any more than I wanted to strike him down.

Cranston directed from across the small clearing, sending me a glare that would freeze a steaming tea kettle. He'd never back down, the obsessed look in his eyes desperate for an answer to the prophecy. Desperate to end this war by any means necessary, even if it wouldn't last. And perhaps desperate for a chance to end the life of a different enemy, the Terran prince. I turned to the young soldier, his expression now panicked, filled with indecision. Which side would he choose?

He slowly raised his sword again, the tip quivering with nerves. I wheeled Raven around before he could strike, heading for Cranston. The sound of hooves followed. A ripple of fear pulsed. Was he hunting me down to sandwich me in, or coming to help? I could veer off my course. Track down an Ember instead.

But it was too late. I'd attracted the leader's attention, and he'd started toward me full force. I scanned our small battlefield. The rest of my team fought valiantly, Hugo nearby, unseated from his horse in hand-to-hand combat. The Caelum officer and I were on a collision course, both believing in Cate, but for different reasons. Both willing to fight to the death for her.

He slashed his sword at Raven's chest, grazing his mark. Raven bellowed in pain. I slid off him, despite being more vulnerable on foot, and sent my horse away anyway. I only hoped he was mobile enough to move to safety.

Cranston rounded on me for a second time, still mounted, his height and speed an advantage. I tried to channel the earth, to spray mud and rocks, but to no avail, my mind too scattered, powers too weak. He swung again, our swords clanging as he cantered past.

"Get him!" he yelled at the young soldier who'd pulled his horse up behind me.

I turned to see him raise his weapon. I'd hoped he'd become an ally; instead, he slashed his weapon downward. I blocked the blow, fear as tight as the grip on my sword. The young Caelumite had chosen the other side, and now it was two against one, me with stuttering powers.

I sidestepped, and Cranston barreled toward me, the soldier preparing another swing from behind. I couldn't block them both at once. I ducked, rolling, too low for them to catch me with their weapons. A thud landed beside me. One of them must have dismounted to hunt me down. I twisted, flipping to my feet to face the enemy.

Instead, Cranston lay in the dirt on his side, a sword through his chest. The Caelum Castle guard's hazel eyes round in shock.

"I—" His mouth started moving, but no words came out.

"It's okay," I told him in a soft voice. "Sometimes, the right thing is hard."

He nodded, his throat working to swallow.

"Tell the others that Cranston is dead. You think anyone else will switch sides?"

He nodded again, less confident than I'd like. I scanned the group. We'd made a significant dent, though several Terrans were either injured or dead. The rain had stopped, sending nerves bubbling to the surface. Dev and Hugo fought on, both up against Caelum soldiers. Two Embers now stood between me and the door, and I stalked toward them. Nothing would stop me—I was too close to Cate.

I flung a knife at one, hitting him through the heart. A fireball from the other hurtled toward me, the heat blowing past as I swerved to dodge it in time. *A few more steps*. I launched myself at him with such speed, it surprised both of us, my sword running him through. I yanked it out, barely glancing at the Ember and strode to the door, bloody sword aloft, ready to fight Rowan.

I hesitated for the barest of moments. Was it foolish to burst in without backup? Probably. Every second I waited was another that Cate endured. That *I* endured, wondering if she was hurting, or worse, already dead. The eerie quietness surrounding the cabin unnerved me.

The knob turned under my fingers. Before I became mired in fear, I swung it open with a bang, the sight so surprising I stood frozen, my sword drifting lower.

Cate sat cross-legged on the floor next to an awkwardly supine Rowan, eyes glassy and staring upward, a pool of blood surrounding them. Tears streaked her face as she watched me enter.

"He's dead," she whispered. "I killed him."

CHAPTER 58
CATE

Daniel's frame shadowed the door's opening: broad stance, sword ready to take on the world. But there was no one to fight. Only me. Broken. The blood on the floor mirrored red, purple, black, then back to red. Rowan's image reflected, flickering to my father's, his blond beard soaked in red, purple, black.

I tucked my knees up and rocked. Back and forth. *Rowan. Father. Rowan.*

Daniel knelt beside me. "Where are you hurt?"

His voice echoed from a faraway tunnel. I wasn't injured. Not really. Then why did it hurt so much? I should get up. Someone must need me. No—not someone. *Everyone.*

Footsteps sounded at the threshold. Dev stood in the same manner Daniel had moments ago.

"He's dead," I said. As if he couldn't see for himself. See the vacant expression.

It was all such a waste. Rowan had wanted better for people. His people. The waste of it all… Those women and children all trapped in Ember City. The kidnapped girls. The men who couldn't control their impulses. The charred land. The greed for more.

He'd been caught up in it, a cause doomed from the start. Whether he'd always been unbalanced or the environment triggered something here, somewhere along the way, Rowan had lost himself.

"We're all clear out here," Dev said softly, shuffling. Every crazy thought spinning in my brain must be plastered across my forehead for him to treat me like an egg that might crack at any moment.

A weight fell onto my shoulder. *Daniel.* His fingers squeezed. "Cate. Look at me."

I turned, head a balloon floating above my neck. He brushed a lock of hair from my brow, those cerulean-blue eyes watching me with care. With worry. "How many people die of choking on a hot dog per year?"

Another tear slipped down my cheek. We'd seen a vendor in the airport, and I'd spouted off the statistic without thinking. I didn't want to use those tricks anymore to center myself. I wanted to be strong. But this was part of what it meant to be me. Anxiety and post-traumatic stress mounded, and heaped, and piled, covering me until I felt nothing at all but its weight.

I'd never be free of it. It would keep happening over and over, and I had to cope. Had to drag myself out of my own head until the next time it buried me.

"How many?" he asked again.

"Five," I answered. "Five. Mostly children."

"Exactly. I know that, yet I have no idea how a hot dog tastes." His lips twitched. "Are you back? Just a little?"

I nodded, unsure if it was true. At least I was with him, not deep inside myself. I felt his fingers in mine, warm against my cold ones.

"Let's go," Daniel said. "You need to get out of here."

I stood, my legs numb, squeezing his hand like a lifeline. Dev had stepped outside, and we met him standing a few feet from the door, conversing with Hugo. I gulped lungfuls of fresh air to wash the taint of metallic blood and death from my breath.

Daniel pulled me up short before reaching the others. "You need another moment?"

"No, I'm okay." I forced it to be true.

He released my fingers. "I have some hard truths for you. And I'm sorry."

I thought I was numb and couldn't feel anything, yet an ache bloomed and curled in my stomach. "Tell me."

"The battle is still raging. There are dragons, too. Even without Rowan, we could still lose this thing. *Will* still lose."

He'd maneuvered me so my back was to Dev and Hugo, blocking my view of the downed men scattered outside the cabin. It made no difference; I'd seen them anyway—couldn't unsee them.

"We'll lose without you," he said. "We need your rain."

I'd fallen so deep into my head that I'd forgotten. A sob choked out before I checked myself. Straightened my spine. Lifted my chin and turned on my heel to Dev and Hugo. "It's time to win," I told them. "Get everyone ready to go."

Dev caught hold of my arm, his expression both questioning and sympathetic. I almost cracked again. Almost. "I'm fine."

Hugo exchanged a strange look with Dev, who gave him a curt nod before the larger man disappeared into the cabin.

I put the others out of my mind. Rain had to be my primary focus, and every moment I remained broken was another life that could be lost. I focused on the energy. It was fuzzier, further from reach. I leaned into Daniel. Waited for the molecules to light up like a candle.

"You can do it," he whispered, stroking my back. "With or without me. You can do it."

Warmth grew in my chest, that candle glowing with his words. I thought about what I told Rowan when instructing him to use the energy right before I killed him. About love. And what I didn't say, and maybe should have. That love was the key. The key to peace and fulfillment.

The prophecy wasn't about Cate the Savior. It was about discovering that using the energy with love would bring peace. That hatred tore apart this world. Even the portals knew what the kingdoms hadn't. Forming bonds with each other would save us.

The energy gathered and grew until I pulled the moisture together. Drops fell. Beautiful, wet, fat drops. I pushed them out. Imagined the battlefield. My pain, all my emotions spread with them, I couldn't restrain them, not right now.

"Make sure I don't lose myself," I told him, when I really wanted to say, *Make sure my heart doesn't stop.*

"Cate—no."

"Yes," I gritted out. "I have to."

The rain fell in a steady stream—not in sheets and buckets like it sometimes did, but enough that it would quench the Ember fires. Daniel left me to sit on a boulder while he checked on Raven. Dev sauntered over to keep me company, and I scooted to make room on the rock.

"I knew there was a reason I backed you." He nudged me with his shoulder and held out one palm, letting the drips fall onto it.

"Just the water thing, huh?"

"Yup." He let the "p" echo between us and shouldered me again. "You're the real deal, Catherine, Queen of Caelum. Don't let anyone tell you different. And on that note… you might want to turn around."

"Why?"

"Because Hugo's about to walk out of the cabin with Rowan's head on a stake."

I gasped. "No. You did not."

"I didn't. He did." Dev bit his lip. "He wouldn't do it if it wasn't necessary. The Embers will understand it—that's what they would do. The fastest way to spread the word that he's dead. We need them to lose confidence. We need them to surrender."

I exhaled slowly, breath unsteady. *Focus on the water, Cate.*

Even though Dev told me to look away, I couldn't. It had been Hugo's idea, but I would be responsible for this spectacle. He'd died under my hand, and I should have the decency to witness what I'd done. My nails bit into the rock, stomach roiled, and skull still pounded from the lump Timmley had given me earlier. I dry heaved into the bushes as the head passed, not able to watch a moment longer. Hugo had closed Rowan's eyes, that tiny gesture humanizing him.

After I wiped my mouth and restarted the momentary loss of rain, Dev leaned in and said, "You did a good thing, you know that, right? Killing is the worst part of war. It's awful, and we're all haunted by it, and—"

"Wow, you're really making me feel better." Though understanding we all shared the same horrors actually *did* help.

Daniel strode up next to us, leading Raven. A thin line of red streaked the horse's chest, mostly healed over. "We'd best get going,"

Daniel said. "He seems okay, but I'll take Cranston's horse. Cate, you can ride one of the other Caelum soldiers' mounts."

North's location was likely closer to the battle, but I had no idea where she'd ended up. If we made it out alive, we would find each other. The bond we shared would draw us together. I remembered the words Daniel had tooled into her bridle: *So you'll always find your way home.*

"I hope so, North," I murmured. "I hope so."

CHAPTER 59
LUCAS

The sound of Molly keening echoed, sending goosebumps traveling up my arms. She dropped the Ember, though not high enough to have caused lasting damage, and flapped her wings upward. "How bad is it?" I called. "Find a safe place to land!" I needed to examine the wound and bandage it from the supplies in her saddlebag. Her friend, a sleek blue dragon the color of the ocean on a clear day, followed us, the rest staying with Leo and Big Momma, continuing their attack.

My sweet Molly had left an impression on them. I'd certainly had no luck changing their opinion the last time we'd seen them. They'd joined us to fight and risked injury for her. I gaped behind as Leo's tail spikes impaled two Embers at once. Judging the number of Embers here, we didn't have a prayer without their help.

Molly reached the outskirts of the battle and circled to land a safe distance away. She hovered longer than usual, gently coming to a stop on her hind legs, then lowering herself carefully. I gathered the bandaging from the bag and slid down her green-gray scales. Steam escaped when I came close to the wound, and if I hadn't jumped out of the way, I would have been facing a second-degree burn.

"Mols, I haven't even touched you yet," I scolded. She shifted her weight, giving me access. One front leg had a slice through the leathery black skin, blood oozing. I cleaned it with a canteen of water, white bone visible through the cut. The wrapping soaked through immediately, but it was all I could manage out here. At least it was covered. Molly tossed her head and thankfully avoided more steamy breaths, or worse, fire.

She tipped her head low and nudged me until I wrapped my arms around her. "It hurts, doesn't it?"

She nodded, nearly knocking me off my feet. I slid my hand along her neck to the underside of her jaw and stroked the orange patch. "Do you need to sit this one out?"

She saw her friends in the distance, still dive-bombing the Embers and starting to make a dent in their back line. The blue dragon had landed twenty yards away and watched with large golden eyes. After a moment, Molly lowered herself gently, avoiding placing weight on her injured front leg, the signal for me to climb on.

I patted her one more time before mounting. "Be careful."

We swooped over the battlefield and joined the others. The cobalt dragon I deemed Milo, on our wing. Molly circled, not yet ready to attack. Tension and fear trembled beneath her scales. The Terran army had reached the front lines and fought valiantly in the distance. Just when she decreased her altitude toward the battle, a drop of rain hit. Then another.

Cate.

I sagged against Molly in relief. "She's okay!" I yelled. "She's alive."

The dragons continued to fight from the far side of the battlefield while the Caelumite and Terrans worked their way from the opposite. Molly gained her confidence and began plucking and dropping Embers, being sure to capture them so they weren't able to twist and use their swords against her. Milo flew by her side, watching over her like a blue guardian angel. The rain stopped again, worry clutching my insides.

We circled over the field, flying low to search for Caelumites in trouble, and spotted John sparring with an Ember, with Grace nearby, her dagger drawn. Another joined the fray, outnumbering our friends. Molly beelined to them and swiped up the enemy.

"Watch yourself!" I called down. I wanted to tell them to run to safety, though at the same time, pride that both stepped up to fight for our kingdom held me back.

Not long after, the rain started again, and Rowan entered the battle, head on a pike, carried proudly by a giant of a Terran soldier. The man who'd hunted and stalked Cate was finally dead. Hope coiled itself around me like spun sugar. This could turn the tide. The water. The dragons. The Terrans. And now, Rowan's death.

My thoughts turned to Mya and the chance to tell her in person. I imagined her slow smile of relief at hearing of Rowan's demise. I'd tried not to let myself think of her, dream of her, the probability of never returning too great, though I'd had little success. I chuckled, thinking of her in Terra Castle, stewing that she hadn't snuck out and followed her father to battle. She'd promised me she would stay, understanding her worth in organizing soldiers, rallying troops, and for the kingdom's stability to have an heir safe at home.

Once the Embers realized their leader was dead, they folded in on themselves like an old tent. Their fire continued to be useless with Cate's relentless rain. The dragons were brutal, acting as a major turning point, followed by the second blow of the Terran army. The Embers laid down their weapons while we surrounded them.

After tending to Molly's wound, I let her fly off with Milo in tow. I needed to trust that she'd return to me, though a prickle of doubt remained. Her happiness was most important, and if she chose that life, I'd have to live with it.

Some wanted to slaughter all the Embers, but Cate announced they would be housed within the walls of the two nearby towns, one of which was Quorum, until we devised a plan. John and Grace's home would likely be destroyed, and Cate promised to rebuild. My throat tightened at the thought of the Four Horseshoes being used by the enemy. Nostalgia prompted memories of my recent stay. Sometimes at night, after closing, I would sneak down to the dining room with its sticky floors and scarred wood tables and pretend I wasn't a fugitive. Just a normal bloke enjoying a pint and a tasty midnight snack. Those memories would only be more painful for Grace and her dad.

"We cannot repeat history," King Dryden's voice rang out in the camp, jerking me out of my thoughts of sausages and chips. "They must all be killed."

I stepped closer to Cate, both for her protection and to offer support. Daniel flanked her other side. A warm, unexpected feeling grew in my chest at the sight of him alive.

"I'm not making any rash decisions," Cate said. "If we keep the males separated from the females, won't they eventually die out?"

King Dryden snorted. "You're going to keep them penned up for the next hundred years? The cost of feeding them alone…" He shook his head. "It will be a nightmare of constant fires, fights, and prison breaks. It can't be done. They must die. We can't risk it."

Cate crossed her arms. "We'll meet with the council to decide."

Dryden took a step forward into Cate's personal space, Daniel straightening, ready to intervene. "You think you can waltz into this realm and make decisions after being here mere months?" Dryden asked. "Killing them all is the only answer. The council will agree. At least you have the sense to consult *someone else*." He stared down Daniel, implying how little he thought of his son's opinion.

"In the meantime," Cate did her best to appear unruffled, "we need to send several battalions to Ember City to clean out any lingering men and rescue the kidnapped girls. I've already informed General Dixon."

"First, we herd the fighters into the walled cities." I wanted them contained. Thousands of Embers sitting in the middle of a field made me itchy.

"I'll provide the manpower to guard them once they're in," the king replied.

"Thank you." Cate's voice was curt, but professional. "With some of Caelum's army, of course."

She didn't want to leave Dryden alone with the Embers, fearing he'd kill them all. The man made some valid points. None of us had the stomach to slaughter an entire nation except him. Cate wanted ideas for saving them, and I had a few. Mya and I made a few interesting discoveries in those archives in London.

"The council must come to us," Daniel said. "It'll be easier to handle the Embers if Cate provides rain, even if it isn't continuous, and she can't manage the distance from here to either castle."

"We need new Caelum members appointed," I added to Cate. She had to replace Graftonberg and his cronies.

"I'll inform the Terrans," the king announced before striding away to send a message.

Cate grimaced, watching Dryden leave. "It could have gone worse."

I chuckled. "Isn't that what we always say?"

"Because it's true," Daniel quipped. "I've seen worse." He turned his attention to Cate. "Who would you like on your council?"

"Hanson, Dame Hemlock, Alana, and Count Wellsbrook," she answered without hesitation.

The count and Alana had been on the assembly previously. The dame was a good choice. She possessed more money than practically anyone in the kingdom. Her resources might come in handy.

"Ah, you learned the count's name finally," Daniel smirked at her.

She punched him in the arm. "Be nice."

Daniel leaned in close. "I'm always nice," he whispered. They looked into each other's eyes like a pair of lovesick fools. His lips hovered over hers.

Jealousy panged. It took a moment for me to process my feelings—a yearning for their closeness rather than any desire for Cate. A longing for Mya. "See you guys later," I said, sure that no one was listening.

"Mmmhmm," Cate murmured, all dreamy-eyed. "Hey." She flipped out of her trance. "Tell me later about the dragons, 'kay?"

I waved her off and left to see if Molly had returned. The medics would need help changing her bandages.

A week later, the remaining Ember men were locked in the three nearest border towns, all with stone walls and guards surrounding them. I'd made the trek to Ember City and released the kidnapped girls, stationing even more guards to keep the rest of the women and children from leaving. Grace and John had journeyed with me. I was proud of Grace facing her fears by guiding her father through the ramshackle city.

We confirmed that none of the women could make fire, though they likely carried the gene mutation that their sons would. The girls who'd already given birth were forced to choose between returning to their families alone or staying in the city with their children. Containment became our primary, yet heart-wrenching goal.

Tears streaked Grace's cheeks as we rode away, one of her friends from Quorum still inside. "It's awful. We promised to save them, and this…" her shoulders slumped, "is just awful," she repeated, at a loss for words.

"It's not the final solution," I said.

"But what is? Try as I might, I can't find it. Not anything that isn't inhumane."

"No one wins in war," I responded quietly. "You've lost your house. Some of those girls don't have a place to return to either. Give us time."

She huffed, and at that moment, she seemed every bit her young age.

John rode beside us, taking in our conversation. "Lucas is right. Nobody wins. We're lucky to have made it. You and me?" he waited until Grace raised her eyes to him. "Remember that. We're survivors."

Another tear slipped down her face. "We are lucky. But… why me, not them?"

John held up his horse. "We may never know. But don't waste the opportunities you've been given, Grace McAllister. Don't squander them. Those girls in there wouldn't want—your mom wouldn't—" his voice broke. "It would be a shame. That's all. A shame."

It was the most I'd ever heard John speak. I'd put my walls up when around the others, but the guilt of those left behind had been eating me from the inside. John's words soothed the ragged edges. The women and children couldn't stay there forever. I wouldn't allow it. I was one of the lucky ones, too, and I wouldn't let it go to waste.

A camp had been set up outside Quorum for Caelum and Terran soldiers, along with several large tents for Cate, King Dryden, and a mess hall. The council members had trickled in, with only a few left to arrive, including Dev's father, the Duke of Earlington. I hoped for Cate's sake he didn't bring Emily. That girl proved to be nothing but trouble.

After reporting to General Dixon, I trudged to the muddy outskirts to check on Molly. The clear skies told me Cate must be resting. She started the rain if fires broke out in any of the Ember camps, even in the middle of the night. Otherwise, the water would fall in starts and stops, purposely unpredictable to give Cate a chance to mentally relax.

I rounded a clump of trees to find a figure already standing next to Molly, stroking her nose. Long, dark hair trailed down her back, her forest-green gown elaborately decorated with embroidery. My heart stuttered. She turned, a wide smile spreading, those dimples peeking out. I reached her in three large strides. Mya wrapped her arms around me, and a sense of peace I hadn't felt in months spread like hot cocoa on a winter's day.

"You're going to kiss me before Molly, right?" she asked.

"One time," I murmured into her hair. "I talked about kissing Molly *one time*. You'll never let it go."

She sagged into me, soft and warm. "Never."

Our lips crashed together, first through joy-filled grins, then the urgency and pain of wondering if we'd ever see each other again pressed into every touch. I tugged her hair and exposed her neck, trailing kisses down it.

"You missed me," she whispered between gasps.

"An understatement." I pulled back. "I could barely stand to think of you, honestly."

Her hand flew to her hip in such a purely Mya gesture that a laugh burst out at the sight of her pursed lips, ice-blue eyes narrowed.

"Because you're too distracting." I sent her my most charming smile. She wasn't buying it.

"I love you, Mya. And try as I might not to think about you—not think about having a life with you one day—I could not get you out of my mind. I didn't want to remind myself that if this was the end, I'd be leaving you behind. This battle—it was a death march. Truly. We had no way of knowing whether the Terrans would join us. And if the dragons hadn't come, and Cate hadn't killed Rowan?" I shook my head.

"Say it again." She watched me, searching for an answer I couldn't quite identify.

"Say… Oh."

She nodded slowly, her sharp expression melting into something softer.

"I love you."

To my surprise, a tear skipped down her cheek. "I love you, too."

My palms lifted, not entirely understanding what was happening here. "I thought we did this already. I told you I loved you back in England. You said it back."

She shoved me. Really shoved me, and I wobbled. Molly's head shot up in interest, though she didn't make a move to intervene.

"I was scared, too, you dolt. Scared I'd never hear you say it again. And just because you say it once—"

"Doesn't mean I don't want to tell you every day for the rest of our lives." I reached for her hand.

The vulnerability in her features broke me. "Promise?" she whispered.

"When have I ever broken a promise?"

She thought about it for a moment. "Never."

"Exactly." And I intended to keep it. I wasn't sure how, but I vowed to find a way. She lit up my world, and I didn't want to live stumbling in the dark anymore. I remembered those lost months when Cate was missing, and Dryden wouldn't let me see her. Never again, I promised. Never.

CHAPTER 60
CATE

"They must all die," King Dryden's voice echoed, decisive and commanding. "Including the women and children. You lack the stomach to accept the truth. We must protect our kingdoms. Letting even one live could be catastrophic."

The council had finally arrived and sat around a makeshift conference table in the mess tent. I'd been informed of a fire outbreak in a neighboring town, so my attention was split between the meeting and keeping the rain falling. The strain in my shoulders burned with the stress of too many juggling balls.

"I agree," the count spoke up quietly. Count Wellsbrook was my own choice of council member—perhaps not a good one. But I hadn't wanted yes-men or yes-women, rather a collection of different voices from the kingdom. The count, Lucas, Dame Hemlock, Hanson, and General Dixon formed the Caelumites in the circle. Alana, a neutral party, took it all in, the brackets around her mouth highlighting her age and fatigue. Dryden, Daniel, Earlington, a viscount I didn't know with a sour expression, another new-to-me aristocrat who'd been silent so far, and to my surprise, Mya, joined the Terrans. We lacked a few more, but contacting every member in Caelum would be too time-consuming. Plus, I wanted to be sure their loyalties were with me, not the Graftonberg camp.

"When can we get rid of them?" the Duke of Earlington asked, straightening his plum-colored cravat as if he were at a dinner party instead of a military camp outpost.

Rowan's last words haunted me. *There's good in them.* I'd promised to save the Embers, and it stuck in my throat, sticky and thick. Did I really have to keep a promise to a murderer? Yet, wasn't I one too? Both Dev and Daniel said it wasn't the same. I'd saved thousands of lives with one death. I just—I wanted so badly for the killing to end. I had told no one about my promise. Not even Daniel. The shame of being a weak queen—one that showed too much mercy—flashed hot against my cheeks.

"I don't want to kill them," I blurted through the lump in my throat. The quiet filled the space as if I'd yelled my confession, dominoing into shocked faces, worried glances, uncomfortable shifting, and King Dryden's slow grin at my naivety.

Dame Hemlock cleared her voice, adjusting her half-moon glasses. "I have a solution. One that doesn't involve more deaths."

Everyone's attention turned to the dame in surprise, including me. The king renewed his glare, this time directed at the older woman.

"You might be aware that I own quite a few seafaring vessels," she said.

Lucas had told me she'd made much of her fortune carrying goods up the coastline and fishing in deep-sea waters, along with various inventions from her ancestors. The innovations on her ships allowed them to travel farther than any other vessels and to catch varieties of fish that wouldn't be available otherwise. The large quantities her boats provided even allowed Terrans to buy seafood from Caelumites. Though I wasn't sure what it had to do with the Embers.

"We've been doing some exploring. I've always wondered if there was other life out there. More land, like when the Spaniards discovered the Americas. My crew has been mapping the oceans, and so far, hasn't found anything so huge as that. But they did find land. A series of uninhabited islands, a three-week voyage from our main port." She looked directly at me. "King Dryden is correct. If we leave the Embers here, they will continue to reproduce. Like cockroaches, they'll never go away. Not unless we kill them or find a place far from us."

"Won't they figure out how to build a boat, then just come back?" I asked.

She nodded slowly. "They might. But it took generations for us to construct a ship that can navigate the rough seas. I suspect they'll die off before then."

"Die off?" I asked. "What, they'll starve on this island?"

"I don't believe so. There seems to be an abundance of vegetation and animals." She crossed her hands in front of her. "I propose we send only the males."

"With all due respect, how's that going to help? The women—" the earl started.

"Aren't a threat," she replied. "Have you ever seen a female Ember use fire? Have you ever found them to be aggressive?"

I looked to Mya and Lucas. They'd been in Ember Camp the longest.

"No." Mya chewed on her lip. "The girls showed a lack of discipline because… well, because they didn't get great parenting, but none of them produced fire."

"How did we not know this?" I asked.

"They've always kept their women and children hidden," General Dixon replied. "We've suspected, but it didn't matter. It was the men who were attacking."

"Say we go along with this plan. How do we know the females don't carry the gene?" I asked. "That their sons won't become Embers?"

"We believe it's carried on the Y chromosome. The male chromosome," she replied.

"Believe?" Daniel asked. "Or know."

The dame pursed her lips. "Strongly suspect."

"What about all those mothers being separated from their sons? It's inhumane," I said.

"So is continually attacking us," the count replied.

Lucas raised a finger. "May I?" he glanced at Mya, who gave him an encouraging nod. "When in London, Mya and I did some research. At first, we were trying to find more about Rowan, then we dug deeper, looking for reports of Embers traveling through the portal. It appears that females usually do well, although older records primarily focused on marriage and children. The men struggled, most of the time ending up in prison. They'd join gangs, steal, the usual."

"It's the boys," Mya continued, her speech pressured as if she couldn't keep the secret. "If they went through the portal young enough, before puberty, whatever is triggered in their genes doesn't happen. They grew up to become upstanding citizens."

One of the Terrans spoke up, "And what of Rowan? When did he cross through?"

"He does seem to be an exception," Lucas admitted. "He was born in England to Ember parents. I think it had more to do with his father being snubbed by the society, then dying not long after. He connected the two and became obsessed with his culture."

"And obsessed with proving the Embers were worthy," I said. "That's why he was always saying he's a man of his word. He wanted to build a society for them. He became twisted along the way." I shivered at thinking just how twisted and turned my thoughts away from the bloody scene of his death that I carried every day. Every hour.

Dryden stared down his daughter. "The women still carry the gene, and they'll pass it on. We'll be in the same situation years from now. This is our chance." He sent me one of his signature lethal stares, jaw tightening. "There may never be another Catherine. We must strike now." I was sure he hated to admit how essential I'd been in the Ember downfall.

"Father," Mya said. "Lucas and I were thinking… what if we moved the women and children through the portal? We've been speaking to Alana. She believes there must be a stable portal near Ember City. That's how Rowan came and went so easily."

"He had to learn how. It took him a long time," I said.

"But with Alana's help…" Mya replied.

"I can guide them," Alana agreed. "Our contacts on the other side will help them settle by providing identification and temporary housing. We'll send them in groups."

I thought of Nigel and his penthouse apartment overlooking the Thames, and Emmitt with his precise forging skills, and Sarah and

Bert. Yes, they would help as long as they survived the attack when we went through the portal. "I think it could work," I said.

"It's not enough," Dryden shouted, nearly standing, but opting to settle in his seat. "They might find a way back. The safest would be to eliminate them all."

The kidnapped girls—the ones who wouldn't abandon their Ember babies. This would be a way to save them. Alana could even guide their family members, too. "I would like to try it. Lucas and Mya have both done the research. If Alana can find a stable portal, then that is my vote. Call to motion?"

I swiveled my head around the room, anticipation tingling. We needed to protect those women. We *had* to. Dryden, Earlington, and the viscount all disagreed. The rest voted with me. Daniel, sitting across from me on the Terran side, sent me a reassuring nod.

I exhaled, my strength deteriorating from my emotions, feeding the rain, and saving those girls. Mya and Lucas had approached me before the meeting, though in truth, they hadn't yet spoken to Alana about this crucial point. The entire plan depended on her. She wasn't the same woman as before her injury. Her weakness might have developed from too much time in the other world, or her injuries were too severe to fully recover. A rush of gratitude reminded me she'd long deserved retirement. King Dryden was wrong about plans being hinged on me—we all played a part, every one of our talents needed, especially Alana's.

The king's dark eyes flashed at Daniel. "Of course you'd side with Catherine. I can kick you off the council. You too." He glanced at Mya as if an afterthought. Whatever soothing, convincing energy she sent his way partially worked, at least for her.

Daniel just shook his head with a mocking smile, both in disbelief and frustration. "If you don't want the heir to play a part, I'm happy to leave. These people will do what's right whether or not I'm here."

Challenging his father in front of the group was two-pronged. It showed the council that Daniel could think for himself, and irritated the king into becoming irrational, something the members here wouldn't tolerate. I sent him a not-so-secret tiny smile.

"And what of the Ember men?" Daniel asked. "Can we vote on that as well?"

This plan was riskier. If the Embers ever learned to build a boat that could cross the volatile seas, they could overrun us again. Yet I couldn't stop thinking of Rowan's statement. *There's good in them.* Ninety-nine percent of me didn't believe it. But that one percent chance kept eating away.

"Dame Hemlock, thank you for your generosity," I said. "It's the solution I've been looking for. There have been too many deaths. If you and your crew are willing, I would be eternally grateful."

Around the room, we voted. This time, even my allies were reluctant. The count voted against, as did King Dryden's councilmembers. The vote came to Daniel, indecision wavering in his eyes. He'd fought the Embers for years. Seen their ruthlessness. He might try to convince me I was crazy for trying to save them. Maybe I *was* crazy. He watched the king, knowing if he sided with me, his father may never forgive him.

Anxiety surged. The rain stopped as if pausing to hear the decision, the absence of tattering on the tent roof descending us into eerie stillness. We'd never discussed this new idea. Hadn't plotted and planned for months. He might tip the scales the other direction.

There's good in them. Why couldn't I get Rowan's voice out of my head?

When the silence stretched, Daniel spoke, "I vote for Dame Hemlock's plan. I've seen enough death to last two lifetimes. We save every Ember we can."

CHAPTER 61
DANIEL

Four weeks passed while Dame Hemlock gathered her fleet to the nearest port, the day finally arriving when we would transport them to the coast. Cate grew weary of the military camp, the lack of privacy, and most of all, the constant need to produce rain. She'd been woken up five nights in a row, the Embers restless in their makeshift enclosures. Daily, at least one attempted a breakout, none making it over the walls and into safety before being struck down by a soldier. In this manner, their numbers continued to dwindle, their impulsivity once again their downfall. They'd listened to Rowan, but without their leader, an organized escape never materialized.

Caravans of food arrived, both for our soldiers and the enemy. We wouldn't starve them as they had our prisoners, despite my father being reluctant to provide comforts. We'd argued so much that I hadn't spoken to him in days, even though my tent sat beside his. He continued to insist extermination was the only solution, while I sided with Cate on the more humane answer. It would be easy to give in—simpler than keeping watch and boarding them onto a fleet of ships.

Yet, I'd become sick of killing. Their eyes haunted me. Each person I'd struck down in battle contained a glimmer of humanity. I wasn't so foolish as to believe they could be rehabilitated, which had been tried for centuries without success. Maybe I'd turned soft. Maybe I would sleep better at night knowing I wouldn't contribute to more deaths. Maybe the decision was more about me and every other soldier who'd be saved from participating in mass execution.

"Hey," Cate emerged from her tent where I waited outside, the smudges under her eyes dark against pale, drawn skin. She'd lost more weight, cheeks hollowed, wing-like collar bones protruding beneath her dress.

I pulled her into my arms, sharp angles collapsing in on themselves, softening against me. "Another hard night?"

"Three times," she groaned into my shirt. "I'm about ready to just let the towns burn to a crisp. It's getting ridiculous."

"Lean on me for a while." I guided her to sit beside me. We discovered that, especially when she was tired, she could draw energy from me. I'd started to regain some of my power, finding it easier when with her. Before the battle, we'd hardly found a quiet moment to practice. Now the endless days of waiting drug on. Though frequently interrupted, we spent nearly every waking second together discussing plans for the kingdom, meeting with advisors, and plotting our future.

"Tomorrow's the big day." Her words filled with hope, but her tone flat, unable to muster excitement, knowing she'd be responsible for near constant rain the next week when we traveled to the sea.

The water had begun to depress everyone—the camp constantly muddy, tents barely holding up against the deluge, dampness seeping into our bones. I pulled her in to ease her chill.

"Final stretch." I squeezed her arm.

"Stay with me." She snuggled closer, absorbing my warmth, skin cool against my touch.

I listened for her emotions, both for practice and to gauge if she was as close to breaking as she appeared. Exhaustion pulsed, a sluggish ping in my brain. I searched for anxiety. Feeling none, I let my breath linger on her neck, my lips caressing soft, warm kisses, each sending tingles traveling through me, as if the energy seeped into capillaries, branched into veins, and traveled straight into the chambers of my heart.

A throat cleared. I reluctantly tore myself away to see Alana, arms crossed like a disapproving schoolmarm, with General Dixon beside her, gaze averted. I cursed the lack of privacy for the hundredth time in this camp. Alana had just returned from the portal near Ember City.

"I wish to take the first group through next week," Alana announced. "Rowan let our friends from the society go. Everyone's fine. I've met with Nigel and set a date. A warehouse will be equipped for the women until they can be placed. I don't guarantee they'll all have a better life, especially with so little schooling, but at least they'll have a chance. Sarah and Bert have made outreach connections. The first group will include those whose sons are older, close to the age when their genes might be triggered here. The others, at Princess Mya's request, are beginning school. Teachers were sent from Terra, and classes start this week."

Cate sat up straighter. "I'll have to thank Mya. I don't know why I didn't—"

"Think of it?" Alana interrupted. "I do believe your talents are occupied here. Remember to lean on others, Catherine." She arched a brow.

"Did you send a message to William Brody at Peaceful Pines?" Cate asked.

"Done," Alana responded. "Now I have a request."

My turn to raise my brows. This was new—Alana showing deference to Cate.

"As you know, I've been fortunate to get acquainted with your family quite well," she said.

"Thank you for taking care of them. I've sent word with the outcome of the war."

Cate wanted nothing more than to be with her family, but her attention had to stay focused on the captured Embers and rain.

"Yes, well." Alana pulled her shoulders back. "I'd like to take them to live in Ember City. They can teach the groups about the other side, so it won't come as such a shock. I believe your family would be happier being useful. It was the hardest part about staying in hiding. They wanted to contribute."

Cate's emotions came roaring to life, as strong as I'd felt them since traveling through the portal. Anxiety, pain, loneliness, disappointment, and finally, pride rippled. She'd planned for her family to be with her after this, even discussed in detail which chambers in the castle should be theirs, weighing every pro and con from northern light to proximity to the kitchens.

"If they are willing, of course they can go." Cate's voice came out scratchy and raw. The sacrifices she'd made for the kingdoms, for the enemy, piled and wobbled until they threatened to bury her. The price of the crown was one I was glad I didn't yet carry.

"You okay?" I asked when Alana left, my hand falling to her knee like an anchor.

She nodded, her smile too tight, too stiff. "If you see Mya before I do, thank her."

"I will. She's returning to Terra tomorrow. Father placed her in charge while he travels to the coast with us, if you can believe it. At least that's what Dev told me." I put on a haughty voice to cover my hurt, "The king hasn't deemed me worthy to share his plans."

"Once we succeed, he'll forgive you." Cate absently stroked my palm.

I thought of Father and the progress between us before the battle, and how it'd disintegrated. He would never understand mercy and kindness. Would likely never understand peace, and I suspected it would put us at odds forever. Every time inroads were made in our relationship, his compulsion for dominance and power would sever them. I wouldn't be so foolish as to fall into past mistakes by attempting to please him if it went against my conscience, though a part of me still craved his approval. The kernel of hope that he might gain a redemption story never completely left.

"You're right," was all I could think of to say, even though I couldn't make myself believe it. We were destined to be at odds eternally.

The next day, with rain pelting, we began the march to the coast. The troops were miserable, wet to the bone, even with drundle coats, as we couldn't escape Cate's constant weather keeping the Embers under our control. The following days were much the same. Lucas scouted by air, watching for any rogue prisoners. I felt sorry for him, the elements stronger up in the sky at Molly's speed. He'd periodically join us for a hot cup of coffee and a joke to keep up Cate's spirits. His emotions came strong, perhaps because of our prior connection in the circle, or maybe because he truly was that miserable.

"Only a few more days," I said, the same I'd uttered multiple times like a mantra. No one corrected me, all of them with the same desire to return to their families, a warm fire, and dry clothes.

On the final day, my father joined us. He'd traveled with a small group elsewhere, claiming kingdom business. Affairs he hadn't shared with me. Cate rode ahead on North with the general to give us privacy. Silence stretched. "Only a few more days," I repeated on autopilot, not sure what else to say, then corrected to, "last one."

"Indeed, it is." He clapped me on the shoulder, his stallion a full two hands taller than Raven. His spirits were suspiciously chipper. "I'd like you to come home after this. Increase your responsibilities. I've held the reins too tight. Mya will also take on a greater role. We need to spend more time together, then you'll be ready, son."

This had not been in the plans Cate and I constructed over the last few weeks. Especially since her family would travel to Ember City, I didn't want her to return to Caelum Castle alone. There might still be Graftonberg supporters, and I wasn't willing to leave her.

"Cate's coronation. I'll need to be there," I replied.

The disapproving stare I'd grown to expect bored into me from atop his mount. "I'll attend as well. But it will take time to organize. Come home with me first." His gaze softened. A ping of emotion—longing mixed with regret grazed past. "Please."

Those same boyhood desires of approval unfurled like a flower turning toward the sun. The never-ending dilemma of time spent in Terra versus Caelum followed, nurturing the bloom and giving the idea room to take root. "I'll think on it," I finally replied, delaying my decision, all the while knowing deep down that I'd choose Cate if she needed me. I watched her ahead, draped in a drundle cloak that covered her features, yet her subtle movements—the way she shifted in the saddle, one hand on the reins, the other in motion as she spoke —were as familiar as my own.

Father and I engaged in small talk until he fell back with a Terran general, uncomfortable communicating with his own son. Some things never changed. Though this time, the pang of regret echoed from him as he rode away.

Dame Hemlock's ships filled the harbor, a massive number, enough to create an entire navy if we desired it. I had no idea one woman was responsible for half the seafood consumed in both kingdoms. The fleet had been outfitted with tankards of seawater and hoses to extinguish any fires that might start. We were at the greatest risk while they were still close to shore, and the Embers could swim to land. Hopefully, they'd have enough restraint in the center of the ocean to realize they'd drown.

We loaded the Embers into ships far into the night. Cate retired to a small inn at the harbor for supper to keep up her strength in producing the relentless rain. I remained, assisting in herding the prisoners onto the boats, packing them like stacked wood to fit as many as possible into each ship. Dev kept me company, and we worked in tandem, guiding them down the ramps to the vessels.

"My father was here when we arrived." Dev's voice held a worried undertone.

"Really?" The duke had returned to Terra after the council meeting and wasn't expected.

"Yeah. Kinda weird. Said he had some business with Dryden."

Worry triggered. The king's cheery mood after meeting with Earlington, a snake as slippery as my father. Unease coiled, and I exchanged looks with Dev.

"They're up to something." I shoved an Ember forward down the slippery ramp. This was the last boat to fill. The rain had sputtered a few minutes ago, Cate likely taking a brief rest.

"Surely, they wouldn't try a Caelum attack now. The Terran soldiers probably wouldn't even follow those orders after rubbing shoulders, sharing meals, and guarding the Embers with the Caelum army this last month." My breath hitched. "You don't think they'd try to hurt Cate, would they?"

Dev's worried expression sent me shoving a prisoner a little too forcefully, nearly pushing him into the dark waters. I thought of Cate, unprotected at the inn, her concentration focused on keeping the storm steady. Yet it wasn't steady, was it? The rain had stopped. "You got this?"

He nodded. "Go."

I sprinted up the slick pier, my heart feeling too big for my own chest, thumping wildly out of control. I had to reach her. Was it already too late? Hugo nearly barreled into me, steps away from the inn.

"Good," he huffed, catching his breath, the lantern light silhouetting his large nose, broken one too many times. "I found you."

"I've gotta go. Later?" I tried to skirt around him, but his bulky body blocked me.

"Wait. I have to tell you something."

"My father is trying to kill Cate, I know." I faked left to try to pass him on his right, but he was too quick.

His brows furrowed. "No—I mean, he is?"

I returned his confused expression. "What'd you want to say to me?"

"The duke and the king have recruited some men, one of whom they shouldn't have trusted, because he came straight to me. Earlington has planted explosives on every vessel. Once they sail out of the harbor, they plan to detonate them and abandon ship before they explode. Your father wasn't supposed to be on board, but he took the place of this Terran who talked to me to make sure they don't leave a single Ember alive."

"And Cate?"

He shrugged. "That's all I know."

My gaze fell to the bay, each boat illuminated by lantern light, bobbing in the gentle waves like beacons of hope. Workmen unwound the knots of the final vessel. "Soldiers on board. He's going to kill them, too?"

"It's only the Caelum army traveling with them. Didn't you know? He insisted the Terrans wouldn't be a part of the voyage."

I remembered arguing about it with him a couple of weeks ago. One of our numerous disagreements. I glimpsed the king's gold braiding of his uniform, reflecting in the light on the closest ship.

"Check on Cate," I yelled, turning on my heel and racing back toward the ramp. I searched for Dev, but he'd already gone.

"Dev!" I shouted into the night air. No response. The tired Terran and Caelum soldiers had all left to make camp. The docks now lay empty.

The final boat with the Embers had already moved away to the center of the harbor. They would head out to sea at any moment, and when that happened, I'd never catch them.

A small fishing boat remained at the pier, a two-person dinghy. I climbed in, not bothering to undo the knots, slicing through the rope with my sword. I snatched up the two cracked wooden oars haphazardly flopped over the bench. I'd only been on a rowboat once, in a lake in Terra up near Dev's hunting lodge. We'd fished, laughing at how we scared them all away, and came home with nothing but one tiny minnow. We'd been kids and vowed never to take up fishing again, leaving it to the experts. Now, I deeply regretted that decision, cursing the fish for not biting that day. If they had, perhaps we would have returned. The boat careened left, hitting the dock. At least I'd had plenty of practice swimming in that lake. If nothing else, I could abandon ship.

The first boat sailed outside the harbor, crossing the protective jetty into choppier ocean waters. I rowed harder, willing my arms to pull at equal measure to maneuver the dinghy straight. The next ship slipped out. Father's still a hundred yards away.

"Help," I cried. "Stop!"

They either didn't hear me or someone commanded them to keep going. For the first time, I noticed a group of smaller vessels tucked into a cove on the other side of the bay. I wondered if they would pick up my father and the others after they set the explosions. I can only assume they hadn't been able to recruit engineers for timed detonators and would instead light fuses long enough to allow escape. I heaved the oars harder but was no match for the larger ships. The bow shifted left again, forcing me to even out, losing more time.

Another ship exited the bay, then another.

A traffic jam at the bottleneck through the jetty slowed my father's vessel, the name now visible in gold and purple: *The Marietta,* a fleur-de-lis marking it as a Dame Hemlock ship. Another pull of the oars led me in the correct direction, the water lapping high on the edge as I turned. I paused, letting myself glide and loosening my grip, blisters already bubbling. The only way I would reach the ship is if I could channel energy. Out in nature, as we'd been these last weeks, it had come easier. But the earth's power lay buried under the sea. I searched for it, finding wisps and snatches. I gathered them like a squirrel hoarding nuts in winter for a burst of speed. My tiny fishing boat sailed forward.

Pull. Pull. Pull.

I inched closer to *The Marietta,* now slowed to allow the others to exit the mouth of the bay. Blisters screamed hot at the oars, my shoulders burning with each stroke. Finally, I bumped against the vessel near an attached wooden ladder, which must be for exiting a lifeboat or into another smaller craft. I abandoned my rocking boat and leaped onto the ladder, climbing rung over rung until I reached the top.

I ran straight into an Ember who almost tipped me back overboard. The prisoners' hands were still tied. I fought through the bodies to find the captain, passing stairs leading into the hold below ship, filled with more Embers. A gold-trimmed uniform disappeared below. I abandoned my search for the captain, who I feared might not believe me or be unwilling to overturn the king's orders, and followed my father instead.

He shoved his way through the crowd and down one more set of stairs, not bothering to look behind. Injecting his power into anyone who challenged him, he left me a path of Embers to step over, some dead, some in excruciating pain. Pain I was all too familiar with, phantom tingling crawling over my skin at the memory.

I raced to catch him. I'm not sure what I hoped. Best-case—convince him to call off the explosions. I worried I'd made a mistake in not finding the captain, but it felt like I was tumbling toward something. I stumbled down a narrow set of stairs to the lowest hold. It brimmed with supplies, with winding pathways between containers. His back faced me, hunched over a set of crates stacked high, one on top of the other, blending in with the other barrels and sacks of food.

"Father," I yelled. "Stop."

He straightened, turning to me, fear flashing like lightning across his features. "What are you doing here?"

"Stopping you from making a huge mistake. Don't light that fuse."

He shrugged, casually, as if it didn't matter. "It's too late."

I rushed forward to see for myself. "Just put it out," I cried. When I came closer, the fuse had already snuck through a tiny hole in the sealed crate at the bottom. I searched frantically for water, finding none. I'd have to move the boxes covering the fuse, but Father blocked my path.

"Son. Let it go. We must leave." He started toward me as if to pull me away, and I punched him. He reeled backward, shock crossing his features. Crossing both of our faces—never in my wildest dreams did I believe I'd hit the king.

"Help me. Help me stop it," I huffed.

"I will not."

I launched forward, shoving him with all my strength. But he was stronger, his full power never waning.

"Please." Desperation laced my voice. Panic bubbled like a cauldron. "You don't want to kill them all. You'll be the same as them."

He held his ground as I scrambled with my sword to chop through the box. Metal met metal. He was too fast, the steel of our swords clashing together.

"Son. Listen to me. We have less than three minutes."

I had to try one last time to reach the explosives. I shoved my sword into his with all my might, power surging through me, matching the adrenaline. He fell backward. His head hit a crate with a sickening thud.

No.

My chest froze, unable to take in a breath. Blood seeped from the back of his scalp.

"Father."

His eyes were closed. He wasn't moving. The blade in my hand clattered to the wooden floor. My fingers fumbled to find a thready pulse. Attention ricocheted between the explosives and my father. I tried to heave the first crate away. They'd filled them with rocks, or something equally heavy. A barrier to keep anyone from finding what lay beneath. I'd never clear them in time to stop it.

I retrieved my weapon and looped my arms under Father's and pulled. A narrow zigzagging path led to the stairs. "Wake up. Please wake up."

My feet slid. I tried again, tugging and pulling him past the piles of supplies. When we reached the stairs, Embers jeered, kicking my flank, nearly sending me tumbling back down. I let go of Father, striking out with my sword, but when I returned to him, they continued to attack, realizing I couldn't carry the king and defend myself at the same time. I ignored the boots pounding my chest, back, and legs, pain pummeling me from all sides. One of my ribs broke with a crack, followed by a sharp pain in my chest. My breath turned shallow, wheezing, pressure building, sure signs of a punctured lung. Still, I pulled, finally reaching the top.

"Hey, what's going on down there?" a Caelum soldier called.

"Help!" I answered. "It's the king! He's hurt."

The soldier pushed his way through the Embers. I yanked him close and whispered in his ear, "We have one minute to abandon ship. He's set explosives." If I announced it, the mass chaos would ensure we'd never make it.

The young soldier's head swiveled between the king and me. He turned tail and ran, weaving through the Embers. The panic inside that had started to bubble overflowed. I hooked my arms through him again, tugging through the crowd. They surged forward, eager to kick the king who'd hurt their comrades a few moments ago. My breathing whistled in my ears, only trivial, hollow gulps of air making it through.

I pulled out my sword. "I'll kill you all unless you help me."

"We'll kill him first," someone yelled.

My internal clock knew I'd never get him out alive. I'd likely not make it either. A boom shattered the air. Followed by another, and another. I was too late. The other ships were being destroyed.

I have to leave him.

"I'm sorry, Father," I whispered before forcing my way up to the top deck. Mass chaos greeted me. Seeing the other vessels explode, Caelum soldiers and Embers were jumping overboard, though the Embers had little chance to survive with their hands tied behind their backs. Everyone was shoving everyone else, and I joined the fray, for any moment might be my last. I finally reached the edge, my vision spot-filled and spinning from lack of oxygen. I lurched upward, teetering atop the narrow rail.

Boom! A flash of heat propelled me forward. Then nothing.

Cold. So cold. Flames lilted around me, orange lanterns floating and bobbing. A great shadow blocked out the moon, looming closer, a demon coming to take me from this world. I hadn't done enough. I hadn't stopped my father's plan. Hadn't saved him either. Numbness overtook everything, and I nearly succumbed to the grip and tug of the freezing water. Honey brown hair swished and flickered. A shy smile. Green eyes brimming with love.

Hold on, she said.

I tried. I tried until the black pulled me under, the shadow demon looming.

"Daniel," a voice called. "Daniel, can you hear me?"

Something warm wrapped around me beneath firm ground. *Earth.* It fed my soul, filling and strengthening until I could open my lids. Lucas's worried face hovered above.

"He needs a medic!" he yelled behind him. "Now." He turned back to me. "You're not breathing too well, mate. We were lucky Molly saw you and plucked you out of the water."

A wheeze chuckled out. *Molly.* Not a demon. "I… I—"

"Hey, no talking 'til you're patched up."

"Cate?" I croaked.

"She's fine," Dev said, coming into view.

I let myself drift off, the pain too much to bear. Cate was alive, which was all that mattered. For now. I closed my eyes, the trail of blood my father left as I dragged him across the wooden decks filling my vision. He'd met his end.

And it was my fault.

CHAPTER 62
DANIEL

Cate's coronation was delayed for Father's funeral. I was due to be crowned, too, yet all I wanted was to lick my wounds in peace. Wallow in shame and failure. No amount of coaxing from Mya or Cate could pull me from the depths of depression these last few weeks.

The Embers were dead, with only a few rescued from the water. My father was dead. And somehow… Somehow, I was to be rewarded with a crown. I hadn't even tried my powers again. I wasn't worthy of them.

Mya swept unannounced into my room at Terra Castle. While I slumped in a chair near the fireplace, she ticked off the arrangements that had been completed for the funeral, set to take place in an hour. I couldn't seem to find warmth since my plunge in the harbor. I threw another log onto the fire. Unlike Caelum, we opted to hold the ceremony in our great hall, limiting the number of attendees. The Terran people would pay their respects to an empty box after the funeral. An extensive search yielded nothing, his remains never found. I didn't have the heart to tell them he would have never survived that explosion.

"Daniel, are you listening to me?" Mya asked, leaning against my desk. "You'll have to snap out of it enough to make your speech. I wrote it out for you." She held the paper aloft. "Repeat after me."

I watched her through glazed eyes.

"I accept the Terran crown and will become your next king."

"I... accept..."

Mya turned over her hand in a hurry-up gesture. "Just say it. All you have to do is read the speech."

A rush of gratefulness cut through the listlessness. "Thank you for this. I'll be better. For you. And Cate. I'll get better."

A smile broke. "Of course you will. Hopefully, one day you'll believe me—I'm so proud of you. Proud that you tried to save all those people. Even if they were Embers. No one could have succeeded. Even you. And," she sniffled, her voice softening. "I'm proud that you didn't give up on Father. You wanted to believe he'd change his mind, and I love you for that."

I shoved him.

I left him.

Mya drifted over and straightened the medals on my jacket. Military dress. What a joke. I didn't deserve them. Didn't deserve any of this. She kissed me on the cheek. "Don't be late. I want to see you down there in thirty minutes. No less. Got it?"

"Yes, Mother." I winced at the joke. More guilt piled on that our mom was now a widow. I'd hardly been capable of speaking to her since arriving home, the dark cloud of shame overhanging.

The ceremony started right on time. Mother sat next to me, Mya on the other side. Cate perched one row behind, her presence the only thing keeping me going. I gripped the speech Mya wrote, the words weaving in and out of focus as the pomp and circumstance of the great King Dryden paraded on until it was my turn to take the podium. I trudged up the stairs in a haze.

"King Dryden always wanted the best for our kingdom," I started, mentally applauding Mya for making him sound good while still speaking the truth. The speech flowed, and she'd even written a few funny bits. People believed my deadpan delivery was deliberate and laughed. Finally, I reached the end. The part where I claimed the throne.

I stared out into the crowd, a blur of faces, until I came to Cate's. All I wanted was to be with her. Support her and live our life together, instead of being torn between both of us ruling two kingdoms at once. Father's death happened too soon. We needed more time. Just us without the weight of two crowns. Joining the kingdoms wasn't the solution. Terra and Caelum felt pride in their land, in their heritage, and wished to maintain it. I couldn't force the citizens together to make it easier for me.

Cate gave me a small nod. I wasn't sure how long I'd stood there, assessing. Mya sent me a frenzied smile, her teeth bared in a grimace. She'd been a rock. Organized the underground. Run the kingdom during Father's absence. I don't know what I would do without her.

"It is my duty to assume the Terran crown," I started, the words tumbling out. "But I choose to abdicate the throne." Whispers echoed in a sweeping wave through the space. "Instead, my sister, Mya, will become queen." I hadn't known I would say it until that moment.

Shocked open mouths and wide eyes responded. "I will act as the Terran consort for Caelum. And Sir Lucas Bradbury will do the same for the Terrans. I love my kingdom, and I've seen how much Mya loves it too. She's the mastermind behind this place, especially when given the chance by someone who believes in her. I believe in my sister. And so should you."

Mya's forced grin faded, her expression shifting to disbelief. My thoughts grew clearer the longer I spoke, my future unfolding before me in a path that sparked a flame of contentment.

"Our two kingdoms deserve peace and cooperation. A consult will ensure both sides are heard, while still preserving our royal positions and separate kingdoms, honoring our history. Our legacy. May we finally have peace for many years to come." I took a step back from the podium.

"Long live the queen," I called. It echoed through the hall, and for the first time in a long while, I felt peace.

CHAPTER 63
CATE

Coronation day. It had finally arrived, and I felt ready to lead the Caelum people. Daniel's bombshell had rocked both kingdoms. Some worried he would act as a Caelum puppet king, but he'd remained in the background, satisfied to let me govern. He still battled the demons of his father's death, but seemed happier, more content. He never really wanted to be king, and I'm not sure he ever pictured himself with the crown, unable to imagine his father dying. He and Mya communicated frequently through messengers, and he enjoyed advising her when she asked. When she'd come for the coronation, they'd been like two schoolgirls, heads huddled together, whispering secrets and ideas. A prince consort was the perfect role for him—he was happy to let others shine, and take up causes as he wished.

Lady Amelia, blonde hair artfully piled atop her head, strode into my suite in a wave of perfume and smiles, followed by her entourage. When I'd first arrived in Caelum, directed by my father, she'd readied me for my debut as a princess, and more than that, had gifted me with words I'd kept close, pulling them out like a secret gift when I needed them most. I'd personally chosen her to design my gown.

"See, what did I tell you?" She waved a hand. "You are a diamond, inside and out."

I laughed. "Wait. You said I was coal, remember? I haven't forgotten your speech all those months ago."

"Ah, yes." She fluttered her lashes. "I did say you were coal. A diamond's use is to look pretty, but coal—coal can start a fire, which is just what this kingdom needed." She gestured at one of the girls to arrange the lighting. "And that's exactly what you were. But that statement isn't quite true anymore. Now you will glitter like a perfect diamond—clear and discerning, scattering light to others. And always. You will always be beautiful, inside and out."

She pulled my coronation gown from its bag with a flourish. I gasped. Ombre, dark at the bodice with thousands of beads fading into a full skirt billowing around her in a cascade of cerulean, ocean, and sky blue. Just a touch of teal glimmered at my request, the green a nod to Terra.

"Fit for a queen, don't you think?" She draped the garment over her arm dramatically.

"It's the most beautiful dress I've ever seen."

"Of course it is, dear," she tutted.

It fit perfectly, tight at the waist, but not so much that I couldn't breathe for my speech and the ball to follow. The tiny beads sparkled in the light, shimmering and pouring down to the skirt, which swished and flounced, moving like every girl's dream. The ladies exfoliated and plucked, trimmed and moisturized, clucking over me, lamenting my time in the woods, the mud and rain creating havoc on my skin.

"There," Lady Amelia said, turning me toward a mirror. "You are complete."

They'd let my hair fall down my back, curled into delicate waves. My complexion glowed, and my green eyes popped against their palette of eyeshadow and liner. "Thank you for making me into a diamond." I swayed my hips, watching the skirt swish with me.

"Have you learned nothing? You are always a diamond, even with those hideous trousers I know you love so much."

I grinned. I'd started wearing my jeans occasionally around the castle. Maybe to stir a little controversy, and maybe to remind myself where I came from. Because sometimes, I wasn't the diamond, I was still the coal, and I loved being both.

After they left, I took a moment to look out the window of my tower—at the field that the Embers ravaged in The Great Battle. The smell of smoke and shouting men returned in a moth-eaten patchwork of memories. Deep green grass now covered the land, the trees swaying in a soft breeze. I'd had wildflower seeds scattered a year ago to honor the dead, and they bloomed in an ocean of blues and yellows, each a miniature sign of hope and remembrance from where we'd come.

When I stepped outside my suite, Lucas stood guard, like old times. He was supposed to stand at sober attention, but couldn't contain his grin.

"Who did you bribe to become my military escort?" I teased.

"Everyone. Believe me, the line was looong." He bowed theatrically. "At your service, Your Highness."

I threw my arms around him. "How are things in Terra?"

He shrugged. "Different… but good."

I raised my brows. "And with Mya?"

He shot me a cocky grin. "I'm surprised you even need to ask. Things are definitely good on that front."

I punched him playfully on the arm and rolled my eyes.

"Hey. That was not very royal of you."

"Thank goodness." My smile faded. "You homesick?"

"A little. I should make more time to visit. It's nice to travel on Molly whenever I like without worrying about being shot with an arrow. And did you hear? She has a friend. One of the dragons from the battle stayed. He's a gorgeous thing—blue and sleek. I named him Milo. Molly's a bit smitten, I'm afraid. So is Mya, who is itching to ride him."

"And you? You're still smitten?" I asked.

"With Molly?" He put his hand over his heart as if I'd injured him. He grew solemn. "I am. With both Mya and Molly. And the rest… Terra… I'm adjusting. Like everyone else."

"It seems like I still owe you that parade for saving us with the dragons."

His grin faded. "I don't need one anymore. Things have turned out as they should. I'm honored to be the consort, and once Mya recovered from the shock of taking over as queen, she's been doing a bang-up job." He hesitated. "Thank you. And thanks to Daniel, too. I owe him one. Or about a thousand."

"He doesn't want you to feel indebted." I laughed. "We've come a long way, haven't we?"

"We have, Princess—I mean, Queen."

"How about just Cate?"

He hooked his arm around mine. "Shall we go, Cate?"

Daniel met us at the royal carriage, newly painted in blues and golds. Four white horses, their manes braided with ribbons, stood at attention, ready to take me to the coronation site outside Neva. I'd almost changed the location, with so many recent memories of my father and Graftonberg's funerals, but decided we needed reminders of our past. It was part of Caelum's history, and I would never erase it.

"You look stunning." His smile lit up his eyes, a welcome change from the sadness. He'd started to forgive himself, and my chest filled with pride for the work he continued to do to heal these past few months.

"As do you," I said.

He held his broad shoulders rigid in his green, gold-trimmed military uniform, a special medal of honor given by General Dixon pinned in front. I never failed to be awed that he chose me with his movie-star good looks.

Mostly, I marveled at his heart. He'd gifted it to me, broken and hollow, and bit by bit we filled it up together. He cherished and cradled mine, with its jagged, missing pieces, each replaced carefully by him and my found family here in Caelum. Just like Daniel, I broke with the death of my father, and he held me together while I shattered. The scars of war and death would always be traceable on both our hearts. We no longer hid them from each other. Nor did we hide them from the world. They made us stronger, and they helped us remember.

"You're ready for this." Daniel smoothed a lock of my hair after we entered the carriage. "And I'm ready to be whatever you need."

My fingers trailed along the velvet seats, back and forth to soothe my nerves. An action I found myself repeating from prior trips to Neva. "You're already what I need." I gazed at his chiseled profile until he swiveled to me. "Exactly how you are." I leaned in and kissed him, tugging at his uniform to pull him close.

Soft lips whispered reassurances in my ear, caressed my neck and jaw, and sent shivers laddering down my spine. "I love you, Cate." His hands splayed across my back, pulling me, pulling me ever tighter.

This is where I belonged. In his arms. In this kingdom. Home.

An hour later, I stood in front of the sea of Caelumites, all in blue, commemorating the occasion, and I spoke the words aloud I'd been thinking about with Daniel. How our scars were important to our history.

"Remember the fallen," my voice echoed through the crowd. "I have never been more proud of a people than I am of you. This kingdom fought to survive, came together, and we won." Cheers erupted, louder than a full stadium at the Super Bowl. When they subsided, I continued, "We cannot forget our Terran friends. Without them fighting by our side, there would not be a Caelum, and vice versa. Together, we are stronger. I want to thank you for believing in me. Believing in a girl who came from a place that cherishes freedom and peace just as you do. Even though I'll be crowned your queen today, I also promise to establish a democracy. You fought for us, and every person, man or woman, deserves to have a say in this kingdom. We will elect officials from the people."

More cheers, and I took a second to cherish this moment. My parents traveled from Ember City, eyes shining with tears, Jack nestled beside them. I couldn't wait to spend an entire week with them in the castle after the ceremony. We'll have tea and scones piled with juneberry preserves and clotted cream while snuggled in my favorite sitting room. I'd found a pony just for Jack, and a sparrow in case he develops Caelum powers. Their time in Ember City would be temporary, though essential, and I was proud they'd chosen to help. Another year, and they'd return here for good. Then Jack could enter a proper school, I'd find them their own house… My wide smile broadened at my thoughts careening off topic.

I'd asked Hildy to come from Terra Castle to lead the catering team, but first attend the ceremony, her too-tight bun and dour expression flickering with pride. My other favorites had reserved seating as well —Emma, my maid, and Charlie the falconer. Dame Hemlock nodded approvingly, Hanson on her left. Dev sat by several other Terran aristocrats. I didn't even mind seeing Emily beside him. Well, didn't mind *too* much.

Mya took Lucas's hand as they looked on from the front row. And Daniel, on stage, watched me with wonder. Like I was a queen reserved just for him.

Tears of joy burned hot, but I refused to let them fall. I retreated to the throne, set high on the dais. Crowning me was Alana's last service before retirement. She had plans to live out her old age with Harlow, and I couldn't be happier for her. She'd trained several men and women adept at traversing portals to take over her work in Ember City. The product of clandestine marriages, they too shared powers of both the air and earth and had been hiding their talents from the kingdoms.

Alana handed me a scepter with the largest sapphire I'd ever seen, winking in the light. I initially hoped to be crowned with my mom's favorite tiara, but Lady Amelia insisted I needed a crown for a queen, not a princess. This one, retrieved from the vault, stood taller than a simple tiara, diamonds sparkling in the sun, sending a kaleidoscope of shimmering color across the stage. I thought of Lady Amelia's words. How I would glitter like a diamond—clear and discerning, scattering light to others. They blanketed me with confidence and strength to dedicate myself to this kingdom, spreading a message of peace.

Alana placed the diamonds on my head, and finally, filled with hope, and joy, and promise, I was crowned Caelum's Queen.

Thank you for reading
Heir of Earth and Sky

Make sure to join our Discord
(https://discord.gg/aethon)
so you never miss a release!

THANK YOU FOR READING THE CROWNED

We hope you enjoyed it as much as we enjoyed bringing it to you. We just wanted to take a moment to encourage you to review the book. Follow this link: The Crowned to be directed to the book's Amazon product page to leave your review.

Every review helps further the author's reach and, ultimately, helps them continue writing fantastic books for us all to enjoy.

Also in series:

The Concealed

The Captured

The Crowned

Want to discuss our books with other readers and even the authors?

JOIN THE AETHON DISCORD!

Calling all Romantasy fans: be the first to discover groundbreaking new releases, access incredible deals, and participate in thrilling giveaways by subscribing to our exclusive Romantasy Newsletter.

https://aethonbooks.com/romantasy-newsletter/

For all our Romantasy books, visit our website.

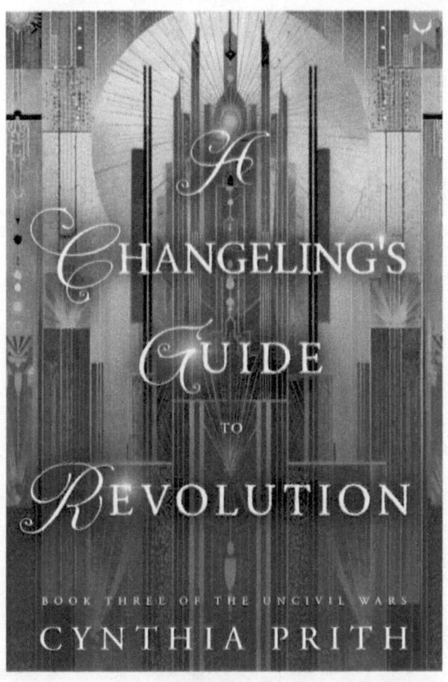

It's time for Unnaturals to reclaim their place in history. On the run from the law, Evelyn ends up smack in the middle of a city turf-war between notorious hotelier Erol King and the Vigil City Police. Furious and feral, still bleeding from a run-in with a government mage that left her nameless and nearly dead, Evelyn refuses to let these bullies win. She throws her all into the fight, saving Erol's life while he saves hers, creating an unshakable bond of debt and promises between them—one Erol seals with a human tooth, proof they couldn't kill her if they tried. Determined to wrest control of her life from human laws and prejudice, Evelyn volunteers to perform in Erol's three-day Solstice Spectacular, an illegal magical show vicious enough to shake the city on its foundations. With the police raids intensifying, and the Mages Union closing in, Evelyn struggles to master her shadowy footwork in time. Worse, her new co-star—Jackson Eden, a sweet and gentle man who treats her like the upstanding lady she isn't—won't quit begging her to run. He offers her a new life with him, anywhere but here, swearing that Erol King is worse than a racketeer and rum-runner. He's a literal monster, one that will sell her out the first chance he gets. But Evelyn knows monsters; she's building a necklace of their teeth. She swore Erol King a promise she intends to keep. Vigil City's going to write her name in lights —or else, in molotov cocktails and curses, she'll autograph these streets herself. **Don't miss this standalone sequel in the Uncivil Wars Series combining the gritty urban fantasy of Laurell K. Hamilton, the romantic fantasy vibes of Hannah Witten, and the glittering glamours of the 1920s.**

Get A Changeling's Guide to Revolution Now!

A Love That Defied Death. A Power That Consumed Gods. A Fate That Demands Blood. With her loves dead and gone, Aelia Springborn awakens in the Underworld—hell-bent on bringing them back. But escaping death is easier said than done. To return to the living, Aelia must place her trust in the Morrigan, a goddess of war and secrets, and navigate the treacherous wastes of No Man's Land. There, she'll face the legions of a fallen queen and her army of lost souls before descending into the bowels of Hell itself to cross the Veil between life and death. While Aelia battles her way through the Underworld, Amolie works tirelessly to forge a bridge between worlds. But to bring her friends back from beyond the Veil, she'll have to pay a price only the gods can demand. Meanwhile, Gideon fights for survival in the brutal Rasa fighting pits, and Baylis and Erissa scour the continent for another Trinity Well—only to discover that to find it, Baylis must strike a bargain with the Wraith King himself. In a world where gods play with mortal fates, love defies the grave, and vengeance burns brighter than the fires of Hell, three souls will bind and rise from the ashes. **Perfect for fans of Sarah J. Maas, Carissa Broadbent, Jennifer L. Armentrout, and Rebecca Yarros, Death Breaker is a darkly romantic epic of gods, monsters, and the woman who dares to break death itself.**

Get Death Breaker Now!

ACKNOWLEDGMENTS

My readers! Thank you for coming along on this ride with me to the end. And for forgiving me for that cliffhanger in *The Captured!* (Hopefully). I may never write a cliffhanger again. Well. Maybe…It's been so exciting how you've shown up for these books and fallen in love with Cate, Daniel, Lucas, Mya, and, of course, Molly. Special shout-out to my street team! I'm not the fastest writer—thanks for sticking with me! For anyone reading this: reviews are the best way to support an author, and I would be so thankful if you took a few moments to do so.

A huge thank you to Aethon Books, Rhett Bruno, and Steve Beaulieu for their continued support. Thank you to editors Kalene Williams and Jennifer Ehrhardt for a fantastic job polishing all three of my manuscripts. I'm grateful to Blue Nose Audio and my two fantastic narrators: Amanda Leigh Cobb and Joe Jameson. Author secret—when I'm having a bad day or a bout of imposter syndrome, I turn on my audiobook! Works every time.

To Wednesday Night Critique Group and their continued support. Dorene McLaughlin is truly the master of the back-of-the-book copy. She's saved me twice now! My beta readers were also incredibly helpful for *The Crowned*. Thanks to Jade, Fatima, MJ, Summer, and my daughter Claire.

As always, I'm grateful for my husband, Michael, for multiple readings, brainstorming, and marketing assistance. Although despite your best efforts, there are still currently no plans for a spinoff, *The Adventures of Molly*. You've endured endless "book talk," and there really should be an award for author husbands. And for author families. Thank you, Brooke and Claire, for your support and patience with

Mom, who seems to always be hiding away on her computer or posting "just one more thing" on social media promoting her books. Lastly, I thank God. This journey has been harder than I thought it would be (much harder), and I'm grateful you've been with me for every step.

www.ingramcontent.com/pod-product-compliance
Lightning Source LLC
Chambersburg PA
CBHW020246030826
48979CB00030B/2637/J

* 9 7 8 1 9 6 4 5 0 5 2 6 8 *